PENGUIN  C

MR. PRESIDENT

MIGUEL ÁNGEL ASTURIAS (1899–1974) was awarded the Nobel Prize in Literature in 1967. A poet, diplomat, and novelist from Guatemala, he studied law in his home country before continuing his studies in Paris, where he encountered the surrealist writings that would deeply influence his work. In addition to being a prolific writer, he worked as a newspaper correspondent in western Europe and later as an ambassador for Guatemala in Europe and Latin America. He wrote numerous works of fiction, poetry, drama, and essays, including the novels *Mr. President* and *Men of Maize*.

DAVID UNGER has received Guatemala's Miguel Ángel Asturias National Literature Prize for Lifetime Achievement. He is the author of several novels, including *The Mastermind*, *The Price of Escape*, and *Life in the Damn Tropics*, and has translated more than a dozen books from Spanish into English. His short stories and essays have been published in *The Paris Review*, *Guernica*, and *Bomb*. Unger is the international representative of the Guadalajara International Book Fair and is the director of the Publishing Certificate Program at the City College of New York, where he also teaches in the MFA program. Born in Guatemala, he now lives in Brooklyn, New York.

MARIO VARGAS LLOSA was awarded the Nobel Prize in Literature in 2010. He has also won the Cervantes Prize, the Spanish-speaking world's most distinguished literary honor, as well as the Jerusalem Prize and many other literary awards. His novels include *The Feast of the Goat*, *Aunt Julia and the Scriptwriter*, *The War of the End of the World*, *The Bad Girl*, *Conversation in the Cathedral*, and *Harsh Times*. Born in Peru, Vargas Llosa now lives in Madrid.

GERALD MARTIN is the Andrew W. Mellon Professor Emeritus of Modern Languages at the University of Pittsburgh. Among his publications are *Gabriel García Márquez: A Life* and a translation and critical edition of Miguel Ángel Asturias's *Men of Maize*. Martin lives in England.

MIGUEL ÁNGEL ASTURIAS

Mr. President

Translated by
DAVID UNGER

Foreword by
MARIO VARGAS LLOSA

Introduction by
GERALD MARTIN

PENGUIN BOOKS

PENGUIN BOOKS
An imprint of Penguin Random House LLC
penguinrandomhouse.com

Originally published in Spanish as *El Señor Presidente* by Costa-Amic, Mexico City

The foreword by Mario Vargas Llosa was originally published in Spanish by
Vintage Español, a division of Penguin Random House LLC, New York

LIBRARY OF CONGRESS CATALOGING-IN-PUBLICATION DATA
Names: Asturias, Miguel Angel, author. | Unger, David, 1950– translator. |
Vargas Llosa, Mario, 1936– writer of foreword. |
Martin, Gerald, 1944– writer of introduction.
Title: Mr. President / Miguel Ángel Asturias ; translated by David Unger ;
foreword by Mario Vargas Llosa ; introduction by Gerald Martin.
Other titles: Señor Presidente. English | Mister President
Description: New York : Penguin Books, 2022.
Identifiers: LCCN 2022000918 (print) | LCCN 2022000919 (ebook) |
ISBN 9780143136385 (paperback) | ISBN 9780525507918 (ebook)
Subjects: LCGFT: Political fiction. | Novels.
Classification: LCC PQ7499.A75 S413 2022 (print) | LCC PQ7499.A75 (ebook) |
DDC 863/.64—dc23/eng/20220426
LC record available at https://lccn.loc.gov/2022000918
LC ebook record available at https://lccn.loc.gov/2022000919

Printed in the United States of America

Set in Sabon LT Std

Contents

MR. PRESIDENT

PART I: APRIL 21, 22, AND 23

PART II: APRIL 24, 25, 26, AND 27

PART III: WEEKS, MONTHS, YEARS . . .

Foreword

Mr. President grew out of "Political Beggars," a short story that Miguel Ángel Asturias wrote in December 1922 before leaving Guatemala for Europe. The novel was first published in 1946 in an edition full of errors that Asturias corrected for the second edition (Buenos Aires: Editorial Losada, 1948). Indeed, he worked longer on this novel than he had on any other of his published books, even though he had abandoned the manuscript for long periods of time. The novel carried this annotation: Paris, November 1923–December 8, 1932.* According to most critics, and the author's own account, this novel was inspired by the dictatorship of Manuel Estrada Cabrera, who ruled as lord and master of Guatemala for twenty-two years, from 1898 to 1920.

At the behest of family friends, Asturias had gone to London in 1923 to study economics. He suddenly had a change of heart and went to Paris to take classes at the Sorbonne with Professor Georges Raynaud. It was in Raynaud's courses that he discovered Mayan culture and spent years translating the *Popol Vuh*, the sacred book of the Mayas. In Paris he wrote poems and the novel *Legends of Guatemala* (1930), and also continued working on *Mr. President*, which was written almost completely in France.

There's a certain confusion about this novel, to which Asturias

*Translator's note: Mario Vargas Llosa's dating of the novel differs from that found in most datings of the composition, which is Guatemala, December 1922; Paris, November 1925, December 8, 1932.

himself contributed. At the time, he championed social and protest fiction, the kind that revealed the horrors that Latin American dictators had committed. On many occasions, he claimed that his book belonged to the genre of politically engaged novels.

Undoubtedly, this is one important aspect of *Mr. President*. The novel deals with prototypical Latin American realist or folkloric themes, based on the dramatic historical circumstance that dictators ruled most Latin American countries. But even though Asturias's novel depicts this constant and recurring reality, it surely isn't its most important aspect, or this lively story wouldn't have stood out from these somewhat unsophisticated novels or survived the test of time.

To be sure, like many other Latin American novels, *Mr. President* fits in the category of the politically engaged novel. It depicts the havoc that dictatorships play in triggering human tragedies, economic catastrophes, and corruption in our countries. But Asturias does this in a unique way, frequently employing subtle, original, and unusual literary devices, without displaying the formal weaknesses and shortcomings often found in Latin American protest literature. More important, he does this in a much broader context than the typical social or political testimonial novel.

Asturias frames his novel as the struggle between good and evil in an underdeveloped society where evil seems to triumph. There isn't a single character in the novel that is saved—not even the young Camila, who is blackmailed into marrying the dictator's favorite confidant: the handsome Miguel Angel Face. She even attends a reception in the Palace of the President, who has imprisoned her father—the exiled General Eusebio Canales, the supposed murderer of Colonel Parrales Sonriente, and who ends up poisoned near the novel's conclusion. All the characters—whether they are soldiers, judges, politicians, wealthy or poor, the powerful or the downtrodden—epitomize evil. They are servile and violent thieves, cynics, opportunists, liars, corrupt individuals, drunkards—in short, among the most repugnant and disgusting of human beings. And probably even the President—who decides who is to live and who is to die and who is a drunkard, a traitor, and the mastermind of hundreds of twisted intrigues—isn't the worst of all. That designation goes to either his Judge Advocate or Major Farfán, who, on orders of the Head of State, perpetuate the most violent, outrageous crimes: the former when he questions, humiliates, and punishes Fedina de Rodas for crimes committed by her husband, Genaro, against the Dimwit; and the latter by detaining Miguel Angel Face at the harbor as he's about to leave for New York on Presidential orders. Miguel is arrested, beaten mercilessly, and buried in an underground dungeon where he has only two hours of light each day. He is fed filth and survives by slowly rotting, dying little by little while his wife, Camila, contacts diplomats and politicians all over the world, even in Singapore, hoping he is safe, only to learn, too late, that Angel Face is also a victim of a monster who controls everything—lives, deaths, and taxes are within his realm—with his little finger.

What is unique and what transforms this demonic book filled with hideous episodes is Asturias's artistry, which is made evident by the novel's formal structure and its original use of language.

Mr. President is qualitatively better than all previous Spanish-language novels. Marvelously controlled, the novel's language owes much to Professor Reynaud's lectures on surrealism and other avant-garde movements in vogue in France while Asturias was writing it. No doubt he was also deeply affected by nostalgia for his far-off country at the other end of the world and the many years he had been away from Guatemala, getting together with his South American friends at Montparnasse's Café de la Rotonde. His work was influenced by automatic writing, the mixing of reality and dreams—nightmares, I should say—an unusual poetic musicality, and the merging of forms that convert history into a grand novelistic and poetic spectacle and where reality becomes street theater and apocalyptical fantasy at every turn.

The first chapter, "In the Portal del Señor," is unforgettable. A swirl of one-legged, one-eyed, blind, crippled beggars have been reduced to the most primitive bestiality and mistreat one another with the deepest misery and savagery. Pelele—the

Dimwit—is one of them; this poor devil is later needlessly killed by Lucio Vásquez. At the book's end, the dictatorship remains intact—of course, the Portal del Señor is destroyed, but the hideous system it symbolizes is not.

Asturias's language is multifaceted and not the Spanish that all the characters in the story utilize. Despite their lack of decency, the upper classes speak a more or less correct Spanish. This is also the case for Angel Face, Camila, a handful of ministers and officers, and even Mr. President. But as the novel explores the language of the lower classes, the richness and innovation of expression increase and shift, introducing invented words, songs, audacious grammatical renderings, astonishing metaphors, rhythms, terms generally associated with native insects, plants, and trees. A provincial world of untamed nature not yet dominated by man is depicted in a country that finds itself isolated and changing slowly, before the advent of cars and airplanes, and in which a trip to New York involves a long train ride and boat journey. Guatemala isn't mentioned even once, but that doesn't matter—everything points to that unfortunate yet beautiful country: the capital is far from the ocean, surrounded by rivers, jungles, and volcanoes. Its hapless citizens would know only hideous dictatorships until long after the novel ends—at least until 1944—and would incorporate into their thoughts and diction an extraordinary glibness, inventing words, fantasizing and improvising as they speak, endlessly creating in everything they say and exclaim, thus transforming reality into enchantment—a hellish one at that—where time goes in circles, around itself, as in a nightmare. Life is depicted as a theatrical tragedy repeated endlessly in which human beings are merely actors and, at times, mythical characters. Chapter XXXVII, "Tohil's Dance," in particular, is more like a painting or mural inspired by the distant ancestors of the K'iche' Maya archeological past, a historical reminiscence that connects to Guatemala's rich history. All the other chapters correspond to an updated present in which a humble, isolated, and primitive people—subjected to the indescribable horrors of a brutal, incarcerating regime—live in abject poverty. But there's something that supports the country's people and keeps them from vanishing: the vital and extraordinary strength with which they withstand mistreatment and humiliation, a tragic existence steeped in muck, jungle, and animals and in the hugely creative way they survive and employ language. Despite the depths of the country's social and political disgrace, its people are capable of creating and taking on a distinct personality, inventing a new language, and the music and rhythms that shape it and make it unique and guarantee its survival.

Asturias achieves something unique in this novel. Its linguistic beauty is part of the historical truth: the Guatemalan way of speaking is innovative and personal. Asturias isn't a mere scribe to that linguistic reality, but also its creator—someone who chooses to dive into the bottomless fountain of how a nation and its people speak, while also managing to cultivate and add something of his own fantasies, obsessions, and excellent ear to give it his personal stamp. *Mr. President* is undoubtedly a work of art, a true tour de force of great originality and creativity, perhaps closer to poetry than to fiction or, perhaps, a rare merging of these two genres.

Many episodes in the novel begin in a realistic vein, but, little by little, Asturias constructs a visionary and metaphorical poetic language, which leads him to discard a realistic, objective landscape for one of legend, dream, theater, myth, and pure invention. This is what makes this novel so unique, so new, and of such high literary value that almost a century later, *Mr. President* continues to be one of the most original Latin American texts ever written.

Asturias's nostalgia for his native land certainly played an important role in the writing of this novel. And yet, the distance between Asturias in Paris and Guatemala gave him a kind of freedom that many Latin American writers living in their homelands did not have—since they were forced to experience a brutality that impeded their ability to write freely—without fear of persecution and censorship. Probably Miguel Ángel Asturias wasn't fully aware of how great a novel he had written, whose magnitude he would never again repeat, because the novels, short stories, and poems he wrote afterward were closer to the narrower, somewhat demagogic literature of "committed" dictator novels that he had earlier championed. He didn't realized that the great merit of *Mr. President* is that he had broken that tradition and raised the politically engaged novel to an altogether higher level.

MARIO VARGAS LLOSA
TRANSLATED BY DAVID UNGER

Introduction

The first lines of *Mr. President* (*El Señor Presidente*), by the Guatemalan author Miguel Ángel Asturias, still have the power to astonish new readers a full century after the author began writing his book: bells tolling at nightfall, swinging from high to low, as if from brightness to utter darkness, night to day, good to evil, ringing outside in the world and deep inside one's ears. The shadow presence of Lucifer, the lord of light and shadow, of malevolence, corruption, injustice. Terror from the very start, which will shortly overwhelm all the characters in the novel, one after another; but also contradiction, the sparks of primeval fire, a fierce libertarian desire communicated through the language itself, and an unexpected, counterintuitive poetic beauty. I was stunned when I first read it, at the age of nineteen, three months after I read James Joyce's *Ulysses* (completed in the year that Asturias's novel was started), in a gloomy English library on a rainy English day. So this was Latin America!

Indeed it was, I would confirm, only two years later, when I saw the tempestuous and contradictory region for myself; no other book would ever have quite the same irresistible impact. It did not occur to me then that what I was reading was already thirty years old. A decade from now, it will be a hundred years old, though for me it will always be youthful.

When the book was published in Buenos Aires in 1948 (after a first Mexican edition, in 1946, which Asturias's mother financed and which went almost unnoticed), it quickly became a Latin American sensation and at that time the most celebrated work of fiction in Spanish American history. Here, at

last, was the great novel of dictatorship for which that neglected region, notorious for its many tyrannical regimes (but
not adequately admired for its unceasing quest for liberty),
had been waiting.

Before long, Asturias's work became the foreign novel of the
year in France, in 1952, and was even published in English, in
London, in 1963, something still highly unusual at the time for
a book from Latin America. Asturias was willingly absorbed
into the postwar existentialist wave of politically committed
literature advocated by Jean-Paul Sartre and Simone de Beau-
voir, the more so after he was forced into exile in 1954, effec-
tively for the rest of his life, by a military coup supported by
the United States. In 1967 he became the first Latin American
novelist to win the Nobel Prize (the Chilean Gabriela Mistral
had won for poetry in 1945), thereby crowning two successful
decades in the public eye.

Yet, from the very moment that he won that prize, four years
after I first read *Mr. President*, Asturias's star began to wane,
and he has never again been at the center of Latin American literary attention. Without an understanding of this extraordinary story, the history and evolution not only of Asturias's
novel but also of twentieth-century literature in Latin America
cannot be properly narrated.

Because the truth is that *Mr. President* was a 1946 or 1948
novel only in terms of its date of publication: it had been written in the 1920s, in Europe, in the age of the literary avant-
garde and silent cinema. And it was not only inspired by one
specific dictatorship, that of Manuel Estrada Cabrera (1898–
1920), in the period immediately before it was written; it
would also become the victim of a second, equally ruthless regime, that of Jorge Ubico (1931–1944), as would its author,
which is why its publication was delayed until after World
War II. Then, after almost two decades of positive reviews, the
novel and its writer would again become victims of history
more widely and of the literary tastes and politics of a powerful new generation fostering its own myths and rewriting history in its own image. Restoring Asturias's novel to its rightful
place in Latin American cultural development and focusing its

achievement are long overdue, both as an act of justice and as a contribution to historical and literary truth.

THE TURBULENT LIFE OF A GUATEMALAN WRITER

The dictator Manuel Estrada Cabrera, a Liberal Party politician in power between 1898 and 1920, is never named in Asturias's novel, because the writer's intention was to universalize the themes of dictatorship and its mechanisms and to investigate their roots in social and economic inequality and the internalization of oppression. Indeed the dictator himself makes very few appearances in the narrative, considering that his political title is the title of the book: Asturias's focus is on not only his physical control of the Guatemalan people through systematic repression, imprisonment, and torture but also his hold upon their minds through the creation of a state of mythological terror that penetrates, through the mystery of power, to the deepest recesses of their consciousness. (The book's original title was *Tohil*, the name of the Mayan god of fire.) Many critics in the decades after the novel was published, given that the details are horrific and the atmosphere both nightmarish and satirical, assumed that the work was in some respects hyperbolic. In fact, the episodes and anecdotes narrated and the methods employed by the President and his regime in the narrative are in no way exaggerated: they are truthful and historical, down to the smallest details. For this reason its central themes, inextricably woven together, are evil, oppression, violence, imprisonment, and death, and—less obviously but unmistakably—their opposites. The novel's mood is one of terror and its methods are those of the dictator: to impose distortions of every kind and to administer shock treatment to the reader's consciousness. Unlike the dictator, however, Asturias seeks to terrorize in order to produce a moral, emotional, and even physical reaction to the reading experience: an antidote, a catharsis. To achieve this, he uses all the technical resources of the avant-garde era of the 1920s, which was also, as mentioned, the age of silent cinema and its narrative modes: melodramatic, gestural, and balletic. This must be understood from the outset: *Mr. President*'s virtues are not those of the traditional realist novel.

The book has a theatrical structure of three parts: "April 21, 22, and 23"; "April 24, 25, 26, and 27"; "Weeks, Months, Years. . . ." It has forty-one chapters, most with spectacularly melodramatic titles, and an epilogue. It has a setting, Guatemala, which is never named, just as the almost mythological President himself is rarely seen and never named. And it has a brilliantly achieved plot that involves the construction of a terrifying narrative prison whose last doors clang shut at the book's conclusion. In other words—as this final detail suggests—it is a novel whose characteristics are not only those of a novel: it is also very like a play, a tightly concocted drama (at times a theater of marionettes), with a pulsating psychic rhythm. Its first two parts accelerate dialectically; the third slows ("Weeks, Months, Years . . ."), then rises briefly to a climax, then slows again into an ambiguous epilogue, which ends, literally, in a cul-de-sac (the previous chapter having ended in a prison cell). It is also a movie (a movie that gives the book the dimensions of a myth), projected onto the screen of the reader's consciousness like a slightly tinted, flickering black-and-white silent film that begins and ends in the darkness, like every archetypal experience at the cinema, or like our daily passage from night to morning and back to night again. And finally, counterintuitively, and perhaps above all, it is a poem: the themes in the inaugural lines are overtly reasserted in the very last lines, as in the most harmonious of narrative poems, but between these moments they open out into a wide array of motifs associated with the nature of being, perception, thought, and kinetic motion, so that almost every sentence and paragraph brings together, through Asturias's political aesthetic, a sense of universal meaning within the contextual moment. Few critics have read the book this way, mainly due to the force of its political subject matter, but its aesthetic dimension is inseparable from its wider meaning.

When Miguel Ángel Asturias was born, in 1899, Estrada Cabrera had been president of the Guatemalan Republic for just a year. He would still be in power as Asturias approached the age of twenty-one. Estrada Cabrera had not only physically controlled the country and its borders for two decades, he had also controlled the frontiers of the writer's own imagination, and that of an entire generation throughout their childhood and youth. This psychic reality underpins the entire conception of Asturias's signature novel.

Asturias's father was a lawyer by profession, like Estrada Cabrera himself, and was forced to quit his post as judge shortly after Miguel Ángel was born, due to political difficulties with the dictator. The family fled to the provinces for a few years of internal exile, after which Asturias's formidable mother, Doña María Rosales, sustained the family by opening a highly successful grocery store and managing the humiliations that this occasioned among the upper classes of Guatemala City. The son on whom she doted enrolled in the law faculty at the University of San Carlos in 1917, a year that would mark the beginning of the end for Estrada Cabrera: Asturias would always maintain that the great earthquakes of the winter of 1917–1918, which destroyed much of the city and forced its inhabitants to camp out together in the streets and squares, made a significant symbolic and psychological contribution to the tyrant's overthrow. (In the novel's epilogue, the consciousness-raising effects of the earthquake are obliquely recorded.) When in 1919 the dictator attempted to have himself reelected in one more phony election, a movement of opposition parties, workers, and students combined to overthrow him, and in 1920 he was captured and arrested. Asturias, who had been highly active in the student movement (he would represent the Guatemalan university students at a conference in Mexico City in 1921, and later in Europe) and who was himself briefly jailed by Estrada Cabrera, interviewed the ex-dictator in prison and was secretary to the tribunal that tried and sentenced him. Asturias graduated in 1922 but practiced law only briefly. In that year he wrote "Political Beggars," a short story that in time would become the first chapter of Mr. President. In 1923 his undergraduate thesis, "The Social Problem of the Indian," was published, the first work of social analysis to appear in Guatemala. Between them, these two works gave an early indication of the themes—politics and indigenism—that would give life and direction to his artistic expression.

Political freedom has been a scarce commodity in Guatemalan history. Lawyers have rarely respected the law. The beautiful, resplendent quetzal, a bird of the Guatemalan cloud forest beloved by the Mayas and a national symbol of independence and liberty since the 1870s, is said to be unable to live in captivity; but the Guatemalan people, especially the Indigenous majority who are the descendants of the Maya, have little experience of political freedom, except in their dreams. By 1923 the novice writer was under serious threat from a new regime that, in the vacuum left by Estrada Cabrera, was dominated by the military. His parents encouraged him to flee to Europe. Asturias moved to London for six months and then to Paris, where he worked as a correspondent for a new and progressive Guatemalan newspaper, *El Imparcial*, studied ethnology at the Sorbonne under Georges Raynaud, a scholar devoted to the study of the Maya; and above all carried out research in the university of life during the era of les Années Folles.

During the next ten years, with Paris as his base, he traveled most of the Old World and met many of the leading Latin Americans of his generation, as well as international celebrities, from Miguel de Unamuno and Vicente Blasco Ibáñez to James Joyce, Paul Valéry, and Pablo Picasso, from Arthur Conan Doyle and Jiddu Krishnamurti to Benito Mussolini. During this period of intense experience, the young writer also worked hard: by the time he returned to Guatemala in 1933, when the plunge in coffee prices following the Great Depression had made it impossible for middle-class Guatemalans to sustain themselves abroad, Asturias had translated into Spanish Raynaud's French versions of the *Popol Vuh*, the so-called K'iche' Bible or creation myth, and the *Annals of the Cakchiquels*, and had written more than five hundred newspaper articles; scores of poems; numerous short stories; the dazzling literary quest for identity titled *Legends of Guatemala* (1930), with a prologue by Valéry; the first draft of a novel about his childhood, *The Bejeweled Boy*; and early sections of what would later become his classic mythological and magical realist novel, *Men of Maize* (1949)—not to mention, with the exception of a few pages added later to chapter XII, *Mr. President*, his most famous novel, at that time still titled *Tohil*. He had completed it by the end of 1932, leaving a manuscript copy behind in Paris with his friend Georges Pillement, who would keep it safe and eventually translate it into French.

The reason for the delay in its publication between 1932 and 1946 was, as previously mentioned, that on his reluctant return to Guatemala in 1933, the country was in the grip of another ferocious dictatorship, that of the fascistic colonel Jorge Ubico, in power from 1931 to 1944. Had Asturias tried to publish a violent protest novel sarcastically titled *Mr. President* during that period, he would have paid for it with his life. Thus it was that a young writer who seemed in 1930 to have the world at his feet, with the newly published *Legends of Guatemala* acclaimed by the great Valéry, now had to endure twelve years of silence, humiliation, and even moments of self-betrayal (Ubico would occasionally force him, Guatemala's outstanding novelist and poet, to attend national events or accompany him on visits to Mayan communities). Those twelve years coincided with the rise of Hitler, Mussolini, and Franco, the defeat of the Republicans in the Spanish Civil War, the Stalinist purges, and the horrors of World War II, one of the most somber periods in all of human history. With *Mr. President* hidden in the darkness, Asturias secretly completed his other great masterpiece, *Men of Maize*, but also concealed it in a trunk and published virtually nothing during this entire period; turned to drink; embarked upon a disastrous marriage that produced two sons, much tortured poetry, and eventually a divorce; and by the time of the Guatemalan middle-class revolution of 1944, appeared to have lost his way in life.

Nevertheless, the new president, Juan José Arévalo, was an old friend who was about to inaugurate the only decade of democratic government in Guatemalan history before the twenty-first century. He sent the aging bohemian off as cultural attaché to Mexico City and then to Buenos Aires, the two most vibrant centers of Spanish American culture. In the former, Asturias widened his acquaintance with Amerindian culture and history, and in the latter, he married an Argentinian divorcée, Blanca Mora y Araujo, who was writing a thesis on him and had the strength of character necessary to sort out his problems and manage his career. The publication of *Mr. President* in Mexico in 1946 had been in an edition hardly anyone read; when it was republished in Buenos Aires in 1948, it became an overnight sensation.

The appearance of the even more audacious and visionary *Men of Maize* in 1949 should have confirmed that in Asturias, Latin America had discovered one of its most distinctive novelists, but that book was considered impenetrable and was put into critical limbo in the shadow of *Mr. President*. At this point, moreover, Asturias himself changed direction, and his writing took a more overtly political and anti-imperialist turn: in fairness one might say that he sacrificed himself for the cause of democratic progress and national emancipation. Between 1950 and 1960 he wrote his notorious Banana Trilogy (*Strong Wind*, 1949; *The Green Pope*, 1954; *The Eyes of the Interred*, 1960), about the exploitation of Guatemalan land and labor by the United Fruit Company (UFC), a series that made him Latin America's best-known "committed" writer in an age heavily influenced by Sartre's existentialism, on the one hand, and by Soviet socialist realism, on the other. In 1954, the basic truth of his historical analysis in these rather curious hybrid novels—a fusion of magical realism with socialist realism—was exemplified by the overthrow, with the connivance of the United States, of the Guatemalan revolution's second government, led by Arévalo's successor, the nationalist Colonel Jacobo Árbenz. (US Secretary of State John Foster Dulles and his brother Allen, the head of the CIA, both had close links to the UFC.) Asturias, who was ambassador in El Salvador at the time, went into exile, where most leading Guatemalan intellectuals have remained ever since (many of them working, ironically enough, in North American universities), and wrote the furiously anti-imperialist stories of *Weekend en Guatemala* (1956), a work that was published in most of the world's leading languages except English.

For the first eight years after the coup, as another series of dictatorships ruled Guatemala, Asturias lived with his wife in Buenos Aires, until in 1962 his support for the still youthful Cuban Revolution led to a brief period of imprisonment, following which he and his wife left for Italy, where they stayed, ever poorer, until 1966, when Asturias was awarded the Lenin Peace Prize by the USSR. That same year, Julio César Méndez Montenegro, Guatemala's first civilian president in a decade and a half, offered the exiled writer the ambassadorship in Paris, and Asturias accepted, hoping to contribute to the peace process in his country. As things turned out, this period saw an intensification of Cuban-inspired guerrilla struggle in Guatemala. Asturias's elder son, Rodrigo, was a leading figure in the guerrilla movement for a quarter of a century, adopting the name Gaspar Ilóm, that of the Indian protagonist in the early chapters of *Men of Maize*. US-led counterinsurgency campaigns were launched everywhere in the region, and especially in Guatemala, where the repression would reach genocidal dimensions with the murder or disappearance of perhaps a quarter of a million mainly Indigenous Guatemalans out of a total population of around seven million.

In 1967, at the height of the so-called Boom of the Latin American novel—led by the Argentinian Julio Cortázar, the Mexican Carlos Fuentes, the Colombian Gabriel García Márquez, and the Peruvian Mario Vargas Llosa—and in the very year that García Márquez's *One Hundred Years of Solitude* was published and Che Guevara was killed in Bolivia, Asturias became the first Latin American novelist to win the Nobel Prize (and thus one of only three writers to receive both the Lenin Peace Prize and the Nobel Prize in Literature) and was able at last to anticipate an old age without political or financial problems. Ironically enough, his refusal to resign from his diplomatic post, despite the increasing militarization of the Méndez Montenegro regime—an agonizing decision for a "revolutionary" writer, who by then had no need for the money or the prestige but believed, following secret discussions with the exiled Árbenz, that staying on was the best way of serving his country—made him a controversial figure in his declining years and made it easy for sometimes unscrupulous critics to consign him prematurely to the past. He died in Madrid in 1974.

THE EXILES OF MIGUEL ÁNGEL ASTURIAS AND HIS NOVEL: A TRAGIC DOUBLE BIND

It was not until the mid-1970s, after the rise of the Latin American literary Boom and the death of Asturias, that the reappearance of the manuscript of *Mr. President* that had been left with Georges Pillement demonstrated that, with the exception of the first few pages of chapter XII, "Camila," Asturias's novel had been completed by 1932 and could have been published the following year. In other words, had it not been for the Ubico dictatorship, *Mr. President* would have been the contemporary of famous and rather rudimentary regionalist novels like *Doña Bárbara* (1929) by the Venezuelan Rómulo Gallegos and *Huasipungo* (1934) by the Ecuadorian Jorge Icaza. We would also have seen more clearly that the 1960s Boom was not a sudden new dawn in Latin American fiction, neither a revolution nor a rupture, but the crystallization and completion of Latin America's own belated version of the Anglo-American and European modernist movements of the 1920s (Joyce, Virginia Woolf, and William Faulkner on the one hand; Marcel Proust, Franz Kafka, and Thomas Mann on the other).

Asturias was born in Guatemala City in the same year that the great Jorge Luis Borges was born in Buenos Aires, 1899. Between them, these two very different writers from two very different countries would provide radically different visions of their continent, the one "Latin Americanist," the other "universalist" or, we would say today, "globalist." Both would be surpassed by the novelists of the 1960s generation, whose sudden and sensational transformation of Latin America's literary image, in the era of Marshall McLuhan's post-Sputnik "global village," was summed up by that controversial but undeniably effective and lasting label: the Boom. It is generally agreed that without Borges, the brilliant sense of structure and lucidity, the almost Cervantean humor and unmistakable irony of, say, García Márquez might not have emerged. Few have acknowledged an equally obvious and even more decisive—because quintessentially Latin American—influence: without Asturias, the so-called magical realist perspective and techniques of *One Hundred Years of Solitude* might not have developed. It was not Gabriel García Márquez who invented magical realism; it was Miguel Ángel Asturias. Thus Borges gave García Márquez the "European," "Western," "universal" aspect to his work; but Asturias gave him the "anthropological," "third-worldist" element, the postcolonial, revolutionary thrust. Because what is magical realism if not the solution to writing novels about hybrid societies in which a dominant culture of European origin is juxtaposed in multiple ways with one or more different cultures that in many cases are "premodern"? An unremarked aspect of Asturias's audacious work is that his viscerally Guatemalan novel was, so to speak, written mostly in Paris; the clash of what would later be called third- and first-world perspectives structures the entire reading experience.

When this novelist from a small underdeveloped republic, who had been broadly and generally admired between 1948 and 1967 for the works that he had written between the 1920s and the 1940s, was awarded the Nobel Prize, his success lasted mere hours, minutes, seconds—a parricidal drama that no one had anticipated, whose script had previously been invisible, went into immediate production. Some of the Boom writers, but above all many critics and propagandists professionally invested in the new movement, had already decided that the new writers who had emerged in the early 1960s were young revolutionaries (though only Vargas Llosa was really young) without literary fathers (mothers were not much considered at this moment in literary history), writers whose originality had no precedent (we might note that they were all from "big" countries, unlike Asturias), and the particular precedent of Asturias was unwelcome because it undermined the narrative and the micromyths that the Boom writers and their publicists were in the process of broadcasting to Latin America itself and the rest of the world.

Somehow, to be justified, Latin America always has to be new; it always has to surprise us. Asturias, overnight, became an "anachronistic" writer. *Mr. President* was reframed as an exclusively political and excessively committed work. *Men of Maize* (in my view the most visionary novel ever written in Latin America) remained largely unknown and almost entirely ignored. And incredibly, and unforgivably, Asturias, whose direct commitment to broadly political activities on behalf of his small and largely Indigenous republic vastly outweighed the political commitments of the most famous novelists of the Boom, was evaluated according to a selective reading of his past and deemed a "traitor" to the Latin American left because he had accepted an ambassadorship from a regime that, in his view, offered the last best hope for a democratic Guatemala.

Yet it was Asturias who had established what one can broadly call the avant-garde—or even the Joycean—moment in Latin American narrative, a moment that did not begin after World War II, still less during the celebrated and dazzling Boom of the 1960s, but in the period after World War I, during which Joyce wrote his books in Italy, Switzerland, and Paris and the poets César Vallejo of Peru and Pablo Neruda of Chile gave a foretaste of what Latin American literature would become in later decades. In short, the Latin American New Novel actually began in the period when Asturias published his *Legends of Guatemala*, wrote the early chapters of *Men of Maize*, and, above all, wrote *Mr. President*, despite the fact that the novel as a genre is always much slower to respond to new trends and new historical eras than poetry. But Asturias's poetic vision ran fierce and deep, which is why the great Martinican poet Aimé Césaire, at the end of a remarkable poem written in homage to Asturias after his death, declared that the Guatemalan would never be deceased but had been metamorphosed into "a mountain perennially green, on the horizon of all mankind."

To recapitulate (and rewrite history): If it had not been for Ubico (and the writer's beloved mother, who begged him to return to Guatemala in the early 1930s), the merits and the contribution of Asturias's work to an entire epoch of Latin American culture would have been obvious, material, natural, undeniable. *Mr. President* would have been published in 1933, the year Hitler became the Herr Präsident of Germany; Asturias's relationship to the international avant-garde would have been not only evident but also epochally self-evident, as would his absolute originality (which has always been recognized in France, the country where he wrote the novel) and indeed the novel's uniqueness within the Latin American fiction of his time. And a decade later, *Men of Maize* would have been greeted as the equally brilliant and long-gestated follow-up to that earlier landmark and would have received the full attention of Latin American literary criticism instead of dying—let me be more optimistic, hibernating—in the shadow of the more sensational *Mr. President* and of the social realist works inspired by the political urgency of the postwar period. (This more politically committed moment had begun, in Asturias's case, in 1949, before Sartre's influence became widespread, in the very year that *Men of Maize* appeared, with the simultaneous publication of *Strong Wind*, the first volume of his perhaps excessively "committed" Banana Trilogy, born nonetheless of the entirely justifiable moral outrage of humanist anti-imperialism.) Thus in 1967, *Mr. President* was read not in the ways just hypothesized but as a "picturesque relic" (by the Uruguayan critic Emir Rodríguez Monegal, the Boom's most enthusiastic and influential propagandist), and *Men of Maize*, of which not a single serious critical study existed, was dismissed as an obscure "indigenist" novel, in reference to a genre whose high point had been in the 1920s and early 1930s.

And if it had not been for the Boom and its very partial reading of its own prehistory and equally selective choice of its precursors (who included no "political" or "indigenist" writers), it would not have been necessary to suppress Asturias's true antecedents or to call his first two novels anachronistic or to call him a political traitor. It was true that he had been born in a previous era (a generation ahead of Cortázar; two generations ahead of García Márquez, Fuentes, and Vargas Llosa), but he had been as precocious in his own generation as Vargas Llosa would later be considered in his; and in any case he would never have been called anachronistic had he been French,

English, or North American. (*The Great Gatsby* is not anachronistic any more than, say, *Don Quixote* is; it is a great American classic, written, as classics are by definition, in another time.) Instead of anachronistic, he would have been seen as archetypal, in terms of both his literary significance and his political trajectory. But it was not convenient to recognize this in the 1960s, when Asturias, the wrong man, won the Nobel Prize, and it is still not convenient in the present day, in an entirely different context, both culturally and socially (one that is even less political and even less avant-garde). The result was that Asturias, the victim of two temporal time lags, ceased to appear as what he was, the essential bridge between two eras and two generations, and became—was converted into—a missing link (some kind of Neanderthal, perhaps?). Double exile, double jeopardy, double disappearance, double bind.

THE FIRST PAGE OF THE BOOM

And yet: *Mr. President* remains, despite everything, the single most famous dictator novel in Latin American history. It is the region's first fully-fledged surrealist novel and exemplifies more clearly than any other the crucial link between European surrealism and Latin American magical realism, which Asturias himself originated with *Legends of Guatemala*, completed by 1928. (Literary history has not yet appreciated that the true and original home of magical realism is in Central America and the Caribbean.) It was also the first novel to show Latin American political, social, and psychological life as a labyrinth or web of corruption, and indeed the whole tissue of human experience as a web or network of perceptions, emotions, and ideas that have to be deciphered by the reader in order to reconstitute them and make sense of the world. It could achieve this because it was also the first major novel in Latin America to attempt a revolution in literary language, to exploit the relation between myth and language and between both of these and the unconscious; it was also the first to underscore the crucial role of myth in social and political life, to show that myth could be operative at the level of the text itself, and indeed to perceive that a narrative could unfold as a kind of myth. It was the first book—with the partial exception of José Mármol's *Amalia* (1851), about the Juan Manuel de Rosas regime in Argentina—to show that whole cities, even entire countries, could be prisons, or that under a dictatorship, with terror and repression internalized, human consciousness itself becomes a prison, rendering still more invisible all the other biological and psychological determinisms that we cannot entirely know but cannot entirely escape. It was the first important novel to unite the implicit call for a revolution in language and literature— what else was the avant-garde?—with a call for a revolution in politics and society (particularly through the unnamed student), to challenge patriarchy and authoritarianism at the level of consciousness, and thus to question the very basis of Latin American social life and psychic existence—that is to say, the internalization of totalitarianism (before Hitler). It was also the first Latin American novel to understand that Latin America's uneasiness with its hybrid, mestizo, "underdeveloped" identity, combined with the inauthenticity and alienation of what would much later be called postcolonialism, contrived to make melodrama—the stock-in-trade of silent cinema—an unavoidable and indeed characteristic facet of Latin American identity, evident throughout the region, in its boleros, its tangos, and its world-famous telenovelas, or soap operas. (The principal character in *Mr. President*, Angel Face, a darkly self-critical version of its author, is "as good and evil as Satan himself"; in chapter XII, probably the most important section of the novel, the teenage Camila, symbol of the continent's future generations, later Angel Face's wife, experiences the wave effect of cinematographic images as the possibility of some future liberation of consciousness; and the heartbreaking surrealist dream sequences involving the crazed beggar Pelele—a "rag doll"—are Buñuelian in conception and achievement, and his unbearable orphanhood is symbolic of the story of the Latin American lower classes since the Spanish conquest; and all three of these archetypal characters are orphans without mothers, like Latin America itself since its pre-Hispanic societies were conquered and destroyed.) Finally, all of this, in turn, makes *Mr. President* one of the first works to reverse the ideological signs of the century after independence from Spain, a century that had involved an almost unquestioning march toward Europe (especially Paris and London) and its technological progress and modernity, a process that attained its literary culmination in Gallegos's *Doña Bárbara*, published only three years before the completion of *Mr. President*. Such complexity! And yet the book could be read by anyone with a minimal knowledge of literary culture (unlike the later *Men of Maize* and indeed the majority of the Boom novels).

In a brilliant but little-known essay published in 1987, "The First Seven Pages of the Boom," the U.S. novelist and critic William Gass gives his opinion on which were the top seven novels of Latin America's sensational 1960s phenomenon (Ernesto Sábato, *On Heroes and Tombs*; Cortázar, *Hopscotch*; Fuentes, *The Death of Artemio Cruz*; Vargas Llosa, *The Green House*; Guillermo Cabrera Infante, *Three Trapped Tigers*; García Márquez, *One Hundred Years of Solitude*; and José Lezama Lima, *Paradiso*) and quotes their opening lines. But in starting his essay with the first paragraph of *Mr. President*, Gass reveals that he, too, believes that the Boom was inscribed, thirty years in advance, in the first lines of Asturias's novel. It is, indeed, an archetypal Latin American novel; and Asturias is an archetypal Latin American writer; and the first lines of *Mr. President* are the first lines of the Boom.

Nothing has ever more precisely expressed my own feelings upon first reading the novel than the comment by Gabriel Venaissin, a reviewer of the French translation, reproduced on the cover of my first copy of *Mr. President*, bought in 1966 in Buenos Aires in the same bookshop where I bought Sartre's *What Is Literature?* in Spanish:

I doubt if any novel has managed to create a greater sense of asphyxia. But the remarkable thing about this book lies in its having used this universe to attain something else. Asturias invents a language of almost total freedom. Despite his point of departure in a poisoned world, there is not a single instant in which we do not feel ourselves projected toward the sky and the stars, launched toward space, pushed toward liberty from a reality in which liberty is dying at every moment.

I have always found something characteristically Latin American in this contrast between imprisonment and freedom, repression and passionate creativity, reality and utopia.

And I also clearly remember the impact in my own mind, as a student, of the words, toward the end of the book, that run through the mind of the student, newly released from prison, as he sees some of his fellow citizens watching a line of anonymous convicts shamble past. (The student is the representative of what would be a historically decisive new Latin American generation flowing from the movement that began at the University of Córdoba, Argentina, in 1918.) It is a Hamletian variation, based not on the self but on recognition of the other: "The prisoners continued walking by. To be them, and not to be the onlookers so happy not to be prisoners." I believe this is the culminating moment of the text, the point where theory and practice come together, become visible and, above all (it is Asturias's entire endeavor), unavoidable. It is also, manifestly, the moment when the fusion of identification (see Jean-Jacques Rousseau and Claude Lévi-Strauss) and political and ethical commitment (see Sartre) is confirmed as the central message of the novel. *Mr. President*, whose words and images seem to speak to us across a hundred-year abyss, as we come to appreciate that we, too, are short on time, is not only an act of witness and an act of protest, but also a call for moral commitment and an act of faith in the possibility, despite everything, of a better, more creative, and more harmonious world.

GERALD MARTIN

A Note on the Translation

Mexico's Editorial Costa-Amic published *Mr. President* in 1946, fourteen years after Asturias completed it. As it portrayed a dictator and his destructive authoritarian rule, Asturias was rightly afraid that Guatemala's president at the time he finished writing the novel, Jorge Ubico, would consider it an indictment of his own regime (1931–1944). It actually references the 1898–1920 dictatorship of Manuel Estrada Cabrera, though no country or leader is ever named, thus making it a portrait of the archetypal Latin American dictator, both past and present (Paraguay's Alfredo Stroessner, Nicaragua's Anastasio Somoza Debayle, Cuba's Fidel Castro, Venezuela's Hugo Chávez, and Nicaragua's Daniel Ortega come to mind). It was the first Latin American dictator novel—Augusto Roa Bastos's *I, the Supreme* (1974), Gabriel García Márquez's *The Autumn of the Patriarch* (1975), and Mario Vargas Llosa's *The Feast of the Goat* (2000) were to follow—and is considered today the most daring, if not the best. And in a broader sense, without Asturias there would be no García Márquez, Vargas Llosa, Isabel Allende, Laura Restrepo, Laura Esquivel, José Lezama Lima, or Roberto Bolaño.

Mr. President challenges and sometimes frustrates even native Spanish readers. Guatemalan Indigenous vernacular (more than 50 percent of the population speaks one of twenty-three Mayan languages) is sprinkled throughout, and Asturias employs it with often outrageously comical results. He also pierces any illusions of decorum and politeness with his rampant and startling use of colloquial language, surrealism, and magical realist elements. Language explodes out of him as if he were one of Guatemala's many active volcanoes. At the same time,

Mr. President is a plot-driven novel with more than its share of unexpected turns and, also, a failed love story.

Despite its broad acceptance in Latin America and Europe, *Mr. President* has failed to capture a wide readership in English. Frances Partridge's 1963 translation may be partly to blame; although lyrical, it is somewhat dated, full of Anglicisms, mistranslations, occasional paragraph omissions, and an overdose of awkward Latinate constructions that may leave readers scratching their head.

Guatemalan Spanish has changed tremendously in a hundred years, with many words and idioms having fallen into disuse. I encountered more than a few linguistic breaches; by consulting two Guatemalan aficionados of Asturias (they were often equally stumped by some of my 250 or so queries), I was able to bridge gaps, as it were. I have also left in place many Spanish words that have entered American usage. And no contemporary reader of this novel will fail to shudder when encountering the slurs against Jews, Arabs, Chinese, Indigenous Guatemalans, and gay and transgender people that crop up from time to time and that were rampant during the period Asturias is depicting.

Asturias's prose is often overly poetic, and at times repetitious and even redundant. I have tried to establish, in the American vernacular, the proper relation among words, sentences, and paragraphs so that the author's startling images, metaphors, and narrative verve may speak directly to the monolingual reader. I don't believe that a translation, or any work of fiction, for that matter, should be a chore to read. Umberto Eco said in *Experiences in Translation* that "a perfect translation is an impossible dream"; agreed, but it is still a goal worth trying to achieve. Bilingual readers may feel that I have not duplicated all the linguistic and narrative registers of the original, but I hope my translation comes across stereophonically, capturing much of the fire and novelty of the original.

As a self-proclaimed Guategringo—born in Guatemala but raised and educated in the United States—I found translating

Mr. President to have a special personal significance. My work as a translator and fiction writer has been a lifelong attempt to return to my roots, to the land of my birth.

This translation was made possible, in part, by a grant from the New York State Council on the Arts with the support of Governor Andrew M. Cuomo and the New York State legislature. I would also like to thank Jill Schoolman for supporting this project and the Guatemalan writers Denise Phé-Funchal and Javier Mosquera Saravia for clarifying many Guatemaltequismos. I am grateful to the Penguin Classics team—John Siciliano and Marissa Davis, in particular—for the help they have rendered me along the way.

DAVID UNGER

Mr. President

Mr. President

PART I

APRIL 21, 22, AND 23

I

IN THE PORTAL DEL SEÑOR

. . . lluminate, light of aluminum, Light of alighted Stone! Like ears humming, the buzzing of the bells beckoning to prayers persisted, doubletroublestar of light in the shadow, of shadow in the light. ¡Alumbra, lumbre de alumbre, Luzbel de piedralumbre, sobre lapodredumbre! ¡Alumbra, lumbre de alumbre, sobre la podredumbre, Luzbel de piedralumbre! ¡Alumbra, alumbra, lumbre de alumbre . . . , alumbre . . . , alumbra . . . , alumbra, lumbre de alumbre . . . , alumbra, alumbre . . . !

Hidden in the shadows of the icy Cathedral, the beggars staggered by the Mercado's food stands along streets as wide as oceans on their way to the Plaza de Armas, leaving the empty city behind.

Night brought together the beggars and the stars. United only by misery, soon the beggars would huddle to sleep in the Portal del Señor, cursing and insulting one another through clenched teeth. They elbowed and threw dirt on one another like mortal enemies. Scuffling, biting, and spitting, they picked fights with those brothers-in-filth with neither a pillow nor a friend to trust. Without undressing, they hunkered down to sleep like thieves, heads resting on cloth bags stuffed with their riches—meat scraps, ripped shoes, candle stumps, clumps of boiled rice wrapped in old newspaper, oranges, and rotting bananas.

Then they sat up to count their money on the steps facing the Portal's back wall, biting coins to make sure they were real. They talked among themselves, tallying their food and weapons: soon they would take to the streets with rocks in

hand and scapulars around their necks, stopping only to fur-
tively chew on bread crusts. Greedy down to their bones, they
would sooner give their leftover scraps to the stray dogs than
to other beggars as wretched as themselves.

With their coins secured in handkerchiefs—knotted seven
times fast and tied tightly to their waists—they dropped to the
ground satiated and fell into tense, miserable sleep. Famished
pigs, scrawny women, crippled dogs, carriage wheels passed before their eyes in their nightmares. Phantom priests entered
the Cathedral as if going to a grave, preceded by a worm of a
moon on a cross made of frozen shinbones. Sometimes, they
would be shocked awake by the screams of the Dimwit lost in
the Plaza de Armas or the sobs of a blind woman who dreamt
she was hanging on a spike like a side of beef, covered with
flies. Other times, they would wake up to the crack of a whip
as a political prisoner was dragged and beaten by police, while
a group of women always followed close behind, wiping the
tracks of blood with tear-drenched handkerchiefs. Or it would
be the snores of a filthy hypochondriac or the gasps of a pregnant deaf-mute who suspected a baby alive in her womb would
wake them. But the Dimwit's never-ending inhuman cries were
the saddest of all, almost tearing open the heavens.

On Sundays, a drunk who in his sleep cried like a child for
his mother would join this strangest of gatherings. As soon as
the Dimwit heard the word "mother" (both curse and lament
in the drunk's mouth), he would sit up and scan the Portal
from side to side. Once fully awake, his screams would rouse
his friends until his cry merged with that of the drunk.

Dogs barked, voices rang out, and the most mulish of the
beggars would stand up and join the chorus to silence him: *Either you shut up or the police will shut you up.* But the police
wouldn't dare appear. Not one of them had money to pay a
fine. "Long live France," screamed Pegleg. Then the Dimwit
jumped and screamed and became the laughingstock of the
group because this one-legged, cursing cripple made fun of the
drunk all during the week. Pegleg teased both the drunk and
Pelele—the Dimwit's nickname—who appeared dead when
sleeping, though he came back to life at each shout, not noticing

his fellow beggars, piled together on the floor on top of burlap strips, who would then curse and cackle at his crazy antics. Standing far off from his companions' hideous faces, he saw, heard, and felt nothing. Exhausted by so much crying, Pelele would fall into a deep sleep, but as soon as he did, Pegleg would scream:

"Mother!"

Pelele would jack up his eyes like someone dreaming he was spinning into emptiness; his pupils widened as he drew into himself. Wounded to the core, he felt the pooling of his tears. He would fall back to sleep slowly, totally spent, his body almost pulp, nausea whirling in his broken mind. But someone would startle him by saying "Mother" as he closed his eyes and inched toward sleep.

That someone was the degenerate mulatto Widower, who, laughing from his old man's puckered mouth, said: "God bless you, Mother of Mercy, our hope and salvation. Protect us lowly exiles."

Pelele would wake up laughing, amused by his own grief, hunger, pained heart, and tears splashing his teeth while the beggars snatched la-la-la-laughter from the air, la-la-la-laughter from the air. A fat man with stew sauce on his moustache laughed so hard he lost his breath, and a one-eyed man pissed his pants, butting his head against a wall like a goat. Blind men protested that they couldn't sleep through all the noise, and Mosco, a blind man missing both legs, muttered that only fags could amuse themselves like this.

But the complaints of the blind were ignored, and Mosco's comment not even heard—why should anyone listen to his cackling? "Yes, I spent my childhood in the barracks. Mules and officers kicked me into shape and made a man out of me. I learned to work like a horse, which helped me drag a barrel organ down the streets. Sure, I lost my sight, and then my right leg, in a bar brawl, God knows how, and a car chopped off my left leg, but I was too drunk to remember how or where."

The beggars spread the word that Pelele would go nuts whenever anyone mentioned his mother. The poor wretch ran through the streets, squares, courtyards, and markets, trying to get away from people shouting "Mother!" at him, morning, noon, and night like a curse from heaven. He sought refuge in houses, but maids and dogs chased him. People drove him out of churches and stores, indifferent to his exhaustion and to his crazed eyes pleading for pity.

The sprawling city, made larger by his own exhaustion, shrank in the face of his despair. Days of persecution followed nights of terror. People weren't content only to scream at him, "You'll marry your Mother this Sunday, you stupid Dimwit"— they had to beat him and tear at his clothes. Children chased him, forcing him to hide out in the poorest neighborhoods where everyone lived hand to mouth. Just teasing him wasn't enough in such places, so they threw stones, dead rats, and tin cans after him as he ran off in panic.

One day, he came to the Portal from one of these poor areas just as the bells were ringing. Forehead slashed, he wore no hat, though a kite tail had been tied around him as a joke. Wall shadows, dogs running by, leaves falling from trees, and even squeaky wheels frightened him. When he reached the Portal, it was nearly dark and the beggars were sitting facing the wall, counting their money. Pegleg argued with Mosco, the deaf-mute caressed her inexplicably swollen belly, and, in a dream, the blind woman hung from a spike like meat at the butcher shop, covered with flies.

Pelele fell onto the ground half dead. He'd gone days without resting, nights without sleeping. Beggars silently scratched their fleabites, unable to sleep. They heard police walking back and forth along the dimly lit square and guards clicking their arms as they stood at attention in the windows of the nearby barracks like ghosts covered in striped blankets, keeping nightly watch over the President. No one knew where he actually was, because he owned several houses outside of the city. No one even knew how he slept—someone said he held a whip in his hand and kept a phone beside him—and some friends claimed he didn't sleep.

A stranger walked toward the Portal. The beggars curled up like worms. The creak of army boots was met by the sinister hoot of a bird in the porous, bottomless night.

Pegleg opened his eyes—it seemed the end of the world was near—and said to the owl: *Double double toil and trouble; fly into the air, drop down into the muddle.*

Mosco groped with his hands for his face. The air was tense, as if the earth were about to shake. The Widower, seated with the blind men, crossed himself. Only Pelele slept, for once, like a log, snoring.

The stranger stopped. A smile spread over his face. He tiptoed over to Pelele and screamed, "Mother!"

The cry jolted Pelele awake. The Dimwit threw himself at his tormentor, not giving him a chance to pull out his weapon. He gouged his eyes with his fingers, bit into his nose, and kneed him in the balls until the stranger fell to the ground, inert.

The beggars shut their eyes in disgust. The owl flew by once again, and Pelele fled down the darkened street, shaking in panic.

A blind force had put an end to the life of Colonel José Parrales Sonriente, known as the Man with the Tiny Mule.

Dawn was about to break.

II

THE DEATH OF MOSCO

The sun gilded the Second Police Station's projecting roof (some people were walking down the street), the Protestant Chapel (a few doors were open), and a brick building under construction. Groups of barefoot women sat on stone benches in dark corridors, waiting for the prisoners in a courtyard that was, as usual, dripping with rain. They cradled breakfast baskets in the folds of their skirts while bunches of children clustered around them. Babies clung to their pendulous breasts, and the older kids hungrily eyed the loaves in the breadbaskets. The women whispered their troubles to one another, crying as they spoke, drying tears on the ends of their shawls. An old woman, obviously sick with malaria, wept copiously, silently, as if to underscore that her suffering was even more profound. In this dismal place, the ills of life seemed incurable: here, where the waiting women stared out at a couple of barren shrubs, an empty fountain, and a few police officers who cleaned their shirt collars with spit, only God's mercy could save them.

A mestizo police officer walked by, dragging Mosco. He had seized him at the corner of the Colegio de Infante and shook him from side to side as if Mosco were a trained monkey. But the women were far from amused, as they watched the guards bring breakfast to the prisoners and return with scraps of news.

Say what? Don't worry about him; he's doing better.

Say what? Bring him some mercury ointment as soon as the pharmacy opens.

Say what? Don't pay attention to what his cousin says.

Get him a young public defender, 'cause they don't charge as much as a real lawyer.

Don't be jealous, there are no women in here. They brought a fag in the other day.

Give him a laxative. He hasn't been able to take a shit.

Say what? Lazy of her to sell their only chest of drawers.

"Hey, stop!" said Mosco, tired of how the policeman was flinging him about. "I'm not some piece of shit. I may be poor, but I'm honest. Listen to me—I'm not your kid or a stuffed animal—you can't treat me like this. Look at you, going to where we dirtbags hang out so you can stay good with the gringos. Good going. Catching a scor-pi-on without his stinger, a bunch of drunken turkeys. Treating us like dirtbags. When that brownnosing busybody Mister Nosey-poesy came, we'd gone three days without eating, looking out of windows wrapped in muslin like a bunch of weirdos. . . ."

One by one, the beggars were brought to the dark, narrow jail cells known as the Three Marias. Mosco was dragged by his arms and stump legs, like a crab, his voice drowned out by the keys creaking in the locks and the cursing jailers who stank of sweat and stale tobacco.

Now his voice echoed loudly in the underground vault: "Fucking pig. Son of a bitch. *JesusChristPrice*, help me."

His fellow prisoners whimpered like sick, sniveling animals scared of the dark (all they'd ever see again). They were scared shitless, there where dozens had died of hunger and thirst. They suspected they would be boiled down like mongrels and made into pig soap or have their throats slit to feed the police. They saw cannibal faces advancing through shadows lit up like torches, their buttlike cheeks and moustaches drooling chocolate. . . .

A student and a church sexton were in the same cell.

"If I'm not mistaken, sir, you were here first. You came, then I came, no?" The student talked just to say something, to get rid of the knot of tension in his throat.

"I think so," the sexton replied, looking into the dark for the face talking to him.

"I was about to ask why you were jailed."

"Something to do with politics."

The student, shaking from head to toe, stuttered, "Me, too."

The beggars felt around for their bagged possessions, but the prison director had taken everything, even what was in their pockets. The rules were strict. Not even a match was allowed.

"And what's the charge?" the student went on.

"There's no charge. Someone at the top accused me of something." The sexton rubbed his back against the rough wall, trying to scratch off the lice.

"You were—"

"Nope!" the sexton interrupted angrily. "I wasn't anything."

Just then, the door hinges creaked as another beggar came in.

"Long live France," said Pegleg.

"I'm in prison—" the sexton answered.

"Long live France!"

"—for a crime I committed by mistake. Instead of taking down a sign about the Virgin of O from the church door, I took down a poster announcing the birthday anniversary of the President's mother."

"But how did they find out?" the student asked.

The sexton wiped away tears with his fingers. "You got me. My own stupidity. Anyhow, they arrested me and brought me to the Chief of Police. He slapped me around a few times and then gave orders for me to be put in solitary confinement—as a revolutionary."

Crumpled in the dark, the beggars cried out of fear, hunger, and cold. They couldn't even see their own hands. At times, they fell into a stupor. The pregnant deaf-mute's heavy breathing circled about them as if hunting for a way out.

They were released, who knows when, maybe around midnight. A squat man with a wrinkled yellow face—bushy moustache over thick lips, stubby nose, hooded eyes—told them he was investigating a political crime. He asked them all together, and then individually, if they knew who was responsible for the murder of a colonel in the Portal the previous night.

They had been taken to a room lit by a smoking lantern whose weak light seemed filtered through watery glass. What happened? Against what wall? And that rack of weapons fiercer than a tiger's jaw and that police officer's belt full of bullets?

The Judge Advocate leapt from his chair when he heard the surprising responses of the beggars.

"Tell me the truth!" he shouted, banging his fist on the table he used as a desk. His eyes bulged under thick eyeglasses.

One by one, they accused Pelele of carrying out the Portal murder. They described circuitously, but in great detail, the crime their eyes had witnessed.

The Judge Advocate signaled for the police officers who had been listening outside the room to come in and corral the beggars into an empty room and beat them up. A long rope hung from the barely visible central beam.

"Dimwit killed him," said the Widower, hoping to escape torture by spitting out the truth. "Sir, it was Dimwit. I swear to God. It was Dimwit, Dimwit. *Pelele!* Pelele did it!"

"I don't suffer fools. You were told to say that. I'll kill you if you don't tell me the truth! Understand? Understand?!"

The Judge Advocate's voice was drowned out by the blood roaring in the unfortunate wretch's ears. He was hanging by his thumbs, his feet inches above the ground. He kept shouting: "It was Dimwit, I'm telling you! I swear to God it was him! The Dimwit! Dimwit! Dimwit!"

"You liar," he answered, pausing for a breath. "Liar! I'm going to tell you who killed Coronel José Parrales Sonriente. Let's see if you have the balls to deny it. It was General Eusebio Canales and his lawyer, Abel Carvajal!"

His voice met a frozen silence. Then bit by bit, a whimper, a moan, and finally a *yes* was heard. When the rope was loosened, the Widower fell to the ground, unconscious. The mulatto's cheeks, dripping with sweat and tears, looked like chunks of wet coal.

His companions, shaking like dogs poisoned by the police and left to die on the street, confirmed one by one what the investigator claimed. Mosco, his face twisted with fear and nausea, was the only one to deny it. They hung him by the thumbs because he claimed, half buried—his legs belowground, like everyone whose legs have been cut off—that his fellow beggars were lying when they accused someone else of a crime for which the Dimwit alone was responsible.

"Responsible!" The Judge Advocate pounced on the word. "How dare you say that a Dimwit was responsible? You're lying! An irresponsible Dimwit, responsible?"

"Let him tell you himself. . . ."

"Whip him!" said a shrill-voiced police officer, while another cop struck him in the face.

"Tell the truth!" demanded the officer as he whipped the old man's cheeks. "The truth, or you'll hang here all night!"

"Can't you see I'm blind?"

"Then stop blaming the Dimwit."

"But that's the truth, and I have the balls to say so."

Two lashes bloodied his lips.

"Just because you're blind doesn't mean you can't hear and can't tell the truth like the others."

"All right," said Mosco faintly. The investigator smelled victory. "Okay, you dumb fuck. The Dimwit killed him."

"You fool!"

The Judge Advocate's words were lost in the ears of a halfman who would never hear anything again. When they loosened the rope, Mosco's dead body—or rather his torso, since his legs had already been cut off—fell to the ground like a broken pendulum.

"Stupid old liar! His testimony would've been useless anyway, since he was blind," said the investigator, walking past the corpse.

He hurried into a shabby carriage drawn by two skinny horses, a pair of lanterns hanging off it like the eyes of death, to give the President the results of the investigation. The police threw Mosco's body into a trash cart headed to the cemetery. The roosters were already crowing. The beggars, now free, crowded back into the streets. The deaf-mute woman cried out in fear, feeling a child moving in her womb.

III

PELELE'S ESCAPE

Pelele fled down the narrow maze of streets toward the city's outskirts. His frantic screams disturbed neither the breathing of the sky nor the sleep of its residents, who were as alike in death's mirror as they'd be different once the sun rose and the daily round began. Some lacked the bare necessities and worked for their daily bread, while others—taking advantage of the privileges of the idle rich—had more than enough. The latter were the President's friends: owners of forty to fifty houses; moneylenders at 9, 9.5, even 10 percent a month; and officials holding seven or eight different public posts who cashed in on concession stands, pensions, professional titles, gambling halls, cockfighting, Indians, moonshine distilleries, whorehouses, bars, and bribed newspapers.

The beet-red dawn stained the tips of the mountains cupping the city, like dandruff atop a valley. Common laborers were the first to walk down streets shrouded in darkness, ghosts in a soulless world. Office workers, clerks, and students followed a few hours later. Around eleven, when the sun was already high, the important gentlemen came to walk off their breakfast and build an appetite for lunch or rushed to join an influential friend in buying the debt of starving teachers at half price.

Down streets still engulfed in subterranean shadows, the rustling of starched skirts would break the silence—poor girls tirelessly doing morning chores or supporting families as swineherds, butter churners, traders, or girlfriends. And with the turning of the light from rose to white, like a begonia petal, came the pattering footsteps of some skinny secretary. She was ridiculed by ladies of leisure who waited until the sun was hot before leaving their bedrooms to prance down hallways and recount their dreams to their maids, scoff at passersby, caress the cat, read the newspaper, or preen before a mirror.

Pelele hurried off, in a kind of foggy dream, chased by mutts and spikes of fine rain. He ran every which way, mouth open and tongue lolling, snot nosed, panting, his arms waving in the air. Door after door, window after door after window flew by him. Suddenly, he'd stop short and put his hands over his face to defend himself from telegraph poles, but once he realized they were harmless, he'd burst out laughing and resume running like a man fleeing prison, chasing after walls of mist that disappeared the closer he came to them.

When he reached the outskirts of the city, where town gave way to countryside, he collapsed on a pile of trash. Above webs of dead trees, buzzards and blackbirds circled the garbage dump and gazed at him with bluish eyes. Since he was motionless, they swooped down and hopped around on the ground near him, edging closer in a macabre birds-of-prey dance. Glancing back and forth, ready to fly off at the slightest shift of wind or leaf, they closed in on him until they were just a beak away.

A fierce squawk signaled the attack. Pelele jumped to his feet, ready to defend himself. The most daring buzzard sank its beak like a dart into his upper lip, down to his gums, while the others fought for the right to peck out his eyes or heart.

The buzzard didn't care that the victim was still alive. It was about to rip off his lip when the Dimwit rolled down a trash heap, sending up clouds of dust and clumps of solid garbage.

Darkness descended. Green sky. Green landscape. In the barracks, bugles sounded the six o'clock call, the echoing aftertaste of a tribe on the alert or a besieged medieval town. The suffering of prisoners being killed slowly by the passing of years started again. The horizon gathered up its points of light in the city streets like a snail with a thousand horns. People were coming back from meeting the President, either relieved or even more frightened.

The light from the gambling dens flickered in the darkness.

Pelele continued to struggle with the ghost of the buzzard he felt was still attacking him and with the pain of a leg broken by a fall—an unbearable black pain tearing at his life.

All night he moaned softly and loudly, back and forth, like a lame dog. "Ow, ow . . . *ow ow* . . . ow, ow."

Sitting by a pool of water among wild plants sprouting flowers fertilized by the city's trash, the Dimwit imagined huge storms in the cavern of his small skull.

"Ow, ow, ow."

Steel fingernails of fever clawed at his forehead. Flitting thoughts. A world made rubbery by mirrors. Enormous distortions. Delirious tempests. A dizzying horizontal, vertical, or angular escape, newly born and dead, spiraled forth.

"Ow, ow, ow."

Curveofacurveinacurveofacurveinacurveofacurveinacurve of Lot's wife. (Did she invent the Lot-tery?) Trams pulling mules were turned into Lot's wife, and their stillness annoyed conductors, who, not satisfied with whipping and stoning them, invited the male passengers to fire their guns. The proper gentlemen spurred the mules on by unsheathing their daggers. . . .

Owowow.

Dim, dim, dimwit! Dimdimdimwit.

Owowow.

The knife sharpener sharpens his teeth to laugh. Laughter sharpeners. Teeth of sharpeners.

"Mother!"

The scream of the drunkard roused him.

"Mother!"

The moon shone brightly between spongy clouds, whiteness turning the damp leaves into glowing porcelain.

They're carrying off—
They're carrying off—!
They're carrying off the church saints to bury them!
Oh what fun, they're going to bury them, oh they're going to bury them, oh what fun!

*The cemetery is cheerier and cleaner than the city. Oh what
fun! They're going to bury them!*
Ta-ra-ra! Ta-ra-boom-te-ray.

Trampling everything, he leapt from one volcano to another,
from star to star, from sky to sky, half awake, half asleep, from
big mouths to small, with and without teeth, with and without
lips, with fleshy lips, with hair, with double triple tongues, who
shouted "Mother!Mother!Mother!" at him.

Choo-choo. He took the local train to leave town and go as
fast as possible into the mountains that served as stepping
stones for the volcanoes, way beyond the radio towers, way
beyond the slaughterhouses, the artillery storages, a vol-au-
vent full of soldiers.

However, the train returned to its departure point like a toy
on a string. When it arrived—chug-chug, chug-chug—a snif-
fling vegetable seller with basket-wire hair cried out: "Bread
for the Dimwit! Water for the Dimwit! Squawk! Bread for the
Dimwit!"

He ran toward the Portal, chased by the vegetable seller, who
was threatening to toss a gourd of water on him.

When he got there: *Mother!* A cry . . . a jump . . . a man . . .
a night; a struggle . . . death . . . blood . . . escape . . . the
Dimwit . . .

"Water for the Dimwit, Polly wants a cracker! Water for the
Dimwit!"

The pain in his leg woke him. He felt a maze inside his
bones. The sunlight saddened his eyes. Sleeping vines with
their occasional flowers invited him to sleep under their shade,
near a cool spring, which snapped its foaming tail as if a silver
squirrel hid among its ferns and mosses.

Nobody. Nobody.

Dimwit sank again into a night when his pain did battle
with his falling lids. He tried to find a comfortable position for
his broken leg while holding his torn lip in place. Whenever he
opened his burning lids, clouds of blood passed over him. The
shadow of worms became a butterfly fluttering between flashes
of lightning.

He turned his back to the hallucinations ringing in his head like a bell. Ice cream for the dying. The ice cream man is selling the Eucharist for the Last Rites. The priest is selling snow. Ting-a-ling, ting-a-ling. Ice cream for the dying! There goes the Eucharist. So goes the ice cream man! Take off your hat, you dumb fuck! Ice cream for the dying!

IV

ANGEL FACE

Pelele went on dreaming, covered in paper, leather strips, rags, broken umbrellas, straw-hat brims, porous pewter pots, ceramic pieces, cardboard boxes, mashed books, broken glass, tonguelike shoes curling in the sunlight, collars, eggshells, cotton mats, and leftover food. Now he was in a huge courtyard surrounded by masks—he soon realized they were people watching a cockfight. The match was like paper burning. One of the combatants died peacefully while the spectators gazed on, glassy-eyed, happy to see the spurs drenched in blood. The reek of cheap liquor. Gobs of tobacco-stained spit. Entrails. Utter exhaustion. Stupor. Softness. Midday sultry siesta. Someone tiptoed through his dream, not to wake him. . . .

It was Pelele's mother—mistress to a cock breeder who strummed a guitar with flintlike nails and made her a victim of his jealousy and sin. The never-ending story of her troubles: daughter of a who-knows-who and victim of the child she gave birth to, under the influence of a mesmerizing moon, so said the midwives. In her agony, she associated her son's bulging head—a melon with a double-moon-like crown—with the bony faces of sick patients and with the fear, disgust, hiccups, and constant vomiting of the drunken cock breeder.

Pelele recognized the rustle of her starched petticoat—wind through leaves—and chased after her with teary eyes.

He found comfort in her motherly breasts. The guts of the woman who had given birth to him absorbed the pain of his wounds like cotton balls. What a deep and trustworthy refuge! What abundance of love. My pretty lily. What a gorgeous, big lily. So much love, so much love.

The breeder was whispering softly into her ear:

> Sure . . .
> Sure . . .
> Sure my sugary sweet,
> I am a sugar cock,
> I am a sugar cock,
> Who stuck his foot
> And dragged his wing.

Pelele lifted his head and murmured: "Sorry, Mami, so very sorry."

And the shadow stroking his face replied tenderly: "Sorry, son, so very sorry."

He heard from a distance his father's voice, like a trickle from a shot of cheap brandy,

> I hooked up . . .
> Hooked up . . .
> Hooked up with a white woman
> And when the yucca is good,
> You only rip out the roots.

Dimwit murmured: "Mami, my soul truly aches."

And the shadow stroking his face replied tenderly: "Son, my soul truly aches."

Happiness doesn't taste of flesh. Nearby, the shadow of a pine tree, refreshing as a river, bent down to kiss the earth. And a bird, which was also a little gold bell, chirped from the pine tree:

"I'm the Apple-Rose of the Bird of Paradise, I'm life, and half my body is a lie, the other half truth. I am both rose and apple. I offer everyone a glass eye and a real eye. Those who see my glass eye see it because they dream; those who see my real eye do so because they can truly see. I am life, the Apple-Rose of the Bird of Paradise. I am the lie in every truth, the truth of all fiction."

Suddenly Pelele left his mother's lap and ran to see the

jugglers going by. Horses with manes like weeping willows ridden by spangle-dressed women. Carriages festooned with flowers and paper streamers reeling along the paved streets like drunkards. A troupe of filthy street musicians, third-rate fiddlers, and drumbeaters. Flour-faced clowns gave out colorful programs announcing a gala performance dedicated to the President of the Republic, the Benefactor of the People, the Head of the Great Liberal Party and Defender of the Studious Youth.

His gaze wandered to a spot along a high vault. The jugglers left him alone in a building built over a bottomless grayish-green pit. Seats hung from the curtains like hanging bridges. Confessionals went up and down from earth to sky, elevators of souls manned by the Angel of the Golden Ball and the Devil with Eleven Thousand Horns. The Virgin of Carmel came out of a doorway, like light through glass, the panes notwithstanding, to ask what he wanted, who he was looking for. And so he stopped to talk happily to her, the proprietress of the house and the honey of angels, the reason for the existence of saints and the pastry shop of the poor. This impressive woman was less than three feet tall, but when she spoke, she seemed to know everything, like a normal grown-up. Using his fingers to talk, Pelele told her how much he liked chewing wax; amid sobriety and laughter, she told him to take one of the lit candles from her altar. Then she gathered the hem of her too long silver dress and took him by the hand to a pool filled with colorful fish. She gave him a rainbow to suck like a *piruli*. Perfect joy. He felt happy from the tip of his tongue to the tip of his toes. This was something he had never had: a gob of wax to chew like incense, a mint sugar stick, a pool of colorful fish, and a mother who sang while she massaged his broken leg: "Health, health, you froggy buttocks, seven farts to you, and seven for your mama." All this while he slept on a trash heap.

Nevertheless, happiness lasts as long as a sun shower. A woodcutter trailed by his dog came down the path of milk-colored earth that ended at a garbage dump. A coat covered the pile of wood on his back. He held a machete in his arms as if it were a child. The ravine wasn't deep, but the shadows of the still setting sun plunged it and the heaps of trash at the bottom—human wastes that reduced fear at night—into darkness. The woodcutter looked around again and swore he was being followed. He stopped farther on, drawn by the aura of someone hiding. The dog howled, stiffening as if he had seen the Devil. A swirl lifted into the air dirty sheets of paper stained with red beets and the blood of women.

The dark blue sky above looked like a tomb. Buzzards crowned it, flying in sleepy circles. Suddenly, the dog took off after Pelele. A gust of fear chilled the woodcutter. He tiptoed behind the dog to look closer at the dead man. He didn't want to cut his feet on the shards of glass, bottle chips, sardine cans. He had to step over piles of reeking excrement and dark patches that floated down gullies like vessels in a sea of trash. . . .

Without dropping his load—his fear was so much heavier—he kicked the supposedly dead body. He was stunned to find it still alive, shuddering in anguish amid the dog's barking and growling. The footsteps of someone walking in the small forest of pines and old guava trees scared the woodcutter. "What if it were a cop? Really, I mean, that's all I need. . . ."

The woodcutter kicked the dog when it barked. "Shut up, you critter. . . ."

He considered leaving, but running would be a confession of guilt. What if the dead man were a cop? Worse still. Turning to the injured man, he said, "Gimme your hand. I'll help you stand up . . . Oh God, they almost killed you . . . Listen, don't be afraid, don't scream, I'm not going to hurt you. I was poking along here, when I saw you in a heap. . . ."

"I saw you digging him out," a voice said from behind. "I came back 'cause I thought I recognized your voice. . . . Let's get him out of here. . . ."

The woodcutter shook his head, almost collapsing in fear. He gasped, but couldn't leave because he was holding a man so injured he could barely stand. It was an angel talking to him—golden marble skin; blond hair; small, slightly feminine mouth in sharp contrast to the blackness of manly eyes. In the light of the dying sun, his gray outfit resembled a cloud. The angel carried a very thin bamboo cane in delicate hands and wore a panama hat shaped like a dove.

"An angel . . ." The woodcutter couldn't drop his eyes. "An angel, an angel," he repeated.

"You can tell he's poor by his clothes," the apparition said. "How miserable it is to be poor. . . ."

"So it goes. Everyone plays his role in life. Look at me: I'm a poor laborer. I have a wife and live in a shack, but I don't find my situation sad," stuttered the woodcutter, as if trying to win over the angel with sleepy words whose power, given his Christian orthodoxy, could transform him into a king by will. And for a moment, he seemed bathed in gold, covered in a red blanket, with a studded crown on his head and a diamond scepter in his hand. The trash heap was a long way off now. . . .

"How strange," said the apparition over Pelele's cries.

"What's strange? In the end, we poor are the happiest. What's the use, anyway? It's true that the schooled and educated are full of pipe dreams. Even my wife is sometimes gloomy 'cause she'd like to wear wings on Sundays."

The injured man fainted a few times trudging down the ever steeper hill. The trees rose and fell like the fingers of Chinese dancers before his dying eyes. The comments of the men who carried him buzzed in his ears. A huge black spot clung to his face. His body shuddered several times, launching images of burnt ashes. . . .

"So your wife wants to have wings on Sundays?" said the ghost. "If she had them, they would be of no use to her. . . ."

"That's it. She wants them so she can go for a stroll. And when she's pissed at me, she asks the air for wings. . . ."

The woodcutter stopped to wipe the sweat off his brow with his coat sleeve. "He weighs a ton."

Soon the ghost said, "That's why her feet are and aren't enough. If she had wings, she wouldn't fly."

"Of course not. And not because of her looks but because a woman is a bird that can't live outside a cage. And I don't have enough pieces of wood to waste breaking them on her back." Saying this, he remembered he was talking to an angel and decided to change his tune. "With divine intervention, don'tcha think?"

The stranger said nothing.

"Who would hit this poor man?" the woodcutter asked to change the subject, angry with himself for his words.

"There's always someone. . . ."

"Aren't there friends everywhere? This one, yes, he's been hit . . . like killing a snake. A cut to the throat and straight to the garbage dump."

"Surely he has other injuries. . . ."

"Slashed lips . . . You see? So no one would hear about this crime."

"But between sky and earth—"

"—you took the words right out of my mouth."

At the top of the ravine, the trees were full of buzzards. Fear, more than pain, silenced Pelele; between corkscrew and sea urchin, he wrapped himself in a blanket of deadly silence.

The wind blew over the city, across the plateau, to the familiar, spinning countryside. . . .

After glancing at his watch and throwing the injured man a few coins, the ghost hurried off, bidding the woodcutter a friendly goodbye.

The cloudless sky glowed. The lights at the edge of town that gazed toward the countryside were like matches in a darkened theater. Serpent trees appeared out of the darkness near the first huts: muddy hovels smelling of earth, wooden huts smelling of mestizos, big houses with ugly lawns smelling of horse stables, and inns where the sale of hay was customary; a servant with her lover in the Matamoros Castle barracks and muleteers talking in the darkness.

The woodcutter laid him down by the first houses. He pointed toward the hospital. Pelele half-opened his lids, looking for some relief, something to stop his hiccupping. But his dying man's gaze, sharp as a thorn, focused on the closed doors of the deserted street. Far off, bugles sounded, proof that a nomadic people had been pacified. Bells tolled three at a time for the souls of the dead believers: Pit-y! . . . Pit-y! . . . Pit-y! . . .

A buzzard dragging its wings in the darkness terrified him. The wail of the injured bird was like a threat. Pelele trudged off, resting against walls, motionless, quivering walls, moan after moan, not knowing where he was going, fighting an icy-breathed wind. His hiccups startled him.

When he reached his shack, the woodcutter dropped the firewood, as usual, in the courtyard. His dog had beaten him home and now jumped about friskily. He pushed the dog away. Without taking off his hat, he opened the jacket hanging on his shoulders like bat wings. He went up to the open fire in a corner where his wife warmed tortillas and told her what had happened.

"I met an angel in the garbage dump. . . ."

The firelight flickered on the bamboo walls and straw roof like the wings of other angels.

A vinelike white smoke snaked its way out of the hut.

V

THAT PIG!

Dr. Barreño was talking to the President's Secretary. "I must tell you, Mr. Secretary, I've been visiting the barracks for the last ten years as an army surgeon. I must tell you that I've been the victim of unspeakable abuses. I've been arrested, for the flimsiest reason. . . . Let me explain: A strange illness hit the Military Hospital; ten or twelve men died each and every morning; ten or twelve every afternoon; and ten or twelve at night. The Chief Health Army Officer asked me and my colleagues to investigate why soldiers, more or less in good health, would check into a hospital and die. After performing five autopsies, I was able to establish that these unfortunate men were dying from a hole the size of a penny in their stomach. I didn't know the source of their illness initially, but later discovered that they were being given a purgative of sodium sulfate purchased from a local soda factory. Obviously, the purgative was tainted. My colleagues didn't agree with my diagnosis and that's why they weren't arrested—they thought an unknown disease needing further study had caused the deaths. I'm telling you that a hundred forty men died and we still have two barrels of sodium sulfate left. Just so the Chief Health Army Officer can make a few extra bucks. And there will be more deaths to come. . . ."

"Dr. Luis Barreño," screamed a secretary in the Presidential Staff.

"Mr. Secretary, I will tell you what the President says."

The Secretary took a few steps toward the door with Dr. Barreño. In addition to being curious, he was interested in how the doctor had constructed his theory, systematically, in a mo-

notonously dull fashion, matching the gray hair on his head
and the dry-steak face of a man of science.

Standing with his head held high, the President greeted him
with one arm at his side and the other crossed behind his back.
Before the doctor had a chance to speak, the President said, "I
must tell you, Don Luis, that I'm not in the mood to listen to
any medical quackery that might discredit my government.
My enemies better know this, because the second they drop
their guard, I'll cut off their heads! Now get out of here. Scram.
And send in that other damn pig!"

The doctor backed out of the room, hat in hand and a huge
wrinkle on his forehead. He was as pale as if he were at his
own funeral.

"Mr. Secretary, I'm finished, completely finished. All I heard
was 'Get out of here. Scram. And send in that other damn pig!'"

Someone who had been writing at a corner table stood up.
"I'm that other damn pig." He went into the Presidential Office through the same door Dr. Barreño had exited through.

"I thought he was going to strike me. . . . You should've
been there. Seen it," the doctor went on, mopping the sweat
running down his face. "You should've been there. But I'm
wasting your time. I can see you are a busy man, Mr. Secretary. I'm leaving, okay? And thanks so much. . . ."

"Goodbye, my little doctor. It was nothing. Have a nice day."

The Secretary was putting the finishing touches on a document the President was about to sign. The city was dressed in
orange muslin, crowned in stars like an angel of praise. The illuminated bell towers released the lifesaving "Ave Maria" into
the streets.

Barreño walked into his house wondering how to throw off
such a crippling blow. As he shut the door, he glanced at the
nearby roofs, thinking how easily a criminal hand could reach
over and strangle him. He took refuge behind the bedroom
wardrobe.

His coats hung gloomily, corpses wrapped in naphthalene.
They reminded Barreño of the murder of his father, killed
walking down a lonely road many years back. The family was
forced to accept a fruitless judicial investigation that had con-

cluded the wicked act. An anonymous letter followed that more or less implied a farce. "My brother-in-law and I were riding back on the road between Vuelta Grande and La Canoa around eleven p.m., when suddenly we heard shots: pum, pum, pum, five times. Horses came toward us at full gallop and we took cover in a nearby outcropping of trees. Horseback riders almost crashed into us. Once it was quiet, we went on our way, though our horses kept rearing up. We decided to dismount, guns in our hands, and see what had happened. We found a man lying facedown, dead, and a wounded mule, which my brother put out of its misery. We decided to go to Vuelta Grande and file a report. We found Colonel José Parrales Sonriente, the Man with the Tiny Mule, sitting and drinking at a table with a bunch of friends. We took him aside and told him what we had witnessed. First we heard the shots, then. . . . He listened to us, shrugged his shoulders, and glanced back to a huge, melting candle. 'Go straight home,' he said unflinchingly. 'I know what I'm talking about. Never mention this matter again. . . .'"

"Luis! . . . Luis . . ."

In the wardrobe, one of his coats fell off the hanger like a bird of prey.

"Luis!"

Barreño shot up and went out to turn the pages of a book in his library. His wife would have been scared shitless if she had found him hiding in the wardrobe.

"It's not a joke. You'll either die or go blind reading. I've told you a thousand times. You don't seem to understand that you need tact more than knowledge to succeed. You're wasting your time studying—what's the point? Tell me, what's the point? There's none. Won't even get you a pair of socks. What the heck! What the heck."

Both the light and his wife's voice calmed him down.

"What's the point of all this studying . . . Studying for what? So they'll say you were brilliant after you die? They say that about everyone. Bah! Leave the studying to empiricists. You already have a degree. Isn't that enough? And don't look so upset. You need customers, not bookshelves. We would be better off if you had a patient for each of those fat books. I'd prefer to see your clinic full, the telephone ringing off the hook at all hours, seeing patients . . . Do something with your life. . . ."

"You think that *doing something*—"

"Do something worthwhile . . . And don't tell me you need to wear your eyes out for that. Other doctors don't know half of what you know. They only care about their reputation. Mr. President's specialist here, Mr. President's specialist there . . . that's how you make something of yourself."

"Well . . ." Barreño focused on the word as if to bridge a memory gap. "You won't believe this—hold on, my girl—but I've just been with the President. Yessir, been with the President. . . ."

"Oh my. What did he say? Did he receive you properly?"

"Not really. 'Cutting off my head' is all I heard him say. I was scared and, what's worse, I couldn't find the door to leave."

"He berated you? You wouldn't be the first or the last. Usually he beats people." And after a long pause, she added, "Your fear has always done you in."

"Sweetie, show me someone who's courageous facing a wild beast."

"No, sir, that's not what I mean. I'm talking about doing surgery, about never becoming the President's doctor. You would have to lose your fear for that. You need courage to be a surgeon. Believe me. Courage and determination in using a knife. A tailor unwilling to waste material will never be able to fit a dress properly. And a dress is worth a lot, as you know. Doctors, however, can practice on the poor Indians in a hospital. Don't worry about the President. Come and eat. He's in a bad mood because of that awful Portal murder."

"Shut up, will you, or I'll slap you in the face, something I've yet to do. It wasn't a murder. There's nothing awful about someone getting rid of the hateful hangman who killed my father, a defenseless old man on an empty road."

"That's according to an anonymous letter. Be a man! No one believes an anonymous accusation—"

"If I believed in anonymous—"

"You're not a man. . . ."

"Let me speak! If I trusted rumors, I wouldn't stay here at home." Barreño looked through his pockets feverishly. His face was somber. "You wouldn't be in my house. Here, read this. . . ."

White as a sheet apart from the vermilion powder on her lips, she took the paper from her husband and read it quickly. "Doctor, please console your wife, now that the Man with the Tiny Mule has gone to a better place. Signed: a few friends who wish you well."

She gave the paper back to her husband, laughing painfully— splinters of the sound filling test tubes and beakers in Barreño's small laboratory like a poison to be analyzed.

"Lunch is served," said the maid at the door.

The President signed the order in his Palace office, assisted by the little old man—that pig—who had entered the room as Dr. Barreño left.

That pig was a poorly dressed man with pink baby-mouse skin. His hair was like cheap gold; his blue, worried eyes sunk behind egg-yolk-colored glasses.

The President attached his signature, and the old man, wanting to dry the paper quickly, knocked over the inkwell onto the newly signed sheet.

"You pig!"

"Sorry, sir!"

"You pig!"

One buzz, two buzzes, three buzzes. Footsteps and another assistant appeared.

"General, give this man two hundred lashes right away!" roared the President. He walked over to his House Palace. Lunch was already served.

The "pig's" eyes filled with tears. He couldn't say anything, knowing it was useless to ask for forgiveness. Parrales Sonriente's murder had put the President in a foul mood. His cloudy eyes imagined his wife and children coming to his defense: a worn-out woman and half a dozen bony kids. His scrawny hand patted his coat, searching for a handkerchief. He couldn't scream to let off steam; all he could do was cry bitterly. Like anyone else, he didn't think the punishment was unjust; on the contrary, he was happy to be whipped so next time he wouldn't be so clumsy. If only he could scream to let off steam, to teach himself to do things right and not spill ink over signed documents.

His teeth stuck out of his tight lips like a comb. His hollow cheeks made him look anguished, like a man condemned to die. He was sweating, and his shirt stuck to his back, scaring him in a most frightful way. He'd never sweated so much. . . . And unable to scream! The nausea of fear forced him to to to shiver, shake. . . .

The President's aide-de-camp took him by the arm, sunk as he was in a weird torpor. His eyes stared, his ears buzzed with a terrible sensation of emptiness, his flesh weighed down on him, terribly so. Doubled over, he grew weaker by the second. . . .

Minutes later, in the dining room, a voice said, "May I enter, Mr. President?"

"Yes, come in, General."

"I'm bringing you news about that pig who couldn't bear the two hundred lashes."

The servant began to tremble, holding the plate from which the President grabbed a French fry.

"And why are you trembling now?" her master asked. Then he turned to the general, who stood at attention, cap in hand. "Thanks, now get out of here."

Holding the plate, the servant ran after the man and asked why he hadn't been able to withstand two hundred lashes.

"Why? Because he died first!"

She went back, plate in hand.

Almost in tears, she turned to the President, who was eating calmly, and said: "Sir, he couldn't bear the two hundred lashes because he died first."

"So what? Bring me the next course."

VI

A GENERAL'S HEAD

Miguel Angel Face, the President's confidant, came to see him after the dessert (like Satan, he was both good and evil).

"Please forgive me, Mr. President!" he said, standing by the dining room entrance. "So sorry, Mr. President, for my lateness, but I was helping a woodcutter who found a wounded man in the garbage dump. I couldn't get here sooner. The wounded man wasn't anyone important, just a simple fellow!"

The President was dressed in full mourning attire, as usual: black shoes, black tie, black hat. His toothless gums hid under a gray moustache that reached the corners of his mouth. His cheeks were ruddy, his eyebrows tweezed.

"Did you take him to the hospital?" he asked, relaxing his frown.

"Sir?"

"What? No one who believes he's a friend of the President of the Republic leaves a poor wretch wounded by who knows whom on the street."

He turned at the creak of the dining room door.

"Come in, General. . . ."

"With your permission, Mr. President . . ."

"Are they ready, General?"

"Yes, Mr. President."

"Take care of it yourself, General: Give my condolences to the widow. Give her three hundred pesos to help pay for the funeral, in the President's name."

The general stood at attention, cap in hand. Not blinking, almost without breathing, he bent to take the money on the table. Minutes later, he was driving off in a car with the coffin carrying the body of "that pig."

Angel Face went on. "I considered taking the injured man to the hospital, but then thought that a Presidential order would ensure better treatment. And since I was coming here on your orders anyway to express my horror at the cowardly murder of Parrales Sonriente . . ."

"I'll give the order."

"Just what I expect from a man who others say shouldn't be ruling this country."

The President jumped as if he had just been stung.

"Who says so?"

"I do, Mr. President. Many of us believe that a man of your distinction should govern a country like France or democratic Switzerland or industrious Belgium or marvelous Denmark . . . But France . . . France above all . . . A man of your stature would be perfect to steer the future of a country that produced Gambetta and Victor Hugo!"

An almost imperceptible smile appeared under the President's moustache. He cleaned his glasses with a white silk handkerchief, not taking his eyes off Angel Face. After a short pause, he changed the subject.

"Miguel, I asked you to come to handle something for me tonight. The authorities have ordered the arrest of that scoundrel General Eusebio Canales, whom you know well, tomorrow at daybreak. For various reasons, besides his being one of Parrales Sonriente's killers, it would serve the government if he were to escape capture and not end up in prison. Go tell him what you know and advise him to flee this very night. You can help him escape, because like every good soldier, he believes in honor and would prefer to die than run away. If he's caught tomorrow, he'll be executed. This conversation stays between us. And be very careful. I don't want the police to know you are helping him. Arrange things so nothing is discovered. Go now."

His confidant left, a scarf hiding half his face (like Satan, he was both good and evil). The officers guarding the President's dining room saluted him. Maybe it was just a feeling, or maybe they had overheard that he held a general's life in his hands.

Sixty hopeless individuals yawned in the receiving chamber, waiting for an audience with Mr. President. Carpets of flowers decorated the streets near the Palace and the House Palace. Groups of soldiers were hanging lanterns under their commanding officer's orders, tiny flags and blue-and-white paper chains at the front of the neighboring barracks.

Angel Face didn't notice the party preparations. He had to find the General, come up with a plan, and help him escape. Everything seemed simple until the dogs living in the thick forest that separated the President's House Palace from his enemies began to bark. It was a forest of ears, responsive to the slightest disturbance—now a hurricane stirred the leaves. Not even the smallest noise could escape the gluttony of those millions of membranes. The dogs kept barking. A network of invisible threads, more hidden than telegraph wires, sent messages from each leaf to the President, allowing him to spy on the darkest secrets of his citizens.

If only it were possible to make a pact with the Devil, sell one's soul to him for the police to be deceived and for the General to escape! But the Devil doesn't commit charitable acts, although anything might be at stake in the President's strange request. The General's head—and something else. He repeated this phrase as if he truly carried in his hands the General's head—and something else.

He reached General Canales's home in the La Merced neighborhood. It was a massive corner house, nearly a hundred years old, with the majesty of an ancient coin. Eight balconies hung over the main street and there was a carriage gate at the back. Angel Face considered waiting—he heard voices inside—for someone to open the door. But the policemen walking on the sidewalk across the street dissuaded him. He glanced toward the windows every so often to see if he could signal anyone inside.

He saw no one. He couldn't stay on the sidewalk without awakening suspicion. He noticed a rickety bar on the corner across from the house. Better to go there and have a drink. A beer perhaps.

He went inside, mumbled a few words to the female barkeeper, and glanced around. He saw the outline of a man on a bench against a wall, hat pulled over his brow, almost hiding his eyes, scarf around his neck, jacket collar pulled up, wide trousers, high boots with the clasps unfastened—rubber tops, yellow leather, brown fabric. Angel Face lifted his eyes absent-mindedly and glanced at the bottles in rows on the shelf, the glowing S filament of the light bulb, a poster advertising Spanish wines (Bacchus riding on a barrel among potbellied monks and naked women), and a portrait of Mr. President, looking much younger than he was now, with railway cars on his shoulders and an angel laying a laurel crown on his head. A tasteful portrait.

Every once in a while, he glanced back at the General's house. It would be a problem if the man on the bench and the barkeeper were more than friends. He unbuttoned his jacket, crossed his legs, placing his elbows on the bar as if he had all the time in the world. What about another beer? He paid with a hundred-peso bill. Maybe the barkeeper wouldn't have change. She opened the cash register, looked through the filthy bills, and banged it closed. Indeed, no change. The same old story of going out into the streets to find some. She pulled her apron over her bare arms and went outside, not without signaling to the man on the bench to keep an eye on the customer: *Careful—he might try to steal something.* A stupid precaution, as just then a young woman stepped out of the General's house as if dropped from the sky.

Angel Face saw his chance.

"Young lady," he said, running after her. "Would you mind letting the proprietor know that I have something important to tell him?"

"My father?"

"You're General Canales's daughter?"

"Yes, sir. . . ."

"Well, please forget what I said. . . . Go ahead . . . let's walk together . . . here's my card. Tell him to please come to my house as soon as possible. I'm going home now, and will wait for him there. His life is in danger. . . . Yes, at my house, as soon as possible. . . ."

The wind blew away his hat. He grabbed for it two or three times, as if chasing after a fleeing hen, until he finally seized it.

He went back to the bar more to gauge the reaction to his sudden departure than to get his change. He found the man on the bench pushing the barkeeper against a wall, trying to steal a kiss with his greedy mouth.

"You wretched policeman. No wonder Puke is your last name—"

Hearing Angel Face, the man let her go.

Angel Face grabbed the bottle the barkeeper was brandishing and smiled at the man on the bench. "Easy now, my lady. What's all the fuss? Here, keep the change. Make up, you two. Nothing's gained by fighting. You might rouse the cops, especially if our friend here—" he said, happy to intervene.

"Lucio Vásquez, at your service."

The barkeeper spoke. "Lucio Vásquez? Better known as Filthy Puke! Why call the police? Everyone is always sending for them! Let 'em try to come in! Just let 'em. I'm no Indian slave and I ain't afraid of anyone. Do ya hear, mister? Not scared of the threat of going to the Casa Nueva Prison."

"I'll have you thrown in jail or a whorehouse if I want!" Vásquez mumbled, spitting the phlegm he had pulled up from his nostrils.

"You think you have that kind of pull, *chon*?"

"Hey, let's make up now!" said Angel Face.

"All right, sir. I'm done talking."

Vásquez had a disagreeable, feminine voice, a kind of wimpy falsetto. He was head over heels with the barkeeper—he fought her day and night for a heartfelt kiss. That's all he wanted. But she refused on the grounds that a kiss was only the beginning. Entreaties, threats, little presents, real or fake tears, serenades, two-step dances. Nothing worked with a barkeeper who gave nothing back, not even to keep the peace. She'd say, "Anyone who tries to make love to me is in for a heap of trouble."

"Now that you two have settled down," Angel Face went on, as if speaking to himself, rubbing his forefinger on a small nickel coin glued to the bar counter, "I'll let you in on what's going on with the lady from across the street."

He was about to tell them that a friend wanted him to ask her if she would accept a letter, when the barkeeper interrupted, "We've already seen how you've taken a fancy to her. . . ."

He suddenly had a better idea. . . . *Fancy to her . . . against the wishes of her family . . . pretend he wanted to abduct her . . .*

He kept rubbing the nickel coin on the counter, but now with more energy.

"You're right," Angel Face replied. "But I'm screwed because her father doesn't want us to marry—"

"I don't want to hear anything about that old man," Vásquez interrupted. "He always has the sourpuss of a poorly paid blacksmith. It's not my fault that I'm under orders to follow him wherever he goes!"

"That's how rich people act," groused the woman.

"And that's why," Angel Face explained, "I've decided to go off with her. We've decided to elope this very evening."

Vásquez and the woman smiled.

"Let's celebrate," Vásquez said, "this is getting really good." He offered Angel Face a cigarette. "Care for a smoke?"

"No, thanks . . . well . . . to be polite . . ."

The barkeeper poured three drinks while the men lit up.

The liquor burned its way down their throats. "So, I can count on you both? No matter what, I'll need your help. And it has to be tonight."

"It's got to be before I go on duty at eleven," Vásquez said. "But this girl here—"

"*This girl?* You've got some nerve to call me that."

"La Masacuata here," he said, glancing back at the barkeeper, "can substitute for me. She's equal to two men—unless you want me to send a replacement. I'm supposed to meet a friend at a Chinese restaurant later."

"Why are you always hanging around with that milquetoast Genaro Rodas?"

"Milquetoast?" Angel Face asked.

"He looks like a corpse, colorless . . . I'm forgetting how to talk: he's as colorless as a corpse!"

"Who cares?"

"I don't see a problem."

"I'm sorry to intervene, sir, but there is a problem. I didn't want to tell you, but Genaro Rodas's wife, Fedina, is going around saying that the General's daughter is going to be god-mother to her child. In other words, Genaro Rodas, your buddy, isn't a good replacement."

"Bullshit."

"Everything's bullshit to you."

Angel Face was grateful to Vásquez for his good advice, but thought better of it because Milquetoast, as the barkeeper pointed out, would have a stake.

"My dear Vásquez, it's too bad you can't help me out."

"I'm sorry not to be available. Had I known earlier, I could've gotten time off."

"Will some spare change help?"

"Money's not the issue. I just can't help you tonight," he said, touching an ear.

"What can't be done, can't be done. I'll come back later, quarter to two or one thirty. With love you have to strike while the iron is hot."

He said goodbye at the door, lifted his wristwatch to his ear to see if it was working—how thrilling is the beat of the second hand!—and hurried off with his black scarf covering his pale face. He held the General's head in his hands—and something else.

VII

THE ARCHBISHOP'S ABSOLUTION

Genaro Rodas leaned against a wall to light his cigarette. As his match struck the box, Lucio Vásquez appeared. A dog vomited into a church grate.

"This damn wind!" growled Rodas, seeing his friend.

"How ya doing?" Vásquez asked. They began walking together.

"Okay. And you?"

"Where ya going?"

"*Where am I going?* You make me laugh. Hadn't we planned to meet here?"

"Oh, I thought you'd forgotten. I want to fill you in, but I need a drink. I really do need a drink. Let's go by the Portal—something's bound to be open there."

"I don't think so, but we can go anyway. Since they barred beggars from sleeping there, you don't see hide nor hair of a cat!"

"All the better. Let's take a shortcut by the Cathedral, no? What a God-awful wind!"

After Colonel Parrales Sonriente's murder, the toughest members of the Secret Police had been assigned to the Portal. Vásquez and his friend walked all through the arcade, climbed steps that led to the corner of the Archbishop's Palace, and went down by the Hundred Doors. The column shadows lay on the ground where the beggars once had slept. A set of ladders revealed that the building was being painted from top to bottom. The first item in the Mayor's plans to show his unconditional support for the President of the Republic was to clean and paint the building, which had been the scene of that awful murder, but was also where Arab and Jewish merchants had set up their disgusting bazaar reeking of burnt garbage. "Let them pay for it. They're partly responsible for Colonel Parrales Sonriente's death, since they live where the crime was committed." Because of this vindictive approach, the merchants would have ended up poorer than the beggars who slept on their doorsteps, had it not been for the help of influential friends who offered to pay for the Cathedral's painting, cleaning, and improved lighting with National Treasury Bonds bought at half value.

But the Secret Police presence rained on that parade. The merchants whispered, *Why so much scrutiny?* Hadn't the bonds been converted to cans of paint? Hadn't they bought paintbrushes as bushy as the beards of the Prophets of Israel? Wisely, they increased the number of bars, bolts, and locks on their shops.

Vásquez and Rodas left the Portal by the side closest to the Hundred Doors. The silence absorbed the echoes of their heavy footfalls. Farther up the street, they slipped into the Lion's Awakening. Vásquez greeted the bartender, ordered two drinks, and sat with Rodas at a tiny table behind a screen.

"Any news about my screwed-up situation?" asked Rodas.

"Salud!" Vásquez raised his glass filled with cheap liquor.

"To your health, old man."

The bartender standing near them added mechanically, "To your health, gentlemen!"

They both swallowed their drinks in one gulp.

"No news to report . . . ," Vásquez spat out after swallowing the last gulp, diluted by his bubbly saliva. "The Assistant Director gave the job to his godson. By the time I mentioned you, he'd already given it to that piece of shit."

"No kidding."

"Where a captain rules, a sailor has no sway. . . . I told him you wanted to join the Secret Police, that you were pretty sharp and reliably underhanded."

"And what did he say?"

"What I've just told you. He had hired his godson. That

shut me up. What could I say? It's tougher now to get into the Secret Police than when I joined up. Everyone knows where the future lies."

Rodas shook off his friend's words with a shrug and a curse. He'd come with the hope of getting work.

"Listen, man, don't be so down in the mouth over this. I'll let you know when another cushy job opens up. I swear, on my mother's life, as soon as something new comes up. There are more jobs than ants in an anthill. I don't know if I told you"— Vásquez paused and looked around nervously—"I'm no fool, better keep my mouth shut."

"Okay, so don't tell me. What do I care?"

"It's complicated. . . ."

"Look, man, don't tell me. Do me a favor and keep your mouth shut. You don't trust me, that's crystal clear."

"Hey, brother, you sure are touchy."

"I don't like people who don't trust me. You're like the women I know. I'm not questioning you so you'll talk!"

Vásquez stood up to see if anyone could hear him. He drew closer to Rodas, who seemed to be sulking, offended by his friend's caginess. "I don't know if I told you," he said, almost in a whisper, "that the beggars sleeping in the Portal on the night of the murder have already let the cat out of the bag. Everyone knows who killed the Colonel." And, talking louder, he added: "Who do you think?" Lowering his voice again, he said: "None other than General Eusebio Canales and his lawyer, Abel Carvajal."

"Are you kidding me?"

"The order for their arrest went out today. Now you know the whole shebang."

"So that's it, huh?" Rodas said, more calmly. "The Colonel rumored to kill a fly at a hundred yards, the man everyone feared. Not killed by a gun or a knife, just with his neck twisted like a chicken. All you need in life is determination. What balls it took to kill him."

Vásquez proposed another round. "Don Lucho, two more shots!"

The bartender filled their glasses, revealing his black silk suspenders.

"Down the hatch," said Vásquez. He spat and added through his teeth, "Bottoms up before the hen flees the coop. I despise a full glass, you know! Salud!"

Somewhat distracted, Rodas rushed to raise his drink. When his glass was empty, he said, "The fools who sent the Colonel to the next world wouldn't be so dumb as to come back to the Portal. No how, no way."

"Who said they're coming back?"

"What?"

"Seek and you shall find everything you want! Ha-ha. You make me laugh."

"Where'd you get that? I'm saying that it's useless to wait for whoever offed the Colonel to come back to the scene of the crime and be captured. . . . Or do you think he'd come to the Portal to see those handsome Middle Eastern faces . . . huh huh?"

"You don't know what you're talking about!"

"Don't start with your theories."

"What the Secret Police do in the Portal has nothing to do with the murder. I swear to God! You have no idea what we're up to. We're waiting for a rabid man!"

"Go on!"

"Do you remember the mute everyone teased by shouting 'Mother' at him? That tall, bony guy with twisted legs who runs through the streets like a dimwit? Remember? You couldn't have forgotten him. Well, he's the one we're waiting for. No one's seen him for three days. We're going to make chopped liver out of him!" Vásquez said, touching his gun.

"You're pulling my leg!"

"I'm not, man. It's the truth. That rabid dog has bitten dozens of people and the doctors prescribed that he be injected with an ounce of lead. How's that sit with you?"

"You think I'm stupid, but you're dead wrong. I ain't so dense. The Secret Police are waiting for the men who wrung the Colonel's neck. . . ."

"Hell no! You're more stubborn than a mule. They're waiting for the mute with rabies, the rabid mute that's bitten hundreds of people. Don't you get it?"

Pelele's moans slithered through the streets. Dragging himself
along, sometimes crawling on hands and knees, pushing himself along with a big toe, his stomach dragging over rocks,
sometimes tensing the thigh of his one good leg while using an
elbow to push his body along. Soon the square appeared. The
wind rustling through the park trees seemed to harbor vulture
cries. Pelele was so scared he lost consciousness now and
again. Worries danced in his bowels and his dry, fat, thirsty
tongue was like a dead fish among ashes. His inner pants legs
were so wet that they felt like soggy scissors.

He went up the Portal gradually, pulling himself along like a
dying cat. He huddled in the shadows, mouth open and eyes
glazed, his body rags caked in dirt and blood. Silence merged
with the footsteps of some late-night strollers, the clicking of
rifles, the padding of street dogs as their snouts sniffed the
ground, hunting for bones among the husks of half-eaten tamales blowing along the edges of the Portal.

The bartender gave them another double shot of rum.

"Why won't you believe me?" said Vásquez, spitting, his
voice rising. "Wasn't I telling you that today, around nine tonight, or maybe nine thirty, before meeting up with you, I was
flirting with La Masacuata when a guy came into the bar for a
beer? She served him right away. The guy ordered a second
beer and pulled out a hundred-peso bill. She went to look for
change. I kept an eye on him since I was suspicious of him
from the moment he walked in . . . I could tell that he was up
to something. Poof! Just then a girl came out of the house
across the street. She was barely out the door when the guy
started tailing her. But I couldn't follow them anymore, 'cause
just then La Masacuata came back, and I started trying to
make her. . . ."

"And the hundred-peso bill?"

"Hold on. We were smooching when the guy came back for

his change. We were in each other's arms. He skulked into us and said he was nuts over General Canales's daughter. He was planning to take off with her tonight. General Canales's daughter had come out just to check signals with him. I can't tell you how hard he tried to get me to help him abduct her, but I've got guard duty at the Portal."

"What a story, my man!" Rodas spat out a wad of saliva.

"I've seen lover boy standing around the President's Palace many times. . . ."

"Damn. They must be family."

"No way. Not how the crow flies. What I found strange was his rush. He knows something about the General's impending arrest and wants to make off with her before the soldiers nab her father."

"You've hit the nail on the head."

"Let's put another shot down the hatch and get the hell out of here."

Don Lucho filled their glasses. They swallowed their drinks and then spat on the butts of cheap cigarettes on the floor.

"How much do we owe you, Don Lucho?"

"Sixteen twenty—"

"Each?" Rodas gasped.

"Hell no. For the both of you!" answered the bartender. Vásquez placed sixteen bills and four coins in his hand.

"See you later, Don Lucho."

"Till the next time, Don Luchito."

The bartender walked them to the door.

"What the hell. It's so fucking cold!" Rodas exclaimed, going out into the street, sticking his hands into his pants pockets.

They walked to the prison shops at the corner closest to the Portal. Feeling happy, Vásquez stretched his arms as if disposing of a worrisome load and stopped.

"Now's the time for the lion to awaken and shake his fiery mane!" he said, stretching. "It can't be easy for a lion to be a lion! Do me a favor and cheer up, eh? This is my night to be happy, my night to be snappy, I'm telling you, my happy, snappy night!"

Repeating these words over and over in a sharp, shrill tone, he transformed the night into a gold-belled black tambourine. He seemed to be shaking hands with invisible friends in the air and encouraging the puppeteer and his puppets to come alive and tickle his throat. He burst out laughing, trying to dance with his hands in his waistcoat pockets. Then his laughter became a groan. His happiness turned into pain. He doubled over to keep the contents of his stomach from flying out of his mouth. Then he grew silent. His laughter hardened in his mouth like dental plaster. He glimpsed Pelele and heard his dragging feet break the Portal silence—echoes resounding by two, by eight, by twelve. Pelele whimpered softly, then loudly, like a wounded dog. His scream shattered the darkness when he saw Vásquez approaching him with a gun, ready to drag him by his broken leg toward the stars setting by the corner of the Archbishop's Palace.

Panting and sweating, Rodas watched it all without moving. Pelele rolled down the stone steps after the first shot. The second shot finished him off.

The Arab and Jewish merchants flinched between blasts. No one saw anything, yet a saint looking out from a window in the Archbishop's Palace helped the unfortunate man to die. As the body rolled down the steps, the saint raised his amethyst ring and gave him absolution, opening for Pelele the door to the Kingdom of Heaven.

VIII

THE PORTAL PUPPETEER

Soon after the gunshots and Pelele's yowls, Vásquez and his friend ran off. The streets, poorly dressed by the moonlight, ran after one another, not knowing exactly what had happened. The trees in the plaza desperately snapped fingers because they couldn't propel through the air or along telephone wires what had truly occurred. No, it wasn't in the Jewish Merchant Alley, curling and zigzagging as if designed by a drunk! It wasn't in the Escuintilla Alley, long ago made famous by the cadets who brandished their swords dressed as police officers and rogues, as if reenacting tales of musketeers and chivalry. Nor in the King's Alley, the gamblers' favorite haunt, where no one could pass without saluting the King. It wasn't in St. Teresa's Alley, a steep road leading to a gloomy neighborhood. Nor in the Rabbit's Alley, nor near the Havana Fountain, nor down Five Streets, nor in the Martinique area.

It had happened in the Plaza Central, where the water flushing constantly through public toilets sounded like weeping, where sentinels clicked their rifles again and again and night wheeled over the Cathedral's icy vault and took over the sky.

The wind pulsed intermittently like blood after a shot to the temple, unable to dislodge the leaves stuck like obsessive ideas to the crowns of trees.

Suddenly a door opened in the Portal and a puppeteer peered out. His wife had pushed him into the street with the curiosity of a fifty-year-old girl, so he could tell her what was happening. What were those two blasts? The puppeteer drew no pleasure in coming to the door in his underwear on the whims of Doña Venjamón, as his wife was called, probably because his name was Benjamin. He didn't like it when his busybody wife, anxious to know if an Arab or Jew had been killed, stuck her fingers like spurs into his ribs so he would poke his neck out as far as he could.

"Look, woman, what do you want from me? I can't see a thing! Why do you care?"

"What? Did something happen in the Arab and Jewish quarter?"

"I can't see anything. What's the fuss?"

"Stop mumbling, for the love of God!"

When the puppeteer didn't wear his dentures, his mouth slurped like a suction cup.

"Hold on. Now I see what's happening!"

"Benjamin, I don't understand a word you're saying," she whimpered. "Get it? I can't understand you."

"Hmmm, I see now . . . there's a crowd of people gathering at the corner of the Archbishop's Palace."

"Let me by. You're blind. You're absolutely useless. I can't understand a word you say."

Don Benjamin let his wife by. She came to the door half dressed, with one breast sticking out of her yellow cotton nightgown and the other entangled in the scapular of the Virgin of Carmel.

"They're carrying a stretcher," Benjamin finally said.

"Oh, good, that's good. So it's over there, not by the Jews and Arabs, where I thought it happened. Why didn't you say so, Benjamin? That's why the shots sounded so near."

"I see, saw, them carrying a stretcher," the puppeteer repeated. His voice seemed to come from the bowels of the earth when he spoke from behind his wife.

"Shush. I don't understand a word you're saying. Why don't you go back and put on your dentures? It sounds as if you're talking to me in English!"

"I saw, see, them carrying a stretcher."

"No, they're just now bringing it!"

"No, girl, it was there before!"

"They're bringing it now! I'm not blind, you know."

"I don't know, but I saw it there. . . ."

"What? What? The stretcher? Don't you understand . . . ?"

Don Benjamin was barely three feet tall, skinny, and hairy as a bat. He couldn't see what the crowd and the police officers were looking at over the shoulder of Doña Venjamón, a woman of unusual girth, who took two seats on the tram (one for each of her buttocks) and who needed eight yards of cloth for a dress.

"You're the only one that can see," Don Benjamin ventured to say in the hopes of escaping the blindness of a total eclipse.

As if he had said *"Open, sesame,"* she wheeled around like a mountain and fell on top of him.

"I'll pick you up, abracadabra," she yelled. And, lifting him from the floor, she carried him to the door in her arms like a child.

The puppeteer spat green, purple, orange, and multicolored phlegm. While he kicked his wife's bosom and stomach, four drunks walked across the square in the distance, carrying a stretcher with Pelele's body. Doña Venjamón crossed herself. The public toilets wept for the dead man, and the wind blew through the ashy park trees, screaming like vultures.

"I'm giving you a nurse, not a slave, the priest should've said to me—damned be him—on our wedding day," growled the puppeteer once his feet were back on the ground.

His better half let him speak—though "half" is misleading, as he was barely half a tangerine and she was larger than a grapefruit. She let him speak partly out of respect, and partly because she didn't understand what he said without his dentures.

Fifteen minutes later, Doña Venjamón was snoring as if her lungs struggled to survive under such a mass of flesh. Meanwhile, her husband, eyes ablaze, cursed the day he married her.

But his puppet theater took advantage of that strange situation. The puppets ventured into the field of tragedy. Tears dripped out of their flinty cardboard eyes thanks to a syringe, which fed a system of small tubes connected to a bowl of water. The puppets had only been able to laugh before—or if they wept, it was only in smiley grimaces, with none of the bleak emotion of the tears now trickling down their cheeks, forming rivers on their previously cheerful faces.

Don Benjamin, imagining that the children would cry during the upsetting parts of the show, was surprised when they laughed even more wholeheartedly than before. The children laughed at the weeping . . . they laughed at the hitting. . . .

"Makes no sense, makes no sense," Don Benjamin concluded.

"Makes all the sense in the world," Doña Venjamón contradicted him.

"Nonsensical, nonsensical, nonsensical!"

"Super sensical, super sensical, super sensical!"

"Let's not quarrel!" Don Benjamin suggested.

"Let's not quarrel!" she agreed.

"Still it makes no sense . . ."

"Super sensical, super-duper sensical!"

When Doña Venjamón argued with her husband, she always added extra syllables to his words, almost like escape valves to keep her from exploding.

"Super nonsensical," the puppeteer cried, about to tear out his hair in frustration.

"Dupersupersensical! Superdupersensical!"

Either way, there was no debating that the system of using a syringe and making the puppets cry to amuse the children was a big hit in the Portal Puppet Theater.

IX

GLASS EYE

After adding up their sales, getting the evening newspaper, and sending their last customers on their way, the city's smaller shops closed their doors a bit after sundown. Groups of boys gathered on street corners, amusing themselves watching huge bugs circle the streetlamps. Each insect caught was put through a series of tortures by sadists who lacked the pity to take them out of their misery. Young couples in the throes of love embraced at windows. A bayoneted police patrol and groups with sticks walked the quiet streets, following their leaders in single file.

Some nights played out differently. The flying bugs' peaceful torturers split into teams and battled one another instead, as long as they had sufficient ammunition—stones—to throw. As for the lovers, the girl's mother would show up and put an end to the sweet talk by sending the boy, hat in hand, on his way, the Devil in pursuit. To vary things, the patrols preferred to stop a passerby, pat him down from head to foot, and cart him off to jail; even if unarmed, he was a suspect, a tramp, a conspirator (as the patrol leader would say) because *I didn't like his looks.*

At this time of night, the poorer neighborhoods seemed under the spell of an endless solitude and the filthy misery of Chinese shops, stamped by the kind of religious fatalism that revealed God's will. The gutters reflected the moon rising like a flower from the horizon. Water dripped from drinking fountains, counting out the endless hours of people who felt themselves condemned to sin and servitude.

Lucio Vásquez said goodbye to his friend in one of these poor neighborhoods.

"So long, Genaro," he said, winking to ensure secrecy. "I'm off to see if it's not too late to help abduct the General's daughter."

Genaro hesitated, unsure of what to say. Then he walked home and rapped on the door.

"Who's there?" someone barked from inside.

"It's me," Genaro replied, bending his head as if speaking to a short person.

"Which me?" said a woman, opening the door.

Fedina de Rodas raised a candle to see his face. She wore a nightgown and her hair was a mess.

As Genaro came in, she lowered the candle, noisily barred the door, and went back to their bedroom at the back of the shop without saying a word. She raised the candle to the clock to show that no-good rascal the hour at which he was coming home. Genaro stroked the cat sleeping on the front counter and tried to whistle a happy tune.

"Why so cheerful?" Fedina asked, rubbing her feet before getting into bed.

"No reason!" Genaro replied sharply, lost like a shadow in the shop's darkness, afraid his wife would detect worry in his voice.

"You and that cop with the girly voice are thicker than thieves."

"Not so!" he shouted. With his floppy hat pulled over his eyes, he walked into the bedroom.

"You liar. I just saw you two saying goodbye. I know what's up: Nothing good comes from a friend who has a half-hen, half-rooster voice. You're pals just to see if he can get you into the Secret Police. A job for do-nothings. You've no shame!"

"What's this?" Genaro asked, changing the subject and taking a little skirt out of a box.

Fedina grabbed it like a white flag from her husband's hands. She sat on the bed and very excitedly told him that it was a gift from General Canales's daughter for having asked her to be the godmother of their first child.

Rodas hid his face in the shadow over their son's cradle. He was in a bad mood. Without hearing what his wife said about the baptismal preparations, he put his hand up to block the candlelight in his eyes. He then quickly pulled back his hand, shaking it to cleanse the reflection of blood stuck to his fingers. The shadow of Death flew up from his son's cradle as if it were already a coffin. The ghost was egg white, with cloudy eyes—it had no hair, no eyebrows, no teeth, and it twisted itself like the spirals that rise from the censer bowls at funerals. Genaro heard his wife's voice in the distance. She was talking about her son, the baptism, the General's daughter, about inviting the next-door neighbor, the fat man who lived in front, other neighbors from around the corner, the restaurant friend, the butcher, the baker.

"How happy we'll all be!" Then she snapped at him. "What's wrong, Genaro?"

"Nothing's wrong!" he shouted.

His wife's scream splashed little black spots on the ghost of Death, dots that made its skeleton visible against the corner of the dark room. It was a woman's skeleton, but the sagging breasts hairy as hanging rats on her rib cage were the only feminine details.

"What's wrong, Genaro?"

"Nothing's wrong!"

"Is that why you go out and come home half asleep with your tail between your legs? A devil of a man who can't stay in his own home."

His wife's voice made the skeleton vanish.

"No, nothing's wrong."

An eye passed over the fingers of his right hand like light from a small lamp. From pinkie to middle finger, then over to the ring finger, from the ring finger to the index, from index to thumb. An eye . . . a single, solitary eye. It seemed to be throbbing. He squeezed his hand shut trying to crush it, his nails piercing his own flesh. But when he opened his hand, it reappeared on his fingers, no bigger than a bird's heart and more terrifying than hell. Sweat like hot beef broth formed on his temples. Who was looking at him with this eye in his fingers jumping around like a roulette ball, tolling like a bell at a funeral?

Fedina pulled him away from the cradle where their son slept.

"Genaro, what's wrong?"

"Nothing!" He sighed, adding: "It's just an eye chasing me, an eye chasing me. I look down at my hands . . . It can't be! They're my eyes, some eye. . . ."

"Commend yourself to God!" she said through her teeth, not understanding his gibberish.

"An eye . . . yes, a round, black, lashed, glassy eye!"

"You're drunk!"

"How can I be? I haven't had anything to drink!"

"Nothing? Your breath stinks of liquor."

In the bedroom half of the room—the other half was the shop—Rodas felt lost in a cellar full of bats, spiders, snakes, and crabs. He was far from any relief.

"You must've done something to have the Eye of God watching you," added Fedina, yawning.

Genaro leapt onto the bed fully dressed, shoes and all, and got under the sheets. Next to his wife's body, now the beautiful body of a younger woman, the eye began to dance. Fedina blew out the light. It made things worse: the eye grew rapidly in the dark. In a split second, it covered walls, floor, ceiling, houses, his entire life, his infant child. . . .

"No," replied Genaro to something his wife had said. Frightened by his screams, she relit the candle and tried to dry the cold sweat on his forehead. "It's not God's eye, it's the Devil's eye. . . ."

Fedina crossed herself. Genaro begged her to blow out the candle. The eye became a figure eight, turning from light to dark, then it made a thundering noise. It was about to crash into something. Then it exploded against some footsteps out in the street. . . .

"The Portal! The Portal!" cried Genaro. "Yes! Yes! Light! Matches! Light! For God's sake! For the love of God!"

She stretched her arm across him to reach the matchbox. Carriage wheels ground in the distance. Genaro put his fingers inside his mouth and talked as if underwater. He didn't want to be alone, so he called his wife to calm him. She put on a long skirt and went out to make him some coffee.

Hearing her husband's scream, Fedina hurried back into bed. "Has he seen an evil spirit or what?" she asked, watching the candle flame flicker with her beautiful black eyes. She remembered the worms they had found in the stomach of Henrietta, a girl from the Theater Inn; in a hospitalized Indian's skull that had a loofah for a brain; in the spirit Cadejo, who kept you from sleeping. Like the mother hen who opens her wings for her chicks when she sees a vulture flying, she got out of bed and put a St. Blas medallion around the neck of her baby, reciting the Trisagion Prayer.

But the prayer startled Genaro as if he'd been beaten. He jumped out of bed with eyes tightly shut and found his wife by the cradle. He got down on his knees, hugged her legs, and told her what he had seen.

"He rolled down the steps, toward the bottom, bleeding from the first shot. His eyes were wide open. His legs were spread, his gaze fixed . . . a cold, frozen stare, something I've never seen before. An eye seemed to take everything in like a flash of lightning and stare at us. I can't shake off the look of that eye, the long lashes on my fingers, oh God, help me!"

The baby's cry shut him up. Fedina took the flannel-swaddled baby out of the cradle and gave him her breast. She couldn't get away from her husband, who was moaning on the floor, clinging to her legs. He disgusted her.

"Worst thing is that Lucio—"

"Isn't he the guy with the funny voice?"

"Yes, Lucio Vásquez."

"The one they call Velvet?"

"Yes."

"And why in heaven's name did he kill Pelele?"

"He was under orders. The guy had rabies. But that's not all. There's an order to arrest General Canales. A man Lucio knows is going to run off with his daughter tonight—"

"Miss Camila? Our child's godmother?"

"Yes."

On hearing this incredible news, Fedina burst into tears the way simple people cry deeply and profusely over the troubles of others. Her tears fell onto the head of her cooing baby, hot as the water grandmothers carry to church to warm the baptismal fonts.

The baby fell fast asleep. Night passed, and they were still lying there as if under a spell when the first light of day drew a gold line under the door and the baker's daughter knocking on doors nearby broke the shop's silence.

"Bread! Bread! Fresh bread!"

X

THE PRINCES OF
THE ARMY

General Eusebio Canales, alias Chamarrita, marched out of Angel Face's house as if he were about to lead an army. As soon as he closed the door and was alone on the street, his military gait turned into that of an Indian running to sell a hen at market. He sensed spies hot on his heels. He pushed down on his groin; his hernia made him nauseated. He mumbled odd words as he let out syllables of despair; his heart contracted and skipped a few beats. It got so bad that he had to press his fist into his chest, his eyes vacant, his thoughts in a whirl; he pushed down on his ribs as if they were plaster limbs that he could force to continue functioning.

He turned a corner that had seemed so impossibly distant a minute earlier. And another corner . . . only one more . . . he was so tired that it seemed far off . . . He spat phlegm. His legs almost gave out under him. A banana peel. A carriage trundled by at the end of the block. He was trundling. He saw a carriage, houses, lights . . . He walked faster. He had no choice. Then he turned the corner that minutes earlier had seemed so distant. And then another corner, only one more . . . He was so tired it seemed far off. He clenched his teeth so his knees wouldn't give way. He was hardly progressing. Knees stiff, weakening, An unbearable itch rising at the base of his spine and the back of his throat. He would have to drag himself back on all fours, on his elbows—anything to help him escape death.

He slowed down. The street corners were deserted—they

multiplied in the sleepless night like doors with transparent screens. He was behaving ridiculously to himself and to others, whether they saw him or not, belying the fact that he was an important public servant, always, even in the dark of night, exposed to the judgment of his fellow citizens.

"What will be will be," he mumbled. "My duty is to wait at home, especially if what that scoundrel Angel Face has just told me is true."

And then he added: "Running away would be a confession of guilt." His echoing footsteps tapped over and over . . . "Running away is a confession of guilt . . . I won't do it." His echoing footsteps tapped over and over . . . "It is an admission of guilt . . . I won't do it!" His echoing footsteps tapped repeatedly. . . .

He put a hand on his chest as if to tear away the cement of fear that Angel Face's words had placed there. His medals of honor were missing . . . "Running away is to admit 'I am guilty,' but I won't do it . . ." Angel Face's finger was pointing to a road of exile as the only means of escape . . . "You've got to save your skin, General! There's still time!" Everything he was, everything he was worth, and everything he loved with a child's affection—his country, family, memories, traditions, his daughter, Camila—everything spun around that fatal finger. If he destroyed his ideals, the whole universe would spin out of control.

After a few more steps, only confused tears remained of that spinning vision. . . .

"Generals are the Princes of the Army," he had once said in a speech. "What a fool! I've paid dearly for that little phrase. Why didn't I say that we were the Princes of Foolishness? The President will never forgive me for that 'Princes of the Army' comment. Now that he has me in his claws, he's getting rid of me by accusing me of killing a colonel who always paid my gray hairs the utmost respect."

A thin, crooked smile formed under his white moustache. He was making a place within himself for another General Canales, one who strode slow as a turtle, dragging his feet like a penitent in a procession, silent, sad, lifeless, with the odor of burnt firecrackers on his body. The real Chamarrita, the

General who had stormed out of Angel Face's house, at the top of his military career, shoulders muscular against a background of the glorious battles waged by Alexander the Great, Julius Caesar, Napoleon, and Bolívar, had been replaced by a caricature of a general: a General Canales striding without golden spangles, plumes, and braids, without boots or blazing spurs. Alongside this crow-colored, deflated interloper—this pauper's burial—the other authentic and true Chamarrita seemed, without arrogance, a rich man's burial, complete with cordons, tassels, wreaths, plumes, and solemn salutes. The disgraced General Canales advanced toward a defeat that history would ignore, passing up the other general, who remained behind like a puppet bathed in blue and gold light, his tricorne hat pulled over his eyes, sword broken, fists hanging down, and medals and crosses rusting on his chest.

Canales didn't slow down. His eyes shifted away from the image of himself in full uniform, feeling morally defeated. He was grieved to see himself an exile, dressed in a gatekeeper's trousers and a coat, either too large or too small, too tight or too loose. He walked over the ruins of his own life, trampling his golden braids as he walked down the streets.

"But I'm innocent!" he repeated with total conviction. "I'm innocent! Why should I be afraid . . . ?"

"For that very reason!" his conscience replied, in Angel Face's own words. "For that reason . . . Another rooster would crow if you were guilty. Your crime is noteworthy because it guarantees the state the support of its citizenry. Your country? Save your skin, General, I know what I'm saying. Screw your country and your stupid burial shrouds. Laws? They're good for nothing! Save your skin, sir, otherwise death awaits you!"

"But I'm innocent!"

"Don't ask whether you're innocent or guilty, General. What counts is the President's support. An innocent man, without the President's support, is worse off than a guilty person."

He closed his ears to Angel Face's words, and muttered words of vengeance, drowning in his own heartbeats. Then he remembered his daughter. She must be waiting for him with her heart in her mouth. The clock on the La Merced tower tolled one. Stars studded the clear sky. Not a shred of clouds. When he reached the corner of his house, he saw windows casting anxious reflections halfway down the street.

"Camila will stay with my brother Juan until I can send for her. Angel Face offered to take her there tonight or early tomorrow morning."

He didn't need to use his key; the door opened as soon as he arrived.

"Daddy!"

"Shush . . . Come . . . Let me explain . . . We've no time to lose. I'll explain . . . Tell my servant to harness one of my mules to the carriage. . . . We need money . . . and a gun . . . I'll have my clothes shipped later . . . just the bare essentials . . . don't know what I'm saying or if you understand me! Have my bay mule saddled and get my things together while I write a letter to my brothers. You'll be staying with Juan for a few days."

A lunatic would have frightened Camila less than seeing her father, normally so calm, in this nervous state. He couldn't speak; the color of his face came and went. She'd never seen him like this. Driven by haste, worried to death, unable to hear well or say anything but "Oh my God!," she went off to wake up the servant to saddle the mule, a magnificent creature with sparkling eyes. She then went to pack his bag (towels, socks, bread . . . butter, but forgot the salt). In the kitchen, she roused her nanny, who, once awake, sat on a wooden basket and nodded at a fire that was now ashes, near a cat who raised its ears whenever it heard something.

The General was writing quickly when the maid came into the room and closed the windows and shutters.

The silence that ruled the house—not the silken silence of peaceful nights, but the black-carbon-paper silence that copies happy dreams—was lifeless, as stiff and annoying as a strange new garment. It was interrupted only by the General's coughs, his daughter running back and forth, the sobbing maid, the scary opening and closing of wardrobe, cupboard, and bathroom doors.

A short man with a wrinkly face and a dancer's body is writing silently without lifting his pen—he seems to be spinning a spiderweb:

> To his Excellency Señor Presidente
> Constitutional President of the Republic

*In accordance with the instructions received, General
Eusebio Canales has been closely watched. At this time,
I have the pleasure of informing Mr. President that
he was seen in the house of one of his Excellency's friends,
that of Señor Miguel Angel Face. Both the maid (who was
spying on the General and the cook) and the cook (who was
spying on the General and the maid) have informed me
that Angel Face and General Canales met for approximately
three-quarters of an hour. They both said that General
Canales left in an agitated state. Following instructions,
we have doubled the guard at Canales's house, reiterating
the order that he should be shot if he attempts to
escape.*

*The maid—the cook doesn't know this—has supplied
additional information. Her master said to her—she told me
over the telephone—that Canales had come to offer his
daughter in exchange for a successful plea on his behalf to the
President.*

*The cook—the maid doesn't know this—said that when
her master left, he was in a very good mood and ordered
her to go out as soon as the stores opened and buy a large
quantity of canned goods, liqueurs, cookies, and candies,
since a woman from a good family was coming to live
with him.*

*This is the information I wish to provide the President of the
Republic. . . .*

He dated and signed the letter—his signature a dartlike flourish—
and before lifting pen from paper—his nose itched fiercely—he
added:

Further to the message sent this morning re: Dr. Luis Barreño:
Three people visited his office this afternoon, two of whom
seemed to be in bad shape. In the evening, he and his wife
strolled in the park. Re: Lawyer Abel Carvajal: This afternoon
he went to the American Bank, to a pharmacy across from the
Capuchin monastery, and to the German Club. At the latter,
he spoke for a long time with Mr. Romsth, whom the police
are tailing on a separate matter, and returned to his house
around seven thirty. He didn't go out again, and, according to
instructions, the number of guards watching him has been
doubled.

—Signed as above. Dated as above. Sworn.

XI

THE ABDUCTION

After saying goodbye to Rodas, Lucio Vásquez raced over to La Masacuata's bar to see if he was in time to help abduct the young woman. He hurried by the La Merced fountain, a terrifying, dangerous place, according to locals, and a rumor mill for women threading the needle of gossip while dirty water trickled into their jugs.

"Abducting someone is something," thought Pelele's killer. "Thank God, my tour of duty ended early in the Portal so I can give myself over to this pleasure. Holy Mother of God, if I relish stealing objects or robbing a chicken, imagine my pleasure at stealing a girl?"

La Masacuata's bar finally came into view. He began sweating when he saw the La Merced clock . . . it was almost time, if his eyes were to be believed. He greeted a couple of policemen guarding Canales's house and dove into the bar like a rabbit going down a hole.

La Masacuata was lying down in her bedroom, nerves on edge, waiting for 2:00 a.m. She squeezed her legs together, twisted her arms, which were uncomfortably crushed beneath her. Hot ashes oozed from her pores; she thrashed left and right on the pillow, unable to sleep.

Hearing Vásquez knock, she leapt from bed to door, gasping for air, panting as if she had just scrubbed down horses.

"Who's there?"

"It's me, Vásquez."

"I wasn't expecting you."

"What time is it?" he asked, coming in.

"One fifteen," she replied without looking at the clock. She was sure that the person waiting until two was counting minutes, aware of when five, ten, fifteen, twenty minutes had passed. . . .

"Why does the La Merced clock say it's a quarter to two?"

"The church clock always runs fast."

"Has the guy with the money come back?"

"Not yet."

Vásquez hugged the barkeeper, sure she'd slap back his caress. Instead, La Masacuata was gentle as a dove; she let him embrace her and their lips met, as if sealing the pact that tonight they would go all the way. The candle, the only light in the room, illuminated the Virgin of Chiquinquirá's picture by a paper rose bouquet. Vásquez blew on the flame; the barkeeper stumbled. The image of the Virgin vanished in the darkness and their two bodies rolled on the floor like twined ropes of garlic.

Angel Face approached from the direction of the theater. A group of thugs followed him.

"As soon as the girl is in my arms," he told them, "you can loot the house. I swear you won't go away empty-handed. Be very careful—and remember, keep your mouth shut even if you are tempted to boast about this later. If you can't do this right, don't do it at all."

A patrol stopped them as they turned a corner. Angel Face talked with the commanding officer while his men surrounded the other policemen.

"We're on our way to serenade a lady, Lieutenant."

"So where do ya think you're goin'?" he replied, his sword tapping the ground.

"Near here. To the Callejón de Jesús."

"And where's your marimba and guitars . . . ? A weird sort of serenade without instruments, if you ask me."

Angel Face discreetly slipped a large bill into the officer's hand. Just what was needed.

La Merced was at the end of the block. The church was tortoise shaped, with two little eyes—windows—in the cupola. Angel Face told his companions to arrive at La Masacuata's bar at different times.

"We'll meet at the Two Step Tavern!" he said aloud, as they separated. "The Two Step. Careful, guys, don't go elsewhere. It's by the mattress shop!"

Their footsteps faded as they took different streets. The plan was for a couple of Angel Face's thugs to climb onto the roof of General Canales's house when the La Merced clock struck two. This was the signal for the General's daughter to go to a window at the front of the house and scream for help because thieves were trying to get in. This would alert the police watching the house. Amid the uproar and confusion, the General would slip out through the garage door in back.

A fool, a madman, or a child would never have come up with a more harebrained plan. It made absolutely no sense. If the General and Angel Face found it acceptable, it was because each had a secret plan up their sleeve. For Canales, Angel Face's protection ensured certain escape, and for the latter, success relied on the President, whom he informed by telephone of the time and specifics of the General's departure.

April nights in the tropics are the widows of the hot March days: dark, cold, scruffy, and gloomy. Angel Face arrived at the tavern diagonally across from Canales's house, counting the avocado-colored police shadows scattered here and there. He walked around the block. Then he hunched down to enter the below-street-level doorway to the Two Step; uniformed guards stood at the door of each neighboring house, and countless Secret Police agents walked nervously up and down the sidewalks. It felt dangerous.

"I'm taking part in a crime," he said to himself. "This man will be killed as soon as he walks out of his house." The more he thought about his plan, the more ominous it seemed; the idea of abducting the daughter of a man about to die seemed as hateful and repugnant as it seemed pleasant—even satisfying—to help the General escape. For a heartless man like himself, it wasn't decency that made him feel disgust at the idea of ambushing a trusting and unsuspecting citizen in the very center of town—on the contrary, the General would be thinking he was under the protection of the President's confidant. In the end, this "protection" was just a ruse of refined cruelty to

poison the victim's last terrifying moment, when he would realize he had been duped, trapped, and betrayed. The crime would
have the dubious guise of legality, the final effort of the powers-
that-be to prevent the escape of an alleged criminal, who, anyway, would be arrested the next day.

Angel Face's disapproval of such a despicable and diabolical
plan made him bite his lips. He felt himself, in good faith, to
be the General's protector and thus to have certain rights over
his daughter—rights that he should have lost by taking on his
usual role as blind tool, hired assassin, and hangman.

A strange wind blew across his plateau of silence. A thirsty
wild plant sprouted from his eyelashes; the dryness of spiny
cactus, parched as trees unquenched by rain. Why is desire expressed like this? Why are rain-laden trees so thirsty?

The idea that he might turn back, let Canales know, stop
the crime, passed through his brain like a flash of lightning (he
even visualized the daughter's grateful smile). But he was now
at the tavern door, and his own thoughts and the presence of
Vásquez and his men revived his courage.

"Let's go, I'm ready. Yes, sir, I'm ready to do anything, hear?
I won't back out. I've got nine lives. I'm the son of that courageous Moor."

Vásquez was trying to deepen his feminine voice, to make his
words sound manlier. "If you hadn't brought me good luck,"
he said loudly, "I wouldn't be talking like I am now, that's for
sure. You strengthened the love between La Masacuata and
me, and now she's behaving toward me as she should."

"I'm so glad you're here feeling so brave. That's how I like
my men!" gushed Angel Face, shaking the hand of Pelele's
killer. "Dear Vásquez, your words have returned the optimism
the police took from me—there's a cop at every door!"

"Come and have a shot! It'll make you more courageous."

"It's really not for me! This isn't the first time I've had my
back against the wall. I'm thinking about the girl. I wouldn't
want them to nab and arrest us as soon as we get her out of the
house!"

"Look here. Who's gonna nab you? Not one cop will be on
the streets the second they're free to loot the house. I'll bet my

life on it. As soon as they realize they can steal, they'll claw their way in, bet your boots on that!"

"Wouldn't it be wise if you talked to them, now that you were kind enough to come? Let them know you're incapable of . . ."

"Bull! No need to say anything to them. As soon as they see the doors wide open, they'll think: 'What's the harm?' Even if they catch sight of me, they all know what kind of a man I am, since the time Antonio Libélula and I broke into a priest's house. He was so scared when he saw us drop into his room from the attic and light a lantern that he gave us the key to the drawer where he hid his silver and gold, wrapped in a handkerchief so it wouldn't clink if it fell. He pretended he was sleeping. Yes, sir, I certainly got away that time. Now, these guys are determined," Vásquez went on, pointing to the group of unlucky, silent, filthy thugs drinking glass after glass of moonshine, swallowing the liquor in one gulp, and spitting it out in disgust as soon as their lips left the glass. "Yes, sir, these guys are raring to go!"

Angel Face raised his glass to invite Vásquez to join him in toasting love. La Masacuata poured herself an anisette and the three of them drank together.

In the darkness—they didn't light a lantern, to be safe—the only illumination in the room came from the Virgin of Chiquinquirá's candle. The disreputable bodies in the bar projected improbable shadows, elongated like gazelles against the straw-colored walls. The bottles on the shelves resembled colored flames.

They kept their eyes on the clock, spitting on the floor as if their phlegm were bullets. On the side, Angel Face leaned his back against the wall near the Virgin's image. His big black eyes moved around the room, pursued by a thought that assaulted him at decisive moments like a pesky fly: to be married and have kids. He smiled inwardly, remembering the story about the political prisoner condemned to die who, twelve hours before his execution, was visited by a judge advocate. He'd been sent by the President to offer him anything, even his life, if he changed his plea.

"My wish is to bear a son," the prisoner had answered immediately.

"Granted," the judge advocate had said. Smiling at his cleverness, he sent him a prostitute.

The condemned man sent her away without touching her. When the judge returned, he said: "Aren't there enough sons of bitches already?"

Another smile tickled Angel Face's lips. "I've been a school director, newspaper publisher, diplomat, senator, mayor, and now, as if it were nothing, the head of a band of thugs. *That's life in the tropics!*"

The La Merced clock chimed twice.

"Hit the streets!" shouted Angel Face. He took his gun out and told La Masacuata as he left: "I'll be back soon with my trophy."

"Let's go!" shouted Vásquez, climbing like a lizard up a window of the General's house, followed by two thugs. "And woe to any deserter!"

The church clock also chimed twice in the General's house.

"Coming, Camila?"

"Yes, Daddy."

Canales wore riding trousers and a spotless blue waistcoat stripped of its gold braids. His gray hair stood up. Camila fell into his arms, almost fainting, without shedding a word or a tear. The soul can understand happiness or disgrace only if it is anticipated. You have to chew a handkerchief repeatedly, salty from the tears, ripped to shreds tooth by tooth. This was all either a game or a nightmare for Camila—it couldn't be, it simply couldn't be true. What was happening, both to her and to her father, couldn't possibly be true. General Canales took her into his arms and said goodbye.

"This is how I hugged your mother when I went to fight for our country in the last war. The poor thing got it into her head that I wouldn't be returning; it was she who went off and didn't wait for me."

Hearing footsteps on the roof, the old soldier pushed Camila away from him and strode over the flower beds and flowerpots in the courtyard toward the back entrance. The scent of each azalea, geranium, and rose bid him farewell, as did the gurgling water jars and the lit bedrooms. The houselights flicked off, as if the circuit connecting them to other houses had been cut. Fleeing was not worthy of a soldier. The thought of returning home to lead a liberating revolution, however, was worthy of a soldier . . .

As planned, Camila went to a window and called for help. "Thieves are breaking in," she screamed. "They're breaking in."

Before her voice was absorbed by the hugeness of night, the first officers guarding the front of the house came in, tooting their long, hollow whistles. Metal clashed against wood and the front door opened wide. Plainclothes police appeared on the corner, having no idea what was happening. They came, just in case, with sharpened daggers in hand, hats pulled over foreheads, and coat collars covering their necks. The open door, like a fast-moving river, swallowed them up.

So many things that the master of the house knows nothing about.

Vásquez cut the electric wires on the roof, turning corridors and rooms into a single elastic shadow. His henchmen lit matches to find wardrobes, dressers, and chests of drawers. They went through them from top to bottom, snapping off locks, shattering glass doors with gunshots, and smashing fine wood to splinters. Others went to the living room and overturned chairs, desks, and corner tables holding framed pictures—playing cards lost in darkness. Thugs smashed a tiny grand piano left open; it groaned like a wounded beast each time they struck the keys.

In the distance, a chorus of forks, spoons, and knives dumped on the floor laughed and clanged, followed by a scream silenced with a single blow. The nanny La Chabelona hid Camila in the dining room, between a wall and a breakfront. Angel Face shoved her to the ground. The old lady's braids got caught on the handle of the silverware drawer, throwing the contents to the floor. Vásquez silenced her with a metal bar. He hit her repeatedly; nothing, not even her hands, was seen.

PART II

APRIL 24, 25, 26,
AND 27

XII

CAMILA

She spent hour after hour in her room gazing into the mirror. "The devil will come if you don't stop ogling over yourself!" her nanny shouted.

"Is he more devilish than me?" answered Camila. Her disheveled hair formed black flames, her wheat-colored face glowed with coconut butter cleansing cream, and her slanted jade eyes could make ships crash. Her nickname was Asian-Eyes Canales. She wore her school uniform buttoned to the top, but she was grown-up now, less ugly, more capricious and defiant.

"I'm fifteen," she told the mirror. "I'm just a little donkey surrounded by tons of uncles, aunts, and cousins who swarm around me like insects."

She pulled her hair, screamed, made faces. She hated always being with a swarm of relatives. Always the little girl. Going with them to the bus stop. Going everywhere with them: to twelve o'clock Mass, to the Cerrito del Carmen Church, to horseback-riding lessons at the White Horse Stable, to visit the Colon Theater, to climb up and down El Sauce ravine.

Her uncles were whiskered scarecrows with rings jangling on their fingers. Her cousins were sloppy, plump, and heavy as lead. Her aunts were repulsive, or so it seemed to her. A cousin gave her a cone filled with colorful candies, as if she were just a child—this exasperated her. Her uncles would caress her with their stinky tobacco hands, pinch her cheeks to turn her face right and left even though she stiffened her neck so they would stop. Her aunts kissed her through veils, making her feel she had a spiderweb stuck with spit to her cheeks.

Sunday afternoons she would either nap or sit in the living

room, bored of looking at the old pictures in the family album and the portraits arranged on the silver-topped tables, marble consoles, and red-silk-papered walls. Her father purred like a cat as he stared out the window onto a deserted street or answered the greetings of the few friends and neighbors who walked by every once in a blue moon. They would tip their hats. He was General Canales, and he answered in a booming voice: "Good afternoon . . ." or "See you later . . ." or "What a pleasure to see you" or "Take good care of yourself."

In the photos of her just-married mother, only her face and fingers were visible—every other feature was a mystery. Her body was hidden by the latest-fashion ankle-length dress, gloves rising up to her elbows, furs draped around her neck, and a hat dripping with ribbons and feathers under a lace sunshade veil. Her big-breasted aunts looked as stuffed as living room furniture in their pictures, hair sculpted under tiaras that covered half their foreheads. There were photos of her close friends, too—one in a Manila shawl with hair combs and a fan; others dressed up as Mayan natives in embroidered, colorful Indian blouses, sandals on their feet and clay jars on their shoulders; others posing like Madrileñas, with fake beauty spots and jewelry. All these pictures made Camila very sleepy. They spread a kind of torpor that foreshadowed the following dedications: "This portrait will follow you like a shadow." "This pale witness of my affection will be with you at all hours." "If forgetfulness erases these words, the memory of me will also vanish." At the bottom of other photographs, a few words were written between dried pressed violets and faded ribbons: "Remember, 1898," "My Much Adored," "Beyond the Grave," or "Your Mystery Friend."

Her father greeted the few walking down deserted streets; his voice boomed through the living room as if he were actually responding to the inscriptions: "This portrait will follow you like a shadow." "I am so happy. Please be well. . . ." "Goodbye, take good care of yourself. . . ." "If forgetfulness erases these words, the memory of me will also vanish." "It's a pleasure. Regards to your mother."

Sometimes a friend would escape the photo album and stop at

the window to talk to the General. Camila would watch them from behind curtains. It was a man who resembled a conquering hero: young, slender, with long lashes, wearing gorgeous checkered trousers, a buttoned overcoat, and a hat somewhat between a bolero and a derby—the I-am-uninhibited attitude of the turn of the century.

Camila smiled and swallowed her words: *You'd be better off staying as you were in the photograph. You would appear old-fashioned, people would snicker at your museum outfit, and yet you wouldn't be potbellied, bald, with fat cheeks and talk as if you had marbles in your mouth.*

From the shadows of the dusty velvet curtains, Camila's green eyes would peer from a window on this typical Sunday afternoon. Nothing would soften the iciness of her glazed eyes as she stared from the living room onto the streets.

From the balcony stretching over the street, her father would kill time talking to a friend he clearly trusted. His elbows would rest on a satin cushion, and he would not wear a coat, only a linen shirt with dazzling sleeves. His bilious friend would have a hooked nose, a thin moustache, and a gold-knobbed cane. What a lucky break. He was strolling by when the General had stopped him with "What a surprise to see you here in the La Merced neighborhood! What luck!"

Camila recognized him from the album. It wasn't easy. She stared long and hard at the photo of a young man with a handsome nose, a sweet round face. How true it is that time flies—and is cruel. Now his face was angular, with prominent cheeks; thin, hairless brows; and a sharp jaw. As he spoke to her father in a halting, cavernous voice, he would often raise the knob of his cane to his nose as if to smell the gold.

The vast world was in motion. She was in motion. Everything motionless inside her was in motion. Surprising words danced on her lips when she saw the ocean for the first time. But when her uncles asked what she thought of this marvelous scene, she answered with bored indifference: "I knew what it would be like from photographs."

The gusting wind tugged at the wide-brimmed pink hat in her hands. It was like a hoop or a huge round bird.

With open mouths and popping eyes, her cousins stared in amazement. The deafening waves drowned her aunts' words. "How gorgeous! Truly incredible! So much water! It seems to be raging. And there, see? The sun is sinking below the horizon. We didn't leave anything on the train, did we, in our haste to get out? Have you looked to see if everything's here? Let's count the suitcases!"

Her uncles carried trunks filled with light garments perfect for the beach—summer clothes wrinkly as raisins. They hefted tons of cheap coconuts the women had bought at the stations along the way. They walked to the hotel in single file, loaded with baskets and clothes bundles.

"Yes, I know what you mean," finally said a cousin with the longest legs (a rush of blood made Camila's dark cheeks turn slightly pink when she realized someone was answering her), "but I see it differently. You meant to say that the sea resembles images you've seen in films, only bigger."

Camila knew about the moving pictures at the Hundred Doors, near the Portal, but she had no idea what they were like. After what her cousin had said, she could easily imagine them as she looked back at the sea. Everything moving. Nothing constant. Picture following picture, merging together, snapshots jumping to form a fleeting image, a state neither solid, liquid, or gas, but which captured ocean life. A luminous state, both in the moving pictures and in the sea . . .

Toes squirming inside her shoes, eyes darting, Camila continued watching what her eyes couldn't stop remembering. If initially she had felt her eyes emptying to take in the immensity, now that same immensity filled them. It was the rising tide filling her eyes.

Followed by her cousin, she walked slowly across the beach—trudging through sand wasn't easy—to get closer to the waves. Instead of offering her a polite hand, the Pacific Ocean offered a gloved slap that soaked her feet. Surprised, she barely had time to backtrack. Her pink hat, lost, shrank into a small dot carried off by the waves. This elicited a spoiled child's cry, carping to her father: "Oh, sea!" *A mar, amar, to love.*

Neither she nor her cousin realized that, for the first time in

her life, she had said the word *amar*—to love—as she grumbled at the sea. The tamarind-colored sunset froze the dark
green water.

Why did she kiss her arms on the beach and sniff her salty,
sun-drenched skin? Why did she smell the forbidden fruit,
sniffing it with sealed lips? "Acidity is bad for young girls," her
aunts lectured in the hotel. "So are wet feet and running and
jumping around like a filly." Camila kissed both her father
and nanny without smelling them first. She held her breath
when she kissed Jesus's feet—which resembled torn roots—at
La Merced. Without smelling what you kiss, a kiss tastes of
nothing. Her salty flesh bronze as sand, pinecones, and quince
begged for her kiss and made her nostrils widen, excited and
eager. From discovery to action, she didn't know if she was
sniffing or biting when, at summer's end, the cousin who
talked about moving pictures and whistled Argentine tangos
kissed her on the lips.

When they returned to the capital, Camila insisted her
nanny take her to the movies at the Hundred Doors, around
the corner from the Portal. They went without her father's permission, snapping fingers and singing holy hymns all the way
there. When they saw how full the theater was, they almost
went back home. They took two seats near a white curtain,
where images flashed from time to time like a sun reflector.
They were testing the electricity and the lenses. The projector
made a sputtering sound like when the streetlamps turned on.

Suddenly the theater was dark. Camila felt as if they were
about to play hide-and-seek. Everything on the screen was
blurry. Figures jumped around like grasshoppers, shadowy
people who seemed to chew when they talked—their steps
were a series of jumps and their arms seemed to leave their
sockets when they moved.

Camila was reminded of the time she and a boy had hidden in
a skylit room, so she forgot about the movie. A Souls in Purgatory kerosene lamp faced an almost transparent celluloid Christ
in the room's darkest corner. They had lain flat on the floor
under a bed, which seemed to creak. It was an old piece of furniture that couldn't be moved around much. "Coming!" came

from the second courtyard. "Coming!" from the first courtyard. "Coming! Coming!"

When she heard the person seeking say, "I'm coming with a thrumping!," Camila had wanted to burst out laughing. The boy she was hiding with looked at her harshly, to make her stop. She had glared back at him with equally harsh eyes, but then she couldn't hold back her laughter when she heard someone open a night table drawer and a sickening smell entered her nostrils. Her eyes were filling with fine sand that turned into water when she felt something striking her head.

As when she had played hide-and-seek, she walked out of the movie with tears in her eyes, bumping into people getting out of their seats and running for the exits in the dark. They ran until they reached the Portal. That's when Camila realized that everyone was leaving to avoid being excommunicated from the Church. On the screen, a woman in a dress that hugged her body tangoed with a long-haired, moustached man wearing a wide, colorful tie.

Vásquez went out into the street still holding his weapon—the iron bar with which he had silenced La Chabelona was massive. All at once Angel Face appeared carrying the General's daughter in his arms and he disappeared into the Two Step just as the police were making off with the loot.

Those thugs who hadn't taken expensive furnishings made off with wall clocks, full-length mirrors, sculptures, a table, a crucifix, a tortoise, chickens, ducks, doves—anything God had created. Men's clothes, women's shoes, porcelain dishes, flowers, images of saints, basins, trivets, lamps, a chandelier, candleholders, medicine bottles, portraits, books, umbrellas for rain, and chamber pots for piss.

La Masacuata was ready to bar the door.

Camila had no inkling that a stinking, rotten-mattress-smelling hovel existed only a few yards from the house where she had lived so happily, spoiled to heaven by the old soldier (hard to believe he had been happy just yesterday) and looked after by her nanny (hard to believe she'd been wounded). Courtyard flowers lay trampled on the ground—the frisky cat and canary were dead, crushed cage and all. When Angel Face took off the black scarf from around her eyes, Camila realized she was miles from home. Two or three times she passed a hand before her face, looking around to figure out where she was. Her fingers suppressed a cry when she realized her desperate situation.

It was not a dream.

"Young lady, at least you're not in danger here. How can we calm your fears?" Surrounding her inert, heavy body, she heard the same manly voice that had brought disastrous news to her that afternoon.

"Fear fire and water!" said La Masacuata. She ran to unearth a few live embers among the ashes under the clay pot, which was her stove. This gave Lucio Vásquez the chance to sip his potent brandy. He swallowed without tasting, as if drinking rat poison.

The barkeeper revived the fire by blowing, repeating over and over: "Fire liar, liar fire." Against the back room's wall glowing red from the embers, Vásquez's shadow passed behind her on its way to the courtyard.

"This is where he told her," Lucio shrilled, "there isn't anyone who wouldn't come for a hundred . . . for a thousand, too. He who drinks rat poison dies of rat poison. . . ."

La Masacuata dropped a live ember into a bowl of water. It hissed and bubbled like a scared person—the black coal floated like a fruit seed from hell before she took it out of the water with tongs.

After a few sips of this potion, Camila's voice came back. "Where's my father?"

"Don't worry. Drink a bit more of the charcoal water. Nothing's happened to the General," Angel Face replied.

"Are you sure?"

"I think so."

"What if some misfortune—"

"Don't even think it!"

Camila glanced at Angel Face again. A face often reveals more than words, but her eyes got lost in his black, empty eyes.

"You're just feeling helpless," La Masacuata said, dragging

the bench where Vásquez had sat earlier, when Miguel had paid for his beers with a large bill the first time he entered the tavern.

Had that afternoon been years or hours ago? Angel Face glanced at the General's daughter, then at the flame lighting up the Virgin of Chiquinquirá's face. The idea of blowing out the flame and doing what he wanted with the girl darkened his face. One puff and . . . she would be his by force or desire. When he glanced at Camila's pale, teary face, her disheveled hair, and her nearly angelic body, he changed his mind. He took the cup from her with a fatherly gesture and said, "Poor girl."

The barkeeper's coughs coincided with Camila's second round of tears—she would give them privacy. But the coughs turned into curses when she saw Vásquez lying flat in the tiny courtyard smelling of roses in the back of the building, completely soused.

"Boy, you're a worthless drunk," La Masacuata scolded him. "You bring out the worst in me. The second I blink, off you go. All that bullshit about loving me. Yes . . . that's right . . . I turn my back and you grab a bottle . . . You think I get them for free? That I pay nothing? You're just a common thief . . . Get the hell out of here, before I throw you out!"

Lucio grumbled, his head bouncing on the ground, as the barkeeper hauled him out by the feet.

A gust of wind slammed the courtyard door shut. Then it was quiet.

"It's okay, it's all over," Angel Face whispered into Camila's ear. She was crying rivers. "Your father's in no danger. You're safe as long as you stay here. I'll protect you . . . It's all over . . . You can stop crying . . . Crying will only upset you more. Shush. Look at me and I'll explain everything."

Camila's weeping subsided. Angel Face stroked her hair and took the handkerchief in her hands to dry the tears. Morning light filtered under doors and between objects like pink whitewash. People smell each other before seeing them. The trees were going crazy from all the yapping birds, not able to scratch themselves. The fountains yawned repeatedly. The morning air flung aside night's black tresses, the tresses of the dead, to create a golden light.

"You've got to stay calm or you'll ruin everything. You'll put yourself, your father, and me in danger. I'll come back tonight and bring you to your uncle's house. Time is on our side. We must be patient. It takes time to set things right. Some things take more time than others."

"I'm not worried about myself. I feel safe after what you've told me. I am grateful. I understand that I should stay here. I'm just worried about my father. I just need some proof he's really all right."

"I promise to bring you news."

"Today?"

"Yes, today."

Before leaving, Angel Face came back and caressed her check affectionately. "Re-lax!"

General Canales's daughter lifted her tear-filled eyes. "Bring me news."

XIII

THE ARRESTS

The morning bread hadn't reached their door when Genaro Rodas's wife went out. God only knew if the loaves would be delivered. She left her husband fully dressed in bed, limp as a rag. Her baby slept in the basket that doubled as his cradle. It was six in the morning.

The La Merced clock tolled as she knocked on the door of Canales's house. "I hope they'll forgive me for coming so early," she thought, rapping the knocker. "Are they going to open or not? The General needs to know what Lucio Vásquez told my crazy husband last night at the Lion's Awakening."

She stopped knocking. While waiting for the door to open, she remembered that the beggars claimed the General was responsible for the Portal murder. They'll come to arrest him later this morning. Worse, someone's going to abduct his daughter. . . .

"That's really a tough place to be," she told herself, as she kept knocking.

Her heart tightened. "And if they arrest the General? Well, after all, a man can bear it. But if they take his daughter? God help us! That would be awful. I'd bet anything that there's a bitter, dishonest, shameless country bumpkin behind all this. . . ."

She knocked again. House, street, and air echoed the noise like a drum. She was furious that no one opened the door. She spelled out the name of the tavern to pass the time: T-H-E T-W-O S-T-E-P. There were few letters, but then she noticed the painted, carved figures, a man and a woman, on the sides of the door. *Come dance the Two Step* floated over the woman. *No, thanks! I prefer the Bottle Dance!* hovered above the man with a bottle in his hand.

Tired of knocking, she pushed on the door. They either weren't in or were not answering. Her hand just kept pushing. Was it only latched?

She pulled her embroidered shawl around her shoulders and crossed the vestibule. Her heart beating loudly, she went down a corridor barely knowing what she was doing. Like a bird struck by buckshot—blood draining, breath weakening, eyes crisscrossed, wings and legs paralyzed—she saw overturned flowerpots, quetzal feathers stomped on the ground, screens and windows broken, mirrors in hundreds of pieces, destroyed wardrobes, locks forced open; papers, dresses, furniture, and rugs in shreds. Everything aged in a single night; all turned into a disgusting ball of lifeless garbage, filthy, no privacy, utterly soulless.

La Chabelona paced about, her skull cracked, like a ghost among the ruins of an abandoned nest, looking for her charge.

"Ha-ha-ha," she laughed. "Hee-hee-hee! Where are you hiding, my dear Camila? I'm coming to find you . . . Why don't you answer me? . . . I'm gonna get you . . . Coming . . . *coming to find you. . . .*"

She imagined they were playing hide-and-seek. She looked for her everywhere—in corners, among the flowerpots, under beds, behind doors, turning everything upside down like a whirlwind. . . .

"Ha-ha-ha-ha! . . . Hee-hee-hee-hee! Ho-ho-ho-ho! I'm going to get you! Come out, dear Camila, I can't find you. Come out, my dear Camilita, I'm tired of looking for you! Ha-ha-ha-ha! Come out! . . . I'm gonna get you! . . . Hee-hee-hee-hee! Ho-ho-ho-ho! . . ."

Searching everywhere, she reached the fountain. When she saw her reflection in the still waters, she screamed like a wounded monkey. Her laughter was a fearful tremble of her lips—her hair covered her face and her hands covered her hair—until she sank slowly onto the ground, trying to escape that unbelievable vision. She whispered broken apologies, wanting to be forgiven for being so ugly, so old, so short, so disheveled. She screamed again. Through her ragged, cascading hair and the bars of her fingers, she'd seen the sun leap from the roof and fall upon her, ripping away her shadow, which she now saw on the courtyard tiles. Raging mad, she stood up and attacked her shadow and reflection in the fountain, striking the water with her fists and the tiles with her feet, wanting to wipe them off. Her shadow twisted like a flogged creature; despite her furious stomping, it was still there. Her reflection shattered into pieces in the fury of the beaten water, but once the waters calmed, it reappeared. She howled like a rabid beast, sensing her inability to destroy the charcoal film on the stones, which fled her kicking as if it actually felt the blows while she pounded and slapped the gleaming, fishlike dust in the water.

Her feet bled, her arms hung tired at her sides, and her shadow and reflection were still there.

Twisting with rage, she dove headfirst into the fountain in one last desperate attempt. . . .

Two roses dropped into the water . . . the thorns had plucked out her eyes. . . .

Writhing on the ground like her very own shadow, she finally ended up lifeless at the foot of an orange tree wrapped in a blue jasmine vine.

A military band marched down the street, playing fierce, warring tempos. What desires for triumphal arches! And despite the trumpeters blowing loudly together, the neighbors failed to open their eyes willingly that morning. They were like heroes tired of seeing useless embers disrupting the wheat fields' golden peace, unwilling to seek a happy holiday by praying humbly for God to remove evil thoughts, curses, and deeds against the President of the Republic.

After a short nap, La Chabelona bumped into the band. She was blind. Camila tiptoed over to cover her eyes from behind.

"Dear girl, I know it's you. Let me look at you," she stammered. Camila's hands were hurting her, so she lifted her fingers to her face to remove them.

The wind noisily whipped the stalks down the street. The music and blindness of a child's game reminded her of the Pueblo Viejo School, where she first learned to read. Skipping time, she saw herself all grown up, sitting in the shade of two mango trees. Then time skipped again, and she saw herself riding an oxcart across a flat field smelling of hay. The wheels creaked like a double crown of thorns, drawing blood from the beardless driver who had made a woman out of her. The tamed oxen munched as they continued pulling the marriage bed. Heavenly rapture in spongy fields . . . But the memory faded quickly and she saw a throng of men rushing the house like a waterfall, panting like black beasts. Hellish screams, blows, wickedness, cruel laughter, the piano screaming at the top of its lungs as if its teeth were being yanked out in one pull. Camila vanished like perfume, and she felt a blow to the head accompanied by a strange cry and total darkness.

Fedina found the nanny on the courtyard floor, her cheeks bathed in blood. Her hair was a mess, her clothes ripped: she was fighting to keep off flies that invisible hands were throwing in her face. Fedina fled through the house like someone who had seen a ghost.

"Poor thing! Poor thing!" she muttered to herself repeatedly.

She found near the window the letter the General had written to his brother Juan asking him to look after Camila. Fedina didn't read the whole letter, tortured as she was by La Chabelona's screams—which seemed to spring from fractured mirrors, shattered windows, broken chairs, forced breakfronts, fallen pictures—and also because she wanted to take to her heels and leave all this behind. She dried the sweat off her face with a folded handkerchief, which she then balled up in a hand bedecked with cheap rings. She slipped the letter into her bosom and ran into the streets.

Too late. Soldiers had surrounded the house. An officer nabbed her at the door. The nanny, tormented by flies, let out another scream from the courtyard.

La Masacuata and Camila urged Lucio to keep a lookout from the Two Step door. He held his breath when he saw soldiers clasping the wife of Genaro Rodas, to whom he had disclosed, after too many drinks, the plan to arrest the General.

A soldier approached. "They're looking for the General's daughter," La Masacuata guessed, with her heart in her throat.

Vásquez agreed, his hair standing on end. The soldier told them to shut the place down. They closed the doors and went over to the barred windows to observe the street activities.

Vásquez felt energized in the dark. Using fear as a pretext, he began stroking La Masacuata. As usual, she wouldn't have any of it and smacked him.

"You sure are prickly."

"You think so? Sure, pal, sure. You expect me to let you touch the merchandise for free? Didn't I tell you last night that this hussy was going around saying that the General's daughter—"

"Shush! Someone might hear you!" interrupted Vásquez. They both stooped to look out into the streets through door cracks.

"Don't be an ass. I am whispering. . . . Didn't I say that this hussy was going around saying the General's daughter was going to be the godmother of her brat? It'll go to hell if you breathe a word of this to Genaro."

"Fuck!" he said, coughing up something stuck between his throat and nose.

"You're disgusting. A fool with no manners."

"Oh, and you're so dainty?"

"Ass!"

Just then someone got out of a decrepit carriage.

"It's the Judge Advocate," said Vásquez.

"What's he doing here?" La Masacuata asked.

"He's come to arrest the General."

"Dressed like a peacock? Gimme a break! Why don't you grab one of the feathers off his head?"

"No way! You're a busybody! He's dressed like that 'cause he'll then go see the President."

"Lucky guy! If they didn't arrest the General last night, I'm fucked."

"The plan was to arrest him last night!"

"Why don't you shut your trap?"

The Judge Advocate exchanged a few words with a captain who went into Canales's house, followed by a squad of soldiers. The captain held an unsheathed sword in one hand and a gun in the other: he resembled an officer from a Russo-Japanese War poster.

A few minutes later—it seemed years to Vásquez, who watched with his heart in his mouth—the captain came back out. His face was twisted, pale, troubled as he told the Judge what he had seen.

"What's this? What's this!" the Judge Advocate shouted.

The captain's words were garbled by the folds of his tormented mouth.

"What? What? Who's escaped?" roared the Judge. Two veins popped in his forehead like black question marks. "And they've . . . they've looted the house?"

He stormed in, followed by the captain. He surveyed the damage quickly and came back out to the street. His fat hand angrily grasped the hilt of his sword. He looked so pale that it was hard to tell his lips from his moustache, thinner than a fly's wings.

"I want to know how he escaped!" the Judge said, standing by the front door. "That's why telephones exist: to capture the government's enemies. Unlucky fool! I'll hang him the second I find him. I wouldn't want to be in his shoes!"

An officer and a sergeant dragged Fedina over to him. His gaze split her in two.

"Bitch!" he shouted without lifting his eyes. "We'll make you spill the beans! Lieutenant, take ten soldiers and put her where she belongs! Where she can't talk to anyone, you understand."

A frigid shout filled the air—an oily, lacerating, inhuman cry.

"Dear God, what are they doing to that poor Man on the Cross?" groaned Vásquez. La Chabelona's increasingly sharp cries drove a stake into his chest.

"Man on the Cross?" the barkeeper repeated sarcastically. "Don't you know it's a woman screaming? I suppose you think men sing like female blackbirds!"

"Shut your mouth!"

The Judge ordered a search of the neighboring houses. Teams of soldiers followed corporals and captains. They went through courtyards, bedrooms, private quarters, attics, and fountains. They climbed roofs, rummaged through chests of drawers, beds, rugs, breakfronts, barrels, wardrobes, and trunks. Rifle butts struck anyone slow to open. Dogs barked ferociously next to their ashen-faced masters—each house exploded with barking.

"What if they come and search here?" Vásquez whispered, hardly able to speak. "We'd be in a real pickle! We'll get nothing out of this deception!"

La Masacuata ran to warn Camila.

Vásquez followed. "I think she ought to cover her face and leave." He went back to the door without waiting for an answer.

"Wait! Hold it!" he said, putting his eye back to the crack. "The Judge has canceled the search order. We're safe!"

The barkeeper came to the door to see with her own eyes if Lucio was right.

"Well, well, Lord have mercy!" she whispered.

"Who is it?"

"The nanny, can't you see?" She pulled her body away from Vásquez's lecherous hands. "Be still, damn it! Be still. What the hell!"

"Poor thing. Look what they've done to her."

"As if run over by a tram."

"Why do eyes go to the corners when you're dying?"

"Stop! I can't look at this."

A soldier took the nanny from Canales's house on orders of the captain with the drawn sword. The Judge could no longer question her. She was hardly more than a human relic, who, twenty-four hours ago, had been the soul of a house where the only political movements were those of a canary scheming for birdseed, a spout making concentric circles in fountain water, a general's endless game of solitaire, and Camila's whims.

An official followed the Judge Advocate back to his decrepit carriage. The vehicle vanished in smoke at the first turn. Four ragged, filthy men brought a stretcher to carry La Chabelona to the morgue for the postmortem.

Soldiers returned to their barracks and La Masacuata re-opened her bar.

Vásquez sat at his usual place, making little effort to disguise how upset he was at the arrest of Genaro Rodas's wife. His head was hot as a kiln. He farted from all the alcohol he had drunk; waves of intoxication flooded his body. He wondered about the General's escape.

Fedina went off with the arresting soldiers, who kept pushing her off the sidewalk into the street. She let them mishandle her without complaining, but after walking for a long time, she lost patience and slapped one of them in the face. She hadn't expected a rifle butt to strike back at her. Then another soldier hit her so hard from behind that she lost her footing, chomped down on her own teeth, and saw stars.

"Filthy cowards! Is that what your weapons are for? You should be ashamed!" said a woman returning from market with a basket full of fruits and vegetables.

"Shut up!" a soldier shouted.

"In your face, you murderer!"

"Hey, lady, why don't you just run along? Go on now. Or do you have nothing else to do?" shouted a sergeant.

"I'm not a pig ready for slaughter like you!"

"Shut up!" the sergeant answered. "Or I'll bash your face in!"

"My face, eh? That's brave of you! You're just street urchins, all skin and bones, with elbows sticking out and the seat of your pants worn. Look at yourselves in the mirror and you'll shut your dumb mouths. Dirty lice that you are . . . insulting people for the heck of it."

The frightened passersby watched Fedina's unknown defender until she receded into the distance. But the prisoner went on walking toward the prison surrounded by officers; she was a tragic figure, sweating, out of sorts, sweeping the street with the fringes of her cottony shawl.

The Judge Advocate's carriage arrived at Abel Carvajal's house. The lawyer was leaving for the President's Palace wearing a top hat and a morning coat. The Judge Advocate leapt from carriage to pavement, stumbling as he went, rocking the carriage behind him. Carvajal had already gone back in, closed his house door, and was carefully pulling off a glove when his colleague arrested him. Dressed elegantly, he let a group of soldiers escort him down the middle of the street to the Second Police Station, whose walls were festooned with flags and paper chains. They took him to the cell where the student and sexton were imprisoned.

XIV

LET THE WHOLE WORLD BURST INTO SONG!

Daybreak emerged, radiating April's freshness—outlining roofs and fields with light and bringing the darkened streets back into view. Mules carrying clanking milk cans almost galloped, urged on by the shouts and whips of muleteers. The sunlight reached the cows milked in the entryways of wealthy home-owners and on the street corners where the poor lived. The customers—either energized or about to pass out, with sleepy, glassy eyes—waited for milk from their favorite cow, tilting their bottles artfully to get more liquid and less froth. Women carrying fresh bread in baskets passed by, waists twisted, legs stiff, heads sunk into their chests. Their bare feet alternated between steady and slippery steps under the weight of the bas-kets, piled one on top of the other like pagodas. The fragrance of sweet sesame pastries trailed them.

The national holiday began, an alarm clock that created ghosts of wind and metal, a concert of smells, and colorful sneezes, while church bells tolled timidly to announce the day's first Mass. The chiming suggested chocolate and canoni-cal cakes on normal weekends; on national holidays it smelled of forbidden fruit.

National holiday . . .

The neighbors' delight rose from the streets with an odor of fertile earth. They emptied pails of water out windows to tamp down the dust stirred up by the troops that carried the na-tional flag, smelling like a new handkerchief, to the Palace. The wealthy, dressed in fancy clothes, passed by in carriages wearing their Sunday best, generals brandishing uniforms smelling of mothballs—the former wearing satiny headwear and the latter with plumed tricorne hats. Minor officials, whose importance was determined by the amount the state would one day pay for their funeral services, trotted by.

Dear Lord, heaven and earth are filled with Thy glory! The President could be glimpsed way in the distance, surrounded by advisors and loved ones, grateful to a nation that responded in this way to his governance.

Dear Lord, heaven and earth are filled with Thy glory! Women felt the divine power of a Dearly Beloved God. The clergy's most powerful members paid homage to Him. Lawyers imagined they were participating in a King Alfonso the Wise competition. Diplomats—excellencies from the Tiflis Governorate, perhaps—put on grand airs as if at Versailles's Court of the Sun King. Domestic and foreign journalists preened in the presence of Pericles the Second.

Lord, Lord, heaven and earth is filled with Thy glory! Poets imagined they were in Athens, so their verses announced to the world. A sculptor of saints imagined he was Phidias. He smiled and rubbed his hands upon hearing the name of the Eminent Ruler praised in the streets. Lord, Lord, heaven and earth are filled with Thy Glory. A composer of funeral marches, a devotee of both Bacchus and the Holy Burial Procession, stuck his drunk tomato face over his balcony to try to sober up.

If artists imagined they were in Athens, Jewish bankers believed they were in Carthage as they wandered through the parlors of the President, who deposited both his trust and national savings into their bottomless coffers at zero percent interest, a transaction that allowed them to profit so much they were converting gold and silver coins into foreskins. Lord, Lord, heaven and earth are filled with Thy glory!

Angel Face (like Satan, he was both good and evil) waded among the guests.

"The people want you to appear on the balcony, Mr. President."

"The people?"

The Leader seemed to question this term. Silence encompassed him. A deep sadness, which he angrily suppressed as soon as he sensed it, weighed him down. He got up from his chair and went out onto the balcony.

Surrounded by advisors, he faced the people: a group of women had come to commemorate the happy anniversary of the day he had escaped death. When one of them saw the President, she began her prefatory remarks.

"Like Jesus, he's the son of the people.

"Son of the peo-ple," she repeated. "Of the people. In this radiantly beautiful day, the sun lights up the sky, protecting your eyes and your life. It reveals the holiness that occurs in the heavenly vault, the shadow without forgiveness from whence a criminal hand, who—instead of planting fields the way you taught us, Lord—planted a bomb at your feet. Despite having incorporated all European scientific safeguards, it left you unharmed. . . ."

Vigorous applause drowned out the Talking Cow, as the speaker was unkindly called. A series of proclamations fanned the air around the Leader and his entourage.

"Long live the President!"

"Long live the President of the Republic!"

"Long live the Constitutional President of the Republic."

"Let our applause echo for now and forever. Long live the Constitutional President of the Republic, the Benefactor of Our Country, the Head of the Great Liberal Party, the Liberal-Hearted Protector of Our Scholarly Youth . . ."

The Talking Cow went on: "Our flag would have been titter-tattered" ("in titters and tatters," her speechwriter corrected under his breath) "had those evil sons of our nation succeeded, their crime supported by the President's enemies. They never considered that the hand of God was protecting your valuable life, with the support of all those who recognize you as the First Citizen of Our Nation: those who surrounded you then, who surround you now, will surround you forever and ever.

"Yes, gentlemen—ladies and gentlemen. More than ever, today we realize that if that dastardly deed had succeeded—the memory of that sad day lives in all of us—our nation would have lost its father and protector, been orphaned by evil hands working in darkness to force a dagger into the chest of our democracy, as our great statesmen Juan Montalvo wisely said.

"Thanks to your survival, our flag continues to wave unsullied above us. And this is why the quetzal, born from the ashes of the hands that declared the independence of America without shedding a single drop of blood, is on our coat of arms. Indian hands fought until death for the triumph of liberty and law.

"And that is why, gentlemen, we come together today to celebrate the Protector of the poorest classes, the person who watches over us with a father's love and who leads our nation, as I said before, to the front line of progress that Fulton fomented with his steam engine, with which Juana Santa María defended Honduras, the land of the *lempira*, by setting fire to the munitions dumps. Long live our republic! Long live the Constitutional President of the Republic, Head of the Liberal Party, Benefactor of the Nation, Protector of defenseless women, children, and education!"

The Talking Cow's words were lost in a blaze of hurrahs and extinguished by a sea of applause.

The President then said a few words, his right hand clutching the marble balcony. He stood so as not to put his chest in view, glancing from left to right at the spectators, knitting his brow, squinting to recognize faces. Men and women alike wiped away tears.

"Won't you come back inside," Angel Face said, hearing the President sniffle. "The cry of the people has stirred your feelings."

As soon as the President came into the company of friends, the Judge Advocate hurried to tell him about General Canales's escape and to be the first to congratulate him for his stirring speech. But like the others, he stopped dead in his tracks, overcome by a strange supernatural fear; instead of offering the President his outstretched hand, he gave it to Angel Face.

But Angel Face turned his back on him, and the Judge Advocate instead heard a series of explosions followed by a hail of bullets—then screaming, jumping, running, the toppling of chairs, women panicking. Soldiers scattered like grains of rice, hands trying to open cartridge belts, rifles loaded, machine-gun fire, broken mirrors, officers, cannons sounding.

A colonel disappeared upstairs, gun in hand. A second colonel ran down a spiral staircase, clutching his gun. It was nothing. A captain ran to a window, clutching his revolver. A second captain stood guard at a door, gun in hand. It was nothing. Absolutely nothing! But the air was frigid. News spread through the disorderly rooms. It was nothing. Little by little, the guests formed groups; some peed in their pants out of fear, others lost gloves, others recovered their color but were scared mute. Some recovered their speech, but not their color. Still, no one could say when and where the President had gone.

At the foot of a small staircase, the military band's first drummer lay on the ground. He had rolled down from the second floor, drum and all, setting off the general panic.

XV

AUNTS AND UNCLES

Angel Face walked out of the Palace with the Supreme Court's Chief Judge—a little old man in a top hat and tails who looked like a mouse from a children's book—and a congressman chipped like an old statue of a saint. They were arguing over whether the Grand Hotel or a nearby tavern would be better suited to drive away their panic over the crazy drummer: both of them would happily have sent him to be executed, to hell or a worse place. The congressman preferred the Grand Hotel, the most aristocratic of places to knock back a few drinks and frivolously bounce back and forth the obligations of the state like a billiard ball. The Judge, however, spoke as a lawyer pronounces a sentence: "True wealth avoids appearances, and that is why, my good friend, I prefer a drink in this humble inn, in the ease and comfort of friends, to a luxury hotel. Not everything that glitters is gold."

Angel Face left them arguing at the Palace corner—when two such experts argue, it's better to wash one's hands of the whole ordeal—and headed toward Juan Canales's house in the El Incienso neighborhood. It was of utmost importance for Juan to pick up his niece at the Two Step. "It doesn't matter whether he goes alone or has someone fetch her," he said to himself. "As long as she stops being my responsibility, as she was yesterday, when she meant nothing to me." Two or three people turned down the street and ceded passage to greet him. He thanked them without seeing who they were.

The General's brother lived by El Incienso, in a house close to the Coinage, the name given to the Mint, a building as solemn as the gallows. Chipped bastions reinforced the flaking walls; looking into iron-barred windows, you could see rooms that resembled cages for wild beasts. Here the Devil's millions were stored.

When Angel Face knocked, a dog barked. It was obvious from the barking that the dog was tied up.

Angel Face came into the house—he was as good and evil as Satan himself—holding his hat, happy to be where he would bring the General's daughter. The barking dog unnerved him. He heard Juan Canales, a rosy-faced, cheery, potbellied man, say, "Come in! Come in.

"Do come in, I beg you, this way, sir, if you would be so kind! To what do I owe the pleasure of your visit?" Don Juan said, robotically. His tone hid the anxiety he felt in the presence of the President's studded earring.

That bad-tempered dog gave an awful welcome. Angel Face glanced around. He stared at a series of portraits of the Canales brothers and realized that the General's was missing. A mirror, at the far corner, reflected the spot where the portrait had hung against wallpaper as yellow as an old telegram.

The dog, Angel Face observed, was the house guardian as in years of yore, while Don Juan exhausted his barrel of stock phrases couched in niceties. The dog was the Defender of the Tribe. Even the President had a kennel of imported hounds.

Don Juan Canales, having pulled out all the polite words in his repertoire, dove like a good swimmer into the deep end, gesturing frantically in the mirror.

"Here, in my house," he began, "my wife and I, your humble servants, have completely disapproved the behavior of my brother Eusebio. What a story! A crime is always detestable, and even more so when you consider who's involved: a person beyond reproach, a man who was a credit to our military and, most of all, as I'm sure you know, a friend of our esteemed President!"

Angel Face kept the chilled silence of someone watching a man drown who could not be saved by any means. Don Juan seemed afraid to accept or reject what the visitor was saying.

Realizing his words had fallen on deaf ears, he lost his nerve and began beating the air with his hands, trying to find the ground under him. His head was on fire. He felt implicated in the Portal murder and all that it implied politically. His innocence meant nothing. How complicated it all was, very complicated. *It's a crapshoot, my friend, just a crapshoot.* This phrase summarized the situation in the country, as Old Fulgencio used to scream. Fulgencio was a good man, a devout Catholic, an art collector selling lottery tickets on the street. Instead of seeing Angel Face, Juan Canales stared at the silhouette of Uncle Fulgencio's skeleton, whose bones, jaws, and fingers seemed held in place by jittery wires.

Old Fulgencio gripped his black leather case under a bony arm. He smoothed his face wrinkles, slapped his buttocks under baggy pants, stretched his neck to speak with a voice that came out of his nostrils and his toothless mouth: "The only law in this country is the lot-lot-tery. It can send you to p-p-rison or get you ex-ex-ecuted. You can become a co-con-gressman, a dip-dip-lomat, even President of the Republic, a gen-gen-eral, a min-min-ister. What's the use of studying, if it's all a crapshoot? The lot-lot-tery, my friend, the lot-lot-tery, buy a tick-tick-et from me!" And that twisted skeleton, that trunk of warped vines, shook while laughter shot out of his mouth like a list of winning lottery numbers.

Angel Face merely watched him in silence, asking himself what that cowardly, detestable man had in common with Camila.

"Someone said—actually someone told my wife—that they want to implicate me in Colonel Parrales Sonriente's murder!" Juan went on, struggling to pull a handkerchief out of his pants pocket to mop the thick sweat rolling down his forehead.

"I don't know about that," Angel Face replied dryly.

"That would be a travesty. From the start, my wife and I disapproved of Eusebio's behavior. Besides, I don't know if you know, but my brother and I see very little of each other lately. Hardly ever. Actually never. We walk by each other like strangers: Good morning, good morning; good afternoon, good afternoon. That's it. Hello, goodbye, nothing more."

Don Juan's voice trembled. His wife had been watching from behind a screen, but thought it was time to come out and save her husband.

"Introduce me, Juan!" she exclaimed, appearing. She greeted Angel Face with a nod and a polite smile.

"Oh yes, of course," answered her husband anxiously, standing next to Angel Face. "It's my pleasure to introduce you to my wife."

"Judith Canales."

Angel Face heard her name but didn't remember if he had said his.

This visit had gone on too long, because an inexplicable force now stirred his heart. Words that had nothing to do with Camila were lost in his ears, leaving no trace.

"But why don't these people mention Camila?" he wondered. "If they talked about their niece, I would listen. If they mentioned her, I would tell them not to worry, that Don Juan isn't being implicated in any murder. If they talked about her. . . . But I am so foolish. She and them, I, no, there's no reason to be here, I don't have anything. . . ."

Judith sat on the sofa and wiped her nose with a lace handkerchief, waiting for something. "You were saying? I interrupted you. So sorry."

"Of . . . !"

"If . . . !"

"Have you . . . !"

All three spoke at the same time. After a few polite and comical "Please continue, please continue"s, Don Juan suddenly said (*Idiot!* his wife's eyes screamed at him), "I was telling our friend here that you and I were outraged—just between us—that my brother Eusebio was one of Colonel Parrales Sonriente's killers. . . ."

"Oh, yes, yes, yes!" agreed his wife, pushing up her rather large breasts. "Juan and I were saying that the General, my brother-in-law, should never have stained the honor of his uniform with such a dastardly dead. And worst of all, we've been told that they want to implicate my husband in this."

"I explained to Don Miguel that we've been estranged for a long time, that in a sense, we're almost enemies . . . Yes, mortal enemies. He couldn't lay eyes on me, not even in a picture, and I even less on him."

"Not quite so bad. But the stuff of families—resentment and quarrels," added Judith, sighing.

"That's what I thought," Angel Face broke in, "but don't forget, Juan, that there's always an indestructible bond among brothers—"

"What? What are you hinting, Don Miguel? . . . That I'm an accomplice?"

"Excuse me?"

"Don't even think it!" Doña Judith hastened, lowering her eyes. "All bonds are destroyed when money issues crop up. It's sad, but it happens every day! Money trumps blood ties."

"Let me speak! I was saying that among brothers there's an indestructible bond, because despite the profound differences between Don Juan and the General, the latter, seeing himself ruined and forced to leave the country, told me—"

"He's a crook if he implicated me in his crimes! Oh, what a slur!"

"But that's not it!"

"Juan! Juan! Let the man speak!"

"He told me he relied on your help so his daughter would not be orphaned. He asked me to come and talk to you about her staying in your house. . . ."

Now it was Angel Face's turn to feel his words falling on deaf ears. He thought he was speaking to people who didn't understand Spanish. Between the clean-shaven, potbellied Juan and Judith, with her huge wheelbarrow breasts, his words reflected no more than if he had spoken into a mirror.

"It's up to you to decide what should be done for the girl."

"Yes, of course!" As soon as Juan realized that Angel Face wasn't arresting him, he returned to his normal demeanor. "I don't really know how to respond; you've taken me quite by surprise. . . . Having her stay here is out of the question. . . . You know you shouldn't play with fire. . . . I am sure that this unfortunate girl would be happy here, but my wife and I are not in a position to lose friends who would hold it against us if we welcomed into our respectable home the daughter of an opponent of the President . . . besides, everyone knows that my infamous brother offered—how should I put it?—yes, offered her to a close friend of the Chief of State for—"

"Simply to avoid being locked up!" interrupted Judith, letting the peaks of her enormous breasts sink into the ravine of another breath. "Like Juan said, he offered his daughter to a friend of the President, who would then give her to the President himself, who obviously rejected this disgraceful proposal. And then the Prince of the Army—his nickname after his famous speech—finding himself in a dead end, decided to escape and leave us with her ladyship. That's it! What can you expect from a man who brings a plague of suspicion on his own family and who discredits our family honor! Don't think we haven't suffered because of these shenanigans. Our hair has almost turned white—may the Lord and the Virgin Mother be our witness!"

Anger flashed across the bottomless pits of Angel Face's eyes.

"Well, there's nothing more to say. . . ."

"We're sorry you came. We would have gladly come to see you. . . ."

"If it wasn't impossible, we'd cross rivers and mountains to meet you," added Judith.

Angel Face left without saying another word. The dog barked ferociously, dragging his chain across the floor from one end of the room to the other.

"I'll go and talk to another of your brothers," he said in the foyer as he left.

"Don't waste your time," Don Juan slipped in. "If I, a well-known conservative living here, won't have her stay, imagine those liberals. . . . Well, they'll think you've lost your mind or you're simply joking—"

He was almost standing outside when he said these words. He closed the door slowly, rubbed his pudgy hands, paused for a second, then came back inside. Overcome by a strong urge to caress anyone but his wife, he went over to the still barking dog.

"If you're going out, leave the dog alone," Judith shouted from the courtyard, pruning the rosebushes now in the shade.

"Yes, I'm going out now."

"Well, hurry back. I need to go say my evening prayers. I shouldn't be in the streets after six."

XVI

IN THE CASA
NUEVA PRISON

Around eight in the morning (wonderful were the days of the Greek water clock, before the grasshopper clock, before time was measured in leaps and bounds), after the usual paperwork and a list of what she wore was completed, Fedina was thrown into a dungeon that looked like a guitar-shaped tomb. They searched her meticulously from head to toe, from nails to armpits—a most offensive process. They searched everywhere, searched her even more thoroughly after finding a handwritten letter from General Canales tucked into her bosom—the letter she had picked up from the floor of his house.

Tired of standing in this tiniest of hovels, she sat down on the floor—after all, it was better to sit—but then she stood up again. The cold penetrated her buttocks, legs, hands, ears— human flesh can't bear cold like this. So she kept standing, sitting down, standing, sitting down, standing.

She heard prisoners singing as they went out to get some sun in the yard: songs that tasted of raw vegetables despite the boiling heat in their hearts. Some tunes—sung drowsily—were monotonously grim. Then their chained oppression burst into desperate screams. They cursed God, hurled insults, and swore aloud. . . .

One voice in particular terrified Fedina—a discordant voice that repeated the same words over and over:

> From Casa Nueva
> To a cathouse,

Cielito lindo,
There's barely a step.
Now that we are alone,
Cielito lindo
Take me in your arms.

Ay ay ay ay!
Take me in your arms,
From Casa Nueva
To a cathouse,
Cielito lindo
There's barely a step.

The first two lines of "Cielito Lindo" clashed with the rest of the song; still this tiny discord underscored how similar a cathouse was to a prison. The break in rhythm reflecting reality underlined the terrifying truth that made Fedina shake in fear. She was already shaking without feeling the unknown, terrifying fear that she would feel later, when a scratchy recorded voice hiding many criminal secrets penetrated her bones. It wasn't fair that this bitter song was her breakfast. If she'd been flayed alive, she would have felt less tormented than she did in this underground hovel, listening to the prisoners who forgot that a whore's bed was still colder than a jail, even if it offered a little more freedom and warmth.

She took comfort in remembering her son. She imagined him still in her womb. Mothers never feel completely empty of their children. She'd baptize him the second she got out of prison. Everything was arranged. Señorita Camila had given him such a pretty outfit and bonnet. She planned to celebrate the event with tamales and chocolate for breakfast, *arroz a la Valenciana* and a *pepián* stew for lunch, cinnamon water, *orchata*, ice cream, and cookies for afternoon snack. The glass-eyed printer would create gift stamps of the saints to give to her friends. She would order two carriages from Shumann's with horses as big as locomotives and jingling silver-plated harnesses and drivers wearing top hats and tails. Then she tried to rid her brain of such thoughts, should something happen like what occurred to the man who said on the eve of his wedding: "This time tomorrow, you'll taste this little mouth of mine!" The next day, before the wedding, he had the misfortune of someone throwing a brick at his mouth on his way to the church.

Her memories of her son were interrupted when she found herself facing a cobweb of obscene drawings. This depressed her even more. Crosses, holy verses, men's names, dates, and cabalistic numbers were written on the sides of penises of all sizes: the word "God" next to a phallus; the number 13 on an engorged testicle; devils with candelabra horns on their heads; flower petals shaped like fingers; drawings caricaturing judges and magistrates; little boats, anchors, suns, moons, bottles, and little meshed hands; daggers piercing eyes and hearts; suns with whiskered policemen; moons with old maid faces; three- and five-pointed stars; watches, mermaids, winged guitars, arrows.

Panicking, she tried to escape this world of perverted madness, but ran up against more obscenities on the wall. Terrified and mute, she closed her eyes. She was a woman sliding down a slippery slope, seeing cavernous ravines instead of windows. The starry sky resembled wolf fangs.

A horde of ants lugged a dead roach across the floor. Influenced by the obscene drawings, Fedina imagined a vulva dragged by its pubic hair toward a harlot's bed:

> From Casa Nueva
> To a cathouse,
> *Cielito lindo* . . .

The song rubbed little glass splinters into her flesh as if to abrade her feminine modesty.

Celebrations honoring the President of the Republic continued in town. Every night a movie screen was raised like a gallows in the Plaza Central. A hypnotized crowd watched blurred fragments as if witnessing the burning of heretics. Illuminated public buildings stood out against the darkened sky. Droves of people pressed like a turban around the sharp-pointed railing encircling the park. Society's crème de la crème strolled in circles during the nights of celebration, while the common folk gazed in awe at the screen in religious silence. Old men and old women, bachelors, and married couples were packed like sardines and couldn't hide their boredom anymore; from garden benches and chairs, yawn followed yawn as they watched passersby flirt with girls and greet friends. From time to time, rich and poor looked up to the sky: a rocket would burst in the air, releasing threads of rainbow silk.

The first night in a dungeon is terrifying. The prisoner is severed from life, cast into a dark, nightmarish world. Walls fade, ceilings vanish, floors disappear—and yet, there's no sense of freedom. One feels completely dead.

Fedina prayed rapidly: "Oh most merciful Virgin Mary, it's been said that You never abandon anyone who seeks Your protection. I implore Your help and demand Your shelter. I turn to You in confidence, oh Mother of all Virgins. I weep for my sins and kneel before Your feet. Do not reject my prayers, oh Virgin Mary: listen with a kind, receptive ear."

Darkness choked her. She couldn't pray anymore. She fell to the floor and stretched her arms—her oh-so-long arms—to embrace the cold earth, the cold lands, of the prisoners unjustly suffering persecution in the name of justice, the victims, the wanderers. . . .

She repeated the litany:

> *Ora pronobis . . .*
> *Ora pronobis . . .*
> *Ora pronobis . . .*
> *Ora pronobis . . .*
> *Ora pronobis . . .*
> *Ora pronobis . . .*
> *Ora pronobis . . .*
> *Ora pronobis . . .*

She sat up slowly. She was hungry. Who would breast-feed her baby? She crawled over to the door and knocked hopelessly.

> *Ora pronobis . . .*
> *Ora pronobis . . .*
> *Ora pronobis . . .*

A bell tolled twice in the distance.

> *Ora pronobis . . .*
> *Ora pronobis . . .*

In the world where her baby was.

> *Ora pronobis . . .*

She counted twelve strokes. Revived, she tried to imagine she was free—and succeeded. She saw herself at home, among familiar things and people, telling Juanita: "So long. It was so nice to see you!" Going out, she clapped her hands to call Gabrielita, looked down at the fire and nodded reverently at Don Timoteo. Her shop was a living, breathing thing, something built by herself as well as others.

Outside, the celebration continued. The movie screen was erected like a gallows with people walking around the plaza like slaves around a waterwheel.

When she least expected it, the dungeon door opened. The bolts' grinding made her jump, startled as if at the edge of a cliff. Two men felt for her in the darkness and, without a word, pushed her down a narrow corridor. The night wind blew strongly, past two dark rooms and toward a lit room. As she entered it, the Judge Advocate whispered something to his clerk.

"This is the man who plays the harmonium at the Virgin of Carmel," Fedina said to herself. "I thought I recognized him when they arrested me; I've seen him at church. He can't be a bad person!"

The Judge Advocate stared at her, then asked a few questions: name, age, civil standing, profession, address. Fedina answered these questions resolutely. While the clerk wrote down her answers, she tried to ask a question, but just then, the telephone rang. A woman answered it, breaking the silence in the adjoining room: "Yes! How are you feeling? . . . I'm so happy! . . . I had Canducha go and ask you. . . . The dress? . . . The dress is fine, it's the right size. . . . What? . . . No, no, it's not stained . . . I said it's not stained . . . Yes, please do it . . . Yes, yes . . . Yes . . . please come . . . Goodbye . . . Have a nice evening . . . Goodbye."

The Judge Advocate eventually answered Fedina in a cruel, mocking tone. "Don't worry. That's why we're here. To tell people why they've been arrested."

With froglike eyes popping out of his sockets, he switched tones: "But first, I want you to tell me what you were doing this morning at General Eusebio Canales's house."

"I'd gone . . . I'd gone to see the General about something. . . ."

"What about, may I ask?"

"Just a little something, sir. A small issue! About . . . Look . . . I'll tell you everything. I went to tell him that he was going to be arrested for the murder of that Colonel something-or-other who was killed in the Portal."

"And you have the nerve to ask why you were arrested? You bitch! Just a little something? *Just a little something?* You bitch!"

Each word increased his rage.

"Wait, sir, let me explain! Please! It's not what you think! When I got to the General's home, he wasn't there, I swear. I didn't see him, I didn't see anyone. Everybody had left, the house was empty, except for a maid running around screaming!"

"*Just a little something?* That's what you think? When did you arrive?"

"The Merced clock was striking six."

"That you remember! How did you know General Canales was going to be arrested?"

"Me?"

"Yes, you!"

"My husband told me."

"Your husband? What's your husband's name?"

"Genaro Rodas!"

"How'd he know? Who told him?"

"A friend, sir. Lucio Vásquez, a member of the Secret Police. He's the one who told my husband and my husband—"

"And you told the General!" the Judge Advocate precipitated.

Fedina shook her head. "No way, no how!"

"And which way did the General go?"

"For the love of God! I didn't see the General. That's what I'm saying! Don't you understand? I didn't see him, I never saw him! What would I get out of lying? Especially if that's what that guy is writing down!" She pointed to the clerk, who looked back at her, his pale, freckled face like blotting paper used to cover a great many dots.

"Don't worry about what he's writing. Answer my questions. Which way did the General go?"

A long silence followed. The Judge Advocate's voice thundered: "Which way did the General go?"

"I don't know. What do you want me to say? I don't know. I never saw him, I didn't speak to him!"

"Lying is a big mistake. The authorities know everything. And they know you spoke to the General."

"Don't make me laugh!"

"Listen, this is no joke! The authorities know everything— everything, everything!" He rapped the table at each word. "If you never saw the General, where'd you get that letter? It just flew through the air and landed inside your blouse? Is that it?"

"I found the letter in his house. I *snutched* it off the floor when I left. But why am I telling you this? You don't believe a word I say! To you, I'm just a liar."

"'I snatched it.' She can't even talk properly," the clerk grumbled.

"Stop telling tales, señora. Tell the truth! All your lies will earn you a punishment you will remember for the rest of your life."

"I'm telling the truth. If you don't want to believe me, I can't beat it into you as I would into my son!"

"You're going to pay a high price for this, mark my words. Tell me: What's your relationship with the General? What were you, what are you to him? His sister or what? What did he offer you?"

"Me? The General? Nothing. I only saw him maybe twice. But you see, by coincidence, his daughter promised to be my son's godmother."

"That's no reason!"

"She was almost his godmother, sir!"

The clerk whispered: "What poppycock!"

"And if I was upset, lost my head, and ran to where I ran, it was because Lucio told my husband that someone was going to abduct his daughter. . . ."

"Stop lying! You'd be better off telling me where the General went. I know you know. You're the only one who knows and you're now going to tell me, just me. . . . Stop crying! Talk! I'm listening!" Then, softening his voice, he added like a father confessor, "If you tell me where the General is . . . look, listen to me; I know you know. You're going to tell me. If you tell me where the General is hiding, I'll pardon you. You hear? I'll pardon you. You'll be set free and can go straight home in peace. Think of that!"

"Oh, sir, if I knew I would tell you. But I don't know. Unfortunately, I don't know. Holy Mother of God, what can I do?"

"Why deny it? Don't you see you're hurting yourself?"

In the gap between the Judge Advocate's sentences, the clerk sucked his teeth.

"There's no point in treating you nicely, because you're evil." He said these last words more quickly, growing angrier, like a volcano about to blow its top. "One way or another, you're going to tell me. You've committed a very serious crime against the state. You've been arrested because you're responsible for the escape of a traitor, a rebel, a murderer, an enemy of our President. . . . And that's saying a whole lot, quite a lot, quite a lot!"

Fedina didn't know what to do. The words of this diabolical man conveyed a looming threat—almost a death threat. Everything trembled: her jaws, fingers, and legs. When fingers tremble bonelessly, hands shake like gloves. When jaws tremble, unable to speak, they telegraph worry. When legs tremble, someone is standing up in a carriage harnessed to two run-away horses like souls the Devil is about to usurp.

"Sir!" she implored.

"This isn't a game! Tell me! Where's the General hiding?"

A door opened down the corridor. The sound of an infant's obsessive weeping spiraled toward her.

"Do it for your child's sake."

The Judge Advocate had hardly spoken when Fedina lifted her head, glancing left and right to find where the crying had come from.

"He's been at it for two hours. There's no point trying to find him. . . . He's crying because he's hungry, and he'll die of hunger if you don't tell me where the General is."

She dashed toward a door, but was stopped by three brutes, who easily held her in check. Struggling was useless. Her hair flayed to the sides; her blouse came out of her skirt and her petticoat slipped below her knees. Who cared about her clothes? Nearly naked, she crawled back to the Judge Advocate, begging him to let her nurse the baby.

"Sir, for the love of Mary," she begged, wrapping her arms around his feet. "Please let me nurse my baby. He barely has the strength to cry. He's going to die. You can kill me later."

"No Virgin Mary is going to help you here. If you don't tell me where the General is hiding, we'll stay here until your boy cries himself to death."

Nearly mad, she fell to her knees before the guards at the door. Then she rushed back to the Judge Advocate and tried to kiss his shoes.

"Sir, for the sake of my child!"

"For the sake of your child, where's the General? There's no point in prostrating yourself, acting theatrical. If you don't tell me, you will never nurse your son again."

Tired of sitting, the Judge Advocate stood up. The clerk was still sucking his teeth, holding his pen, waiting for the unfortunate woman to finish her statement.

"Where's the General?"

During the cold rainy season, water weeps in the gutters; but this was the blubbering of a frightened child.

"Where's the General?"

Fedina whimpered like a wounded creature, chewing on her lips, not knowing what to do.

"Where's the General?"

Five, ten minutes passed. Drying his lips with a black-bordered handkerchief, the Judge Advocate finally added another threat to his question. "If you don't give me what I want, I'll force you to push the grindstone to make quicklime. Perhaps that will spur your memory."

"I'll do anything you want, only please, let me breastfeed my baby first. Sir, be fair. My baby has nothing to do with this, he's innocent. Punish me any way you want."

One guard pushed her down onto the floor, then another kicked and flattened her. Her tears and her outrage blurred the walls—everything in the room. She could hear only the baby weeping.

It was one in the morning when she started pushing the grindstone so they'd stop beating her. Her little boy was still crying.

From time to time, the Judge Advocate repeated: "Where's the General? Where's the General?"

One.

Two.

Three o'clock. Her little boy was still crying.

It would never be four o'clock. Her boy went on crying.

Finally, it was four. Her boy went on crying.

Countless deep cracks on her hands, widening each time they moved. Her fingertips were raw, sores formed between her fingers, her nails bled. Fedina howled in pain as she lifted and rolled the grindstone over the lime. Whenever she stopped to beg—more for her son than for herself—they'd beat her.

"Where's the General? Where's the General?"

She no longer heard the Judge Advocate's voice in her ears: just her baby, growing weaker and weaker.

At twenty to five, they left her unconscious on the ground. Thick drool issued from her mouth and milk whiter than lime came out of almost invisible sores on her breasts. A few secret tears flowed out of her swollen eyes.

At nearly daybreak, they took her back to her cell. When she awoke, she was holding her dying, ice-cold child, lifeless as a rag doll. Realizing he was in his mother's lap, the boy came back to life and went straight for the breast. But when he began to nurse, he tasted the acidic quicklime. He spat the nipple out and began crying again. No matter what she did, he refused to nurse.

She shouted and banged on the door with her baby in her arms . . . he grew colder and colder . . . how could they let him die like this when he was innocent?

She went back to banging on the door and shouting. "My son is dying! My son is dying! Oh, my love, my little thing, my love! For the love of God! Open the door! For the love of God, open the door! My son is dying! Holy Mother of God! Blessed St. Anthony! Jesus of St. Catherine!"

Outside, the celebration continued. The second day was just like the first: the movie screen was erected like a gallows with people walking around the plaza like slaves around a waterwheel.

XVII

LOVE'S RUSES

"Will he come or won't he?"

"He's almost here!"

"He's already late. As long as he comes—that's what matters."

"You can count on it, as sure as it's dark now; I'll bet my life he'll come. Don't worry."

"Do you think he'll bring me news of Daddy? He said he would. . . ."

"Of course he will . . . All the more reason he's late. . . ."

"Oh, I hope to God he doesn't bring bad news. I'm going . . . crazy . . . I hope he shows up soon so I can stop worrying. I don't want him to come if he's bearing bad news."

La Masacuata listened to Camila lying on a bed in the corner of her small makeshift kitchen. A candle stump burned on the floor in front of the Virgin of Chiquinquirá.

"I'm sure his news will make you happy, given the mess you're in, you'll see. How do I know? I've a sixth sense on matters of love . . . especially when it comes to men. If you only knew. I know that men, like dogs, aren't all alike—toss a bone, and you'll see how many of them show up. . . ."

It was hard for Camila to listen to the barkeeper absent-mindedly pumping the bellows, making swooshing noises.

"Love, my girl, is a cherry snow cone. When you start eating, there's tons of red syrup and you're happy. Then it drips all over and you've got to lick it before the top tips over. Then you're left with a tasteless, colorless clump of ice."

Footsteps echoed on the street. Camila's heart beat so loudly she needed two hands to muffle it. The footsteps passed by the door and disappeared quickly.

"I thought it was him."

"He'll be here soon. . . ."

"Maybe he went to my uncle's house before coming here. Perhaps Uncle Juan will come with him."

"Scram, cat! He's drinking your milk. Shoo him away. . . ."

Camila looked at the cat that was frightened by the barkeeper's scream. It licked its white whiskers near the cup forgotten on the armchair.

"What's her name?"

"Benzoin."

"I had a cat named Droplet."

More footsteps echoed. Perhaps . . .

It was him.

While La Masacuata unbolted the door, Camila smoothed her hair with her hands. Her heart pounded. She felt lifeless, numbed by the seemingly endless day. Her eyes were puffy as if she were sick.

"Señorita, good news!" said Angel Face at the door, appearing untroubled.

She stood by the bed, clasping the headboard. Her eyes were teary, her expression frozen. Miguel caressed her hands.

"First things first: news of your father." He glanced at La Masacuata; without changing tone, he took a different tack. "Well, your father doesn't know you're hiding here. . . ."

"Where is he?"

"Hold on."

"I just want to know he's okay."

"Sit down, sir," La Masacuata said, pointing to a bench.

"Thanks."

"I'm going to grab a little rest—that is, if you don't need me. Since you two have plenty to discuss, I will go look for Lucio. I haven't seen him since he left this morning."

Miguel was about to ask her not to leave him alone with Camila, but she had already gone to change her skirt in the little courtyard.

Camila addressed her: "God bless you for all you've done, ma'am. Poor thing, you're so kind. Everything you say is so sweet."

Then she spoke to Angel Face. "She says you're a good man, very rich and charming. She knows you from a long way back. . . ."

"Yes, she's a doll. Still, I can't talk openly with her around. It's better that she left. I only know that your father escaped. We won't know more until he's crossed the border. Did you by chance tell her anything about your father?"

"No. I assumed she knew everything."

"It's better she know nothing."

"What did my uncle and aunt say?"

"I was trying to get news about your father, so I wasn't able to see them. I left word I would stop by tomorrow."

"Sorry to insist, but I'd feel better staying with them. Uncle Juan is my godfather—like a second father to me."

"You saw a lot of each other?"

"Every day. Well, almost every. He would come to our house when we didn't go visit his, either alone or with his wife. He's my father's favorite brother. Daddy often told me, 'When I'm away, stay with Juan. You should obey him like a father.' This last Sunday we had lunch together."

"If I hid you here, Camila, it was to keep you from the police. And also because we're close by."

The candle's weary flame fluttered like a nearsighted person's gaze. Angel Face seemed shorter, somewhat sickly in that light. Camila seemed pale, more alone, pretty in her yellow dress.

"What are you thinking?" His voice was warm and soothing.

"That my poor father must be suffering, going to dark, unknown places. I just want to say that he's probably hungry, thirsty, and sleepy, with no one to help him. May the Virgin protect him. I've kept a candle burning for him all day."

"Don't worry so much; what will happen will happen. You never imagined you would meet me and that I would serve your father!" She let him take one of her hands in his. Then they both gazed at the Virgin.

Miguel was thinking:

> You would fit perfectly
> In the keyhole of heaven:
> The locksmith carved your body
> On a star, on the day you were born.

These lines ran through his head, revealing the flutter join-ing their two souls.

"You said my father is going far, far away. Do you know when he's leaving?"

"I'm not sure, but probably soon. . . ."

"In a few days?"

"No . . ."

"My uncle Juan, perhaps, has some news. . . ."

"Perhaps . . ."

"You reacted strangely when I mentioned my aunt and uncle. . . ."

"Not at all. On the contrary—without them, my responsi-bility would be greater. Where would I take you, if not to them?"

Angel Face's tone changed when he discussed the General's escape and her uncle. He feared seeing the General escorted back in handcuffs or looking like a cold tamale on a blood-soaked stretcher.

The door opened suddenly. La Masacuata fluttered in. The wooden bar that locked the door crashed to the floor. The can-dle flame flickered in the wind.

"Sorry to interrupt you like this . . . Lucio's in jail . . . A friend was telling me this when someone brought me this note . . . He's in the penitentiary . . . All because of Genaro Rodas! What a poor excuse of a man! We've only had bad news tonight! Every few seconds my heart goes thump, thump, thump. Rodas squealed to the authorities that you and Lucio had abducted the General's daughter. . . ."

Miguel couldn't stop the impending fiasco. A handful of words set off an explosion. His unlucky romance with Camila had been blown to bits in a second, in less than a second.

When he realized what had happened, Camila was already facedown on the bed crying inconsolably. The barkeeper was spilling the beans on an abduction, not realizing that her yapping was tossing their possible love over a cliff. Miguel felt buried alive, open-eyed.

After crying her eyes out, Camila rose like a sleepwalker and asked the barkeeper if she could borrow a shawl so she wouldn't be recognized on the streets.

"And if you're really a gentleman," she said, turning to Angel Face after taking the shawl, "you'd accompany me to my uncle Juan's house."

Miguel wanted to say what couldn't be said; inexpressible words danced in his eyes. His desire had just been struck down by fate. "Where's my hat?" he asked, in a gravelly voice swollen in discomfort.

Before leaving, he glanced one last time at the room where his dream had crashed like a ship into rocks. "I fear," he said, going out, "it may be too late."

"You'd be right if we were going to a stranger's house, but we're going to my home: my uncle's house is my second home."

Angel Face gently held her arm. As if tearing out his very soul, he revealed the bitter truth: "You can forget your uncles. They want nothing to do with you or the General. They have disowned your father. Your uncle Juan said so today."

"But you just told me you hadn't seen him, that you only made an appointment! What's going on? Have you forgotten what you just told me? Now you insult my uncles so you can keep me here like a stolen jewel that's dropped into your hands? I won't believe that my uncles want nothing to do with us—that they wouldn't welcome me into their homes! You've lost your mind. Come! I'll show you how wrong you are!"

"I'm not mad. I'd give my life to avoid your humiliation. If I lied, it was because . . . oh, I don't know. I lied out of tenderness, to spare you the pain you're feeling now as long as I could. I was going to see him tomorrow to reconsider: pull a few strings, beg him not to abandon you to the streets. But that's now out of the question. You want to go there anyway. It's all so hopeless."

The brightly lit streets seemed lonelier than ever. La Masacuata raised the Virgin's candle to give them more light.

The wind blew. The flame seemed to cross itself as it went out.

XVIII

KNOCKS AT THE DOOR

Knock-knock! Knock-knock.

The rapping on the door sped through the house like fire-crackers exploding, disrupting the dog's sleep and waking him up. He barked toward the street.

Camila and Angel Face stood at Uncle Juan's door. Relieved to be there, she said smugly, "Ruby! Ruby! He's barking because he recognizes me!" She shouted, "It's me, Ruby. Don't you recognize me? Run and get them to open the door." She turned to Angel Face. "We must wait!"

"Yes, yes. Don't worry about me. Waiting is fine!" He said this as if everything were crumbling—like someone who has lost it all and doesn't even care.

"Maybe they didn't hear me. I'm going to knock harder."

She shook the hand-shaped gold brass knocker many times.

"The servants must be sleeping or else they'd be wondering who's knocking. That's why my father, a poor sleeper, always says after being up half the night: 'If only I could sleep like a servant!'"

Ruby was the only sign of life in the whole house. His barking came from the hallway and courtyard as he ran crazily back and forth. The knocker clapped like rocks thrown into silence, and Camila's throat tightened.

"How strange!" she remarked, listening by the door. "They must really be fast asleep. I'll knock harder; maybe that will stir them."

Knock-knock! Knock-knock.

"That should do it."

"The neighbors will be the first to come out!" said Angel

Face. Through a fog blanketing everything, they heard doors opening inside.

"Why aren't they coming?"

"Just keep knocking! Don't worry!"

"Let's wait another minute."

Camila began counting in her head: "One, two, three, four, five, six, seven, eight, nine, ten, eleven, twelve, thirteen, fourteen, fifteen, sixteen, seventeen, eighteen, nineteen, twenty, twenty-one, twenty-two, twenty-three . . . twenty-three . . . twenty-three . . . twenty-four, twen-ty-five—"

"No one's coming!"

"—twenty-six, twenty-seven, twenty-eight, twenty-nine, thir-ty, thirty-one, thirty-two, thirty-three, thirty-four . . . thirty-five . . ." She was terrified of reaching fifty. . . . "Thirty-six, thirty-seven, thirty-eight . . ."

Without knowing why, she realized that what Angel Face had said about Uncle Juan was true. Choking in fear, she knocked harder. Knock-knock. Her hand was glued to the knocker. Tap-tap-taptap. . . . It couldn't be! Taptaptaptaptap, taptaptaptaptap . . .

The only response was the dog's endless barking. What had she ever done for them not to open the door? She couldn't imagine. She knocked again, putting fresh hope into each new knock. What if she were left homeless? The mere thought paralyzed her. She knocked again and again, ferociously, as if pounding an adversary's head. Her feet were heavy, bitterness was in her mouth, and her tongue was a scrub pad. Her teeth tingled in fear.

A window creaked open: voices! Her body revived. "They're coming, thank God." She was glad to ditch a man whose black cat eyes sparkled devilishly—a repulsive man, despite being as good as an angel. Just then, the world of house and the world of street, separated by a single door, brushed by her like two dead stars.

You can eat bread safely in your home—bread at home is fresh and makes you wise. A home is a safe place full of socially acceptable things—it's a family portrait where a father wears his best tie, a mother displays her finest jewels, and the children's hair is brushed with genuine eau de cologne. The streets, however, are dangerous and unstable, full of adventure and false as a mirror—where dirty clothes are washed in public.

How often had she played in that doorway as a child? On how many occasions had her father and Uncle Juan discussed business, just before saying goodbye? She had amused herself staring at the eaves of neighboring houses, silhouetted like scaly spines against a blue sky.

"Weren't they just looking out that window? Did you see? But they won't open the door. Or did we knock on the wrong door? How odd!"

She let the knocker go, stepped onto the street, and looked at the front of the house. No mistake, it was Uncle Juan's house. JUAN CANALES, ENGINEER read the metal placard on the door. She puckered her face like a child and started crying, tears galloping out of her eyes. The depressing thought issued from deep inside her that what Angel Face had said at the Two Step was true. She didn't want to believe it, but it was true.

The fog blindfolded the streets and made the stucco walls the color of rotgut. They stank of purslane.

"Will you come with me to see my other uncles? Let's go to Uncle Luis's house first. Is that okay?"

"Whatever you say."

"Let's go." Her tears fell like rain. "They don't want to let me in."

Camila and Miguel turned around. She looked back every few steps—she couldn't give up hope that they'd open the door at the last minute.

Angel Face was glum. He'd come to see Juan again to avenge his previous outrageous behavior. The dog barked as they walked farther and farther away. Soon all hope vanished—no more barking.

They ran into a drunken mailman by the Mint; he tossed letters into the street like a sleepwalker tripping over his feet. Every so often he lifted his arms and cackled like a barnyard hen, struggling to separate uniform buttons from spools of spit. Camila and Angel Face picked up the letters and put them back in his bag, advising him not to toss them out again.

"Thanks—so—much, thank you ver-ry much!" he said, leaning against the wall of the Mint. With the letters back in his bag, and Camila and Angel Face on their way, he started singing:

> To get to heaven
> You need
> A tall ladder
> And a small lat-ter!

Half-singing, half-speaking, he started another tune:

> Oh Virgin Mary
> Rise, rise to heaven,
> Rise, rise to
> Your realm in heaven.

"When St. John lowers his finger, I, Gup-Gup-Gup-Gupmercindo Solares, I will stop being a mailman—stop being a mailman—a mailman.

> When I die
> Who will bury me?
> Only the Sisters
> Of Charity

"Oh, *juin, juin, juilin*. I'll be there for the others, I'll be, I'll be . . . for others!"

The small man with a huge head staggered along in a drunken fog. His uniform was too big for him and his cap too small.

Meanwhile, Juan Canales tried desperately to get in touch with his brother José Antonio. No one answered the switchboard; his grinding telephone crank sickened him. Finally, someone answered and he asked to be connected with José

Antonio Canales's house. He was surprised by his older brother's voice on the line.

"Yes, it's me, Juan . . . I thought you didn't recognize me . . . Listen . . . She and that guy, yes . . . I'm sure, I'm sure . . . Of course . . . Yes . . . yes . . . What did you say? Noooo, we didn't let him in . . . You can imagine . . . And obviously they went straight to your house . . . What, what's that? . . . I imagine so . . . We were shaking, yes . . . You as well? . . . I'm sure your wife doesn't need to get upset . . . My wife wanted to open the door, but I told her not to . . . Of course . . . Of course, that's obvious! And the neighbors are all up in arms . . . Yes, of course . . . And here it was worse. Everyone pulling hair . . . I'm sure they will go to Luis's house . . . Oh, really? He's next on their list."

Angel Face and Camila knocked hopelessly on José Antonio's door. Daybreak spread over the streets—a soft pallor brightening to a lemon tinge, then the color of orange juice, then the dull glow of flames, a newly lit campfire red.

Camila said: "I'll manage somehow."

Her teeth chattered from the cold. Her teary eyes witnessed the arrival of morning with unexpected bitterness. She breathed the air of desperate people and walked stiffly, as if she were not inside her own body.

In the public gardens and courtyards, birds welcomed dawn, a concert trilled to a blue morning sky. The roses awakened. At the other end of town, bells tolling good morning to God alternated with the soft thud of cattle being butchered in shops. Roosters crowed, keeping time with thrashing wings; bread dropped onto trays, making muted sounds; and the voices and steps of evening carousers countered the noise of an old woman opening a door to go to morning Mass or a servant looking for a bread delivery to make a sandwich for someone with a train to catch. . . .

Dawn was breaking.

The crews of Indians that swept the downtown streets during the night were returning to their huts one by one like dressed ghosts. They laughed and joked in the morning silence in a language like the humming of cicadas, carrying brooms under their arms like umbrellas. Their teeth were white as nougat on copper faces. Barefoot. In rags. Occasionally, one of them leaned over the sidewalk to blow his nose, squeezing it with thumb and forefinger. They tipped their hats when they passed a church. . . .

Dawn was breaking. The immense araucaria trees resembled green spiderwebs cast to catch falling stars. Crowds were going to Mass. Strange trains whistled from afar.

La Masacuata was happy to see them returning together. She hadn't slept a wink and was about to bring Lucio Vásquez's breakfast to the Central Penitentiary.

Angel Face said goodbye to Camila, who was weeping.

"See you later," he said, not knowing why he'd said that. He had nothing more to do.

As he left, he felt his eyes fill with tears for the first time since his mother's death.

XIX

PAYMENTS AND CHOCOLATES

The Judge Advocate finished his chocolate rice drink, tipping the cup twice so he could slurp the dregs. He wiped his fly-wing-colored moustache on his sleeve, moved closer to the lamp, and peered into the bottom of the cup to make sure it was empty.

You couldn't say whether this Bachelor of Law was a man or a woman when he took off his collar and sat among filthy piles of papers and law books. Silent, ugly, nearsighted, and gluttonous, he resembled a tree of sealed papers—a tree whose roots fed off all the social classes down to the poorest and most humble. No one had ever seen an appetite like his. When he looked up from the cup, after running his finger around it to make sure he got every last drop, he saw his servant come in through the only door to his room. She was a ghost dragging her feet; her excessively big shoes plopped one behind the other.

"Did you finish your chocolate?"

"Bless you, it was delicious. I love the lumpy dregs going down my throat."

"Where's the cup?" asked the servant, feeling near the books casting shadows on the table.

"There! Can't you see it?"

"While I'm here, those drawers are full of reams of unused paper. If it's okay with you, I'd like to try to sell them tomorrow."

"Sure, but careful no one sees you. People are so difficult."

"You think that I'm that dumb? You have about four hundred

sheets at twenty-five cents each, two hundred at fifty cents each. . . . I counted them while the coal iron was warming up."

A knock on the street door stopped her.

"What an idiotic way to knock!" grumbled the Judge Advocate.

"They always knock like that. Who is it? I can hear them knocking from in the kitchen," the servant said on her way to the door. With her small head and long, faded skirt, the poor thing looked like an umbrella.

"I'm not home!" shouted the Judge Advocate to her. "See who it is through the window."

A few minutes later, the old woman returned, dragging her feet as always. She had a letter in her hand.

"They're waiting for an answer."

The Judge Advocate ripped open the envelope. He glanced at the small card inside and told the servant, softening his tone, "Say I've received the note."

She dragged her feet back to the window to give the message to the boy who'd brought the envelope.

Then she fastened the window shut.

She returned slowly, blessing each door on the way. She'd forgotten to take the dirty chocolate cup.

Her master sprawled on his armchair and reread the card word for word. A colleague, Vidalitas, was proposing a business deal. "Glorious Gold Tooth, the President's friend and the proprietress of a respected brothel, came to my office this morning. She saw a young, pretty girl at the Casa Nueva Prison who she wants for her establishment. She's offering 10,000 pesos. Knowing she's under arrest on your orders, I'm wondering if you would accept this small sum in exchange for the young woman."

"If there's nothing else, I'll go to bed."

"Of course. Sleep well."

"Likewise. May the souls in Purgatory rest in peace!"

While the servant staggered out, the Judge Advocate went over the offer digit by digit: one, zero, zero, zero, zero . . . ten thousand pesos!

The old woman came back. "I forgot to tell you that the priest sent word that Mass will be earlier tomorrow."

"Ah, yes. Tomorrow's Saturday. Wake me when the bells start tolling, you hear? I was up late last night, and I might oversleep."

"I will."

She slunk away, but came back again, half undressed, for the dirty cup. "Luckily, I remembered."

"Yes, no, yes, no, yes, no," she said to herself in her room, struggling to put her shoes back on. In the end, she sighed. "God knows if I took it. . . ." She would have been in bed already if she hadn't found it impossible to leave a dish dirty.

The Judge Advocate didn't even notice the servant return, he was so absorbed in reading his latest masterpiece: the case regarding General Eusebio Canales's escape. Four people were accused: Fedina; her husband, Genaro Rodas; Lucio Vásquez; and Miguel Angel Face. He would take special pleasure prosecuting the latter, with whom he had a score to settle.

The abduction of the General's daughter was the black cloud an octopus releases, a mere ruse to outsmart the watchful authorities, so to speak. Fedina's statement proved this. When she got to the General's house at 6:00 a.m., it was already empty. She told the truth from start to finish. If he had tightened the screw on her, it was to be absolutely sure: what she said made Angel Face irrefutably guilty. If the police declared that the General had come home precisely at midnight and his house was already abandoned by 6:00 a.m., then he must have escaped at two in the morning, while Angel Face was pretending to abduct his daughter. . . .

The President would be disappointed to learn that his confidant had prepared and directed the escape of one of his bitterest enemies! What would he do when he discovered that Colonel Parrales Sonriente's best friend had taken part in the escape of one of his murderers?

Though he already knew by heart the Military Codes of Conduct that dealt with criminal accomplices, he read them over and over again the way one savors a spicy sauce. Joy glowed in his basilisk eyes each time they read the words "death penalty" or "capital punishment."

"Oh, Don Miguelin, Miguelito, you are finally in my hands for now and forever. When you insulted me yesterday at the Palace, little did I know that we would meet face-to-face so soon. Tightening the screw will be my eternal revenge, you'll see!"

He went up the Palace steps at eleven the next morning—his brain feverishly vengeful and his heart icy as a bullet. He carried an indictment and warrant for the arrest of Angel Face.

"Look, Mr. Judge Advocate," the President said after hearing the accusations, "leave your papers here. Listen to me: Neither Señora Rodas nor Miguel is guilty. Set the woman free and tear up the arrest warrant. You imbeciles are the guilty ones. You're totally useless! As soon as General Canales tried to escape, the police should have gunned him down. Those were my orders!

"When the police see an empty house, their fingers start itching to steal! Imagine if Angel Face had taken part in Canales's escape? He wasn't planning it, he was planning his death! But our police are nothing but bags of shit. . . . You can go now. Give Vásquez and Rodas exactly what they deserve. They're just thugs—especially Vásquez, who knows more than he should know. Go now."

XX

BIRDS OF A FEATHER

Genaro Rodas's tears couldn't wash away his memory of the look in Pelele's eyes. Appearing before the Judge Advocate, he could only look down at his shoes. The misfortunes at home, combined with the despondency that affects any calm man denied his freedom, destroyed his last ounce of courage. The Judge ordered his handcuffs off and told him to come closer.

After a long silence that was itself a kind of reprimand, he said: "Son, I know everything. I'm only questioning you because I want to hear, in your own words, how the beggar died in the Portal. In your own words, please."

Genaro spoke in fits and starts, afraid of what he was going to say. "What happened . . . See, what happened . . . For the love of God, sir, please don't hurt me. Please, sir. I'll tell you the whole truth, but on your life, please don't hurt me."

"Don't worry, son: the Law is harsh with hardened criminals, but it's different with a guy like you. . . . Speak up, just tell me the truth."

"Please don't hurt me. Can't you see I'm scared?" He cringed as he spoke, trying to protect himself from a threat against him floating in the air.

"Don't worry."

"What happened? Well . . . It was that night, you know, when I met Lucio Vásquez by the Cathedral and the Chinese shops. Sir, I need work, and this Lucio said he would get me a job with the Secret Police. We met, and glory be, soon enough he invited me for drinks at the Lion's Awakening, a bar a little ways up from the Plaza de Armas. So one drink led to two, then three, four, five, and to make a long story short . . ."

"Yes, yes." The Judge Advocate nodded, glancing at the freckle-faced clerk taking notes.

"So, you see, he didn't get me the job he promised. I told him that was okay. Then . . . oh yes, now I remember! He paid for the drinks. We left together and walked toward the Portal, where Lucio said he was hoping to kill a mute with rabies. I told him I'd leave before that! So we went to the Portal. I was a few steps behind him. He crossed the street, but when we reached the other side, he took off running. I ran after him, thinking that someone was chasing us . . . But then . . . Vásquez pushed someone against the wall. Realizing he'd been caught, this Pelele screamed as if a wall had fallen on him. Vásquez pulled out a gun and, without a word, he fired once, twice . . . Sir, I swear I had nothing to do with it. Please don't hurt me. I didn't kill him! I just wanted a job . . . and see what's happened to me . . . I should have stayed a carpenter . . . Who put the idea in my head to become a policeman?"

Pelele's icy stare was still transfixed in Rodas's eyes. The Judge Advocate said nothing, not varying his expression, and squeezed a silent buzzer. Steps sounded and soon the warden and several guards appeared.

"Look here, warden. Give this man two hundred lashes." His voice remained so steady he might as well have been a bank manager ordering two hundred pesos be given to a customer.

Rodas couldn't understand what was going on. He lifted his head to see barefoot flunkies waiting for him. He understood even less when he saw their calm, impassive faces. The clerk turned his freckled face and blank eyes toward him. The warden said something to the Judge Advocate, who then answered him back. Deaf, Rodas heard nothing. He was about to shit in his pants when the warden screamed for him to go to the next room—a long, vaulted vestibule—and pushed him hard.

The Judge Advocate was still screaming at Rodas, "It's no use treating you well. You only understand cudgels."

When Lucio Vásquez, now a prisoner, entered the room, he thought he was among friends he couldn't quite trust, especially after what he had just heard. It was no small thing to

have contributed, albeit against his will, to General Canales's
escape.

"Your name?"

"Lucio Vásquez."

"Born?"

"Here."

"In the Penitentiary?"

"Of course not. I meant the capital."

"Married or single?"

"A bachelor for life!"

"Answer my questions properly! Profession or occupation?"

"Government sinecure."

"What's that?"

"In the public service. Job for life."

"Have you been arrested before?"

"Yes."

"For what?"

"Murder—during a patrol."

"Age?"

"I have no age."

"What do you mean by that?"

"I don't know my real age. Put down thirty-five, if you have
to put something."

"What do you know about the Dimwit's death?" The Judge
Advocate fired this question point-blank, keeping his eyes on
him. Contrary to expectation, his words had no effect on Vásquez,
who answered quite naturally, rubbing his hands: "All I know
is that I killed Pelele." He put a forefinger to his chest, so there
wouldn't be any doubt. "I killed him."

"Do you think this is some sort of a joke?" the Judge Advocate shouted. "Are you so stupid you don't know this could
cost you your life?"

"Maybe . . ."

"What do you mean by 'maybe'?" The Judge Advocate
didn't know how to react. Vásquez's squeaky, calm voice and
sharp eyes disarmed him. He wanted to move slowly. "Write
this down," he told the clerk, his shaky voice rising. "Put down

that Lucio Vásquez says he killed Pelele, and Genaro Rodas helped him."

"I've already written that," the clerk answered, tightening his lips.

"Obviously, the Judge doesn't know much about things. That statement is worthless. Anyone can see that I wouldn't dirty my hands on an idiot like that . . . ," Lucio objected sarcastically, staying calm.

The Judge Advocate bit his lip. "Show some respect for this tribunal or you'll suffer the consequences!"

"What I'm saying makes sense. I wouldn't be so stupid as to kill that guy for no reason. If I killed him, it was on the President's orders!"

"Shut up, you liar! Ha! My job would be so much easier . . ."

He didn't finish his sentence, because just then the guards brought Rodas back in, dangling by his arms, his legs trailing on the floor like rags, like St. Veronica's veil.

"How many did you give him?" the Judge Advocate asked the warden, who had a whip around his neck like a monkey's tail.

He smiled at the clerk. "Two hundred!"

"Okay . . ."

The clerk came to the Judge Advocate's rescue. "I would give him another two hundred," he muttered, so no one else could hear.

The Judge Advocate took his advice. "Yes, warden, give him another two hundred lashes while I finish dealing with this guy."

Vásquez thought to himself: "What nerve, you old windbag with a bicycle-seat face!"

The warden and the guards retraced their steps, dragging their mournful load. They threw him facedown on a straw mattress in the torture chamber. Four of them held his hands and feet while the others beat him. The warden kept count. Rodas cringed, but otherwise hardly resisted when he received these lashes, unlike during the first set, when he had twisted and howled after each blow. Clotted blood from the wounds that had already crusted after the first whipping now oozed under the blows of the flexible, green, wet quince vines. He let out the smothered cries of a creature not fully aware of the source of his suffering. He buried his head in the straw, face contorted and hair disheveled. His hoarse, piercing cries merged with those of the guard whom the warden flogged for not hitting Rodas hard enough.

"Our job would be so easy, Lucio Vásquez, if we allowed everyone who says that the President ordered him to commit a crime to go free! Where's your proof? The President isn't crazy enough to give an order like that. Where's the proof that you were ordered to go after this poor wretch in such a wicked and cowardly way?"

Vásquez turned white. He put his trembling hands in his pants pockets, looking for an answer.

"You know that a tribunal demands proof to back up your words. Where's your proof?"

"Look, see, I don't have the order anymore. I returned it. The President will vouch for me."

"What? And why did you return it?"

"Because at the bottom it said that I had to give it back after carrying out the order. I wasn't about to keep it! It seems to me . . . you can understand that . . ."

"Be quiet, shut up. Stop hustling me! Giving me the Presidential hustle! I'm not a schoolboy to buy this kind of bullshit, you crook. A person's testimony is no proof, unless prescribed as such by a legal code, like when a policeman's testimony is accepted as truth in a court of law. But I'm not about to give you a course on the Penal Code. Enough is enough! And I've heard enough!"

"Well, if you don't want to believe me, go ask the President. He'll tell you. Wasn't I with you when the beggars accused—"

"Shut up or I'll flog you till you do. I don't see myself asking the President! What I do know, Vásquez, is that you know more about this matter than you're willing to say. For now, you're facing the noose!"

Lucio lowered his head as if the Judge Advocate's words had just cut it off. The wind blew furiously against the windows.

XXI

GOING IN CIRCLES

Angel Face angrily ripped off his tie and collar. "There's nothing more stupid," he thought, "than the foolish explanations people give for the behavior of others. Behavior of others! Others! A rebuke is often no more than an annoying murmur. It silences the good and amplifies the basest actions. What a pile of shit, painful as a hairbrush striking a sore. And this veiled, fine-haired rebuke goes deeper, and disguises itself as a familiar, friendly, or charitable comment. Even the servants gossip. To hell with all these busybodies."

All the buttons popped on his shirt just then as if his chest had been torn open. His housekeeper told him in great detail what people on the street were saying about his love affair. Angel Face knew that one always hears first from the servants about bachelors not wanting a wife who simply believes everything bad said about them, or the gossip about a schoolgirl who works too hard to win a prize.

He drew the curtains before finally taking off his shirt. He needed to sleep or at least to be in a darkened room that might insist on being the continuation of the previous day. "Sleep!" he said, sitting on the edge of his bed—no socks and shoes, shirt open and pants unbuttoned. "I'm such an ass. I still have my coat on!"

He walked on his heels with his toes pointing up so his soles wouldn't touch the cold concrete floor. He hung his coat on a chairback and hopped on one foot, heronlike, until he reached his bed again. And bang! He went under the sheets and covered himself, pursued . . . by a brutish frozen floor. His pant legs flew into the air and spun like the hands of an enormous clock. The floor more ice than concrete. How awful! Ice mixed with salt. Ice made of tears. He had leapt into his bed as if from an iceberg into a lifeboat.

He wanted to escape everything that had happened. He considered that his bed was an imagined island surrounded by half-light and pulverized by stationary events. He lay down to forget, to sleep, to cease to exist. He was tired of arguments assembled and disassembled like machine parts. To hell with the twists and turns of common sense. Better to dream, to fall into an unreasoning sleep, a sweet, azure-colored mindlessness that turns green, then black, distilling itself in the body, making a person tenser.

Oh, desire. A desire possessed and then dispossessed like a gold nightingale imprisoned in a cage made by the ten fingers of our hands. A wholesome, restorative sleep that enters through the mirrors of the eyes and leaves through nostrils. This is what he desired—the peaceful sleep of the past. Soon he realized that sleep hovered over him, above the roof: it was the clear space of day, that inerasable day.

He turned onto his stomach. No use. Onto his left side, to quiet his heartbeats. Then onto the right side. Same thing. More than a hundred hours separated him from his perfect dream, so he fell into sleep without the tug of love. His instincts accused him of suffering these tortures because he had not taken Camila by force.

Life's darkness loomed so close that killing himself seemed the only escape. "I will cease to be!" he thought and his whole body trembled. He put one foot over the other. He was consumed by the lack of nails on the cross from which he hung. "Drunks have the air of hanged men when they walk," he said to himself, "and the hanged men have the air of drunks when they jitter or the wind blows over them." His instincts betrayed him. "A drunk's sex. A hanged man's penis? You, Angel Face, with a turkey beak penis!"

"A beast makes no mistakes in this ledger of sexual acts," he thought. "We piss children into graveyards. Judgment Day trumpets—well, maybe it won't be a trumpet. A gold scissor

will cut that never-ending stream of children. We humans are
like pork tripe stuffed with the minced meat a butcher uses to
make sausages. When I harnessed my desire to save Camila
from my intentions, I left part of myself unstuffed. That's why
this trap makes me feel empty and restless, sick and furious. A
man stuffs himself with a woman—minced meat like pork
tripe—to be satisfied.

"How vulgar!"

The sheets clung to him like a tight skirt. Agonizing skirts
drenched in sweat.

"The Night of Sorrows tree must feel the pain of its leaves!
Oh, my head hurts. The carillon's watery sound. *The Dead
City of Bruges*. Silk corkscrews around his neck . . . Never . . .
Somewhere nearby, a neighbor's playing a gramophone. I've
never heard it before. I didn't know it existed. Always a first
time. There's a dog in the house in back. Maybe two dogs. But
someone has a gramophone. Just one. Between the trumpet
blasting and the dogs in back obeying their master's voice is
my house, my head, me. Being nearby and distant is what de-
fines a neighbor. That's the bad part of neighbors. But what
work do they do, besides playing music and speaking ill of everyone else? I can imagine what they say about me, those assholes! What do I care what they say? But not about her! If I
find out they've said anything against her, I'll accuse them of
being Liberal Youth members. I've threatened to do it many
times, but today I think I will. That'll screw their lives forever!
But maybe I won't—they're such scum. I can hear them going
around saying: *He abducted the poor girl after midnight,
dragged her to a whorehouse, and raped her. The Secret Police
barred the door so no one could stop him!* They'll imagine the
scene of me undressing her, tearing off her clothes—Camila's
body trembling like a bird in a trap. *He made love to her*—
they'll say—*without caressing her, with eyes closed as if committing a crime or swallowing a purgative*. If they only knew
it didn't happen like that, that here I am, half sorry for being
so chivalrous! If they only knew how wrong they were. It's the
girl they want to think about. Imagining her with me or with
themselves. Taking off her clothes, doing to her what they think

I did. The stuff about the Liberal Youth is too light a sentence for this angelic pair! I've got to come up with something worse. Since they're both bachelors—yes, resigned bachelors—it would be better to hitch them to two whores that hang around the President. That would do, yes, even if one of them's pregnant. What the hell! Better still. When the President wants something, what's the point of looking at the bride's belly? Let these scaredy-cats get hitched. . . ."

He curled up in bed with his arms between his legs and buried his head in his pillow, seeking respite from his mind's torturing flashes. Physical shock awaited him at the cold bed corners, giving him temporary relief from his wild and reckless thoughts. He sought these welcome, painful sensations even more by stretching his legs out of the sheets until they touched the brass bars at the foot of the bed. Then he gradually opened his eyes, breaking the gossamer seam between his lashes. He was suspended from his eyes, fixed to the ceiling with suction cups. His bones were flaccid, his ribs mere cartilage and his head soft putty . . . A cottony hand knocked on the doors . . . The cottony hand of a sleepwalker . . . The houses are trees made of knockers . . . Cities are forests of trees full of knockers. . . .

Leaves of sound fell as she knocked . . . The trunk of the door stood intact after the leaves of intact sound fell . . . There was nothing for her to do but knock . . . nothing for them to do but open the door . . . But they wouldn't open. She could've knocked the door down. Knock following knock, she might have brought down the door . . . knock after knock, then silence. She could've knocked down the house. . . .

"Who is it?"

"I have the news of someone's death."

"Yes, but don't bring it to him. He's probably sleeping. Put it there by his desk."

"Joaquín Cerón died last night after receiving the Holy Sacrament. His wife, children, and relatives have the sad duty to inform you and to beg you to commend his soul to God and to accompany the body for burial today at four p.m. in the

General Cemetery. Mourners are asked to meet at the cemetery gate. *Callejón del Carrocero Funeral Home*."

He had accidentally heard a housekeeper read aloud the news of Joaquín Cerón's death.

He brought an arm out from the sheets and folded it under his head. Joaquín Cerón marched before his eyes wearing feathers. He snatched four wooden Sacred Hearts and clapped them like castanets. Doña Judith sat in the back of his head looking dragonlike: her cyclopean breasts squeezed into creaking corsets made of sand and wires, her hair in Pompeian style with a huge *manola* comb. The arm under his head cramped and he stretched it slowly, as if a scorpion were in his clothes. . . .

Slowly, ever so slowly . . .

Hundreds of ants rode an elevator toward his shoulder . . . Hundreds of magnetized ants rode an elevator toward his elbow . . . The cramp continued through the tube of his forearm in the darkness . . . His hand was an open faucet . . . A faucet of double fingers. He felt ten thousand nails all the way to the floor. . . .

"Poor girl, knock after knock and then nothing . . . Such monsters, such stubborn mules. If they open the door, I'll spit in their faces . . . Just as two plus three makes five . . . and five more makes ten . . . and nine, nineteen, I'll spit in their faces. At first, she knocked excitedly on the door and at the end, it was like drilling the ground . . . She wasn't knocking but digging her own grave . . . Awakening without hope! I'll go visit her tomorrow . . . I can do that . . . With the pretext of bringing her news of her father, sure . . . Or . . . If I get news today . . . I could . . . even if she doubted my words. . . ."

"I do believe you! It's true, undeniably true, that my uncles disowned my father and told him they didn't want to see hide nor hair of me in their homes." Those were Camila's thoughts as she stretched out on La Masacuata's bed, her back aching like an injured mare's. Meanwhile, in the bar—separated from the bedroom by a wall of old planks, canvas, and straw mats—the customers discussed the day's events between drinks: the

General's escape, the daughter's abduction, Angel Face's passion. The barkeeper pretended she wasn't listening. . . .

A wave of nausea pulled Camila away from that foul riffraff. She felt she was sinking in silence. To cry out would be rash, but not to—to completely lose consciousness—was no good either, so she screamed. She was immediately enveloped in a cold like the feathers of a dead bird.

La Masacuata ran to her at once—what was happening?—and saw her lying like a green bottle, her arms stiff as broomsticks, jaw clenched, lids closed. She grabbed the first bottle of liquor she could, poured a drink, and threw it in her face. She was so worried that she didn't notice that her customers had left. She begged the Virgin of Chiquinquirá and all the saints she knew not to let the girl die in her house.

"When I left this morning, she cried again over what I had told her. What else could she do? When something unexpected occurs, either you cry out of joy or you cry out of sorrow."

These were Angel Face's thoughts as he lay in bed, almost asleep, sensing a bluish angelic fire. His mind drifted as he nodded off—disembodied, shapeless, like a warm breeze, moved by each of his breaths. . . .

As his body sank into nothingness, only Camila remained: tall, sweet, and forbidding as a graveyard cross.

The God of Sleep that plies the dark seas of reality took Miguel on board one of his many boats. Invisible hands pulled him out from the gaping jaws of events, the hungry seas that fought violently over their victims' parts.

"Who is it?" Sleep asked.

"Miguel Angel Face," replied his invisible helpers. Their formless hands emerged from the blackness like white shadows.

"Take him to the ship of"—Sleep hesitated—"lovers who have lost hope of ever loving and are resigned to simply being loved."

Sleep's helpers obeyed. They escorted him to that ship, walking over the film of unreality sprinkling the daily events of life with a very fine dust. But suddenly a clawlike noise wrenched him away from their hands. . . .

The bed . . .

The servants . . .

No. Not a death notice . . . ! A child!

Angel Face rubbed his eyes and lifted his head, terrified. Two steps from his bed stood a child, out of breath, unable to speak. Finally, he stuttered: "A la-dy sent me . . . to tell you . . . to come to the inn . . . because the young lady there . . . is . . . very ill. . . ."

He wouldn't have dressed as quickly if the President had uttered these same words. He dashed out into the street after grabbing the first hat he found on the rack, not tying his shoelaces, and with the knot in his tie crooked.

"Who's ill?" asked Sleep. His men had just fished him out from life's filthy waters, a rose about to wither.

"Camila Canales . . . ," they answered.

"Very well. If there's room, put her on the ship of unhappy lovers. . . ."

"What do you think, doctor?" Angel Face asked, in a fatherly tone, suspecting that Camila's sickness was serious.

"I think her fever is going to go higher. She's developing pneumonia. . . ."

XXII

THE LIVING TOMB

Her son ceased to exist. Fedina lifted his corpse to her feverish face like a marionette; it weighed no more than dry rind. She did this like someone who, in the chaos of a life falling apart before her eyes, loses courage. She kissed and stroked him. Then she got onto her knees and bent down level to the ground to see, in the yellow morning light seeping under the door, what was left of her little boy.

His tiny face was creased like scar tissue. Black circles around his eyes, lips brown as earth: he looked more like a diapered fetus than a child several months old. She stole him away from the light, pressing him against her milk-swollen breasts. She cursed God in a gibberish that combined words and tears. Her heart stopped beating for a few seconds. She hiccupped lament after lament. "My ssss-son . . . my . . . ssss-son!"

Tears rolled down her blank face. She wept until she collapsed, forgetting that her husband would starve to death in prison if she didn't confess. She ignored her physical suffering, the sores on her breasts and hands, her eyes burning, her back bruised by blows, putting off any worry about her neglected business, stunned, not feeling a thing. When she couldn't weep anymore, she felt she was becoming her son's tomb, enclosing him in her womb again; that she was his final, endless sleep. For a split second, pure joy stalled her endless suffering. The idea of being her son's tomb soothed her heart like a balm. She felt the joy Asian women feel when they elect to be buried with their lovers. Her joy was perhaps greater because she wouldn't be entombed with her son. She was the living tomb, the earthly cradle, the maternal lap where both of them, tightly united, would remain suspended until God called for them. Not wiping away tears, she straightened her hair as if going to a party. She snuggled into a corner of the cell and pressed his body, enveloped by her arms and legs, to her breasts.

Tombs don't kiss the dead, so she shouldn't kiss him; on the contrary, they press heavily against them, just as she was now doing. Tombs are straitjackets of pressure and affection, forcing the dead to bear, quietly and motionless, the tickling of worms, the fire of decomposition. The gleam of light under the door would brighten only every thousand years. Shadows, followed by rising light, climbed the walls slowly like scorpions. The walls of bones . . . bones tattooed with obscene drawings. Fedina closed her eyes—tombs are dark inside— and did not speak or moan. Tombs are also silent on the outside.

It was midafternoon. It smelled of cypresses rinsed in rainwater. Swallows. A half-moon. The streets bathed in bright sunlight and full of rowdy children. The schools emptied a river of new lives into the city. Some played tag, running back and forth like flies. Others formed a circle around classmates fighting one another like raging cocks. Noses dripped blood, snot, tears. Other children scampered about, knocking on doors. Still others invaded candy stores before they were out of caramelized guava, coconut pastries, almond tarts, and sugar candies, or they swung like pirates over baskets of fruit, leaving them behind like empty, rickety boats. Those kids who swapped things, collected stamps, or smoked, trying to hold in the puff, stayed behind in the schoolyard.

Three young women and an old fat one alighted from a carriage in front of the Casa Nueva Prison. You could see what they were just by looking at them. The young women wore cretonnes of outlandish color, red stockings, and yellow spiked-heel shoes; petticoats inched above their knees, revealing long, dirty lace underwear. Their blouses were open to the navel and their hair coiffed in the Louis XV style, with oodles of greasy curls tied to the sides with green or yellow ribbons. Their cheeks glowed red as the lights at brothel doors.

Wearing black with a purple shawl, the fat one stumbled as she got out of the carriage. Her chubby hands, covered with sparkling gems, clutched at the door.

"Doña Chonita: Should the driver wait for us?" asked the youngest of the Three Graces. Even the stones of the empty street could hear her shrill voice.

"Yes, he can wait here," answered the old woman.

All four went into the prison, where a guard cheerfully welcomed them.

There were people waiting in the bleak hallway.

"Hey, Chinta, is the Secretary in?" the old woman asked.

"Yes, Doña Chón. He just arrived."

"For God's sake, tell him I must see him. I've brought him an important note."

The old woman was silent as she waited for the guard to return. The building still resembled a convent for older residents. Before becoming a home for juvenile delinquents, it had been a prison of love for women, only women. The sweet voices of Teresian nuns floated like doves along the convent's thick walls. Though there were no lilies, the light was white, caressing and joyful. Thorns of torture flourished under the sign of the cross, and spiderwebs had replaced fasting and sackcloth.

When the guard returned, Doña Chón went in to speak to the Secretary, who had already chatted with the warden. The Judge Advocate had left explicit orders to release Fedina de Rodas to the Sweet Enchantment, as Doña "Gold Tooth" Chón's brothel was known, in exchange for ten thousand pesos.

Two thunderous knocks echoed in the dungeon cell where that unfortunate woman still crouched with her baby. Eyes closed, hardly breathing, she made an effort not to hear. The lock squeaked, followed by a prolonged squealing of rusted hinges that echoed like a lament. The door opened and guards clasped her roughly. She squeezed her eyes tight so as not to see the light—tombs are dark inside. They dragged her off like a blind woman, the little treasure of a corpse pressed to her chest. She was just a beast bought for the most disgusting of trades.

"She's pretending she can't speak."

"She won't open her eyes!"

"She must be filled with shame!"

"She doesn't want her baby to wake up!"

This is what Gold Tooth Chón and the Three Graces said on the ride back. The carriage made a hellish noise as it drove over the unpaved roads. The driver, a Spaniard who looked like Don Quixote, spewed insults at the horses that soon would be going to the bullring where he worked as a picador. Fedina sat next to him as they took the quick way from the Casa Nueva Prison to the whorehouse (as in the song), completely unaware of the world around her, not moving lids or lips, holding in her song with all her might.

Doña Chón paid the driver quickly while the girls helped Fedina down. They pushed her gently, in almost a friendly way, into the Sweet Enchantment.

A few clients, mostly soldiers, were spending the night in the brothel.

"Hey, what's the time?" Doña Chón shouted to the bartender as she barreled in.

One of the soldiers answered, "Six twenty, Miss Turkey-Face."

"Simple Simon! You're here. I didn't see you before."

"My clock says twenty-five past," the bartender interrupted.

The men flocked to the "new" girl. They all wanted her. Fedina kept a gravelike silence, her baby's corpse still wrapped in her arms. She didn't raise her lids. She felt as cold and heavy as a rock.

"Take her to the kitchen and have Manuela feed her. Put her in nice clothes and comb her hair," Gold Tooth ordered the Graces.

An artillery captain with light blue eyes walked up to the "new" girl and squeezed her legs. One of the Graces stopped him. Another soldier tried to embrace her as if she were a palm trunk—his eyes were white and he brandished splendid Indian teeth, like a dog near a bitch in heat. He kissed her, rubbing his whiskey lips against her cold cheeks, salty from so many tears.

After the barracks, the brothel, living it up! The warmth of whores compensated for the cold of flying bullets.

"Hey, Simple Simon, cool your heels!" Doña Chón said, throwing water to calm them down and put an end to Simple Simon's antics.

Fedina didn't counter the lustful gestures. She tightened her eyelids and sealed her lips, offering only blindness and her gravelike silence to their attacks. Her dead son was cradled in her arms as if only sleeping.

They took her to a small courtyard where twilight sank slowly into a fountain. Women moaned, voices crackled. One could hear the delicate whisperings of sick women or school-girls, prisoners or nuns; fake laughter, rasping cries, the pad-ding of shoeless feet. Someone threw tarot cards from a room and they fanned on the floor. No one knew who threw them. A woman with disheveled hair stuck her face out of a hovel and stared at the cards revealing her future. She wiped a tear from her pale cheek.

A red lantern, a beast's bloody eye, lit the street in front of the Sweet Enchantment. Men and stones took on a tragic air, as if awaiting a flashing camera. Men came to that red hue to rinse off their smallpox scars. They exposed their faces shame-fully to the light, to be seen, as if drinking blood; then they returned to the streetlights, to the city's white lights and the clear light of their homes, with the uneasy feeling of people overexposed in a photograph.

Fedina felt nothing. She was dead to everything but her child. She hadn't opened her eyes or lips, and her milky breasts still hugged the corpse. The girls had done all they could to get her out of that state before she reached the kitchen.

Manuela Calvario, the cook, had reigned for years, from the coal bin to the garbage dump, at the Sweet Enchantment. She was some sort of beardless God the Father wearing starched skirts. The cook's flabby jowls puffed up an airy substance, which became words when Fedina appeared.

"Another wench! Where did you dig her up? And what's she holding so tightly?"

The Three Graces mutely gestured to the cook with their hands to indicate that she had just been released from prison.

"Dirty old whore," she added. When the three girls had left, she said: "I'd as soon give you poison as food! Here's a little snack. Come . . . take this . . . and take that!" She hit Fedina several times in the back with a metal rod.

Fedina fell to the ground with her dead child, not answering or opening her eyes. She'd been carrying him for so long he was almost weightless.

Manuela walked back and forth, screaming and crossing herself. As she carried back clean dishes from the sink, she caught a whiff of something awful. She began kicking Fedina and shouting, not holding anything back. "This rotting thing stinks! Get her out of here! Get rid of her! I don't want her here!"

These crazy shouts brought Doña Chón to the kitchen. They forced Fedina to open her arms the way one breaks branches off of a tree. Fedina realized they were trying to take away her child and opened her eyes, howled, and fell unconscious.

"The child stinks! He's dead! How awful!" screamed Manuela. Gold Tooth gasped. She phoned the authorities while the prostitutes poured into the kitchen. Everyone wanted to see and kiss the child, kiss him over and over. They passed him back and forth. A mask of rotten drool covered his wrinkled little corpse face, which did stink. There was loud weeping.

Major Farfán went off to get official permission to plan a wake. The largest bedroom was emptied; the girls burned incense to remove the smell of stale semen from the wall hangings. Doña Manuela burned tar in the kitchen, and the child—withered, dry, and yellow as the bacteria that grows on lettuce—was put on a black tray surrounded by flowers and linen.

All of them lost a child that night. Four huge tapers were lit. The odor of tamales, cheap liquor, rotten meat, cigarette butts, and piss floated in the air. A half-drunk woman, revealing a bare breast and chewing a cigar as much as she smoked it, repeated, drenched in tears:

> Sleep, my child,
> My little pumpkin head
> If you don't sleep
> A wolf will eat you dead!
>
> Sleep, my sweet,
> I've things to do,
> Wash your diapers
> Sew some clothes for you.

XXIII

THE PRESIDENT'S REPORT

1. Alejandra, Bran's widow, residing in this city and owner of La Ballena Franca Mattress Shop, claims that since her business shares a wall with the Two Step Tavern, she observed several individuals frequently gathering there, especially at night, on the Christian pretext of visiting a sick woman. She brings this information to the President's attention because she believes General Eusebio Canales is hiding in that tavern—according to conversations she's heard through the wall. She claims that these persons are conspiring against the state and against the President's precious life.

2. Soledad Belmares, city resident, says she has nothing to eat because she has no means of support. Because she is foreign-born, no one will lend her money. Given her circumstances, she begs the President to free her son Manuel Belmares H. and her brother-in-law Federico Horneros P. Her country's ambassador can verify that they aren't mixed up in politics; that they only came here to earn a living doing honorable work; and that their only crime was accepting a letter of reference from General Eusebio Canales to help them find work at the train station.

3. Colonel Prudencio Perfecto Paz states that his recent trip to the border was undertaken for the sole purpose of evaluating the land, the roads, and the footpaths and to decide which places should be occupied; he describes in minute detail a plan outlining strategic, favorable positions, should there be a revolutionary uprising. He confirms that there are people on the border waiting for such a thing; that Juan León Parada and others are awaiting orders and that they possess the necessary matériel,

including hand grenades, machine guns, low-caliber rifles, dynamite, and other items for constructing land mines; that there are approximately twenty-five or thirty armed revolutionaries who can attack the country's Armed Forces at any moment; that he hasn't been able to confirm that Canales is commanding these troops, and that if he is, they will certainly invade unless measures are taken to arrest the agitators; that he is prepared for any sort of invasion set for the beginning of next month, but that his sharpshooters lack sufficient weapons and have only .43-caliber ammunition; that with the exception of a few sick soldiers under his care, the troops are healthy and are receiving daily training from six to eight in the morning and a head of cattle each week as provisions; and that he has requisitioned sandbags from the port garrison to use as bunkers.

4. Juan Antonio Mares thanks the President for his help in getting medical assistance. Having recovered, he is once more ready to serve; he seeks permission to come to the capital to share information he's gathered regarding Abel Carvajal's political activities.

5. Luis Raveles M. states that, finding himself sick and without the necessary medication, he requests permission to return to the United States and to be assigned to any Republic Consulate, excluding the one in New Orleans or in any previous post, as the President's loyal servant; that at the end of January he was extremely fortunate to find his name on an appointment list, but that when he was about to enter the vestibule, he noticed a certain mistrust on the part of the General Staff, who had changed the order of names; that when it was apparently his turn, an officer took him into another room and searched him as if he were a revolutionary, saying that he did so based on information that Abel Carvajal had paid him to assassinate the President; that when he returned to the vestibule, his audience had been canceled; that he has done everything he could to speak to the President and tell him certain things he cannot put on paper, but that he has been unable to do so.

6. Nicomedes Aceituno writes to say that upon his return to the capital, after one of his many business trips, he found that a sign emblazoned with the President's name on a water tank had been almost completely destroyed—six letters were missing and others couldn't be read.

7. Lucio Vásquez, imprisoned in the Central Penitentiary by order of the Judge Advocate, begs for an audience.

8. Catarino Regisio sets forth that as manager of Eusebio Canales's La Tierra Ranch, he saw four friends visit Canales during August of the past year. After a night of drinking, Canales told them that he had two battalions at his disposal for the revolution: one was under the command of Major Farfán, one of the friends, and the other belonged to a lieutenant colonel who remains unnamed. Since rumors of a rebellion continue to circulate, he is informing the President in writing, given that he was not able to do so personally, after having requested several audiences.

9. General Megadeo Rayón forwards a letter he received from Father Antonio Blas Custodio, in which he states that Father Urquijo slandered him after the Archbishop replaced him at the San Lucas parish. Together with Doña Aracadia de Ayuso, this prelate stirred up his parishioners with his lies; the presence of Father Urquijo, a friend of lawyer Abel Carvajal, might lead to serious consequences, and this is why he offers these facts to the President.

10. Alfredo Toledano, residing in this town, says that since he suffers from insomnia, he always goes to bed very late at night. This is why he witnessed Miguel Angel Face, one of the President's loyal friends, knocking loudly on the door of the house of Don Juan Canales, brother of the General with whom he shares a last name, and who never misses a chance to speak ill of the government. He informs the President, should it be of interest to him.

11. Nicomedes Aceituno, business traveler, states that the bookkeeper Guillermo Lizazo, in a fit of drunkenness, was the person who defaced the President's name on the water tank.

12. Casimiro Rebeco Luna states that he has been held for nearly two and a half years in the Second Police Station; poor and with no relatives to help him, he begs the President to set him free. He is accused of having removed a flyer announcing the President's mother's birthday from the door of the church where he served as sexton, on orders of the state's enemies; this is a lie, and he did remove a flyer, but it was the wrong one, since he is illiterate.

13. Dr. Luis Barreño begs the President for permission to study abroad in the company of his wife.

14. Adelaida Peñal, a ward of the Sweet Enchantment brothel, wishes to inform the President that Major Modesto Farfán told her, while drunk, that General Eusebio Canales was the only authentic general he had ever met in the army and that he had fallen out of favor because the President was afraid of capable leaders; no matter what, the revolution would succeed, he said.

15. Mónica Perdomino, a patient in bed 14 at the General Hospital's San Rafael Ward, declares that since her bed was next to that of Fedina de Rodas, she heard her mention General Canales in a delirious state; since her own head isn't screwed on right, she hasn't been able to figure out what the woman actually said, but says that it would be a good idea for someone to keep an eye on her. As a humble admirer of his government, she informs the President thus.

16. Tomás Javelí announces his marriage to Arquelina Suárez, an event dedicated to the President of the Republic.

April 28

XXIV

THE BROTHEL

"*Bit-ch!*"

"*I-wha— But— But— Daaar-ling—*"

"*Take what—away?*"

"*No-thing, no-thing!*"

"*No-thing, no-thing!*"

"*Wahoo!*"

"Quiet, will you? Shut up! What crap! From the crack of dawn, nothing but chatter and jabber. You're a bunch of animals!" shouted Gold Tooth.

Dressed in a black blouse and purple skirt, Her Excellency chewed her food like cud in a leather chair behind the counter of the bar.

A little while later, she told a copper-skinned housekeeper with smooth, shiny braids, "Pancha, tell these women to come out. This isn't right. Clients will arrive any second and they should be sitting out here! I'm always chasing after these girls, goddamnit!"

Two girls wearing stockings rushed in.

"Calm down! Consuelo, how cute you are! Chu-Malia's always teasing. And look, Adelaida! I'm talkin' to you! If the major comes, take his sword as payment for what he owes us. How much does he owe us, Snout-Mouth?"

"Exactly nine hundred. On top of thirty-six from last night," the bartender answered.

"A sword isn't worth that much. Not even a gold one. Worse is nothing. Adelaida! I'm speaking to you, not the wall. Understood!"

"Yes, Doña Chón, I heard you," said Adelaida Peñal, between

laughs. She kept fooling around with her friend, pulling her by the hair.

Several Sweet Enchantment girls sat quietly on the old sofas. Tall, short, fat, skinny, old, young, teenagers, well-behaved, shy, blondes, redheads, brunettes, small eyes, large eyes, white, black, brown. Despite their varied appearances, they all shared the same smell, the smell of men, that pungent odor of old fish. Their liquid breasts jiggled back and forth under cheap chemises. Sitting astride, they displayed reedy legs, brightly colored garters, red panties with white or salmon-colored lace and black trim.

Waiting for clients made them short-tempered. They waited like emigrants, cow eyed, huddled near mirrors. To pass the time, they slept, doodled, or swallowed handfuls of mints; others counted specks of fly shit on the blue-and-white paper chains that hung from the ceiling. Enemies quarreled, friends caressed each other softly and without shame.

Nearly all had nicknames. The one with big eyes was called Sea Bream. If she were short, she'd have been called Baby Bream, and if old and stout, Chubby Bream; Pug Nose was the girl with a turned-up nose; Blackie was the brown-skinned girl and Darkie the mulatta; Chinkie was the slant-eyed girl, Blondie the blonde, Stutterer the one who stammered.

There were other nicknames: Crow, Piggy, Big Feet, Honey Tongue, Monkey, Tapeworm, Dove, Bombshell, No-Gut, and Boombox Ears.

A few men came in the early hours of the night to amuse themselves with the ladies, sweet-talking them, stealing kisses, and pinching, always slick and smooth. Doña Chón wanted to slap them. They were as poor as they come, but she tolerated them instead of kicking them out, because she didn't want to upset her queens. The poor queens got involved with these men—protectors who exploited them, lovers who bit them, hungering for someone to care for them.

Inexperienced young men would show up in the early evening. They'd come shaking, hardly able to speak, moving awkwardly like dazed butterflies and wouldn't feel fine until they were out in the streets again. Easy prey. Polite, not mean.

Fifteen years old. "Good evening." "Don't ever forget me." The guilt and bluster that they felt entering the brothel became a bad taste in their mouth once they left, sweetly exhausted from having laughed a lot and made hay in bed. How good they felt to be out of that disgusting house. They munched the air as if it were fresh grass and gazed at the stars as the reflection of their own strength.

The more serious customers arrived later—passionate, pot-bellied, well-known businessmen with an astronomical amount of flesh around their thoracic cavity. The clerk who embraced the girls as if measuring bolts of cloth contrasted with the doctor who seemed to examine them. The journalist, the kind of customer who always left something behind, even a hat, because he was short on money. The lawyer who looked like both a cat and a geranium, given his airs of vulgar and suspicious domesticity. The country boy with milk-white teeth. The hunchback public servant, not attractive to women. The corpulent rich man. The artisan smelling of sheepskin. The wealthy man who slyly patted his pocket watch, wallet, and rings. The pharmacist, quieter and more taciturn than the barber, but less pleasing than the dentist . . .

The room blazed at midnight. The mouths of men and women were on fire. Kisses, lascivious bursts of lips and saliva alternating with bites, confessions with blows, smiles with guffaws, and the popping of champagne with the popping of lead when crooks showed up.

"This is the life!" said an old man, elbows on a table, eyes dancing, feet tapping, and a network of veins bulging in his warm forehead. Growing more excited by the minute, he'd ask one of his partners in debauchery: "Should I go to that woman standing over there?"

"Sure, man. That's why she's here."

"What about the one next to her? I like her even more!"

"Why, of course."

A dark woman seductively walked barefoot across the room. "What about that one there?"

"Which one? The mulatta?"

"What's her name?"

"Adelaida but they call her Piggy. Forget her. She's Major Farfán's girl. I think she's taken."

"Piggy, how she strokes him," whispered the old man. The wench used all her snake charmer skills to seduce the major, putting belladonna around her bewitching eyes to make them more alluring than ever. With fleshy lips, her tongue penetrating his mouth as if licking stamps, she pressed the combined weight of her warm breasts and belly against him.

"Take off that filthy thing!" whispered Piggy into Farfán's ears. And, not waiting for an answer—it was too late for that— she took the sword from his waist and gave it to the bartender.

A whistling train passed, crossing the tunnel in everyone's ears.

Couples danced in and out of tune like two-headed creatures. A man dressed like a woman played the piano. Both he and the piano were missing a few keys. "I'm ugly, buggy, and boring," he answered when people asked him why he painted his face. Not to offend, he added, "My friends call me Pepe, the young men call me Violeta. I wear a low-cut blouse, not because I play tennis, but to show off my lovey-dovey breasts. A monocle to look chic and a frock to distract. Face powder— how shocking!—and rouge hide the smallpox scars on my face, there they are, and there they'll be, scattered like confetti. I don't pay attention to anyone, I'm my own piper."

A train of screams shrieked by. Under grinding wheels, between pistons and gears, a drunk woman the color of bran writhed, soft, livid, squeezing her hands against her groin, the color in her cheeks and lips washed out by her scream.

"Oh, my ovaaaAAries! Oh my ovAAAries! Oh, my o . . . vaaAAAAAries! My ovaries! Oh . . . my ovaries! Oh . . ."

Only those who were too drunk didn't join the group running to see what was happening. In the confusion, the married men asked if someone had attacked her, so they could leave before the police arrived. Others, taking things less seriously, ran back and forth for the simple pleasure of bumping into friends. The group around the woman grew as she turned and twisted, eyes rolling and tongue sticking out. At one point, her false teeth fell out. The spectators went crazy with excitement. A loud laugh shot up when her teeth slid rapidly across the floor.

Doña Chón put an end to this. She'd been elsewhere and now came running like a ruffled hen cackling after her chicks. She grabbed the unlucky shrieking girl by the arm and swept her along the floor all the way to the kitchen. The cook struck her several times with an iron rod and then they buried her in the coal bin. Taking advantage of the chaos, the old man in love with Piggy snatched her away from the major, who was now too drunk to see.

"What a damn bitch, eh, Major Farfán," exclaimed Gold Tooth when she came back from the kitchen. "Her ovaries don't hurt when she's stuffing herself with food and sleeping all day. But when the battle starts, she's like a soldier whining about how his leg hurts. . . ."

A burst of drunken laughter drowned her voice. They laughed as if spitting syrup. Meanwhile, she turned back to the bartender and said, "I was about to replace that braying mule with the big girl I brought yesterday from the Casa Nueva Prison. Too bad she's sick."

"She sure is a fine girl!"

"I already asked the lawyer to see how he can get the Judge Advocate to give me back my money. That son of a bitch isn't going to keep my cash that easily . . . not that easily. . . ."

"I get you. I know you give that lawyer of yours good money!"

"Just another crook!"

"A lecherous one to boot! Go figure!"

"Think what you want, but I promise you he won't skin me twice. They're not busy bees, just a bunch of fat asses. . . ."

She didn't finish her sentence and went to the window to see who was knocking.

"JesusHolyMotherofChrist! Thinking about you and, poof, you show up!" she said aloud to the man at the door with a scarf pulled up to his eyes. He was bathed in the purplish light of the bulb. Without replying to his "Good evening," she screamed to the housekeeper to open the door at once.

"Go, Pancha, open up that door, right quick. Hurry, it's Don Miguelito."

Doña Chón recognized him by instinct as much as by his satanic eyes.

"Well, this is certainly a miracle!"

Angel Face glanced around the room as he greeted her. He calmed down at seeing a big bulk, which was none other than Major Farfán: drool as long as a tail hung out of his mouth.

"A real miracle, because we never see the likes of you visiting us poor folk!"

"Now, Doña Chón, how can that be?"

"You've come here on your own. I was just saying to the saints that I need help, and then you appear."

"Well, you know I'm always at your service."

"Thank you. I've got a real problem, but first let me get you a drink."

"Don't bother."

"It's no bother! Just a little something, anything you want, whatever you hanker for. So you'll think well of us . . . A whiskey would do you good. Bring it to my room. Come this way."

Gold Tooth's private quarters were separated from the rest of the house, in a world apart. There were engravings, sculptures, reliquaries, and pious images on marble tables, bureaus, and end tables. A Holy Family reproduction, astounding in its size and perfect execution. The infant Jesus was as tall as a lily, and the only problem was that He couldn't speak. St. Joseph and the Virgin in a star-studded gown glowed at His sides, the former holding a cup embedded with two expensive pearls and the latter covered in jewels. A dark-skinned, bloody Christ suffered on a vase, and on a wide, seashell-covered surface, a Virgin rose to heaven—a sculpted version of the Murillo painting. The most valuable object was the emerald serpent coiled at Her feet. Sitting in contrast to these pious images were several portraits of Doña Chón at age twenty, when the President of the Republic had offered to take her to Paris. Supreme Court justices and three butchers had gotten into a knife fight over her at a fair. In a far corner, so that guests wouldn't see it, there was a portrait of a survivor with a mop of hair on his head, who in time became her husband.

"Stretch out on the sofa, Don Miguelito. You'll be more comfortable."

"You live well, Doña Chón."

"I do my best. . . ."

"Like in a church!"

"You atheist. Don't make fun of my saints."

"How can I help you?"

"But first drink your whiskey. . . ."

"To your health, then!"

"To yours, Don Miguelito. Forgive me if I don't join you, but my tummy hurts. Put your glass here. On this little table. Here, give it to me. . . ."

"Thank you."

"Well, as I was saying, Don Miguelito, I'm in a lot of trouble. I need your advice, the kind only people like you can offer. Given that one of my ladies isn't of any use to me now, I went to look for another. Someone told me that the Judge Advocate said there was a really fine five-carat woman in Casa Nueva. Since I know what's what, I went straight to my lawyer, Juan Vidalitas, who on other occasions has procured me women. I asked him to write a proper letter to the Judge Advocate, offering him ten thousand pesos for the girl."

"Ten thousand pesos?"

"You heard me right the first time. He answered that as soon as he got the money, which I counted out myself in five-hundred-peso bills, I'd get a written order to bring the money to the prison for the girl. I then found out that she'd been arrested for political reasons. It seems they caught her in General Canales's house. . . ."

"What?"

Angel Face had been following Gold Tooth's story absent-mindedly. His ears were cocked toward the door, so that Major Farfán, for whom he had come, wouldn't slip out. When he heard Canales's name, he felt a stream of fine wires prickling his back. This unfortunate woman was obviously La Chabelona, the servant that Camila had mentioned during her bout of fever.

"Sorry to interrupt you . . . but where is this woman?"

"The rabbit wants his food, eh? Let me finish first. On orders of the Judge Advocate, I went with three of my girls to get her out of Casa Nueva. I didn't want anyone to pull the wool over my eyes. To impress him, I hired a carriage to take us. When I got there, I handed over the order. They read it carefully, talked it over, then they got the girl and handed her to me. To make a long story short, we brought her back here, where they all were waiting. Everyone wanted her . . . so here she is. Why so long faced, Don Miguelito?"

"Where is she now?"

Angel Face was determined to whisk her away that very night. Minutes seemed years as the nasty old woman told her story.

"Quick as a rabbit, eh . . . you rich boys are all alike. But let me finish. From the second we left Casa Nueva, I noticed that she refused to open her eyes or her mouth. I might as well have been talking to that wall there. I thought she was being coy. I also noticed she kept hugging something the size of a baby in her arms."

The image of Camila grew in Angel Face's mind until it split at the waist like the number 8 or a soap bubble pierced by a bullet.

"A baby?"

"That's right. Manuela Calvario Cristales, my cook, found out that the wretched woman was cradling a stinking dead baby in her arms. She called me to the kitchen, and between the two of us, we took it away. We'd barely separated her arms—Manuela almost had to break them—to grab the baby when she opened her eyes like a dead person on Judgment Day. She let out a scream so loud it must've been heard as far away as the Mercado. Then she fell flat on the floor!"

"Dead?"

"We thought so at first. They came for her and took her away, wrapped in a sheet, to San Juan de Dios Hospital. I was so upset I didn't want to look. They say tears came out of her closed eyes like water that's good for nothing."

Doña Chón paused to catch her breath and then went on

muttering: "The girls went to the hospital and asked after her this morning. She seems to be doing poorly. But this is what worries me. As you can imagine, I can't even bear the thought that the Judge Advocate has my ten thousand pesos—I keep trying to think of a way to get the money back. Why in heaven should he keep what's mine? Why? I'd prefer a thousand times to give the money to an orphanage or to the poor!"

"Your lawyer can get your money back for you, but as for this poor woman—"

"Exactly! Twice today—sorry to cut you off—my lawyer, Vidalitas, went looking for him, first to his house and then to his office, and each time he came back with the same answer: there was no way in hell he would return anything! See what a no-good shyster he is? He says that if a cow dies after it's been sold, it's the buyer's loss, not the seller's. Talking about people as if they were animals. That's what he said! I'd really like to give him . . . !"

Angel Face held his tongue. Who was the woman who had been sold? Who was the dead child?

Doña Chón flashed her gold tooth in a threatening manner. "I'm going to see him and give him the kind of thrashing not even his own mother has given him! Let them throw me in jail. God knows how hard it is to make a buck, without having someone make off with it so easily. Filthy old man, who the hell does he think he is? Already this morning I got someone to put dirt from the cemetery at his doorstep. Let's see if that somehow sours his luck!"

"What about the baby? Was he buried?"

"We held the wake in the house; the girls got emotional. They made tamales."

"Party time."

"That's right."

"And what are the police doing about it?"

"Money talks. We got a death certificate and went to bury him the following day in a pauper's grave, in a pretty little coffin with white satin lining."

"Aren't you afraid that some relative will claim him? Shouldn't you post a notice?"

"That's all I need! Who's going to claim him? His father, a man named Rodas, is in jail for subversion and, well, his mother's in the hospital."

Angel Face smiled inwardly; an enormous weight had been lifted off his shoulders. He was no relation to Camila. . . .

"I need advice, Don Miguelito. You're smart: How can I get my money back from that old money-grubber? I'm talking about ten thousand pesos, not a sack of beans."

"I suggest you go see the President and lodge a complaint against him. Ask for an audience. You know he'll take care of it. It's in his hands."

"That's what I thought. I'll send him a telegram tomorrow asking for an audience. Luckily, we're old friends; he had the hots for me when he was only a minister. That was a long time ago. I was young and pretty then, slim as a reed, like in that photo over there. Back then we lived by El Cielito with my grandma, may she rest in peace. Fate had it that a parrot pecked an eye and left her one-eyed. I ended up grilling that parrot—I would've gladly roasted two—and gave it to a stray dog who was stupid enough to eat it and get rabies.

"What I remember most happily from those days is that funerals passed our house. Corpse after corpse went by. And that's why the President and I broke off for good. He was scared of funerals—that wasn't my fault. He was superstitious and very immature. He believed anything anyone told him, whether or not it was good for him. At first, I was head over heels with him and would give him deep, long kisses to help him forget the endless flow of colored coffins. In time, I got tired of this and let him be. What he liked most was for me to lick his ear, though it tasted a bit like death. I can see him now, sitting where you're sitting, with his white silk handkerchief knotted around his neck, wearing a blue suit, a wide hat, and ankle boots with pink spurs. . . ."

"And I suppose that as President he was godfather at your wedding?"

"No way! My husband, may he rest in peace, would have none of that. 'Only dogs need witnesses and godfathers looking over them when they get married,' he used to say. And then they go off with dozens of mutts trailing drool and tongues hanging out. . . .

"Now, we had a photo session. We posed next to a poplar, surrounded by stuffed doves. There was a fancy rug and a tiger's skin on the ground. I stood in profile with my husband's arm around me. The photographer was a real character, with a big moustache and a hunchback. He and the camera lens sparkled to see me so gorgeous. 'Give me a little smile, and hug each other,' he said in a hollow voice. But that was a long, long time ago."

XXV

WHERE DEATH STOPS OFF

The priest arrived at a robe-splitting speed. Others would hurry for much less than this. "What's more precious in this world than a human soul?" he wondered. "For much less, some people would run from the dinner table with rumbling stomachs. Stom-achs. I be-lieve in the Trinity and in one true God, for sure. The stomach is rumbling in me, not in he, me, me, me, in my belly, in my belly. . . . From your guts, sweet Jesus . . . There, the table's set with a white tablecloth, spotless porcelain dishes, and a withered old servant. . . ."

When the priest walked in, followed by female neighbors who believed in séances for the dead, Angel Face tore himself away from Camila's headboard, his footsteps sounding like the gnashing of roots. La Masacuata dragged over a chair for the priest and then they all withdrew.

"I, miserable sinner, confess to God," they said as they left.

"*In nomine Patris et Filii et . . .* How long has it been since your last confession, my child?"

"Two months . . ."

"Did you say your acts of contrition?"

"Yes, Father . . ."

"Tell me your sins. . . ."

"Father, I have lied."

"Over serious issues?"

"No . . . I disobeyed my father and . . ."

(Tick-tock, tick-tock, tick-tock)

"and I confess, Father, that . . ."

(. . . tick-tock)

"I have not gone to Mass."

Sick girl and confessor discoursed as if in a catacomb. Devil, Guardian Angel, and Death were all present. Death emptied his vacant gaze into Camila's glassy eyes. Sitting by the headboard, the Devil spat out spiders while the Angel wept and sniffled in the corner.

"I confess, Father, that I haven't prayed before going to bed or upon awakening . . . I fear, Father, that . . ."

(. . . tick-tock, tock-tock)

". . . that I 've quarreled with my girlfriends."

"Over your reputation?"

"No."

"Child, you have committed grave offenses against God."

"Father, I rode horseback like a man. . . ."

"Other people were with you? Was this cause for a scandal?"

"Just a few Indians were there."

"So you felt you could do what men do? This is a grave sin. Our Lord God created woman to be woman. She should not try to be a man—that's imitating the Devil, who lost his way trying to be God."

Facing the bar—now an altar of bottles of varying colors—Angel Face, La Masacuata, and the ladies waited out front. Avoiding small talk, they exchanged their fears and hopes through their eyes, breathing slowly, an orchestra of sighs oppressed by the idea of death. The half-open door revealed La Merced's atrium, houses, and a few people strolling along brightly lit streets. It roiled Angel Face to see people moving about unaware that Camila was dying: thick grains of sand in a sieve of fine sunlight; shadows expressing common sense; absurd counterintuition of the five senses; walking factories of excrement.

The confessor's voice dragged a chain of words through silence. The sick girl coughed. The air tore the drums of her lungs.

"Father, I confess all the venial and mortal sins I have committed, but don't recall."

Absolution in Latin, the Devil's sudden disappearance, and the return of Angel footsteps that approached Camila like a warm-winged light put an end to Angel Face's anger and inexplicable hatred of everyone that didn't share his concern. It made him conceive—grace works in mysterious ways—of the idea of saving a man who was in grave danger of dying. God, perhaps, might give him Camila's life in exchange, though science now deemed it impossible.

The priest slipped away quietly. He stopped to light a cob cigarette and lift his cassock at the door—the Law required that it be hidden under his cloak in public. He seemed a sweet old man. People muttered that a dying woman had summoned him to confess. The silly women trailed him, and Angel Face ran off to carry out his plan.

The Callejón de Jesús to the White Horse to the Cavalry Barracks. He asked a guard for Major Farfán. He was told to wait while the guard went off to find him, shouting, "Major Farfán . . . Major Farfán!"

His voice vanished in the huge courtyard. "—jor Faán fán . . . —jor fán," answered the broken echoes from the eaves of distant houses.

Angel Face waited by the door, unaware of what was happening around him. Dogs and buzzards fought over a dead cat in the middle of the street, directly across from an officer who watched the ferocious struggle from a barred window, twirling the ends of his moustache. Two women drank fermented cider in a fly-infested corner shop. Five little boys dressed in sailor suits came out of a gate from the house next door, followed by a man pale as quince and a quack doctor and his pregnant wife (mama and papa). A butcher walked between a group of boys lighting cigarettes: his apron full of blood, his shirtsleeves rolled up, and a butcher knife near his heart. Soldiers came and went from the barracks; a serpentine track of bare feet ran from the entrance almost to the courtyard. Keys jingled against a sentinel's rifle as he stood near a guard on an iron chair inside a circle of spittoons.

A white-haired, wrinkled old woman with dry copper skin walked like a doe to the officer. Out of respect for the man, she had covered her head with a shawl. "May I dare ask you, dear sir, for permission to speak with my son? The Virgin will reward you."

The officer spat a stream of stinky tobacco between his rotting teeth before answering. "What's your son's name, ma'am?"

"Ismael, sir."

"Ismael what?"

"Ismael Myson, sir."

The officer spat again.

"But what's his last name?"

"He's My-son, sir."

"Look, come back some other time. We're busy today."

The woman withdrew slowly, without lowering her shawl—it was as if she counted her footsteps as a way to gauge her misfortune. She stopped briefly at the edge of the sidewalk, then turned back again to approach the officer sitting in the chair.

"Excuse me, sir. But I don't live here. I've come from far away, some fifteen miles away. If I don't see him today, who knows when I will? Do me the favor of sending for him."

"I've already told you we're busy. Go away now, don't be a pest."

Angel Face witnessed this exchange. Pushed by the desire to be virtuous so that God might return Camila to him in good health, he whispered: "Send for her son, Lieutenant. Buy yourself some cigarettes with this."

The officer took the money without glancing at the stranger. He gave the orders to send for Ismael Myson. The old lady stared at her benefactor as if he were a Guardian Angel.

Major Farfán wasn't in the barracks. A clerk appeared on a balcony, a pen behind his ear. He told Angel Face that he would be at the Sweet Enchantment at this time because the noble son of Mars split his time between duty and love. Come to think of it, he might even be home.

Angel Face hailed a carriage. Farfán rented a furnished room in the fifth circle of hell: moisture had damaged the unpainted pine door, and Angel Face could gaze into the dark interior. He called his name two or three times. No one was home. Before going to the Sweet Enchantment, he decided to see how Camila was doing. He was surprised by how loud the carriage sounded when the dirt roads gave way to cobblestone streets, trading the sound of hooves for the sound of wheels.

Angel Face went back into the living room once Gold Tooth had finished her story of her love affair with the President. He couldn't lose sight of Major Farfán—and besides, he might get more information on the woman captured in General Canales's house and sold by that Judge Advocate pig for ten thousand pesos.

Dancing was in full swing. Couples swung to the rhythm of a popular waltz. Farfán, stinking drunk, sang along in an unimaginably bad voice:

> Why do the whores
> Love me so much?
> Because I can sing
> The Flor del Café.

Suddenly he sat up. When he noticed that Piggy was missing, he stopped singing and hiccupped loudly. "So the Sow isn't here, right, you assholes . . . She's busy, isn't she, you shitheads . . . Well, I best be going . . . I'm off . . . I'm off . . . Why shouldn't I go? I best be going. . . ."

He struggled up, using a table, the chairs, and the walls to stand. He staggered toward the door. His servant ran to open it.

"I am def-i-nite-ly on my way! The whore will come back, won't she, Chón?

"But I'm off! There's nothing for us career soldiers to do but drink ourselves to death. Instead of cremating us they can distill us! Long live the pillow and the oven!"

Angel Face hurried to catch him. He angled along a wire of road like a tightrope walker—right foot in the air, then left foot, now again the right, now both feet. . . . About to fall, he found his footing and said: "That's real good, as the mule said to the harness."

The open windows of another brothel lit up the street. A long-haired pianist played Beethoven's *Moonlight Sonata*. No one heard him in the empty room, except the chairs arranged like guests around a baby grand the size of Jonah's whale.

Wounded by the melody, Angel Face stopped. He propped the major against a wall like the puppet he was and came closer to merging his broken heart with the music. He came back to life among the dead—a dead man with warm eyes suspended far from the earth—while the streetlights' eyes closed one by one and dew dripped from the roofs like nails about to crucify drunks or refasten coffin lids. The piano, this box of magnets, brought together the fine grains of music. After holding the notes and then letting them go, the arpeggios that released the fingers to knock on love's door closed forever. Always the same fingers played, always from the same hand.

The moon appeared on the cobblestone sky and slid toward the sleeping fields. As it fled, it left dark grooves that frightened birds and the souls of those who felt the world was vast and mysterious when love—born small and empty—dies out.

Farfán awoke atop a bar counter. Someone was shaking him the way one shakes a tree for fruit.

"You don't recognize me, Major?"

"Yes . . . no . . . maybe . . . maybe. . . ."

"Try and remember."

"Aaah . . . ohhhhh!" yawned Farfán, getting down from the counter like a beaten mule.

"Miguel Angel Face, at your service."

The major saluted.

"Sorry, I didn't recognize you. You're always at the President's side."

"That's right! I hope it's okay I shook you awake like that."

"Don't worry."

"You have to return to the barracks, but first, I need to speak to you in private. Luckily, the owner of this . . . place, this bar, isn't here. Yesterday I looked for you like for a needle in a haystack, in the barracks, at your home. You can't repeat what I'm about to tell you."

"Word of honor . . ."

Angel Face gratefully shook the major's hand. With eyes glued to the door, he whispered softly, "I happen to know there's an order to get rid of you. The Military Hospital has received instructions that next time you show up drunk, you're to get a fatal dose of a sedative. Your favorite whore at the Sweet Enchantment has told Mr. President of your revolutionary outbursts."

Nailed to the floor by Angel Face's words, Farfán lifted his clenched fists. "The bitch!" After pretending to hit her, he bowed his head, appalled. "Dear God, what can I do?"

"For the moment, stop drinking. That way you'll avoid the immediate danger and, ah . . ."

"I hear you, but it won't be easy. What were you going to say?"

"You should avoid eating in the barracks."

"There's no way I can repay you."

"Just with your silence."

"Of course, but that's not enough. Still, an opportunity might arise. You know that I owe you my life."

"I'd also like to advise you, as a friend, to find a way to praise the President."

"Oh, yeah!"

"It will cost you nothing."

Both silently added to these words: *To commit a crime, for example, To find the most effective way of getting the Leader's goodwill,* or *To insult openly defenseless people, To show the superiority of force over public opinion,* or *To get rich at the expense of the nation,* or . . .

A murder would be ideal; killing someone would be proof of loyalty to the President. Two months in jail, for appearance's sake, and then quickly a public position of trust—like what's given to those with a lawsuit pending, so they can be conveniently sent back to prison if they don't behave correctly.

"It will cost you nothing."

"You're so kind."

"No, Major, don't thank me: my decision to save your life is to offer God something in exchange for the health of someone who is very, very sick. Your life in exchange for hers."

"Your beloved, I presume."

The most beautiful verses from the Song of Songs floated in

the air for a second, beautifully embroidered, among trees full of cherubs and orange blossoms.

After the major left, Angel Face pinched himself to see if he was really the man who had driven so many to their deaths. Here he was, in the sacred blue of the morning, pushing a man toward life.

XXVI

WHIRLWIND

Angel Face shut the door and tiptoed into the darkened back room, letting his meeting with the vulgar major fly away like a brown balloon. Had it been a dream? The difference between dream and reality is purely rhetorical. Asleep or awake—which was it? In the half darkness, he felt the ground moving under him. Flies and a clock had kept Camila company as she lay dying. The clock scattered rice-grain beats to mark a path for her return, when she stopped living. Some flies scurried on the walls, removing death's iciness from their tiny wings; others buzzed feverishly without resting. He stood in silence by her bed. The sick girl was still delirious.

Dreams full of illusions . . . pools of camphorated oil . . . stars talking slowly to one another . . . the invisible, salty, naked contact with emptiness . . . hands like double hinges . . . the uselessness of hands in hands . . . in Retuer Soap . . . in the garden of a read book . . . in place of a tiger . . . in the parrot's great beyond . . . in God's cage. . . .

In God's cage, a rooster's Mass, a rooster with a moon drop on his cockscomb . . . pecking at the Host . . . lighting and snuffing, lighting and snuffing . . . The Mass is sung . . . It isn't a rooster, but celluloid of a flash of lightning at the entrance to a street party for little soldiers . . . Lightning from the White Rose Bakery, near Santa Rosa . . . Foam of rooster beer in the Gallito neighborhood . . . By the little rooster. . . .

> We will lay out her corpse
> Matatero, tero, la!
> Since she isn't happy here
> Matatero, tero, la!

A drum beats where noses aren't blown, tracing drum-sticks in the wind academy, it is a drum . . . top, it isn't a drum; it's a handkerchief knocking on a door and the hand of a brass knocker! The knocks penetrate like drill bits, perforat-ing all sides of the house's intestinal silence . . . knock . . . knock . . . knock . . . house drum. Each house has its own door-knocker to call its dwellers and when it's closed, they're living death . . . shebang of the house . . . door . . . shebang of the house. . . . The fountain water becomes all eyes when it hears the doorknockdrum angrily telling servants . . . "Knock-ing again!" and the walls echo back over and over again: "Knocking again! Go ooopen!" "Knocking again! Gooo ooopen!" and the ashes grow restless, not able to stir the cat, the lookout, with a soft shiver sent behind the bars of the grate, and the roses grow agitated, innocent victims of the inflexibil-ity of thorns, and mirrors speak lively like a rapt medium through the souls of the dead furniture: "Knocking! Goooo open!"

The whole house wants to go out like a body shaking in an earthquake to see who is knocking, knocking, and knocking on the door-knocker; casseroles casseroling, flowerpots dancing sinuously, pails pailing! pailing! plates with a china cough, cups, silverware sprayed like the laughter of German silver, empty bottles preceded by a bottle dripping candle-wax tears that serves and doesn't serve as a candlestick in the farthest room, prayer books, blessed branches that, when they sound, think they're defending the house against storms, scissors, shells, por-traits, old locks of hair, oil cruets, cardboard boxes, matches, nails . . .

Only her uncles pretend to sleep among the aroused inani-mate objects, on queen-size bed islands, under the armature of mattress covers stinking of cud. The door drum vainly takes bites out of the expansive silence. "They keep knock-ing," mutters one of the uncle's wives, the one with a genuine mask face. "But it's risky to open," her husband answers from the dark. "What's the time? Aw, man, and I was in such a deep sleep! . . . Still knocking! 'It's risky to open!' What will the neighbors say?" "It's risky to open." "Because of them, we should go out and open—what will they say about us—? you can imagine! They keep knocking . . ." "It's risky to open." "How outrageous! Where in heaven have you seen such rudeness, such impoliteness?" It's risky to open."

The uncle's harsh voice softens when sounding in the servants' throats. Ghosts smelling like calves come gossiping at the master's bedroom: "Sir! Madam! They're knocking like . . ." and they go back to their cots and bedbugs to sleep, echoing repeatedly: "Oh, but it's risky to open! It's risky to open!"

Knock, knock, drum of the house . . . darkness in the street . . . The dogs fill the sky with barking, building a roof for stars, black reptiles, and clay washerwomen whose arms soak in the foam of silver lightning bolts. . . .

"Papa! Sweet Papacito, Papa!"

Deliriously, she calls her father, her dead nanny in the hospital, her uncles who refused to receive her in their homes as she was dying.

Angel Face puts his hand on her forehead. "To heal is a miracle," he thinks, caressing her. "If I could yank out your sickness with the warmth of my hand!" Who knows the source of his pain—the inexplicable grief of parents seeing a toddler die, a tickling tenderness that drags its creeping anguish under the skin, into the flesh, without knowing what to do. Mechanically, his thoughts joined his prayers. "If only I could go under her eyelids and remove her tears . . . merciful after so many rejections . . . in eyes the color of wings of hope . . . May God save you . . . we exiles cry for you. . . .

"It's a crime to live . . . each and every day . . . when you are in love . . . please grant us today, oh Lord. . . ."

He thought of his home as if it were a stranger's. His home was there, with Camila, but where Camila was not his home. And if Camila were not there? He felt a vague grief rambling over his body. . . . And if Camila weren't there?

A truck went by, shaking everything. Bottles clacked on the tavern shelves, a door latch rattled, neighboring houses shook. Angel Face was so scared he thought he was sleeping standing up. Better sit down on a chair by the medicine table. Ticking clock, the smell of camphor, the light of candles lit for Merciful Jesus and All-Powerful Jesus of the Light, the table, the towels, the medicines, St. Francis's rope belt that a neighbor brought to scare off the Devil, all disintegrating slowly, quietly, sleep's descending scale, momentary dissolution, delicious discomfort with more holes than a sponge, invisible, half liquid, almost visible, almost solid, latent, crossed by the blue shadows of dreams:

Who's strumming a guitar? . . . Bonebreaker in an obscure dictionary . . . *Bonebreaker in the dark cellar* goes the agronomist's song . . . Sharp cold among the leaves . . . From all the pores of the earth, four-sided wing, comes an endless, devilish laughter . . . Laughing, spitting, what in heaven are they doing? It's not night and Camila's shadow leaves her, the shadow of that skeletal laughter of the mortuary stir-fry . . . Laughter breaks off from the blackened, bestial teeth, but as soon as it hits the air, it becomes vapor and rises to form clouds . . . Fences made of human guts divide the earth . . . Far off, the sky is divided by fences of human eyes . . . A horse's rib is a violin for the blowing hurricane . . . He sees Camila's funeral passing . . . His eyes swim in the foam carried off by the bridles of rivers of black carriages . . . The Dead Sea will soon have eyes. . . .

Her green eyes . . . Why do the white gloves of stable boys stir in the shadows? Behind the procession, an ossuary of children's thighbones is singing: "Moon, moon, take your fruit and throw the peels into the lagoon." That's how each little soft bone sings: "Moon, moon, take your fruit and throw the peels into the lagoon!" Hip bones with eyes like buttonholes. "Moon, moon, take your fruit and throw the peels into the lagoon." Why does life go on? . . . Why does the tram keep going? . . . Why doesn't everyone die? . . . After Camila's burial, nothing matters, everything is superfluous, false, doesn't really exist . . . Better for him to laugh . . . Laughter makes the tower lean . . . Pockets are checked for memories . . . Mere dust from when Camila lived . . . Trivial things . . . A string . . . Camila is probably at this moment doing . . . A thread . . . A dirty card . . . Belonging to that diplomat who imports wine and dry goods without paying duty and then sells them in the Italian's shop . . . Letthewholeworldsing . . . Shipwrecked . . . The lifesavers of white crowns . . . Letthewholeworldsing . . . Camila not moving in his arms . . . Meeting . . . The hands of bell ringers . . . Streets are tolling . . . the emotion drains blood . . . livid, silently joining in . . . Why not offer her his arm . . . She lets herself down with the spiderwebs of touch and leans on a missing arm . . . she has only a shirtsleeve . . . On the telegraph wires . . . looking at the telegraph wires wasted time, and from a Jewish Merchant Alley shack come five men of opaque glass to cut off his path . . . all five have a thread of blood issuing from their temples . . . he struggles desperately to get to where Camila waits for him, smelling of postage stamp glue . . . the Cerrito del Carmen Church in the distance. . . .

In his dream, he fights to escape . . . he grows blind . . . he weeps . . . he uses his teeth to rip the fine cloth of the shadow that cuts him off from the human anthill on the small mound where he installs himself under a straw awning to sell toys, fruit, and toffee . . . He shows his claws . . . he bristles . . . He runs through a gutter to rejoin Camila, but the five glass men cut off his path. . . .

"They're dividing her into little pieces in the Corpus!" he shouts. "Let me by before you destroy her completely . . . She's dead and can't defend herself." "Can't you see?" "Look! Each shadow has a fruit and each fruit has a piece of Camila strung on it!" "How can you believe your eyes? I saw her buried and was certain it wasn't her, she is here in the Corpus, in this cemetery smelling of quince, mango, pear, and peach, and they have made white doves from her body, dozens, hundreds of them, cotton doves strangled by colorful ribbon with exquisite sayings like *Remember Me, Eternal Love, Thinking of You, Love Me Forever, Never Forget Me . . . !*"

His voice is canceled by the strident voices of small trumpets and drums made of cheap intestines and stale bread; among the noise of people, potato steps that drag feet like four-seat carriages with children running after them; in the ringing of steeple bells, in the burning sun, in the heat of blind candles at noon, in the resplendent guards.

The five glass men come together to form a single body . . . Paper made of sleeping smoke . . . They stop being a solid mass in the distance . . . They're drinking soft drinks . . . A flag of soft drinks between hands restless as screams . . . Skaters . . . Camila glides among invisible skaters atop a public mirror impartially reflecting good and evil . . . The fragrance of her aromatic voice nauseates when she speaks to defend herself: "No, no, not here!" . . . "But why not here?" "Because I'm dead!" "What does it matter?" "It matters that . . . !" "What matters, huh?" Between the two of them passes a current of cold air and a column of men wearing red trousers . . . Camila chases after them . . . He follows her the first chance he gets . . . The column suddenly stops at the first pum!pum!pum! of the drum . . . The President approaches . . . a golden man . . . Tan-tara! . . . The crowd backs off, trembling . . . The red-trouser men are playing with their heads . . . Bravo! Bravo! A second time! Do it again! How well they do it! The red-trouser men don't obey orders, they obey the crowd and juggle their heads again . . . Three movements! One! Take off your head! . . . Two! Thrown into the air for stars to comb . . . Three! Catch it in their hands and put it back on . . . ! Bravo! Bravo! Once more! Do it again! That's right! Do it again! . . . Everyone has goose bumps! Slowly the voices die down . . . The drumbeat sounds . . . Everyone is seeing what they don't want to see . . . The red-trouser men take off their heads, toss them into the air, and let them fall . . . The skulls crash onto the ground, facing two rows of motionless bodies with their arms tied behind their backs.

Two loud knocks on the door wake Angel Face. What an awful nightmare! Luckily, reality is different. The person returning from a burial, like someone escaping a nightmare, feels the same sense of well-being. He flew to see who was coming. News about the General or an urgent Presidential message?

"Good morning—"

"Good morning," replied Angel Face to a tall person with a

small, pink, bowing face. He tried finding his eyes through thick glasses.

"Excuse me. Can you tell me if this is where the musicians' cook lives? She's a lady dressed in black. . . ."

Angel Face slammed the door in his face. The nearsighted man kept staring. Realizing she wasn't there, he went next door.

"Goodbye, Tomasita! Good luck!"

"I'm going to the square!"

The two of them spoke at the same time. La Masacuata said at the door, "Fun time!"

"Stop it!"

"Don't let anyone steal you."

"Stop it. Nobody wants a skirt who speaks her mind!"

Angel Face opened the door. "How'd it go?" he asked La Masacuata, just back from the prison.

"Nothing's new."

"What did they say?"

"Nothing."

"Did you see Vásquez?"

"Yeah, sure! They brought him breakfast in a basket and took the basket away."

"So he's not in prison?"

"I almost collapsed when the basket came back untouched. A man told me he had been sent on a work detail."

"The warden?"

"I gave him a piece of my mind. Touching my cheek, coming on to me!"

"How's Camila?"

"So-so . . . poor thing is just so-so!"

"Not well, huh?"

"She's lucky! I'd love to check out without knowing how cruel life can be! I feel sorry for you. You should go pray to Jesus of La Merced. Who knows? Maybe a miracle will happen! Before reaching the prison, I lit a candle and prayed: 'Look here, little buddy. I've come to You. You're the Father of us all, so listen to me. That girl's life is in Your hands.' Then I turned to the Virgin and said: 'I'm asking You for the same favor. I lit this candle in Your name, trusting in You. I'll come back soon to remind You of my prayer.'"

Half asleep, Angel Face recalled his dream. Surrounded by the men in red trousers, the owl-faced Judge Advocate argued with a faceless man, kissing and licking him, swallowing him, shitting him out, and swallowing him again. . . .

XXVII

THE ROAD TO EXILE

General Canales's mule seemed drunk tired as it trotted in the early-evening darkness under the dead weight of its rider. Canales grasped the pommel of the saddle. Birds flew over the forest; clouds went up and down the mountains just as the rider had before sleepiness overcame him. He traveled across muddy slopes, through thickets full of brambles, and along goat tracks that evoked witches and thieves.

Night came dangling its tongue of damp earth. A large shadow soundlessly lifted the General from his mule, led him to an abandoned shack, and left him there. The shadows must've gone to be briefly among the cicadas that chirped chirped chirped and then came back into the hut, stayed briefly, then vanished like smoke. The shadow man went out to report his find and returned to make sure the General was still there. The starry landscape followed his lizard footsteps like a faithful dog stirring a rattling tail in the silence of night: cricricri, cricricri, cricri, cri!

Finally, he returned to the shack for good. The wind danced among the forest branches. It was daybreak in the night school where frogs taught the stars to read. An atmosphere of happy digestion. The five senses of lights. Objects took shape for the man squatting by the door—he was a shy, religious man struck dumb by the beauty of daybreak and the perfect breathing of the sleeping rider. Last night the person who had dismounted the rider had been a huge shadow, but in daylight he was most definitely a man.

As soon as it was light, he gathered kindling, placing the damp wood in the shape of a cross. He lit the old ashes, damp wood, and twigs with a piece of ocote. The green kindling squawked like a parrot sweating, contracting, laughing, crying. The rider sat up, not fully awake, terrified by what he saw: gun in hand, he jumped to the door, willing to trade his life at whatever cost.

Ignoring the gun barrel aimed at him, the man silently pointed to a coffeepot just beginning to boil on the fire. The rider didn't drop his gun. He slowly looked outside—the shack was surely surrounded by soldiers, but he saw only a wide clearing starting to lose its rosy hue. In the distance, a blue lather. Trees. Clouds. The trilling of birds. His mule snoozed by a large fig tree. Not blinking, he stood still to make sure he was actually seeing what he saw; he heard no sound but the harmonious concert of birds and a gliding stream that left no more than a smooth chirp in the air, like powdered sugar falling into a wooden bowl of hot coffee.

"You aren't the authorities?" asked the man who had dismounted him, suspiciously hiding forty or fifty cobs of corn behind him.

The rider glanced at the man. He shook his head back and forth, his lips glued to his coffee cup.

The shadow man glanced around the room like a lost dog and addressed the rider politely as Tatita.

"I'm running away."

The man put down his corn and poured his guest more coffee. Canales felt embarrassed.

"Same as me, Tatita, sir. I'm running away with this corn, but I'm no thief. This was my land till they robbed me of it and my mules."

The General was curious about what the Indian said. He wanted to know how someone can steal and not be a thief.

"I'll show you, Tatita, how I steal without being a thief. Him you're looking at was the owner of a nearby piece of land and eight mules. I had a house, a wife, and kids. I was as honest as you."

"What happened?"

"Well, some three years ago, a political commissioner came and told me to donate some of my pine logs for the President's holiday. So I did, sir, what else could I do? When he saw my mules, he locked me up. I couldn't speak to anyone. He and the mayor, a mestizo, divided my mules between them. And when I tried to defend what was mine by my own blood and tears, the commissioner said I was a fool. If I didn't shut up, he'd handcuff me. Sure, Mr. Commissioner, do what you want with me, but my mules are mine. I hardly got the words out when the guy hit me so hard in the head I almost died!"

A bitter smile came and went under the old, now disgraced soldier's moustache. The Indian continued speaking softly, without changing tone: "When I got out of the hospital, someone from town came to tell me that my children were in chains. If I paid three thousand pesos, they'd let 'em free. My children were youngsters, so I begged the commander to keep 'em in jail and not put 'em in the army—I would get him the money. I went to the capital and met with a lawyer, who introduced me to a stranger, who offered me three thousand pesos for my land. That's what they said, but not what they did. A clerk ordered me off my land, saying it wasn't mine anymore because I'd sold it to the stranger for three thousand pesos. I swore to God it wasn't true, but they believed the lawyer, not me, and I had to give up my land. Worse, they put my kids into the army and kept my three thousand pesos. One son died protecting the border, the other one was so injured, he'd be better off dead. Their mother, my wife, died of malaria. And that's why, mister, I steal without being a thief, even if they beat me to death or throw me in jail."

"That's what we soldiers are defending!"

"Say, what, Tatita?"

A storm raged in Canales's heart, as when a good man confronts injustice. He suffered for his country, its corrupted blood. There was an ache in his skin, his bones, the roots of his hairs, under his nails, between his teeth. What was true? Having used his cap, not his brain, to think. To keep a group of thieves, exploiters, and arrogant traitors in power is so much sadder than to die of hunger in exile. What God do soldiers serve if His regimes betray ideas, the earth, the human race?

The Indian stared at the General as if he were some weird fetish, without understanding what he had said.

"Let's go, Tatita, before the soldiers come back."

Canales suggested that the Indian cross the border with him: without land, he was a rootless tree. He would make sure he was well paid.

They left the shack without putting out the fire and took off through dense forests, cutting the undergrowth with machetes. A mountain lion roamed ahead of them. Shadow. Light. Shadow. Light. The pattern of leaves. Behind them, the shack glowed like a meteor. Midafternoon. Still clouds. Motionless trees. Desperation. White blindness. Stones and more stones. Insects. Fleshless bones hot like recently ironed undergarments. Decomposition. Birds fluttering, circling overhead. Thirst and water. The tropics. Change without time passing, the same heavy heat, never changing . . .

The General wore a handkerchief on his neck to keep the sun off. The Indian walked at his side, in step with the mule.

"If we walk through the night, we can reach the border tomorrow. I'd risk going on the main road since I need to visit some friends in Las Aldeas."

"The main road? Are you crazy, Tatita? You'll run into the mounted police!"

"Be brave! Follow me! Nothing ventured, nothing gained. Those friends of mine may prove useful!"

"No, Tatita!" Suddenly alarmed, he added, "Listen! Don'tcha hear that?"

Several horses were approaching, but then the wind died down. They seemed to be turning back.

"Shush!"

"It's the mounted police, Tatita; I know what I'm talking about. And now we have to go *this* way, even if we need to make a big circle to get to Las Aldeas."

The General got off his mule and veered slightly to follow the Indian. As the ravine swallowed them up, they felt like they were inside a snail shell, protected from the threats all around them. Suddenly, it grew dark. The shadows seemed to gather deep inside what seemed a sleeping temple. Birds and trees became mysterious omens in the gentle, fluctuating wind. They saw a cloud of reddish dust rising toward the stars just where they'd been when the police had galloped past.

They trudged all night.

"Las Aldeas is just over this hill, boss."

The Indian went ahead with the mule to alert Canales's friends that he was coming. They were three spinster sisters who spent their lives between hymns and tonsils, from novenas to earaches, from face to butt aches. They feasted on the news and nearly passed out. They were afraid to be with him in the living room, so they gathered in their bedroom.

In small towns, guests came in shouting, "Ave Maria! Ave Maria," all the way to the kitchen. The old soldier told them his tale of misfortune in a slow, muffled voice, dropping a tear when he mentioned his daughter. They, in turn, cried, grief-stricken. For a brief moment they forgot their own sorrow—the death of their mother—for whom they were all dressed in black.

"We'll help you escape," said the eldest. "I'll go out and see what our neighbors are up to. Now, we need to remember which of them are smugglers. . . . Yes, I remember! All the passable routes are monitored by the state."

She then looked her sisters in the eye.

"Like my sister says, your escape is in our hands, General. You'll need some provisions," said the middle sister, going out.

The youngest was so scared that she forgot her toothache. "I'll try to cheer you up with some nice conversation, since you're going to spend the afternoon with us."

The General looked gratefully at the three sisters—what they were doing for him was priceless. In a low voice, he apologized for causing them so much trouble.

"General, don't worry!"

"Don't talk like that, General."

"Ladies, you are so generous. I know I'm putting you in danger just by being here. . . ."

"But what are friends for? We are mourning our mother. . . ."

"Oh, oh, what did the sweet thing die of?"

"My sister will explain. I need to go and get things ready," said the eldest, breathing deeply. She went into the kitchen to put a rolled corset in her coat while the middle sister went to the hog and chicken coops to get provisions.

"We couldn't take her to the capital. No one here suspected she was ill. General, you know what that's like. She got sicker and sicker. Poor thing. She died weeping . . . she felt she was leaving us alone in the world. We couldn't do anything. But look what happened to us. We couldn't pay the doctor for his fifteen visits—the bill came to the total value of this house, which was the only thing we inherited from our father. Just a second—let me see what your servant wants."

Canales fell asleep as soon as the youngest went out. Eyes closed, body light as a feather . . .

"What do you need, boy?"

"Do you know where I can go take a shit?"

"Over there, by the pigsty."

The peaceful countryside hatched the sleeping soldier's dream. He was grateful for planted fields, for the tenderness of green grass and wildflowers. The morning passed, carrying the fear of partridges that hunters spray with buckshot; the dark fear of a burial sprinkled with holy water by a priest; the deceits of a young bucking bull. Important events had occurred in the dovecotes of the women's courtyard: a seducer's death, courtships, and thirty couples cavorting under the sun. As if nothing had happened.

As if nothing had happened, said the doves to the houses' tiny windows. *As if nothing had happened*.

They woke the General at noon for a lunch of beef broth, stewed chicken, parsley and rice, beans, plantains, and coffee.

"Ave Maria . . ."

The political commissioner's voice interrupted their lunch. The women turned white, not knowing what to do. The General hid behind a door.

"Don't be scared, girls, I'm not the Devil with Eleven Thousand Horns! How easily someone who really likes you can frighten you!"

The women couldn't say a word.

"And not even asking me to come in and sit down . . . even if it's on the floor!"

The youngest brought the most important village official a chair.

"—thanks muchly, you hear: But, ah, who was eating with you? I see there's a fourth plate here."

All three stared at the General's plate at the same time.

"It was, you know . . . ," stuttered the eldest, twisting her fingers nervously.

The second sister came to the rescue. "You might not understand, but ever since Mama died, we put down a plate for her so that we don't feel so lonely."

"Well, it seems you are turning into spiritualists on me."

"Won't you join us, Commissioner?"

"God bless you, but my wife just served me lunch. I didn't take my siesta, because I received a telegram from the Interior Minister to bring charges against you if you don't pay the doctor. . . ."

"But, Commissioner, that's not fair and you know it. . . ."

"You may be right, but where God commands, the Devil serves. . . ."

"Of course," the three sisters exclaimed, tears in their eyes.

"I don't enjoy coming here to make you more miserable. But you know, either pay nine thousand pesos, or give up the house, or . . ."

The doctor's hateful stubbornness was clear in the way the commissioner turned on his heels, walked off, and gave them his back as stiff as a ceiba trunk.

The General heard them crying. They locked and barred the door, afraid that the commissioner would come back. Their tears splashed onto the chicken dishes.

They sat back down to finish their meal.

"How cruel life is, General! How lucky you are to leave this country, never to return!"

"What will he do if you don't pay?" said Canales, addressing the eldest.

Without drying her tears, she turned to her sisters. "One of you tell him."

"He threatened to take Mama out of her grave," stammered the youngest.

Canales stopped eating. "What?"

"Just what you heard, General. Dig her out of her grave . . ."

"But that's perverse!"

"Tell him that."

"Well, you do understand, General, that the village doctor is an out-and-out scoundrel. We'd been warned, but since you only learn from experience, we were taken for a ride. What choice did we have? It's hard to imagine people so evil. . . ."

"More radishes, General?"

Canales took the bowl from the second sister and served himself. The youngest went on talking. "He tricked us. When a patient is seriously ill, he has a crypt built, knowing that the last thing the family is thinking of is the burial. Then when the patient dies, as happened to us, we accepted his offer to have her buried in a crypt instead of in the ground, without knowing what we were getting ourselves into."

"He knew we were guileless!" said the eldest, her voice choked by tears.

"When we got the bill, General, all our hearts nearly stopped. Nine thousand pesos for fifteen visits. Nine thousand pesos or this house. Apparently, he has plans to marry and—"

"And if we don't pay him—the monster told my sister—we will have to 'take our shit' out of the vault!"

Canales banged his fist on the table. "What a crook!"

He banged his fist again, shaking plates, silverware, and glasses. He opened and closed his fingers as if to strangle that filthy crook, but also to choke a shameful social system. That's why, he thought, the poor are promised the Kingdom of Heaven. What crap! So they'll put up with thieves like this. Enough of this Kingdom of Deceit!

"I promise to make a total revolution from top to bottom, from bottom to top. The people must rise up against these parasites, these opportunists, these lazy good-for-nothings that would be better off working the soil. We will raze, demolish, and destroy this system. . . . Off with the heads of God and all His puppets."

A family friend who was a smuggler planned the General's escape for ten that night. Before leaving, he wrote several letters, including an urgent one to his daughter. The Indian would take the main road, playing the role of carrier. There were no good-byes. The mule's hooves were wrapped in rags and off he went.

The sisters leaned against a dark alley wall, weeping. When the General reached the main road, a hand held back his mule. Dragging steps echoed.

"I was scared to death," mumbled the smuggler. "I could hardly breathe. But don't worry; the soldiers are heading to where the doctor is serenading his honey."

At the end of the block, the brilliant flames of an ocote torch joined and parted the outline of houses, trees, and five or six men standing under a window.

"Which of them is the doctor?" asked the General, gun in hand.

The smuggler reined his horse, lifted an arm, and pointed to a man strumming a guitar.

A shot tore through the air and a man fell to the ground like a banana cut from the bunch.

"Damn! Look what you've done. We had better get the hell out of here . . . or we're finished. Spur your mule!"

"It's what . . . all of us . . . must do . . . if we want . . . to change things . . . in this country!" said Canales, his voice interrupted by his horse's clops.

The pounding hooves woke up dogs, who woke up hens, who woke up roosters. The roosters woke up people, who returned reluctantly to life, coughing, stretching. Afraid.

The serenaders lifted the doctor's corpse. People came out of nearby houses holding lanterns. The fiancée couldn't cry. She stood stunned, half naked, a Chinese lantern in her pale hand, eyes lost in the darkness of the murderous night.

"We're almost at the river, General. We're going to cross where only the brave cross, I'm telling you. Oh, if we could only live forever. . . ."

"Who's afraid?" answered Canales, trailing the smuggler on a jet-black horse.

"That's the spirit! You're faster than a swinging monkey when someone's on your tail! Hold on good and tight, don't get bucked."

The landscape was in darkness, the warm air was sliced by gusts as cold as glass. The river mangled the shoreline reeds as it rushed by.

They got off their steeds and descended into a gorge. The smuggler tied them at a spot where he could easily find them when he returned. Between shadows, patches of river reflected a starlit sky. Strange vegetation floated by with talc-colored eyes and the white teeth of speckled trees. Water gurgled over sleepy, buttery banks that reeked of frogs.

The smuggler and general hopped from dry spot to dry spot in silence, guns in hand, their shadows following them like alligators and alligators following them like shadows. Clouds of insects stung them, winged poison in the air. There was an odor of sea trapped by a jungle net, with all its fish, stars, madrepore corals, caves, currents. Loofahs hung over their heads like slimy octopus tentacles. Even wild animals wouldn't go where they were going. Canales glanced around, lost in the inexorable brush, unreachable and destructive as the souls of his countrymen. An alligator that had obviously tasted human flesh attacked the smuggler; he barely managed to jump out of the way. The General wasn't so lucky: he tried going back and stopped for a split second on the shore, where another alligator waited for him with open jaws. Crucial moment. A deathly shiver ran down his back, his hair stood on end. He couldn't shout, just ball his fists. Three rapid shots and three echoes rang out. When he saw the wounded alligator flee, he jumped to safety. The smuggler fired again. No longer afraid, the General ran and shook the smuggler's hand, burning his fingers on the gun barrel.

The sun was rising when they said goodbye at the border. Alligator-shaped clouds with sparks of light on their backs sailed over emerald fields, the dense mountain forest that birds had transformed into music boxes.

PART III

WEEKS, MONTHS, YEARS . . .

XXVIII

CONVERSATION IN THE SHADOWS

First voice: "What day is it?"

Second voice: "Hmmmm. I wonder. What day?"

Third voice: "Wait . . . I was arrested on a Friday . . . yes . . . Friday . . . Saturday . . . Sunday . . . Monday . . . Monday . . . But how long have I been here? Really. What day is it?"

First voice: "Sorry. Do you know how . . . ? As if we were far, very far away . . ."

Second voice: "They buried us forever in a tomb of the Old Cemetery. . . ."

Third voice: "Don't say that!"

First two voices: "Let's not—"

"—talk like that."

Third voice: "Don't stop talking. Silence scares me. I'm very scared. I feel a hand stretching in the shadows is going to grab me by the neck and strangle me."

Second voice: "Tell us, damn it, what's going on in the city. You were the last one there. What are the people up to? How are things going? Every so often, I imagine that the entire city is in darkness, like we are, behind very high walls and with the streets in the deadly mud of winter. . . . I don't know if you two agree, but at the end of the rainy season, I always have the feeling that the earth won't ever dry. I get so hungry when I talk about the city—I want to eat California apples."

First voice: "Holy or-an-ges! I would prefer a hot cup of tea."

Second voice: "And to think that everything is normal in the city, as if nothing happened and we weren't locked up here. The tram's still running. What time is it?"

First voice: "More or less . . ."

Second voice: "I have no idea . . ."

First voice: "It must be around . . ."

Third voice: "Talk. Keep talking. Keep talking as if it's what you want most in this world. Silence scares me. I'm very scared. I feel a hand stretching in the shadows is going to grab me by the neck and strangle me." Gasping for breath, he added: "I didn't want to tell you, but I'm scared they're going to whip us. . . ."

First voice: "Bite your tongue! A whipping must hurt so much!"

Second voice: "Even the grandchildren of whipped children feel shame!"

First voice: "You only talk of sin. Better shut up!"

Second voice: "Sextons think everything's a sin!"

First voice: "What crap. Look what they've put into your head!"

Second voice: "I mean sextons think everything's a sin in the eyes of others."

Third voice: "Talk. Don't stop talking. Keep talking as if it's what you want most in this world. Silence scares me. I'm very scared. I feel a hand stretching in the shadows is going to grab me by the neck and strangle me."

The lawyer Carvajal had joined the student and the sexton in the same dungeon cell where the beggars had been locked up for a single night. "My arrest," Carvajal went on, "was carried out in the worst way. The maid went out to buy bread in the morning and came back with the news that soldiers were surrounding the house. She told my wife, who then told me, but I didn't think anything of it, figuring that it had to do with the theft of some illegal rum. I shaved, showered, ate breakfast, and got dressed to go congratulate the President. A real dandy was I. . . . 'Hi, mate, what a coincidence!' I said to the Judge Advocate when I saw him in full uniform at my door. 'I came looking for you,' he replied. 'Hurry up. It's getting a bit late.'

"I walked a few feet with him. He asked me if I knew why soldiers were around my house, and I said I didn't. 'Well, since

you're acting all naïve, let me tell you why, then, you hypo-
crite,' he answered. 'They're here to arrest you.' I looked him
in the face and realized he wasn't kidding. One of the officers
grabbed me by the arm and a detail escorted me. That's how I
ended up in this dungeon wearing tails and a top hat."

After a few seconds, he added: "Now it's your turn to talk.
I'm scared of the silence, very scared. . . ."

"Hey, hey, what's this?" the student yelled. "The sexton's
head is ice-cold."

"Why do you say that?"

"Because I'm touching him. He's a bit lifeless. . . ."

"Not touching me. Watch what you're saying. . . ."

"Who is it, then? Just you, sir!"

"No!"

"As I was saying . . . there's a dead man among us."

"He's not dead. He's me—"

"But who are you?" the student interrupted. "You're cold
as ice."

A very weak voice: "I'm one of you."

The first three voices: "Oh, oh, oh . . ."

The sexton told Carvajal his miserable story. "I walked out
of the sacristy," (he saw himself walking out of the clean sacristy, smelling of censers, old wood, ornamental gold, ashes,
and the hair of the dead) "across the church," (he saw himself
crossing the church, embarrassed by the presence of the Holy
One, motionless flies, and votive candles) "and went to the
chancel screen to remove the flyer announcing the Virgin of
O's days of mourning on orders of a church monk, because it
was an old flyer. But since I can't read, which is my defect, instead of taking down that flyer, I tore off the one announcing
the jubilee of the President's mother, my mistake. Dear Lord . . .
that's all I did. . . . And they arrested me and put me in this
dank dungeon on accusations of being a revolutionary!"

Only the student didn't say why he'd been jailed. To discuss
his frail lungs hurt him less than to speak ill of his country.
His delight in physical pain let him forget he had seen the light
in the eyes of a shipwrecked man, that he had seen a light
among corpses, that he had opened his eyes in a windowless

school he had entered. They had put out his tiny light of faith and in exchange gave him nothing: darkness, chaos, confusion, the astral grief of a eunuch. Little by little, he recited quietly the poem of generations sacrificed:

> We anchored in the port of nonbeing,
> without lights in the masts of our arms
> and soaked in salty tears,
> like sailors returning from the sea.
>
> Your mouth is my delight—kiss me—
> your hand in mine—still yesterday.
> Ah, uselessly life sails over
> the frozen channel of our hearts.
>
> Saddlebag ripped and honey spilled,
> the bees flew through space
> like meteors. The rose of the wind
> Had yet to lose its petals;
> The heart jumped over graves.
>
> Ah, rrumr-rum rumbling cart!
> The horses go through the moonless night
> roses in their bodies to their hooves,
> as if returning from the stars
> and not from the graveyard.
>
> Ah rrumr-rum rumbling cart,
> funicular of tears, rrum
> between feathered brows, rrum
>
> Riddle of dawn in the stars
> illusions of turns on the road
> and how far, how early from the world!
>
> Waves of tears struggle during high tide
> to reach the shore of eyelids.

"Talk. Keep talking," Carvajal said after a long silence. "Please keep talking!"

"Let's talk of freedom," muttered the student.

"What an idea!" the sexton broke in. "To talk of freedom in a prison cell."

"But don't the sick talk of health in hospitals?"

The fourth voice suddenly muttered: "There's no hope of freedom, my friends. We're condemned to suffer as long as God wills it. The people who yearn for the good of the country are far off. Some of them beg next door, others rot in the earth in common graves. Streets will one day stop seeing these horrors. Trees don't bear fruit as they once did. Corn doesn't provide sustenance. Sleep doesn't lead to rest. Water doesn't refresh. The air can't be breathed. Plagues follow pestilence, pestilence follows plagues, and soon an earthquake will destroy everything. We are a cursed country. Heavenly voices shout when it thunders: *Vile, filthy creatures! Accomplices of wickedness!* Hundreds of men have had their brains blown away by murderous bullets on prison walls. The Palace marbles are drenched in the blood of innocent people. Where can we look to find freedom?"

The sexton: "To God Almighty!"

The student: "Why? Isn't He deaf?"

The sexton: "Because this is His Holy Will!"

The student: "What a shame."

The third voice: "Talk. Don't stop talking. Keep talking as if it's what you want most in this world. Silence scares me. I'm so scared. I feel a hand stretching in the shadows is going to grab me by the neck and strangle me."

"Better pray. . . ." The sexton's voice spilled Christian resignation into the dungeon air.

Carvajal, who came from a liberal neighborhood that wanted to burn priests, muttered, "Let us pray."

But the student broke in. "What's the use in praying? We shouldn't be praying. Let's tear down that door and join the revolution."

Two arms, belonging to someone he couldn't see, embraced

him tightly. He felt the brush of a tear-soaked beard against his cheek. "Former teacher of the San José de los Infantes School: Die in peace! There's hope for a country as long as its youth talk like this!"

The third voice: "Talk! Keep talking. Keep talking!"

XXIX

WAR COUNCIL

Charges of sedition, rebellion, and treason against Canales and Carvajal kept growing until it was impossible to read the whole transcript in one sitting. Fourteen substantiating witnesses swore under oath that on the night of April 21 at the Portal del Señor, where dirt-poor beggars normally slept, they saw General Eusebio Canales and his lawyer, Abel Carvajal, attack a military officer, who was later identified as Colonel José Parrales Sonriente. They saw how these two men strangled him to death, despite his ferocious, lionlike resistance. He was unable to grab his weapons to defend himself against a superior force. Furthermore, they swore that after the killing, Carvajal more or less said the following to General Canales: "Now that we've gotten rid of the Man with the Tiny Mule, the barracks commanders will have no problem handing over their weapons and recognizing you, General, as the head of the Armed Forces. We must hurry—it's almost daylight, and we need to inform those waiting for us at my house to proceed with the arrest and execution of the President of the Republic and the formation of a new government."

Carvajal was speechless. Each page of the indictment revealed a new surprise. He would've laughed if the charges had not been so serious. He kept reading, sitting at a window facing a small courtyard. The room he was in, devoid of furniture, was reserved for those sentenced to death. He had been left alone with the transcripts to prepare his defense, even though the General War Council would convene that same night to decide his future. But they had left it until the last moment.

His whole body trembled. He read without understanding

or stopping, tormented by the darkness spreading over the document. Words became damp ashes as pages fell apart in his hands. He didn't have the chance to read much of it. The sun was setting, the light was growing dim, and a starry anguish clouded his eyes. The last line, two words, a heading, a date, and a signature. . . . He vainly tried to read the page number; night squirted black ink on the sheets of paper. Exhausted, he fell on the hefty tome—instead of having him read it, they had tied it around his neck just in time to throw him down a deep hole. The chains of prisoners arrested for petty crimes jangled throughout the hidden courtyards. Farther on, one could hear the muted sounds of cars driving down city streets.

"Dear God, my poor frozen body needs more warmth. My eyes need more light than all the people in the world about to be illuminated by the sun. If they knew of my punishment, they would be more merciful than You, my Lord, and return the sun to me so I could finish reading. . . ."

He counted and recounted all the pages he hadn't read. Ninety-one. He passed his fingertips desperately over the cover of the thick-grained sheets, trying to read them as if they were written in Braille.

The night before, they had transferred him in the dead of night—in a sealed, heavily guarded carriage—from the Second Police Station to the Central Penitentiary. Nevertheless, he had been happy to be on the streets, to hear himself and feel himself on the streets—for a split second, he dared to think they were taking him back home. This last word, "home," dissolved in his bitter mouth like a tickle or a tear.

Thugs found him with the document in his hands and the sweet flavor of the street in his mouth; they snatched away the papers and dragged him into the room where the War Council convened.

"But, sir!" Carvajal said to the general presiding over the council. "How can I defend myself if I'm not given enough time to read all the charges against me?"

"Sorry, we can't do anything about that," he answered. "The time between cases is short; the hours fly by and we're in a rush. We've been summoned here for the task at hand."

What followed was for Carvajal a dream—half ritual, half comedy. As the protagonist of this drama, he gazed at them from a seesaw of death, overwhelmed by the hollow void surrounding him. He wasn't afraid, he felt nothing; his worries vanished inside his sleeping skin. Some would say he was courageous.

The country's flag covered the tribunal table as the Law demanded. Military uniforms. The reading of documents. Many papers. Many oaths. The Military Code like a rock on the table over the flag. The beggars sat on the witness stand. Peg-leg with a happy drunkard's face—stiff, curly haired, well-groomed, toothless, following the tribunal president's every word and gesture. Ferocious Tiger followed the proceedings with a gorilla's dignity, picking his flattened nose or his big teeth in a mouth that stretched nearly from ear to ear. The Widower—tall, bony, sinister—smiled at the tribunal, twisting his corpselike face. Lulo, a chubby, wrinkled dwarf, emitted sparks of laughter and fury arising from hatred of how he was treated, closing his eyes and covering his ears so they'd know he didn't want to see or hear anything. Fancy Pants Don Juan, slight, suspicious, smelling like a rich, half-dressed man: sheathed in his requisite frock coat, a wide cravat splashed with tomato sauce, patent leather shoes with twisted heels, false cuffs, a dickey on his chest. His straw hat lent him elegance, but he was as deaf as a garden wall. Hearing nothing, Don Juan counted the soldiers posted every two feet along the walls of the room. Next was thick-nosed Ricardo the Musician—his head and half his face wrapped in a multicolored handkerchief, bits of food caught in his small whisk beard. He talked to himself, eyes fixed on the swollen stomach of the deaf-mute woman drooling on the benches and picking lice from her left armpit. Next to the deaf-mute sat Pereque, a Black man with a single small washbasin ear. Next was La Chica-miona, thin as a rail, one-eyed, with hair on her upper lip, stinking like an old mattress.

After reading the prosecutor's charges, a soldier, his tiny, crew-cut head emerging from a military jacket two sizes too big, stood up and asked for the death penalty. Carvajal glanced again at the members of the court, trying to guess if they were rational people. The first one was drunker than a skunk. His dark hands, outlined against the flag, resembled those of a peasant in a court play at a small-town fair. Next was another dark-skinned officer, also drunk. And finally, the tribunal president, the most drunk of them all, on the verge of passing out.

There was nothing he could say in his defense. He mumbled a few words but realized no one was listening. No one at all. His words stuck in his mouth like wet bread.

The sentence had been drawn up and written in advance. It seemed portentous compared with the simple executioners who were going to announce the punishment—puppets made of gold or salted meat bathed from top to bottom in the slush of oil lamps—or with the frog-eyed and serpent-shadowed beggars casting black moon spots on the orange tile, or with the soldiers sucking their chinstraps, or with the silent furniture taken from a house where a crime had been committed.

"I protest the sentence!" said Carvajal, his voice stuck in his throat.

"Stop dreaming," quipped the Judge Advocate. "There are no appeals or peals here. Finders keepers, losers weepers!"

A huge glass of water, which he now had in his hands, helped him swallow what he wanted to expel from his body: the idea of suffering, the machine of death, the crash of bullets against bones, blood flowing over living flesh, cold eyes, warm rags, the earth. Scared, he put the glass back down and kept his hand stretched out until he found the strength to move it. He didn't want to smoke the cigarette they offered him. His hands shook as they scratched his neck; his frozen stare scanned the room's whitewashed walls, unconnected to the pale cement of his face.

They carried him, more dead than alive, down a drafty corridor, his mouth tasting of cucumber, his legs collapsing, a tear in each eye.

"Here, have a drink," said a lieutenant with heron eyes.

He raised the glass to his mouth—it seemed huge—and drank.

"Lieutenant," a voice said in the darkness, "tomorrow you'll be hearing the drumroll. We're under orders not to pardon any political criminal."

A few feet farther, they locked him in a ten-by-six-foot dungeon with twelve other prisoners condemned to death. They were packed like sardines, unable to move, pissing and shitting standing, stepping on their own excrement. Carvajal was Number 13. As the soldiers drew away, the gasping of that suffering mass filled the silence of the cell. The distant cries of another confined prisoner were the only other sound.

Two or three times, Carvajal caught himself mechanically counting the cries of that poor wretch condemned to die of thirst: seventy-two, seventy-three, seventy-four!

The stench of crushed excrement and the lack of oxygen dizzied him. He lurched away from the others, counting screams along the edges of the hellish cliffs of despair.

Lucio Vásquez paced back and forth in another cell, yellow from jaundice, his nails and eyes the color of the underside of an oak leaf. He bore his misery by imagining getting revenge on Genaro Rodas, who he felt was responsible for his troubles. He was kept alive by this remote hope, sweet and black as molasses. He would wait for eternity—so much blackness packed his wormy chest in this darkness—for revenge. Just the thought of a knife ripping Rodas's guts and leaving a hole as big as an open mouth relieved his spiteful thoughts. Vásquez savored revenge, spending hour after hour still as a yellow clay worm: *Kill him! Kill him!* And he would dash the shadows with his hand as if his enemy were near, feeling for the cold handle of a knife. Like a ghost practicing his motions, he hurled himself on top of an imaginary Rodas.

The scream of the thirsty prisoner brought him back to the present.

"*Per Dio, per favori* . . . water! Water! Water! Water. Tineti needs water. *Per Dio, per favori* . . . water, water, water."

The prisoner threw himself against the door of his cell, which was sealed with bricks from wall to wall.

"Agua, Tineti! Agua, Tineti! Agua, *per Dio*, Agua, *per favori*, Tineti!"

Without tears or saliva, with nothing damp or fresh to

drink, his throat a bush of burning thorns, his mind spinning
in a world of lights and white spots, he still tamped out his
endless cry: "Agua, Tineti! Agua, Tineti! Agua, Tineti, agua,
Tineti!"

A Chinese man with smallpox scars watched over the prisoners. Every hundred years he would pass by like the last
breath of life. Did this strange, half-godlike being really exist
or was he a figment of the imagination? The crushed excrement and the cries of the sealed-up prisoner made their heads
spin. Maybe, just maybe, that benevolent angel was just another astonishing vision.

"Agua, Tineti! Agua, Tineti! *Per Dio, per favori*, agua, agua
agua!"

Soldiers came and went, their leather sandals stamping the
tiled floor. Some laughed heartily and screamed back at the
prisoner. "Italiano, Italiano! *Per* did you dirty yourself, green
parrot, qui *parla* just like a *chente*?"

"Agua, *per Dio, per favori*, agua, *signori,* agua, *per favori!*"

Vásquez brooded on his revenge. The Italian's cries left the
air as parched and thirsty as sugarcane husk. A shot at last cut
off his breath. The executions had started. It must have been
three in the morning.

XXX

MARRIAGE IN EXTREMIS

"Deathly ill person in the neighborhood!"

A spinster came out of every house. "Deathly ill person in the neighborhood!"

A woman called Petronila, who preferred to be called Berta, came out of the Two Hundred House with a face like a military recruit and the manners of a diplomat. Next came Silvia, Petronila's chickpea-faced washerwoman friend, dressed like a Merovingian. Then Silvia's friend Engracia, wearing a corset— her armor—that strapped her flesh, her shoes squeezing her corns, and a watch chain's necklace hanging like a gallows rope around her throat. Then came a cousin of Engracia, no bigger than Engracia's leg, with a heart-shaped viper's head and a manly, withered voice, given to forecasting disasters in the almanac and prophesying the coming of comets, the arrival of the Antichrist, and the time, according to prophets, when men will climb trees to escape the ardent pursuit of women willing to climb trees to get them down.

Deathly ill person in the neighborhood. What fun! This wasn't their idea, but still they screamed it, smiling cheek to cheek. They declared these words softly, knowing that no matter how much their scissors cut, they would have plenty of extra material to make a full-length dress for themselves.

La Masacuata waited for them.

"My sisters are ready," said Petronila, not saying what they were ready for.

"If anyone needs clothes, you can count on me," Silvia observed.

And Engracia, little Engracia, who smelled of beef broth

when she didn't smell of hair spray, spoke in broken syllables because her corset choked her: "Thinking of her, I prayed for the souls of the dying after my Hour of Prayer!"

They whispered in the back of the shop, trying not to disturb the silence encircling the invalid's bed like a pharmaceutical product or worry the man watching over her day and night. He was an ordinary man, a very ordinary man. They tiptoed to her bed more to see the man than to see how Camila, a ghostly figure with long eyelashes, a very thin neck, and disheveled hair, was doing. Since they were suspicious—such devotion implies love—they wouldn't leave until they were able to get the barkeeper to spit out the secret. He was her lover! Her lover! Her lover! Her lover! That was it, no? He was her lover! All but Silvia, who, as soon as she found out Camila was General Canales's daughter, disappeared discreetly and did not come back, repeated the golden word. No way was she going to get involved with the government's enemies: "He may be her lover and a friend of the President, but I am my brother's sister. My brother is a congressman and I won't put him at risk. God help her!"

In the streets, she repeated, "God help her!"

In carrying out his act of mercy, Angel Face ignored the spinsters who came not only to visit the sick woman, but also to console her boyfriend. He thanked them without hearing their words or gestures of support, since he was only conscious of Camila's uncontrollable, agonizing groans. Grief crushed him as he felt her body turning cold. He felt it was raining; his limbs stiffened, entangled by the invisible spirits in a space larger than life, where everything—air, light, shadows—was separate and alone.

The doctor arrived, interrupting his vicious circle of thoughts.

"So, doctor?"

"Only a miracle will save her!"

"You'll come back and look in on her later?"

The barkeeper kept working, not wasting a second. She washed the laundry for her neighbors early in the morning, then went to the Penitentiary to bring Vásquez his breakfast. News of him was scarce. When she got back, she soaked, rinsed, and hung the clothes. While they dried, she ran home to straighten up and do some other chores: change the invalid's sheets, light candles for the saints, get Angel Face to eat a little something, wait for the doctor, go to the pharmacy, endure the spinsters, who seemed like presbyters to her, and argue with the mattress owner.

"Mattresses for fatsos!" she shouted from her doorway, waving a rag in the air to shoo the flies. "Mattresses for fatsos!"

"Only a miracle can save her!"

Angel Face repeated the doctor's words. A miracle, the arbitrary persistence of mortals, the victory of the crumbs of humanity over the sterile Absolute. He felt the urge to scream at God for a miracle, while the world slipped through his useless, hostile, uncertain arms.

All awaited the end. A dog's howl, a hard knock, the tolling of the Merced bells, led neighbors to cross themselves and cry between breaths: "She's now at peace! Her time has come. Her poor boyfriend . . . What can be done? God's will be done! In short, this is our fate!"

Petronila recounted what had happened to a friend of hers—a man who had never lost his adolescent face—who taught English and other strange subjects and was known only as Teacher. She wanted to know if it was possible to use supernatural means to save Camila. Teacher should know, as he also taught theosophy, spiritualism, magic, astrology, hypnotism, and occult sciences on the side. He was also the discoverer of a method known as "a system of witchcraft to find hidden treasures in Haunted Houses."

Teacher was incapable of explaining his devotion to the unknown. When he was a young man, the Church had beckoned him, but a married woman more experienced and disciplined than he was had intervened when he was about to recite the Epistles, forcing him to hang up his cassock and other priestly habits, looking a bit foolish and alone. He left the seminary for business school and would have happily finished his studies if he hadn't had to escape his accounting instructor, who fell madly in love with him. Mechanics—the drudgery of

working in the ironworks—opened his grimy arms and he
ended up blowing bellows in a shop near his home. But he
soon quit, unused to a kind of work that ran against his natural instincts. Why did the only nephew of an extremely wealthy
woman have to work if she had hoped he would enter the
priesthood?

"Go back to the Church," she used to say. "Stop yawning day
in and day out. Go back to the Church. Can't you see you're as
daffy and weak as a baby goat and that earthly things don't ap-
peal to you? You have no interest in being a soldier, musician,
bullfighter! If you don't want to be a priest, why don't you teach
English, for example? If the Lord didn't choose you, you should
choose your students; English is easier and more useful than
Latin. Teaching English will make your pupils imagine you're
speaking English, even if they don't understand a single word
you say. If they don't understand, all the better."

Petronila lowered her voice, as she did whenever her heart
was on her sleeve.

"A lover adoring her, worshipping her, Teacher! Despite abducting her, he respects her, hoping the Church will bless their
eternal union. You don't see that every day."

"And even less often nowadays, my child," said the tallest
woman of the Two Hundred, who seemed to have climbed a
few extra rungs of her own body. She held a bouquet of roses
in her arms.

"A lover, Teacher, who is devoted and undoubtedly will die
when she dies."

"So, Petronila, is it true"—Teacher spoke slowly—"that the
doctors have declared themselves incapable of saving her?"

"Yes, sir, completely incapable; they've given up on her
three times."

"And you, Nila, do you believe only a miracle can save her?"

"For sure! And her lover's heart's breaking. . . ."

"Well, I've got the key. I can trigger a miracle. Only love can
oppose death since both are equally powerful, according to
the Song of Songs. And if, as you say, the young woman's lover
adores her, loves her with all his heart and soul and plans to

marry her, then the Sacrament of Marriage can save her. According to my theory of grafting, this is what we should do."

Petronila nearly fainted in Teacher's arms. She aroused the whole household, went to her girlfriend's house, and told La Masacuata to speak to the priest. That very day Camila and Angel Face were married on the threshold of death. Into his own feverish right hand, he took hers—long, delicate, and cold as an ivory paper cutter—while the priest recited marriage vows in Latin. Engracia, the Two Hundred House members, and Teacher, dressed in black, were witnesses.

When the ceremony ended, Teacher cried: "Make thee another self, for the love of me!"

XXXI

SENTINELS OF ICE

In the prison courtyard sparkled the bayonets of the guards, who sat in two rows across from one another as if traveling on a dark train. Many carriages passed by before one suddenly stopped. The driver's body leaned back to pull hard on the reins, rocking from side to side like a dirty rag doll. He cursed between his teeth, almost losing balance. Wheels screeched as brakes ground along the smooth, high walls of the ominous-looking building. A potbellied man whose legs barely reached the ground got down slowly. Feeling the carriage relieved of the Judge Advocate's weight, the driver squeezed a cigarette butt between his dry lips—what a relief to be left alone with the horses!—and loosened the reins so the carriage was parked alongside a garden as stony as treason. Just then, a woman threw herself at the feet of the Judge Advocate, pleading for his intercession.

"Please stand up, woman! I'm not going to hear your plea like that. Do me the favor of standing up. I don't have the honor of your acquaintance—"

"I'm the wife of Carvajal, the lawyer. . . ."

"Please get up—"

"Sir, I've been looking for you day and night, at all hours, everywhere, at your house, your mother's, even your office, without finding you. Only you can tell me what's happened to my husband. Where is he? What's happened to him? Please tell me if he's still alive! Please tell me he's alive!"

"As it happens, ma'am, the War Council has an urgent meeting tonight to hear his case."

"Ohhhh."

Her lips trembled from so much joy that she couldn't join them. "He's alive!" The news offered hope. "Alive . . . And since he's innocent, he'll soon be free. . . ."

But the Judge Advocate, a frozen look on his face, added, "The country's political situation doesn't allow the government to show its enemies leniency, madam. That's all I can tell you. Go ask the President to spare your husband's life. He may be sentenced to death and shot, according to the Law, within twenty-four hours. . . ."

"The La . . . la . . . la . . ."

"The Law supersedes the individual, madam. Only the President can pardon him."

"The La . . . la . . . la . . ." She couldn't squeeze the word out. Pale as the handkerchief her teeth gnawed on, she stayed quiet, motionless, vacant, tugging her fingers impulsively.

The Judge Advocate disappeared between two rows of bayonets. The street became tired and empty after the commotion of carriages with elegant ladies and gentlemen returning from visiting the city's most fashionable promenade. A tiny tram sparked and whistled down a side street and limped away along the rails.

"The La . . . la . . . la . . ."

She couldn't speak. Two ice-cold prongs gripped her neck. The rest of her body slipped down from her shoulders to the ground. She was nothing but an empty dress, with head, hands, and feet. The rattle of an approaching carriage echoed in her ears. The horses seemed to swell like tears as they arched their necks, compressing their flanks. She stopped the carriage, ordering the driver to take her to the President's country home as fast as possible. She was in such a rush—a desperate hurry— that though the horses were at a full gallop, she criticized the driver for not making them go faster . . . She should be there by now . . . Faster . . . She had to save her husband . . . Faster . . . faster . . . even faster . . . She snatched the whip from the driver . . . she had to save her husband . . . the horses galloped faster under her cruel whip . . . The whip burned their flanks . . . She had to save her husband . . . She should be there by now . . . But the wheels seemed to spin in place . . . not going anywhere . . . spinning around sleeping axles, not moving forward . . . She had to save her husband . . . Yes, yes, yes, yes, yes . . . her hair was flying loose—to save him—her blouse came out of her skirt—to save him . . . But the carriage wasn't going anywhere, she felt the front wheels spinning, the back wheels staying in place . . . the carriage stretched like camera bellows and every second the horses seemed smaller and smaller . . . The driver had taken the whip back from her . . . They couldn't go on like this . . . Yes, yes, yes, yes . . . yes . . . no . . . yes . . . no . . . yes . . . no . . . But why not? Why not? . . . yes . . . no . . . yes . . . no . . .

She took off her rings, brooch, earrings, and bracelet and put them all into the driver's coat, all his, as long as he didn't stop the carriage. She had to save her husband . . . But they never arrived . . . To arrive, arrive, arrive . . . but they never arrived . . . To arrive, beg for his life and save him, but they hadn't arrived . . . They were stuck like telegraph wires, or rather going in reverse like telegraph wires, like thorn and thistle fences, like fallow fields, like golden clouds of twilight, abandoned crossroads, motionless oxen.

Finally, they turned toward the President's country home along a stretch of road that divided trees from ravines. Her heart nearly choked her. The road ran between the little houses of a clean, almost deserted village. They began to see carriages returning from the Presidential quarters—landaus, sulkies, buggies—occupied by similar faces and outfits. Nearby noises of wheels on cobblestones, the sound of horses' hooves increased . . . But they still hadn't arrived . . . they hadn't arrived . . . Along with the unemployed bureaucrats and fat, well-dressed soldiers on leave that arrived in carriages came farmers on foot, summoned urgently by the President months ago; villagers with shoes like leather bags; schoolteachers who stopped often to catch their breath—eyes blinded by dust and wearing moth-eaten shoes, skirts rolled up to their knees—and Indian committees, who, though composed of officials, understood little of what was going on around them.

To save him, yes, yes, yes, but would they ever arrive? The first thing was to get there, get there before the President ended his audiences, get there to beg for his life, to save him, but when would they arrive? They had only a short distance to go, just outside the village. They should be there, but the village seemed endless. This was the road where images of Jesus and the Virgin of Sorrows were carried on Holy Thursday. The hounds, saddened by trumpet music, howled and howled when the procession passed in front of the President, who was standing on a balcony under a canopy of purple tapestries and bougainvillea. Jesus passed in front of Caesar, beaten down by the weight of a wooden cross, but men and women paid homage to Caesar. Suffering was not sufficient, weeping hour after hour was not enough, it wasn't sufficient that families and towns aged in despair: to increase the public shame, it was necessary for the image of a suffering and cloudy-eyed Christ to pass before the President under a disgraceful golden canopy, between rows of puppets and the pounding of pagan music.

The carriage stopped at the gate of a magnificent home. Carvajal's wife ran along a road of thick trees. An officer blocked her path.

"Señora, señora."

"I've come to see the President."

"The President isn't receiving visitors. You'll have to go back. . . ."

"Yes, yes, he'll see me. You see, I'm the lawyer Carvajal's wife. . . ." She slipped out of the soldier's grip. He ran after, telling her to halt. She managed to reach a poorly lit little house in the shadow of sunset. "They're going to execute my husband, general!"

A tall, dark man, festooned in gold braids, walked along the corridor, hands behind his back, along what seemed to be a doll's house.

She went bravely up to him: "They're going to execute my husband, general!"

The soldier chasing her kept saying that it was not possible for her to see the President.

Despite his good manners, the general answered harshly: "The President is not receiving visitors, señora, so please do us the favor of leaving. . . ."

"Oh, general! Oh, general! What will become of me without my husband? What will become of me? No, no, general! He will see me! Let me by, let me by! Please announce my visit! They're going to execute my husband!"

Her heart thumped under her dress. They wouldn't allow her to kneel. Her eardrums buzzed with the silence of their reply.

Dead leaves crackled in the twilight, afraid the wind would blow them away. She sank onto a bench. Men of black ice. Ice in their veins. Her sobs sounded like starched tassels, almost like knives, on her lips. Saliva ran down the edges of her mouth like a boiling groan. Her weeping watered the bench as if it were a grinding stone. They yanked her away from where the President might be. A passing patrol, smelling of sausage, olive press, and peeled pinewood, made her shiver from fear. The bench disappeared in the darkness like a plank into the sea. She walked back and forth so as not to drown in darkness with the bench; to remain alive. Two, three, many times the guards posted among the trees stopped her. They blocked her way and threatened her with their rifle butts if she persisted. She ran left and right, frustrated at every turn, stumbling on rocks, injuring herself on thornbushes. More heartless guards blocked her passage. She begged, fought, stretched her hand like a beggar and, when no one listened to her, she ran in the opposite direction.

The trees swept a shadow toward a carriage, a shadow that had barely put a foot on a step when she suddenly rushed back like a lunatic to beg again. The driver woke up and nearly dropped the jewelry that warmed his pockets as he took out a hand to grab the reins. Time passed so slowly; he was dying to see his sweetheart. Earrings, rings, bracelet . . . He had enough to hock. He scratched one foot with the other, pulled his hat over his eyes, and spat. Where had so much darkness and so many toads come from? Carvajal's wife came back to the carriage like a sleepwalker. Once seated, she ordered the driver to wait a bit; perhaps they'd open the gate . . . in half an hour . . . in an hour. . . .

The carriage drove off silently; was she deaf or were they

still stopped? The road angled to the bottom of a ravine from a steep hill, only to rise again like a firecracker toward the town. The first dark wall. The first white house. A poster for the illusionist Onofroff in a wall hollow . . . Everything seemed welded to her grief . . . air . . . everything. A solar system in each tear . . . centipedes of dew fell from the roofs to the narrow sidewalks . . . her blood seemed stanched . . . "How are you? . . . Actually, I'm not well . . . not well at all . . . And tomorrow, how will you be? . . . The same, and day after tomorrow the same. . . ." She asked and answered her own questions . . . "And all the days after tomorrow. . . .

"The weight of the dead makes the earth revolve at night just as the weight of the living makes it revolve by day . . . When there are more dead than living, night will be eternal, will have no end, for the living won't be heavy enough to bring day. . . ."

The carriage stopped. The road continued, but not for her, since she was at the prison where, undoubtedly . . . She walked slowly along the wall. She wasn't mourning, yet she already felt she had a bat's touch . . . Fear, cold, disgust; she overcame everything to go along the wall echoing the sound of gunfire . . . After all, while she stood there, they wouldn't dare shoot her husband; with a hail of bullets, with weapons, men like him, people like him, with eyes, a mouth, hands, hair on their heads, fingernails, with teeth in their mouths, with a tongue, with a throat . . . It wasn't possible to kill men like that, people with the same color skin, the same tone of voice, the same way of seeing, hearing, going to bed, waking up, making love, washing their faces, eating, laughing, walking, with the same beliefs and the same doubts. . . .

XXXII

EL SEÑOR PRESIDENTE

Angel Face received orders to go right away to the Presidential quarters. He worried over Camila's condition and seemed more determined—a newly found humanity reflected in his worried eyes—yet he wavered like a cowardly snake between going and not going: The President or Camila, Camila or the President?

He could still feel the barkeeper shoving his shoulder softly and the texture of her supplicating voice. He might even be able to put in a good word for Vásquez. "Go, and I'll stay here and care for her."

Once outside, he took a deep breath before hailing a carriage to go to the President's house. The horses' hooves clattered on the cobblestones, the wheels turning in a liquid flow. The Red Pad-lock, the Bee-hive, the Vol-can-o . . . he carefully spelled out the names of the stores he passed. The signs were more visible at night than during the day . . . the Sandy Bog . . . the Rail-road, the Hen and Chick-ens . . . Sometimes he saw Chinese names: Lon Ley Lon and Co. . . . Quan See Chan . . . Fu Quan Yen . . . Chon Chan Lon . . . Sey Yon Sey. . . . He kept thinking about General Canales. "They must've sent him the latest report. . . . It couldn't be! Why couldn't it be? They captured and killed him, or they didn't kill him, but brought him back in handcuffs. . . ."

A cloud of dust suddenly rose up. The wind was a bullfighter toying with the carriage. Anything could happen. The carriage went faster once it was in the countryside, like a body passing from a solid to a liquid state. Angel Face squeezed his knee-caps and sighed. The carriage noise was overpowered by the thousand other noises of the slow, deliberate, clinking night. He thought he heard a bird fly by. They passed a handful of houses. Half-dead dogs barked. . . .

The Under-Secretary of War waited for him at his office door. He shook hands, dropping the cigar he was smoking into a bowl and escorted him to the President's quarters unannounced.

"General," began Angel Face, taking the Under-Secretary by the arm, "do you know why the boss called for me?"

"Don Miguelito, I have no idea."

He certainly knew. An abbreviated laughter, followed by smirks, confirmed what the Under-Secretary's evasive answer had led him to suppose. When he reached the door, he saw a forest of bottles on a round table and a plate of *fiambre*, guacamole, and red peppers. Several overturned chairs were on the floor. The white opaque glass windows emblazoned with red crests tried to keep out the light from garden lamps. Fully armed officers stood one at each door and soldiers stood one at each tree.

The President approached from the far end of the room—the ground seemed to advance under his feet and the house over his hat.

"Mr. President," Angel Face greeted him. He was about to say that his wish was his command, when he was interrupted.

"Ni mier . . . va!"

"Do you mean the Goddess Minerva?"

His Excellency hopped to the table, ignoring Angel Face's praise of the Goddess Minerva. "Miguel, did you know that the man who discovered alcohol was looking for an elixir to prolong life?"

"No, Mr. President, I didn't know that," Angel Face answered quickly.

"It's strange, but you can find it in Swett Marden's writings—"

"It's not strange for a man of your vast knowledge, Mr. President. No wonder you're considered one of the world's leading statesmen. Not me."

His Excellency lowered his eyelids to suppress the spinning of the room caused by too much drink.

"Damn, I do know a lot!" He then let his hand drop to the black forest of whiskey bottles. He offered Angel Face a drink.

"Bottoms up, Miguel." Something caught in his throat; he choked on his words. He pounded his chest with his fist to breathe more easily. The muscles of his thick neck tightened; the veins in his forehead bulged. Angel Face helped him to some soda water and, after a few burps, he was able to speak again.

"Ha! Ha! Ha! Ha!" he laughed, pointing to Angel Face. "Ha! Ha! Ha! Ha! At death's door. . . ." Explosions of laughter. "At death's door. Ha! Ha! Ha! Ha!"

Angel Face turned pale. The glass of whiskey trembled in his hand.

"The Pres—"

"—IDENT knows everything," His Excellency interrupted. "Ha! Ha! Ha! Ha! At death's door and on the advice of a mental reject—like all spiritualists. . . . Ha! Ha! Ha!"

Angel Face used his glass as a buffer to keep from screaming and drank the whiskey. He was seeing red, about to throw himself on his master and stuff that awful laughter down his throat—the flame of his alcohol-saturated blood. A train passing over him would have caused less pain. He felt disgusted—but continued acting like a trained dog, an intellectual happy with a filthy morsel, willing to do anything to save his life. He smiled to conceal his hostility. Death hovered in his velvety eyes; he felt like a poisoned man sensing that his face was swelling.

His Excellency swatted at a fly.

"Miguel, do you know the fly game?"

"No, Mr. President . . ."

"Oh, it's true that you*uuuu* . . . at death's door. Ha! Ha! Ha! He! He! He! He! Ho! Ho! Ho! Ho!"

Roaring with laughter, he chased the flitting fly, running from one side to the other—shirttail flying up into the air, zipper open, shoes unlaced, mouth dribbling, and eyes leaking some kind of yolky goo.

"Miguel," he said, gasping for breath without catching his prey, "the fly game is lots of fun and easy to learn. You only need patience. We used to play it for pennies in my village when I was a kid."

When he mentioned his village, he frowned and his brow darkened. He went over to the country's map behind him and punched the village's name.

He seemed to be remembering the childhood streets where he had walked, a poor boy, unjustifiably poor, where he had lived as a young man, forced to earn a living while the sons of wealthier families went from one party to the next. He saw a nobody in a hole, ignored by his classmates, isolated from everyone, under the lamp he studied by at night while his mother slept in a narrow cot and the mutton-smelling wind buffeted the empty streets. Then he saw himself later in his third-rate lawyer's office, among whores, gamblers, shit-sellers, cattle thieves, despised by colleagues who handled celebrity lawsuits.

He drank too much, shot after shot. His puffy eyes shone against his jade face, and the nails of his small hands had black half-moons.

"Ungrateful beasts!"

Angel Face held him by the arm. His face swept over the cluttered room, his expression full of corpses. "Ungrateful beasts!" he repeated, more softly. "I loved and always will love Parrales Sonriente. I was going to make him a general because he trampled our citizens, made them shiver and shake. And if it hadn't been for my mother, he would have finished them off and avenged me for all I bore against them, things that only I know. . . . Ingrates! . . . And I won't forget—because I can't forget—that they murdered him, while people around me are plotting against me. Friends are deserting me, my enemies are multiplying, and. . . . No! No! Not a single stone of the Portal del Señor will remain standing."

The words slid from his lips like cars on a slippery road. He leaned on Angel Face's shoulder, pressing a hand to his stomach. His temples pounded, his eyes were yellow, his breath like ice before he vomited a stream of orange fluid. The Under-Secretary came running in with a tin bowl with the republic's coat of arms embossed on the bottom. Most of the vomit landed on Angel Face. When the President finished retching, both men dragged him to a bed.

"Ungrateful beasts! Ungrateful beasts!" he cried over and over.

"Congratulations, Don Miguelito, congratulations," murmured the Under-Secretary as they went out. "The President ordered the newspapers to publish your wedding announcement, with his name at the top of the list of witnesses."

They reached a hallway. The Under-Secretary raised his voice. "And this despite not being so pleased with you at first. 'A friend of Parrales Sonriente shouldn't have done,' he told me, 'what Miguel has done. At the least he should have asked me before marrying the daughter of one of my worst enemies.' They're preparing the earth for you, Don Miguelito, preparing the earth for you. Naturally I tried to get him to see that love is blind, a mess, and a hopeless, deceitful thing."

"Thank you very much, general."

"Come look at this," the Under-Secretary went on jovially, laughing a bit, pushing him toward his office with friendly taps on the back. "Come and look at the newspaper! Her uncle Juan gave us this picture of her. Well done, my friend, well done!"

Angel Face dug his nails into the newsprint. In addition to the Supreme Godfather's, he saw the names of Juan Canales and his brother José Antonio.

"'Huge Society Wedding.' Last night the beautiful Camila Canales and Mr. Miguel Angel Face celebrated their betrothal. Both parties"—from here his eyes dropped to the list of patrons—"a marriage witnessed under the Law of Our Excellency the Constitutional President of the Republic, in whose house the ceremony was performed, attended by various ministers of state and witnessed by generals"—he skipped over their names—"and the esteemed uncles of the bride, Don Juan Canales, engineer, and Don José Antonio, with the same last name. A photograph of Señorita Canales is on *El Nacional*'s Society Page. We take pleasure in congratulating them and wishing them great happiness in their new home."

Angel Face didn't know where to rest his eyes. "The Battle of

Verdun continues. The Germans are expected to launch a desperate offensive this evening."

He shifted his eyes from the page of telegrams and reread the caption under Camila's face. The only person he loved was now playing a role in a farce in which all of them were taking part.

The Under-Secretary yanked the newspaper out of his hands.

"You can't believe your eyes, right? You lucky man!"

Angel Face laughed.

"But, friend, you better get going. Take my carriage. . . ."

"Thanks, general. . . ."

"Tell the driver to take you home quickly and come back to pick me up. Good night, and my congratulations! Take the newspaper to show your wife. Tell her that her humble servant congratulates her."

"I'm grateful for all you've done. Have a good evening."

Angel Face's carriage took off as soundlessly as a shadow pulled by phantom horses. Chirping crickets formed a canopy over the solitude of bare fields smelling of mignonette flowers: it was the odor of the warm solitude of the first corn planting, the pastures soaked in dew and the orchard walls thick with jasmine.

"Yes, if he continues making fun of me, I'll strangle him," he thought, hiding his face in the seat behind him, afraid the driver would guess what he was imagining: a pile of frozen meat with the Presidential banner across the chest, the pugnosed face motionless, hands inside fake cuffs revealing only fingertips, and patent leather shoes dripping blood.

His combative mood resisted the carriage jolts badly. He'd have preferred to be still, like a murderer in a cell trying to reconstruct the crime; he needed to be in stillness, to foil his volcanic ideas. His blood tingled in his veins. He thrust his face into the cool night, wiping off the President's vomit with a handkerchief doused in sweat and tears. "Ah, if I could only wipe away the laughter he vomited on my soul!" he cursed and cried angrily.

A carriage with an officer brushed past them. The sky blinked over its endless game of chess. The horses stormed toward the city in a cloud of dust. "Check to the queen!" Angel Face said to himself, watching the dust left by the officer racing to bring the President one of his girls. He seemed a messenger of the gods.

The goods unloaded in the central train station made a shattering noise, while the steam engines coughed. A Black man leaned from a high floor over a green terrace; drunks staggered down the street; and in a cart driven like a heavy artillery wagon after a military defeat, a miserly-looking man played music.

XXXIII

DOTTING THE I'S

Carvajal's widow went from house to house, but everyone welcomed her coldly. They dared express no grief over her husband's death for fear of being accused of being an enemy of the state. In some houses, servants came to the window and shouted rudely, "Who are you looking for? The masters are out!"

The ice from these visits melted once she arrived home. She shed an ocean of tears at the sight of her husband's portrait, with no companions other than her young son and a deaf servant, who repeated loudly to the boy, "A father's love is best, forget about the rest," and a parrot who said over and over, "Royal parrot from Portugal, dressed in green, and oh so frugal! Shake hands, Polly. Good morning, sir! Polly, shake hands. Buzzards are in the laundry. It stinks of burnt rags. Blessed be the Holy Sacraments on the altar, the Virgin Queen of Angels, and the Virgin conceived without the stain of original sin! Oh my! Oh my!"

She needed signatures for a petition to ask the President for her husband's body but was afraid to discuss it with her neighbors. They received her so rudely, almost out of duty, amid coughs and ominous silences. . . . And she was back home with no signature on the petition under her black shawl other than her own.

They turned their faces away or met her at the door without even saying the well-worn welcome of *Come in*. She was treated as if she had a contagious disease, some invisible illness worse than poverty, worse than the Black Plague, worse than yellow fever. Yet they flooded her with "anonymous letters"— that's what the deaf servant called them—letters she found under the kitchen door near a dark, rarely frequented alley-way. Notes written by trembling hands, deposited under cover of darkness, in which she was called a saint, a martyr, an innocent victim, at the same time as they praised her unlucky husband to the skies and described Colonel Parrales Sonriente's crimes in horrifying detail.

Two more anonymous letters were found under the door next morning. The servant carried them wrapped in her apron, as her hands were wet. The first said:

Señora, this isn't the best way to express to you and your grieving family the deepest respect I have for your husband, our esteemed fellow citizen Abel Carvajal. Allow me, however, to express myself in this way since I can't put certain truths down on paper. One day I will reveal my identity to you. My father was a victim of Colonel Parrales Sonriente, a man for whom all torments in hell await, the hired killer whose misdeeds history will reveal, should someone be willing to dip his pen in pit viper poison and reveal them. This coward murdered my father on a dark street many years ago. As expected, there was no investigation, and the details of the crime would have remained a mystery if it hadn't been for an anonymous person who contacted my family with details about his horrendous murder. I don't know if your husband, such an upstanding citizen, a hero bearing a statue in the hearts of his fellow citizens, was actually the avenger of Parrales Sonriente's victims (many rumors are circulating). I believe it's my duty, however, to express my condolences and to assure you, señora, that we also grieve the disappearance of a man who saved our country from so many gold-braided crooks who use US gold to reduce it to a state of blood and filth. I Kiss Your Hand, Cruz de Calatrava.

She was empty and drained, paralyzed by a deep-seated inertia that kept her bedridden, as motionless as a corpse for hours. The only movement she managed was to bring a few items to her night table so she wouldn't have to get up. She had panic attacks whenever the door opened, someone used the broom, or someone made a noise near her. The darkness, silence, and filth shaped her abandonment, her desire to be alone with her grief, with that part of her being that died when her husband died. Little by little, it was taking over her body and soul.

Madam, with all due respect, she read aloud the second anonymous letter:

> *I found out from friends that you stood against prison walls on the night your husband was shot. If you heard and counted the shots, nine in total, you wouldn't know which bullet tore him from this world, God rest his soul. Under an assumed name—we can't reveal our names, given the times in which we live—and never doubting the pain it caused you, I decided to bear witness to all I know about his murder. A skinny, dark-skinned man who had mostly white hair covering his rather broad forehead walked in front of your husband. I haven't discovered his name. Your husband's very sunken eyes conserved, despite the grief his tears revealed, a great human kindness, indicating a noble and generous soul. The lawyer tripping over his own steps followed him without raising his eyes from the ground. Perhaps he didn't even see it, his forehead drenched in sweat as he walked with one hand across his chest as if to keep his heart from dropping out. When he reached the courtyard and saw himself surrounded by soldiers, he raised the bottom of his hand to his eyelids to make sure he was seeing what he saw. He was dressed in a faded outfit that was much too small for him: his coat sleeves barely reached his elbows and his pants squeezed his knees. He wore dirty, old, torn clothes, which all the prisoners pass down to one another once they are buried or which they trade with guards for favors. His striped shirt had a button made of bone. His shirt had no collar. He didn't wear shoes. The presence of his misfortunate fellow prisoners, also half naked, gave him strength. When they finished reading his death sentence, he lifted his head. His pained eyes gazed across the bayonets and he mumbled*

something no one heard. The old man at his side tried to
speak, but the officers silenced him with sabers that appeared
bluish in the light of daybreak and in the hands of drunk
soldiers. On the walls, a preaching voice echoed: For Love of
Country! . . . *then one, two, three, four, five, six, seven, eight,*
nine shots. I don't know how many, but I counted them on my
fingers—since then, I have had the strange impression I have
one too many fingers. Eyes closed, the victims twisted and
twirled, trying to feel their way to escape from death. A curtain
of smoke separated us from a handful of men who bunched
together as they fell so as not tumble alone into the abyss. The
murderous shots echoed like wet firecrackers, delayed and
stuttering. Your husband was lucky to die after the first shot.
We could see the unreachable blue sky above, mixed with the
faint sound of bells, birds, and rivers. I found out that the
Judge Advocate was in charge of burying each of the . . .

She turned the page impatiently: *each of the . . .* But the sentence ended there. No more sheets of paper. The letter came to
a sudden end, the thought unfinished. She reread all the pages
in vain, looked at the envelope and the unmade bed, lifted the
pillow, looked all over the floor and table, turning everything
inside out, eaten by the desire to know where her husband had
been buried.

The parrot continued talking in the courtyard. "Royal parrot
from Portugal, dressed in green and oh so frugal! Here comes
the lawyer! Hurray, royal parrot! Any second now, says the
deceiver. I won't weep, but I won't forget!"

The Judge Advocate's housekeeper left Carvajal's widow at the
door while she attended to two women screaming in the vestibule.

"Listen, will you listen," one of them said. "Tell 'im I didn't
wait for him, 'cause, damn, I'm not a dumb old Indian to freeze
my ass off in a place as cold as his face is ugly. Tell 'im I came
to see if he would be so kind as to return the ten thousand
pesos he took from me for the Casa Nueva girl that didn't get
me out of my hole, because the day I brought her, she fainted.

Tell 'im that this will be the last time I come. Tell 'im I'm going
to go file a complaint with the President."

"Gee, Doña Chón, calm down. Let me get rid of . . . the
young wo—" the housekeeper tried to say, but she was interrupted. "Shut up now. Tell 'im what I just told you, get it, so he
then doesn't come to me with the excuse that I didn't warn
'im. Tell 'im that Doña Chón and her maid came and waited
and waited and when they realized he wasn't going to show
up, we said what we did and left like rabbits. . . ."

Deep in thought, Carvajal's widow had no idea what was
going on. Wearing black, like a corpse in a coffin with a glass window, she was invisible except for her face. The servant touched
her shoulder—the old woman had a spiderweb's touch—and told
them to come in, which they did. The widow uttered words as
indistinct as the mumbling of a tired reader.

"Yes, ma'am. Please leave your letter. When he comes—he'll
be here soon, he should've been here by now—I'll give it to
him and make sure he knows it's urgent."

"On your life!"

When Carvajal's widow left, a man in a brown suit came in,
followed by an Indian soldier with a Remington rifle on his
shoulder, a dagger at his waist, and a bullet pouch hooked to
his belt.

"I'm in a rush," he said to the housekeeper. "Is the lawyer
in?"

"No, he's not."

"And where may I wait for him?"

"Sit down here. Have your soldier sit here as well."

Prisoner and soldier sat in silence on the bench that the gruff
housekeeper indicated.

The courtyard smelled of wild verbena and cut begonias. A
cat crawled across the terrace. A mockingbird tried to fly inside its wooden cage. A fountain, dazed from dripping so
much, gurgled sleepily in the distance.

The Judge Advocate glanced at the door, jingling his keys
before putting them in his pocket. The prisoner and his guard
stood up when he appeared.

"Genaro Rodas?" he asked, sniffing the air. Every time he

came in from the street, he smelled the stench of cat shit in his house.

"Yes, sir. At your orders."

"Does your guard understand Spanish?"

"Not so well," Rodas replied. He turned to the soldier and asked, "Hey, bud, do you understand Spanish?"

"Just a bit."

The Judge Advocate spoke to the soldier. "Stay here. I need to talk privately with this man. He'll be back shortly. We need to talk."

Rodas waited at the office door. The Judge Advocate walked ahead to put a handgun, a dagger, a truncheon, and a casse-tête on a table piled high with books and papers.

"You must already know your sentence."

"Yes, sir, I—"

"Six years and eight months, if I'm not mistaken."

"But, sir, I wasn't Lucio Vásquez's accomplice. He did what he did without me. When I realized what was happening, Pelele was already rolling down the steps of the Portal, covered in blood, half dead. What could I do? What could I do? It was an order. According to him, it was an order—"

"He's already been judged by God. . . ."

Rodas turned to glance at the Judge Advocate, not quite believing the look on his sinister face. "He's not a bad guy, really. . . ." Rodas breathed out softly, whispering a few words in memory of his friend. Between beats, the message went all the way into his veins. "Well, it's too late now. We called him Velvet because he was smooth and fast."

"He was sentenced as the perpetrator and you as his accomplice."

"But I have a defense."

"Your lawyer provided one, knowing what the President wanted. He asked that Vásquez be sentenced to death and you to life imprisonment."

"Poor man. I can at least say what happened."

"And you might go free. The President needs people like you jailed for political reasons. It's about keeping an eye on one of his friends, who he suspects betrayed him."

"Whatever you say . . ."

"Do you know Miguel Angel Face?"

"Just by name. He abducted General Canales's daughter, didn't he?"

"Yes. You'll recognize him because he's handsome: tall, well-built, black eyes, light-skinned face, hair like silk, and very fine features. A wildcat. The state needs to know everything about him: whom he visits, whom he greets on the street, where he goes in the morning, afternoon, and night. Everything about his wife, too. I'll give you instructions and money for this."

The prisoner's eyes stupidly followed the Judge Advocate, who picked up a quill pen from the table, dipped it in an inkwell with a statue of Themis between the two pools of ink, and handed it to the prisoner. "Sign here. You can start packing. Tomorrow I will set you free."

Rodas signed. Happiness danced like fireworks in his body. "You have no idea how grateful I am to you," he said, going out. He went up to the guard, almost gave him his arm, and walked back to jail as if going up to heaven.

The Judge Advocate was even happier, holding the paper that Rodas had signed.

Received the sum of $10,000 pesos in national currency from Doña Concepción Gamucino, aka "Gold Tooth," owner of the Sweet Enchantment brothel, as payment for my grief and for having corrupted my wife, Señora Fedina de Rodas. By taking advantage of her good faith and that of the authorities, she was made a servant and subsequently enrolled as one of the girls in her establishment. Signed Genaro Rodas

The housekeeper called from the door, "May I come in?"

"Yes, please do."

"Do you need anything? I'm going to the store for candles. By the way, two women from a brothel came looking for you. They said that if you didn't return the ten thousand pesos you took from them, they'll tell the President."

"Anyone else come?" the Judge Advocate barked unhappily. He bent down to pick up a stamp from the floor.

"A woman dressed in black who was probably the wife of the man shot—"

"Which man?"

"Carvajal."

"What did she want?"

"The poor woman left a letter. Apparently, she wants to know where her husband is buried." The Judge Advocate gazed unhappily at the black-bordered piece of paper. "I told her I would help her. I felt sorry for her. She left feeling somewhat hopeful."

"I've told you over and over that I don't like it when you're kind. You shouldn't give them hope. When will you understand that? The first thing you should know is that in my house, you don't offer hope to anyone, not even to the cat. You'll keep this job if you do what you're ordered. The President insists that no one should offer hope—you should step on people no matter what. When this woman comes back, return her letter, nicely folded, and tell her there's no way to know where he's buried. . . ."

"You'll get sick if you get upset. I'll tell her exactly what you want, as if God were giving the orders." She left the room, paper in hand, dragging one foot after the other, her petticoat making a rustling sound.

When she reached the kitchen, she balled up the request and threw it into the fire. The paper writhed in the flames as if it were alive and became thousands of golden wireworms above the ashes. A cat crawled along the shelves of canned spices extending out like a bridge and leapt onto a stone bench. She rubbed the housekeeper's sterile body, stretched her four legs, and rested her golden eyes, full of diabolic curiosity, on the center of the fire.

XXXIV

LIGHT FOR THE BLIND

Camila stood in the middle of a room, supported by her husband's arm and a cane. The main door faced a courtyard smelling of poppies and cats. The window looked out toward the town. A smaller door led to another room.

They had brought her home, still recovering, in a wheelchair. Though the sun lit the green fires of her eyes and air filled her lungs like a heavy chain, she wondered if she were the one now walking. Her feet seemed too large; her legs were stilts. Like a newborn, she walked in another world with open eyes, lacking form. Spiderwebs impeded the movement of ghosts. She had died in a dream without ceasing to exist and had come back to life to find that she couldn't distinguish dream from reality. Her father, her home, her nanny, La Chabelona, formed part of her earlier existence; her husband, a temporary house, and the servants were part of this second life. It was her and it was not her, that person walking around the room. When she spoke about herself, it was about a person leaning on the cane of her previous life, familiar with invisible things. If left alone, she would get lost in this other life, her mind adrift, her hair frozen, her hands resting on the long skirt of a newlywed with noise-clogged ears.

Soon she was moving about, but not less sick because of it, absorbed in thinking about all the things that had happened since her husband first kissed her cheek. It was too much for her to take in, but she clung to the change as the only reality in a world much too strange for her. She enjoyed the moonlight on the ground, the moon gazing at the cloud-topped volcanoes, and stars like gold lice in an empty pigeon loft.

Angel Face felt his wife shivering inside her white flannel gown. She shivered not from cold, as people normally shiver, but as angels shiver. He took her step by step back to the bedroom. The huge head carved above the fountain . . . the still hammock . . . the water as motionless as the hammock . . . the damp flowerpots . . . the wax flowers . . . corridors patched with moonlight. . . .

They went to bed and talked to each other from across a wall. A small door connected their rooms. Buttons came out of sleepy buttonholes, making the soft sound of cutting flowers. Shoes dropped with the rattle of anchors, and stockings separated from the skin like smoke peeled from chimneys.

Miguel talked to her about the objects of his personal toilet on a table beside his towel rack, trying to create the silly intimacy of a happy family in a huge uninhabited house. He wanted to stop thinking about the narrow little door, like the door to heaven, leading from one bedroom to the other.

He collapsed into bed, released from his weight. For a long time, he stayed still, slapped by rolling waves and the mystery of what kept forming and unforming between them. He abducts her to make her his own by force, and then out of blind instinct, love develops. Renouncing his original plan, he takes her to her uncle's houses and they bar the door. He has her in his arms again, and, as people say, he can make her his without affecting what's already lost. Made aware of things, she wants to escape, but her illness keeps her from escaping. She grows sicker by the hour. She worries, but Death will come and cut off the knot. He knows this and is resigned for brief moments, even though more often he's rebelling against these blind powers. But the call of death frustrates his hope, and fate waits till the last moment to bring them together.

First childhood, when she couldn't even walk, then adolescence, after standing up and taking the first steps. During a single night, color has returned to her lips and her breasts swell her lacy bodice. She gets upset and breaks into a sweat each time the husband she never imagined draws close to her.

Angel Face jumped out of bed. He felt separated from

Camila by something that was neither his fault nor hers, by a marriage to which neither had consented. Camila closed her eyes. His footsteps went away toward the window.

The moon poked in and out between gaps in the floating clouds. The road flowed like a river of white bones under shadowy bridges. Now and then everything seemed garbled, the patina of an ancient reliquary, and then reappeared, glowing in golden threads.

A massive black eyelid interrupted this game of floating eyelids. Its huge lash detached itself from the highest volcano and spread like a horse spider over the city's skeleton, reducing it to darkness. Dogs shook their ears like door-knockers, night birds stirred, a moan and a groan flew from one cypress to the next. The winding and setting of clocks was heard. The moon vanished completely behind a volcanic crest and a fog settled over the houses like a bride's veil.

Angel Face closed the window. Camila's slow, clipped breathing came from her bedroom as if she had fallen asleep with her head under garments or a ghost sat on her chest.

Sometimes they went to the baths. The tree shadows speckled the white shirts of peddlers selling brooms, clay pots, mockingbirds in wooden cages, pinecones, charcoals, firewood, and corn. They traveled together, crossing huge distances on tiptoe without ever resting their heels. The sun sweated with them. They panted. Swung their arms. Vanished like a flock of birds.

Camila stopped in a hut's shadow to watch coffee being picked. The pickers' hands worked inside the metallic foliage like starving animals: they rose and fell, tied and knotted, as if tickling the coffee shrub, grabbing beans the way one unbuttons a shirt.

Angel Face put his arm around her waist and led her along a path under the warmth of sleeping trees. They were aware of their heads and torsos; the rest of their bodies, legs and hands, floated with them among orchids and colorful lizards, in a dark honey twilight that deepened in color the farther into the forest they walked. He felt Camila's body through her thin blouse, as one feels the milky, damp kernels of young corn. The wind ruffled their hair.

They reached the pool through early-morning creepers. The sun was sleeping on the water. Invisible forms floated among the shaded ferns. The bath attendant came out of a zinc-roofed hut, chewing black beans; he nodded, and while he swallowed, the beans in his mouth popping in his cheeks, he looked at them, demanding their respect. They requested two bath huts. He went to get the keys, came back, and opened two rooms divided by a wooden partition. They kissed before going separately into their own huts. The attendant, whose eyes were crusty, covered his face so they wouldn't get an infection.

They both felt strange, apart from each other, the forest full of noises. A cracked mirror watched Angel Face undress quickly. He was a man, when it was better to be a tree, a cloud, a dragonfly, a bubble, or even a finch! Camila screamed when her feet touched the bath's icy waters on the first step, and screamed again even louder on the second, third, and fourth steps, and then plop! Her Indian blouse puffed out like crinoline, like a balloon, but the water soaked into the blue, yellow, and green material, revealing her body: firm breasts and stomach, the soft curve of her hips, a supple back, thin shoulders. Her dive over, Camila seemed upset, rising to the surface. The fluid silence of the valley stretched its hand to a butterfly-colored snake, a Siguamonta, a strange spirit that inhabited the baths. But then she heard her husband's voice asking if he could come in, and felt assured.

The water splashed around them like a happy creature. They saw the silhouettes of their bodies like enormous spiders in the mirror of cobwebs reflected on the walls. The smell of *suquinay* bushes, the presence of distant volcanoes, the dampness of little frog bellies, calves breathing as they nursed in pastures transformed into milky white lakes, the coolness of waterfalls born laughing, the restless flight of green flies. An impalpable silent veil, the trill of a motmot, and the stirring of a *shara* bird enclosed them.

The attendant came to their doors and asked if the horses from Las Quebraditas were for them. It was time to dress and depart. Camila combed her hair and felt a worm in the towel she had placed over her shoulders so her hair wouldn't wet her dress. Her scream, Angel Face's arrival, and his removal of the worm happened simultaneously. She was not happy; the forest frightened her, her sweaty breathing, her sleepless torpor releasing worms.

The horses flicked away flies with their tails near an *amate* tree. The boy who had brought them walked up to Angel Face, hat in hand.

"Good morning—oh my, it's you. What are you doing here?"

"Working. Ever since you did me the favor of getting me out of the barracks nearly a year ago."

"How time flies."

"So it seems. Boss, the sun seems to be speeding up and the falcons have yet to fly over."

Angel Face asked Camila, who was paying the attendant for the bath, if she was ready to go.

"Whenever you like."

"But aren't you hungry? Don't you want to eat? Maybe the attendant will sell us something."

"A couple of eggs!" said the boy. He put his hand into his coat, which had more buttons than buttonholes, and took out three eggs wrapped in a handkerchief.

"Thank you," Camila said. "They look so fresh."

"Young lady, don't thank me. Yes, the eggs are really good. The hens laid them this morning and I told my wife, 'Put these aside. I want to bring them to Don Miguel.'"

They said goodbye to the attendant, who was wiping his crusty eyes again and eating black beans.

"I was thinking it would be good if the lady ate the eggs raw 'cause you're going far and she might get hungry."

"I don't eat raw eggs; they make me sick," Camila replied.

"It's just that the lady looks a bit weak."

"You're looking at someone who's been sick in bed for a long time."

"Yes," said Angel Face. "She's been quite sick."

"But now you're going to get better," said the boy, tightening the saddle girths. "Women, like flowers, need water. Your marriage will perk you up."

Camila lowered her lids and blushed, like a plant that finds eyes growing everywhere its leaves should be. She glanced at her husband and they both felt desire, sealing a silent pact that before had been missing.

XXXV

SONG OF SONGS

"What if fate had not brought us together," they said to each other. They felt afraid to test the fate of wanting each other the second they were apart. If they were close, they embraced; if they were in each other's arms already, they embraced more tightly, kissing and gazing into each other's eyes. If they thought about being happy together, they were enveloped by sheer forgetfulness, in blissful concert with trees swollen with sap and with the little bits of flesh wrapped in colorful plumage flying faster than sound.

But serpents studied the situation. If fate hadn't brought them together, would they have found happiness? The destruction of the useless, enchanting Paradise was brought to public auction in the infernal world; spying shadows and the vague voice of doubt sprouted from the damp vacuum of guilt while a calendar spun cobwebs in the corners of time.

Neither Miguel nor Camila could avoid going to the President's party that night in his country residence.

Their house seemed suddenly foreign to them. They didn't know what to do. They were sad to see themselves sitting on a sofa, by a mirror and other furniture, far removed from that wonderful world they had experienced during their first months of marriage. They felt sorry for each other, sorry and ashamed to be who they were.

The dining room clock struck on the hour, but they felt so far away that they would have to take a boat or a hot air balloon to get there. Yet they sat longer. . . .

They ate in silence, glancing at the clock's pendulum, whose ticking seemed to increase as the time for the party approached.

Feeling cold, Angel Face put on a frock coat and placed his arms in the sleeves like someone wrapping himself in a plantain leaf. Camila wanted to fold her napkin, but instead it folded her hands—she was a prisoner between table and chair, lacking the strength to take a first step. She pulled back her feet. The first step had been taken. Angel Face checked the time again and went to their bedroom for his gloves. His footfalls sounded as if in a cave. He mumbled something in a garbled voice. A minute later, he came back to the dining room with his wife's fan. He had forgotten what he had been looking for in the bedroom. Finally, he remembered, but he had already put on his gloves.

"Make sure all the lights are turned off and the doors locked. Then go to bed," Camila told the servants who watched them walk out to the alleyway.

They set off in a carriage, disappearing as their plump horses trotted in a river of jangling coins made by the harnesses. Camila sat deep in her seat under the weight of an oppressive drowsiness, the lights of the streetlamps deadening in her eyes. From time to time, the carriage pitched and lifted her from her seat; little jumps that interrupted her shifting body kept pace with the carriage. Angel Face's enemies believed he was no longer the President's confidant, insinuating that his Inner Circle now called him Miguel Canales, not Miguel Angel Face. Rocked by the flashing carriage wheels, Miguel savored in advance their surprise at seeing him at the party.

The carriage left the paved streets and went down a slope of sand as fine as air, tamping down the sound of noisy wheels. Camila was afraid; she saw nothing but stars in the blackness of the open country. She couldn't even hear the crickets in the damp night mist. Frightened, she flinched as if dragged by a path—or the illusion of a path—to her death, a hungry ravine to one side and Lucifer's wings stretching like a rock in the darkness on the other.

"What's wrong?" Angel Face asked, gently pulling her by the shoulders away from the carriage door.

"I'm afraid."

"Shush!"

"This man is going to flip over the carriage. Please ask him to slow down! Don't you feel what's happening? Open your mouth, say something to him."

"These carriages—" Angel Face began. But he stopped when he felt his wife squeeze his arm as the cab's springs jumped. It felt they were rolling down into a ravine.

"We're okay now," he assured her. "It's all right now . . . the wheels must have gone into a rut. . . ."

The wind screeched above the rocky summits like linen ripping. Angel Face stuck his head through the window to tell the driver to slow down. The latter turned his dark, pockmarked face toward him and slowed the horses to a funereal pace.

The carriage stopped at the edge of a village. A cloaked officer walked toward them, clicking his spurs; recognizing them, he let them proceed. The wind sighed across the dry, stumpy cornstalks. A cow's outline stood out in a corral. The trees were sleeping. Two hundred yards later, two more officers approached the carriage, also allowing them to pass. Their carriage continued until it reached the Presidential residence, where three colonels came toward it.

Angel Face (he was as good and evil as Satan) saluted the President's staff officers. The nostalgia for a warm home floated in the inexplicably vast night. A little lantern on the horizon marked where an artillery fort protected the President of the Republic.

Camila lowered her eyes to a man with a brow like Mephistopheles; his shoulders were hunched, his eyes mere slits, his legs long and thin. As they entered the residence, he lifted his arm slowly and opened a hand as if about to release a dove.

"Parthenius of Bethany," he began, "was taken prisoner in the Mithridatic wars and, once in Rome, taught the Alexandrine language. Propertius, Ovid, Virgil, Horace, and I learned it from him. . . ."

Two elderly women talked in the vestibule while the President greeted guests.

"Yes, yes," one said, passing a hand over her bun, "I've told him he must be reelected."

"And what did he answer you? I'm so curious. . . ."

"He only smiled, but I know he will be reelected. Candidita, he's the best president we have ever had. I need only mention that since he's been in power, my husband, Moncho, has made a very good living."

Behind the women, Teacher lectured a group of friends: "Whoever laughs last, laughs best, and wears a vest. . . ."

"The President wants to see you," the Judge Advocate said to people standing to his left and to his right. "The President wants to see you. He wants to see you!"

"Thank you!" Teacher answered.

"Thank you!" said a Black jockey with bowed legs and gold teeth, assuming the remark was meant for him.

Camila would've preferred to enter unseen, but this was impossible. Her exotic beauty—her vacant, inexpressive green eyes, her shapely body outlined by a white silk outfit, her small breasts, her graceful movement—drew attention. But mostly, it was because she was General Canales's daughter.

One woman remarked to the others, "She's a nothing. Any woman who doesn't wear a corset . . . You can see she's quite common. . . ."

"And whose wedding dress was altered to become a party dress," muttered another woman.

"Women who don't know how to behave do what they can!" added a lady with thinning hair.

"How mean we are! I only mentioned her dress to show how poor they are."

"Of course, they have no money, that's so obvious," said the woman with thinning hair. Then she whispered, "Rumor has it that the President hasn't given him anything since he married that thing!"

"But Angel Face is his confidant."

"Was! Everyone says—I didn't make it up—Angel Face abducted his wife to throw dust in the eyes of the police so that his father-in-law, the General, could escape. And that's how he got away!"

Camila and Angel Face advanced among the guests toward the President. His Excellency was conversing with a priest,

Father Irrefutable, among a group of women who forgot what they wanted to say as soon as the Leader arrived. There were bankers out on bail with suits pending against them; Jacobian secretaries who kept their eyes steadfast on the President, without the courage to greet him when he glanced at them. They dared not move away when he lowered his eyes. Village luminaries, with the torch of their political ideas smothered, still displayed a fleck of humanity in their dignified, offended small minds when they were treated like mice, not lions.

Angel Face approached the President to introduce his wife. The President gave Camila his cold little right hand and rested his eyes on her as he said her name, as if to say, *Take a look at who I am!* Meanwhile, the priest greeted a beauty who had the same name and appearance as Albanio's lover by reciting Garcilaso verses:

> Nature only once wanted to make
> A woman as beautiful as this
> Breaking the mold, for beauty's sake.

The servants served champagne, hors d'oeuvres, salted almonds, candies, and cigarettes. The champagne fired up the party and everything appeared as if in a dream, real in the mirrors and fake in the rooms, like the leafy sound of a crude instrument made from gourds.

"General," the President spoke. "Please escort the gentlemen out. I wish to eat only with the ladies. . . ."

The men left in small, silent groups through doors that opened to a cloudless night—some almost tripped to fulfill the Leader's orders, while others hid their anger in hurried steps. The women glanced at one another without daring to hide their feet under their chairs.

"The Poet can stay," the President proffered.

The officers shut the doors. With so many ladies, the Poet didn't know where to stand.

"Recite, Poet," the President commanded. "Recite something suitable, from the Song of Songs."

The Poet recited the only words of the poem that he could remember.

> Let him kiss me with the kisses of his mouth—
> I am dark, oh Daughters of Jerusalem
> As the curtains of Solomon.
> Do not long upon me that I am dark
> Because the sun has darkened me
>
> A bundle of myrrh is my lover to me
> That rests between my breasts
>
> I sat down under the shadow of desire
> And his fruit was sweet in my mouth
> He brought me to cellar of wine
> And the banner over me was love
>
> I call to you, oh maids of Jerusalem
> Don't awaken or let love flee
> Till she desires it
> Till she desires it
>
> How beautiful art thou, my love,
> Your eyes are like those of a dove,
> Your hair like a flock of goats,
> Your teeth like a flock of sheep,
> That rise up from the waters,
> All are twins
> And there is no barren woman among them.
>
> Sixty are queens and eighty are concubines

The President stood up with a funereal face. His footsteps echoed like those of a jaguar escaping over dry river stones. He disappeared through a door, shaking his shoulders as he drew the curtains apart and passed through.

Poet and audience, withered and empty, remained astonished as if in an atmospheric storm after the sun sets. A servant announced that dinner was served. The doors opened, and while the men waiting in the passageway came back in, shivering, the Poet approached Camila and invited her to dine with him. She was about to take his arm when a hand stopped her from behind. She almost screamed. Angel Face had been hiding in a curtain behind his wife; everyone saw him come out from his hiding place.

The marimba's wooden slats vibrated in time with the playing of the wooden pipes hanging like little coffins below them.

XXXVI

THE REVOLUTION

They couldn't see anything in front of them. Behind them slithered massive, silent reptiles, like paths battling one another in smooth, flowing, cold ripples. The ribs of the thin, dry earth could be counted by the parched swamps. Trees lifted thick branches, bursting with sap, to breathe above the forest. Bonfires lit up the eyes of tired horses. A soldier turned around to urinate. His legs couldn't be seen. Nobody explained why his companions cleaned their weapons with oil grease and bits of petticoats that still smelled of women. Death was taking them away one by one, withering them while laid up in bed, not helping their children or anyone else. It was better to risk your life and see what could happen. Bullets feel nothing when they pierce a man's body; they think that the flesh is air, warm and sweet, perhaps a little plump. They whistle like birds. It was time to take stock, but nobody did. The revolutionaries were busy sharpening machetes they'd bought in a hardware store that had burned down. The sharpened edge appeared slowly, like laughter on a Black man's face.

"Sing, comrade," a voice rang out. "I heard you singing a little while ago!"

> Why did you court me,
> Ingrate, already having a girl
> Better to have left me alone
> To be cut down for firewood.

"Keep singing, comrade."

> *The party on the lagoon*
> *Caught us off-guard*
> *No moon shone this year*
> *And no people showed up.*

"Sing on, comrade!"

> *The day you were born,*
> *Was the day I was born*
> *There was such a party in heaven*
> *That even Daddy God joined.*

"Sing, little comrade, sing!"

The landscape took on the quinine color of the moon, and the leaves shivered. The soldiers waited in vain for the order to advance. The sound of a dog barking indicated the spot where an invisible village stood. It was daybreak. The immobilized troops, ready to attack the first garrison, felt a weird underground force steal away their speed, turning them into stone. The rain turned everything to mush on that sunless morning. It ran down the soldiers' faces and bare backs. Everything was much louder when God wept.

The first news came in bits and pieces and seemed contradictory—whispering voices so afraid of the truth that they withheld all they knew. Something hardened deeply in the soldiers' hearts: an iron ball, a bone splinter. The whole camp bled like a single wound: General Canales was dead. The news formed in syllables and sentences, syllables from a spelling book. Sentences from Funeral Services. Cigarettes and moonshine tainted by gunpowder and curses. It was impossible to believe it, even if true. The older soldiers were quiet, impatient to hear the truth—some of them stood, others lay down or curled up—they threw their straw hats onto the ground and scratched their heads endlessly. The younger soldiers rushed down ravines to get more information. The echoing of the sun drove them crazy. A flock of birds circled in the distance. From time to time, a bullet rang out. Soon it was evening—a sky blistering under the torn cloak of clouds. Campfires were put out. Everything—sky, earth, animals, and men—became absorbed in a solitary darkness. A galloping horse broke the silence with a multiplying clippity-clop, clippity-clop of hooves. From sentry to sentry, the hoofbeats loudened until they finally arrived in their midst; they were dreaming awake when they heard what the rider told them. General Canales had died, just after eating, on his way to lead his troops. Now they were ordered to wait.

"They must have poisoned him with *chiltepe* root. It leaves no trace. How strange for him to die just now," one man said.

"He should've been more careful," another voice said, sighing.

"Ahhhh!" They were deeply upset, their bare heels glued to the ground. "What about his daughter?"

After a long, unpleasant pause, another voice added: "I'll damn her if you'd like! A witch doctor once taught me a curse when we ran out of corn in the mountains and had to go to the coast to buy more. Should I?"

"Sure, why not?" came another voice out of the shadows. "As far as I know, she killed her father."

The horse galloped down the path again—clippity-clop, clippity-clop, clippity-clop. Sentries shouted again, followed by silence. Coyote howls rose like a double staircase to the haloed moon. Another boom sounded.

As everyone repeated what had happened, General Canales came out of his grave to die again: He sat down to eat by lantern at a bare table. You could hear the sound of cutlery, plates, the General's feet moving. He served himself a glass of water, spread out a newspaper, and . . . no other sound was heard, not even a groan. They found him dead on the table, his cheek flat against the newspaper *El Nacional*, his glassy, half-open eyes staring at something that wasn't there.

The men went unhappily back to their daily chores. Tired of living like domesticated animals, they had joined the revolution of Chamarrita—as they affectionately called Canales—to change their lives, and because the General had offered to give back lands that had been stolen from them on the pretext of abolishing communal plots. He offered to share the water supply equally; to do away with punishing them in stockades; to require that everyone receive free tortillas for a minimum of two years; to form farming cooperatives to provide better seeds, imported machinery, purebred livestock, fertilizers, and technicians. To improve and reduce the cost of transportation. To facilitate the export and sale of goods. To empower individuals elected by, and directly responsible to, them, the people. To abolish private schools, institute a graduated income tax, make medicines cheaper, unionize doctors and lawyers, and grant religious freedom to the Indians so that they could worship their own gods without persecution.

Camila heard of her father's death days later, when a stranger telephoned.

"Your father died reading a newspaper article that said that the President was a witness at your wedding."

"That's not true!" she screamed.

"What's not true?" sneered the voice.

"It's not true. He wasn't a witness. . . . Hello? Hello?" The call was disconnected. The caller had put the receiver down very slowly, like someone secretly listening to a conversation. "Hello! Hello! Hello!"

She sank into a wicker chair, feeling nothing. A little while later, she was able to stand up, but everything had changed—color and mood were different. Dead! Dead! Dead! She brought her hands together as if to strike something, then broke into laughter. Her jaws froze and her green eyes welled up.

A water cart went down the street—tears flowed down its spout, and its metal tanks were laughing.

XXXVII

TOHIL'S DANCE

"What can I get you, gentlemen?"

"A beer."

"Whiskey for me!"

"And a brandy for me!"

"So that's—"

"A beer."

"A whiskey and a brandy."

"And some snacks."

"So that's a beer, a whiskey, a brandy, and some snacks. . . ."

"And what about me, guys?" Angel Face said as he returned, buttoning his fly.

"What'll you have?

"Bring me anything. A highball . . ."

"Okay . . . so it's a beer, a whiskey, a brandy, and a highball."

Angel Face pulled up his chair and sat down next to a man well over six feet tall who looked and gestured like a Black man despite being white. His back was straight as a poker, his hands a pair of anvils. There was a scar between his blond eyebrows.

"Mr. Gengis, make room for me," he said. "I want to sit right next to you."

"With pleasure, sir."

"I'll just finish my drink and head off—my boss is waiting for me."

"Okay," said Mr. Gengis. "Since you're meeting the President, you need to stop being a damn fool and tell him that the rumors about you aren't true, aren't true at all."

"That goes without saying," said the man who had ordered the brandy.

"You're right!'" Angel Face said to Mr. Gengis.

"I'd say that to anyone!" exclaimed the American, banging his open hands on the marble table. "Of course! I was there that night and heard with my own ears what the Judge Advocate said—that you were against his reelection and supported the revolution like the late General Canales."

Angel Face did a poor job of hiding his discomfort. Given the way things were, it was foolish to go meet with the President.

The waiter brought the drinks. He wore a white apron that had the word "Gambrinus" embroidered with red thread on it. "That's one whiskey . . . a beer. . . ."

Mr. Gengis downed his whiskey in one shot, without blinking, as if taking a laxative. Then he took out his pipe and filled it with tobacco. "Yes, my friend. These things have a way of reaching the President's ears when you least expect it. That's no fun. This is your chance to make a clean breast of it. I know it's a minefield."

"Thanks for the advice, Mr. Gengis. I'll hire a carriage to get there faster. I'll see you all a bit later."

Mr. Gengis lit his pipe.

"How many whiskeys have you had, Mr. Gengis?" asked one of the men at the table.

"Eight—een!" answered the American, pipe in his mouth, one eye half open and the other one bluer than blue above the match's yellow flame.

"You're so right. Whiskey is amazing!"

"God knows. I couldn't say. Better ask those who don't drink it like me, out of pure desperation!"

"Don't say that, Mr. Gengis!"

"Why not? That's how I feel. In my country everyone says exactly what they think!"

"That's a fine quality."

"Not really. I prefer things here: to say what you don't think as long as it sounds good!"

"So that means that in your country, you don't make things up."

"Absolutely not. All the tall tales are divinely told in the Bible!"

"Another whiskey, Mr. Gengis?"

"Yes, I think I'll have another whiskey!"

"Bravo! That's how I like it! A man willing to die for his beliefs!"

"*Comment?*"

"My friend says you're one of those willing to die—"

"Now I understand. I am not willing to die, but rather willing to live for my beliefs. I'm very much alive. Dying isn't important. I'll die when God wants me to."

"What Mr. Gengis would like is for whiskey to pour from the sky!"

"No. No. Why would I want that? Then they wouldn't sell umbrellas as umbrellas but as funnels." He paused for a moment, his face filled with pipe smoke and his breathing cottony. Everyone laughed. "This Angel Face is a good kid, but if he doesn't do as I say, he won't ever be forgiven and he'll end up in a shithole."

A group of men came, suddenly and silently, into the bar. They were so numerous that the door wasn't wide enough for all of them to enter simultaneously. Most of them stood between tables or by the counter. They were just passing through, so didn't need to sit.

"Shut up," one of them said. He was a rather short, rather old, rather bald, rather crazy, rather hoarse, and rather dirty man. He was helped by two others in gluing a printed poster on one of the bar mirrors using black wax.

FELLOW CITIZENS: *By merely uttering the name of the President of the Republic, we shed light on the Sacred Interests of our Nation with the Torch of Peace. Under his wise rule, he has conquered and will continue to conquer the Inestimable Benefits of Progress at all levels and of Order in all forms of progress!!! As free citizens, conscious of our obligation to watch over our own destiny, which coincides with that of our Nation, and as men of goodwill opposed to Anarchy, we do PROCLAIM that the health of our Republic depends upon*

THE REELECTION OF OUR ILLUSTRIOUS RULER
AND ON NOTHING ELSE BUT HIS REELECTION!
Why would we risk sending our Ship of State into uncharted
waters, when we already have as our captain the most
accomplished Statesman of our times, whom History will
judge to be the Greatest of the Great, the Wisest of the Wise, a
Liberal, a Thinker, and Democrat??? Just to imagine someone
other than Him in this supreme position is a challenge to the
Destiny of the Nation, which is also our own destiny. Whoever
dares to challenge—if there were to be anyone—deserves to be
imprisoned as a dangerous madman. If he weren't altogether
mad, he would be judged a traitor to the Nation in accordance
with the laws of the land!! FELLOW CITIZENS!! THE
BALLOT BOX AWAITS YOU!! VOTE!! FOR!! OUR!!
CANDIDATE!! WHO!! WILL BE!! REELECTED!!
BY!! THE PEOPLE!!!

Reading this notice aloud aroused universal acclaim in the bar; there were shouts, applause, screams. In response to the general acclaim, a sloppily dressed man with long black hair and cloudy eyes answered:

"Patriots, as a Poet I consider my tongue to be that of a patriotic citizen. A Poet is a man who created the sky; thus, I speak to you as the creator of that useless but beautiful thing we call the sky. Please listen to my disorganized gibberish! When that German who was not understood by his fellow Germans spoke—no, I don't mean Goethe, Kant, or Schopenhauer—about the Superman, he was undoubtedly predicting that the Heavenly Father and Mother Earth would be born in the heart of America, the first truly superior man who has ever existed. I am talking, my fellow citizens, about that Balladeer of the Dawns which the Nation calls All-Deserving, Party Chief, and the Protector of Our Scholarly Youth. Naturally, I am referring to the Constitutional President of the Republic, which all of you no doubt realize is Nietzsche's prototype, the Superman. . . . I say and repeat it here from this highest of lecterns."

As he spoke, he banged his fist against the bar counter. "And so, fellow citizens, even though I am not among those who have made politics a field of endeavor, nor one of those who they say invented Chinese parsley for having memorized the deeds of King Chilperic I—it is my disinterested, wholehearted, and honest belief that, as long as there is no other hyper Superman, Super Citizen among us, only being crazy or blind, blind or crazily bound, would we allow for the reins of government to pass from the hands of this uniquely Super Charioteer who now and forever guides the chariot of our beloved country, to another citizen, an ordinary citizen, fellow citizens, who even if he had all the greatest qualities on earth, would still only remain a mere man. Democracy brought emperors and kings to their end in old and tired Europe, but it is more important to recognize, and we do recognize this, that now when it has been transplanted to America, it takes on the almost divine form of the Superman and gives form to a new kind of government: the Super Democracy. And, therefore, gentlemen, I will now have the pleasure of reciting . . ."

"Recite, dear poet," a voice cried out, "anything but an ode."

"My Nocturne in C Major to the Super-Duperman!"

The Poet's wondrous words were followed by other impassioned speakers attacking the vile party, San Juan's dentures, the abracadabra magical speller, and other theological suppositories. Someone in the audience developed a nosebleed and shouted between speeches for someone to bring him a new brick soaked in water so that he could smell it to stop the hemorrhaging.

"By now," Mr. Gengis said, "Angel Face is between a wall and the President. I like how this poet recited, but I think it must be quite sad to be a poet; and yet, being a lawyer must be the saddest thing in the world. It's time to drink another whiskey! Another whiskey for this super-hyper-rail-almost-roader!"

Angel Face ran into the Minister of War as he was leaving Gambrinus. "Where are you off to, General?"

"To see the boss."

"Then let's go together."

"Is that where you're going? My carriage should be here in a minute. Between you and me, I've just been with a widow—"

"I know that you love the merry widows, General."

"Not the waltz!"

"I wasn't talking about music, but about Veuve Clicquot!"

"Not the champagne, but the Widow Clicquot! The final act of flesh and blood!"

"Damn!"

The carriage rolled down the street silently, on paper-blotter wheels. Policemen were posted at the street corners passing along the news: "The Minister of War is coming, the Minister of War is coming."

The President paced back and forth in his office. His hat was pulled down over his forehead, his coat collar turned up over his scarf, and his vest unbuttoned. Black suit, black hat, black boots.

"How's the weather, General?"

"It's a bit cool."

"Miguel isn't wearing a coat?"

"Mr. President . . ."

"Shush! You're shivering and you're telling me you aren't cold? That's not very smart. General, send someone to Miguel's house to get him his coat."

The Minister of War saluted and went out—his sword almost fell to the ground—while the President sat down on a wicker sofa. He pointed for Angel Face to sit in the chair next to him.

"Miguel, I've got to do everything myself here, be involved in everything, because I have to govern a country full of people who are all talk and no action," he said. "And I have to depend on friends to do what I can't do by myself." He paused for a second. "The people who talk the talk are always planning to do or undo something, but because they lack will-power, in the end they do nothing—which neither stinks nor smells good, like parrot shit. That's why the industrialist spends his whole day repeating: *I'm going to build a new factory; I'm going to buy new machines; I'm going to do this, or do that, on and on and on.* And the farmer says: *I'm going to plant a new crop or I'm going to export my goods.* And the writer says: *I'm going to write a book.* The teacher: *I'm going to open a school.* The businessman: *I'm going to start a new business.* And the journalists—those pigs who have fatback instead of souls—*we're going to improve the country.* And just as I said a moment ago, nobody does a damn thing and, naturally, I, the President of the Republic, have to do everything, even if it comes out wrong. You might as well say that if it weren't for me, there'd be no riches, since I'm forced to play out the role of blind Justice in the lottery!"

He stroked his gray moustache with his transparent, delicate, straw-colored fingers. He then changed tone: "This is all to say that I am obliged by circumstances to make use of the services of people like you who are valuable near me, but even more valuable outside the country where my enemies scheme, plot, and pen articles against me, putting my reelection in jeopardy. . . ."

He let his eyes drop like two dazed mosquitoes drunk with blood. He went on, "I don't mean Canales and his followers: death has always been, and will always be, Miguel, my most trusted ally. I mean those trying to influence US opinion for Washington to abandon me. When a caged animal begins to lose its hair, is it time to get rid of him? All right! Am I an old man whose brain is pickled and whose heart is harder than flint? Traitors can say what they want. But that the people should, for political reasons, take advantage of what I've done to save the country from these thieves, these sons of bitches, that's what galls me most. My reelection is in jeopardy and that's why I've sent for you. I need you to go to Washington and give a full report of what's going on in this cesspool of hatred, where the only good guy, as in all burials, is the dead man."

"Mr. President," stammered Angel Face, caught between Mr. Gengis's advice to put all his cards on the table and the fear of losing, through some indiscretion, an assignment that he recognized from the start might be his salvation. "The President knows I am at his service unconditionally for whatever he wants. But if the President will permit me to speak, since I have always wanted to be the last, but the most loyal and faithful, of his servants. Before undertaking this delicate mission, if the President doesn't object, would he mind investigating the truth of the unfounded charges that the Judge Advocate is leveling at me: that I am your enemy?"

"But who listens to that nonsense?"

"The President can in no way doubt my unconditional support for him and his government. Still I wouldn't want him to bestow confidence in me without knowing if the Judge Advocate's accusations are true or not."

"Miguel, stop it! I'm not asking you to tell me what I should do! I am well aware of what's going on and I have here in my possession, on this desk, the charges he brought against you when General Canales fled. I know that the Judge Advocate hates you for something you don't know about: the Judge Advocate and the police planned to abduct the woman who is now your wife and sell her off to the owner of a house of prostitution from whom he received, as you might know, ten thousand pesos. The woman who paid the price for your wife's freedom is a poor creature who has gone completely crazy."

Angel Face sat still, careful not to show his boss what he might be thinking. He buried his feelings in his heart and behind his black, velvety eyes. He remained as colorless and cold as a wicker chair.

"If the President will permit me, I would prefer to stay here at his side and defend him with my own blood."

"You won't accept my proposal?"

"Absolutely not, Mr. President."

"So then all this has been a waste. The newspapers will publish tomorrow the news of your impending departure. You can't back out now. The Minister of War has been ordered to deliver to you the necessary funds to undertake this journey. I will send the money to the station with my instructions."

Angel Face heard an underground clock marking the passage of fatal hours. Through a wide-open window, between black eyebrows, he saw a fire burning next to a greenish-black cypress grove. Walls of white smoke shrouded a courtyard almost blotted out by the night. Groups of sentries stood under the first light of the stars. Four priestly shadows stood at the

courtyard corners, dressed like watery mosses that could predict the future—all four had toad-skin hands more green than
yellow; each had one eye closed on the dark side of the face
and one eye open, finished in lime skin and chewed by darkness. Suddenly a drumbeat sounded—boom, boom, boom—
and men dressed as animals came leaping in corn rows. Down
the branches of the boom, bloodied and vibrating, came crabs
falling from air tombs and worms running from fire tombs.
Men danced so as not to be glued to the earth with the drumbeat or glued to the wind with a sounding drum, feeding the
fire with the turpentine of their foreheads. From the stool-
colored darkness came a little man with a wrinkled squash
face, a tongue between his cheeks, thorns on his forehead, no
ears, and a velvety cord wrapped around his navel adorned
with the heads of warriors and calabash leaves. He blew on
the flames, and, to the delight of the blind opossums, he stole
the fire and chewed it in his mouth like *copal* so as not to burn
himself. A cry from the darkness enveloped the trees. Near
and far could be heard the mournful cries of tribes lost in the
woods, blind from birth, fighting with all their guts—animals
of hunger—their throats—birds of thirst—and their fears,
their nausea and physical needs, complaining to Tohil, the
Giver of Fire, to return the ocote torch lit by the light. Tohil
arrived on a river made of the breasts of doves that flowed like
milk. Deer ran so that the water wouldn't stop flowing—deer
with horns finer than the rain and little hooves that turned
into air on the avian sands. Birds with bones finer than their
own plumes ran to preserve the water's wavering reflection.
Ratatat, ratatat, echoed from beneath the earth.

Tohil demanded human sacrifice. The tribes brought their
best hunters to him, those with straight pea-shooters, those
with slingshots loaded with seeds.

"And do these men hunt other men?" Tohil asked.

Ratatatat! Ratat-tat, echoed beneath the earth. "Whatever
you require," the tribes answered. "As long as you, Giver of
the Flame, return fire to us so that our flesh—the mishmash of
our bones—our air, our nails, our tongue, or our hair will

never freeze again! As long as life stops dying, even if we slit our throats so death will continue to live!"

"This pleases me," Tohil answered. Rat-a-tat! Rat-a-tat, echoed the earth. "I am pleased. I can prevail over hunters of men. There will never be true death or true life! Now dance the *jicara* for me!"

And each hunter-warrior blew his gourd, without breathing, to the beat of the drum, the echoing, the drum of the tombs that set Tohil's eyes dancing.

Angel Face said goodbye to the President after this baffling vision. As he left, the Minister of War called him over and gave him a wad of bills and his coat.

"Aren't you coming, General?" he squeaked.

"If I could . . . Let me catch up with you later, or maybe I'll see you another day. I have to stay here for now, you see." He twisted his head over his right shoulder, listening to his boss's voice.

XXXVIII

THE JOURNEY

A river ran over the roof as Camila packed his trunk. It didn't flow inside the house but drained much farther away, in the wide expanse leading to the countryside or perhaps in the ocean. A fistful of wind opened the window; water rushed in as if the glass had been shattered to bits. The curtains and loose papers rustled about, and the doors banged on their hinges. Still, Camila continued packing. The spaces she was filling in the trunks isolated her, and though the storm threw pricks of lightning onto her hair, she felt nothing complete or different. Everything remained the same: empty, disconnected, weightless, without body or soul—just like her.

"What do you think?" Angel Face asked, shutting the window. "Is it better to live near or far from this monster? That's just what I want! But perhaps I'm only running away!"

"But after what you told me last night about those crazy witch doctors dancing in his house—"

"It wasn't that bad!" A thunderclap silenced him. "Anyway, what could they possibly predict? He's sending me to Washington, after all. He's covering my expenses! Maybe when I get far enough away, things will look different. Anything's possible. You can join me on the pretext that one of us is sick. Then he can come looking for us both any way he likes!"

"And if he doesn't let me go?"

"Well, then I'll come back and keep my mouth shut. We will be no worse off than before, don't you think? Nothing ventured, nothing gained."

"You think everything's simple."

"With the money we'll have, we can live anywhere. I mean

live, really live, not just go on repeating the same old thing: I think with the President's mind, therefore I exist; I think with the President's mind, therefore I am. . . ."

Camila gazed at him tearfully, her mouth full of hair, her ears full of rain.

"What are you crying about? Please don't cry."

"What else can I do?"

"Women always do the same thing!"

"Leave me alone."

"For the love of God: you're going to get sick if you keep crying."

"Leave me alone!"

"You act as if I'm about to die or be buried alive!"

"Leave me alone!"

Angel Face held her in his arms. Two tears, hot as nails difficult to pull out, twisted their way down his rough, masculine cheeks, so unused to crying.

"But you'll write to me . . . ," Camila said.

"Of course."

"As often as you can. We have never been apart. Write to me every day—it will be sheer torture for days to pass without news of you. . . . And be careful! Don't confide in anyone, do you hear me? Don't trust what anyone says, especially any other compatriot—they can't be trusted. . . . But what I most want"—her husband's kisses interrupted her words—"what I most want is . . . for . . . you . . . to write to me!"

Angel Face closed the trunk, not taking his eyes off his wife's adoring and foolish eyes. It was raining buckets; water ran through the gutters like heavy chains.

They were overwhelmed by the distressing thought of the next day, so close by. Without saying a word—everything was ready—they took off their clothes and got into bed, listening to the ticking clock splice their few remaining hours—clippety-clack, clickety-clack—and the buzzing of mosquitoes that kept them from sleeping.

"I just remembered that I forgot to tell them to close the windows so the mosquitoes wouldn't come in. How stupid of me!"

Angel Face answered by pressing her against his chest; she was a baby lamb too helpless even to bleat.

They didn't dare turn off the light, close their eyes, or say a single word. They were so close in the bright light: the voice of talkers creates a distance, eyelids serve only to keep people apart. . . . Darkness was the same thing as being away from each other, and with all that they wanted to say on that last night, no matter how many times they said it, it all would have seemed like mere telegrams.

The noise of servants chasing a hen among the seedbeds filled the courtyard. The rain had stopped; everywhere, water dripped like sand in an hourglass. The hen scurried, crouched, then fluttered away, trying to escape death.

"My sweet little pebble," Angel Face whispered in her ear, smoothing her round stomach with the palm of his hand.

"My love," she answered, pressing her body against his. Beneath the sheets, her legs looked like oars resting on the waters of a bottomless river.

The servants kept running. Shouting. The hen kept slipping out of their hands, shaking and frightened, with its eyes popping, its beak open, its wings spread out like a cross, and its breathing reduced to a thread.

Their bodies were braided, their trembling fingers sprinkling caresses, between dying and sleeping, atmospheric, formless. . . .

"My love!" she said to him.

"My life," he said.

"My life," she repeated back to him.

The hen bumped into a wall or a wall came tumbling down on her—both things happened at once. They wrung her neck. She flapped her wings as if, though dead, she could fly.

"The poor thing crapped all over herself," the cook screamed. Shaking off the feathers dirtying her apron, she went to wash her hands in the fountain now filled with rainwater.

Camila closed her eyes. . . . The weight of her husband's body . . . the flapping of wings . . . the stain . . .

The clock ticked more slowly: tick-tock, tick-tock! Tick-tock! Tick-tock . . .

Angel Face quickly scanned the papers an officer had brought
him at the train station on the President's orders. The city
scratched the sky with the dirty nails of rooftops that faded
farther back. The document calmed him down. He felt lucky
to have wads of money in his pockets, porters catering to him
in a first-class car . . . and to be far away from that man and all
his spying! He half-closed his eyes, trying to concentrate on
his thoughts. The fields came alive as the train passed; they
seemed to be chasing after one another like children: trees,
houses, bridges. . . .

How lucky to be so far away from that man, in a first-class
compartment!

One after the other, one after the other, one after the
other . . . the house chased the tree, the tree the fence, the fence
a bridge, the bridge the road, the road a river, a river the mountain, the mountain a cloud, a cloud the planted fields, the
planted fields the farmworker, the farmworker the animal. . . .

. . . Porters waiting hand and foot, no one spying on him . . .

. . . The animal chasing the house, the house the tree, the tree
the fence, the fence the bridge, the bridge the road, the road the
river, the river the mountain, the mountain the cloud . . .

The reflections of a village ran along the clear surface of a
river and the dark outline of a small owl . . .

. . . The cloud chasing planted fields, planted fields the farmworker, the farmworker the animal, the animal . . .

. . . Without someone spying on him, with money in his
pockets . . .

. . . The animal chasing the house, the house the tree, the
tree the fence, the fence . . .

. . . And with lots of money in his pocket!

A bridge flashed past the mouth of the windows like a violin
bow . . . light and shadow, scales, flecks of iron, wings of swallows. . . .

. . . The fence chased the bridge, the bridge the road, the
road the river, the river the mountain, the mountain. . . .

Angel Face let his head drop onto the cane headrest. His

sleepy eyes followed the flat, hot, unchanging coastal low-lands. He had the confused sensation of being on a train, of not being on a train, of being left behind by a train, behind a train, farther behind a train, each time farther back, each time farther back, each time farther back, still farther behind, each time, each time, each time, each time, time, time. . . .

Suddenly he opened his eyes. He had slept the fitful sleep of a fugitive, jittery like someone who knows that even the air he breathes is a colander of dangers. It felt as if he had found his seat by jumping into the train through an invisible hole—his neck aching, his face in a sweat, and a cloud of flies on his fore-head.

The layered clouds were motionless, swollen from drinking water from the sea. Nails of lightning hid in the gray plush of thunderheads gathering above the vegetation.

A seemingly uninhabited village of toffee-colored houses came into view, then disappeared. Corn husks dried between its church and its cemetery. "Had I the faith that built this church and cemetery—faith and the dead are the only living things." The happiness of an escaping person misted his eyes. This country with a predictable springtime was his country, his mother, his tenderness, and no matter how much leaving these villages behind might bring him back to life, he would always be a dead man among the living while far from them, eclipsed by people and the invisible presence of crosslike trees and gravestone rocks.

Station followed station. The train sped without stopping, rattling over poorly laid tracks. Here a whistle, there a grind-ing of brakes, and farther on a crown of dirty smoke at the top of a hill. The passengers fanned themselves with hats, newspa-pers, even their handkerchiefs—they were suspended in the hot air formed by the thousands of droplets of sweat their bodies released. They were tired of uncomfortable seats, noise, their own clothes itching as if sewn with little insect feet that hopped all over their skin. Their heads itched as if their hair walked on their scalps. The passengers were as thirsty as if they'd taken purgatives. They were sadder than death.

Dusk followed the merciless light. The suffering rains squeezed out of the clouds and the horizon seemed to fill with holes. Way off in the distance, sardines in blue oil glowed inside a can.

A railroad employee went by lighting the compartment lanterns. Angel Face put on his coat and tie and glanced at his watch. In twenty minutes they would reach the port—a century for him, he was so impatient to be safe and sound on a ship. He pressed his face against the window, trying to distinguish in the darkness anything smelling of vegetation. He heard a river gurgling, then a bit farther, maybe the same river again. . . .

The train slowed to a crawl when it reached a town whose streets spread like hammocks in the darkness. The second-class passengers disembarked carrying bundles of cloth, but the train continued until it reached the wharves where waves broke. The unclear light of the Customs Buildings, which stank of tar, came into view. He could feel the drowsy breathing of millions of sweet and sour things. . . .

Angel Face greeted from afar the Port Commander at the station. It was Major Farfán! At such a difficult moment, he was overjoyed to see a friend who owed him his life. "Major Farfán!"

Farfán waved to him and told him through the compartment window not to worry about his luggage. A couple of soldiers would soon be there to take his trunks to the ship. When the train finally stopped, he came aboard and shook Angel Face's hand forcefully. The other passengers simply hurried off.

"Well, what's new with you? How are you?"

"And you, my dear major? Although I needn't ask—I can see it on your face. . . ."

"The President wired me to look after you and help with whatever you need, sir."

"How kind of you, major!"

The car emptied in a flash. Farfán stuck his head out a window and shouted: "Lieutenant, make sure someone gets his luggage. What's the holdup?"

As soon as he spoke, a group of armed soldiers appeared. Angel Face realized too late that he was trapped.

"On the President's orders," Farfán said, with gun in hand, "I am arresting you."

"But, major! If the President . . . It's not possible . . . come . . . let's go . . . let's go together . . . please come . . . let me . . . let me send a telegram!"

"My orders are explicit, Don Miguel. You'd better come quietly!"

"Of course, but I can't miss my boat. I'm on a mission, and I can't—"

"Quiet, please! Give me all your things!"

"Farfán!"

"Hand them over!"

"Listen to me, major!"

"Easy now, let's not make a fuss!"

"Listen to me, major!"

"Let's stop this charade!"

"I'm on the President's top-secret mission . . . if something goes wrong, you'll answer for it!"

"Sergeant, please search this man. Show him who's in charge here."

A man with a face hidden behind a handkerchief appeared from the shadows. He was as tall, pale, and sandy-haired as Angel Face himself. He took possession of his things (passport, cash, cuff links, handkerchiefs, wedding ring engraved with his wife's name and slipped off his finger with a bit of spit). Then he quickly disappeared.

The ship's horn sounded much later. Angel Face covered his ears with his hands. His tears blinded him. He wanted to break down the door, escape, run, fly, cross the ocean, not be the man staying behind! What a muddy river running under his skin, what a burning itch to become that other man, the one traveling to New York with his luggage and his name on Cabin 17.

XXXIX

THE PORT

In the lull before the tide changed, everything was quiet except the crickets—damp with sea spray and ash from the stars on their forewings—the reflection of the lighthouse like a safety pin lost in the darkness, and the prisoner pacing back and forth, hair falling over his forehead, his clothes messy, unable to sit down. He gestured like a man trying to fend off enemies in his sleep, between ohs, ahs, and mumbled words, dragged down by God's hand toward his inevitable doom: open sores, cold-blooded crimes, awaking disemboweled to a sudden death.

"Farfán is my only hope here," he kept repeating. "I'm lucky he's in charge. For all Camila knows, I was shot twice, buried, and left this world untroubled."

The pounding sounded like two feet hammering the floor all along the stopped train car. Soldiers guarded all the tracks. His mind was elsewhere, recalling the little towns the train had passed in the muck of darkness, in the blinding dust of his sunny days, eaten by the fear of church and cemetery, church and cemetery, church and cemetery. Nothing survived but faith and the dead!

The garrison clock struck once. Spiders shook. It was past eleven thirty and the minute hand inched toward a quarter to twelve.

Dead tired, Major Farfán sheathed his right arm, then his left, in his combat jacket. With equal slowness, he began to button it, starting at the navel, without noticing anything: a map of the republic in the shape of a yawn, a towel with dried snot and sleeping flies, a turtle, a rifle, some saddlebags . . .

button by button until he reached the collar. When he got there, he lifted his head. His eyes landed upon something he couldn't look at without saluting: a portrait of the President.

He finished buttoning, farted, and lit a cigarette with the kerosene lamp. He grabbed his riding crop and went into the streets. The soldiers didn't sense his passing; they slept on the ground, wrapped in ponchos, like mummies; sentries greeted him with their rifles and the guard's officer stood up to spit out a worm of ash, all that was left of a cigarette in his drowsy lips. He barely had the chance to flick it backward with the same hand with which he saluted: "Nothing to report, sir!"

Rivers flowed into the ocean like cat whiskers into a saucer of milk. The liquid shadow of trees, the weight of comical alligators, the heat of swampy windows, mashed weeping—it all flowed seaward.

A man with a lantern walked toward Farfán as he entered the train car. Two smiling soldiers worked together to bind the prisoner. They shackled him on Farfán's orders and dragged him into town, followed by soldiers guarding the carriage. Both by voice and gesture, the major demanded obedience from the soldiers, who separately treated him poorly. Angel Face didn't resist; he'd come up with a plan that might be useful later, when he was in the station, without committing himself beforehand. But they didn't bring him to headquarters. As they left the station, they followed a distant track to a wagon with a shit-covered floor. They lifted him up and struck him, as if obeying previous orders.

"Why are they hitting me, Farfán?" he asked the major, who was talking with the man holding the lantern.

His answer was another blow. Turning around, they hit him on the head. His ear bled and he collapsed on all fours in the pile of shit.

He spat out the excrement; blood dripped from his clothes as he tried to protest.

"Shut up! Shut up!" Farfán shouted, lifting his whip.

"Major Farfán!" Angel Face said boldly, not aware of what he was doing. The air smelled of blood.

Farfán was afraid of what he was going to say and hit him

with a whip. The stroke left a mark on Angel Face's cheek. With a knee on the ground, he tried to unbind his hands from the back. "I see . . . ," he said with a trembling and shaking voice. "I see. . . . This will earn you another stripe—"

"Shut up, I said!" Farfán threatened, lifting the whip again. The man with the lantern grabbed his arm.

"Hit me, don't stop now. I'm not afraid. A whip is the weapon of sissies. . . ."

Two, three, four, five lashes fell on the prisoner's face in less than a second.

"Major, easy now, easy now!" said the man with the lantern.

"No, no! I have to make this son of a bitch eat dust. . . . What he said about the army is no light matter! Crook! Shitty crook!" The whip broke, so he hit him with the pistol butt, ripping hair and flesh from his head. At every blow, he repeated in a stifled voice, ". . . army . . . orders . . . you piece of shit . . . take that. . . ."

The victim's lifeless, shit-covered body was carried from one end of the track to the other while the cargo train to the capital was preparing to leave.

"The first time I tried to join the Secret Police," said the man with the lantern "a buddy named Lucio Vásquez—nicknamed Velvet—tried to help me."

"I've heard of him," the major said.

"But it didn't work out, even though he was tight with everyone. Velvet, get it? Smooth . . . and all I got was a prison term and I lost a ton of money that my wife—I was married back then—and I had invested in a small business. My wife, poor thing, was even thrown into the Sweet Enchantment. . . ."

Farfán stirred at hearing the brothel's name. Piggy—who often stank of sex like a latrine—had once excited him, but now left him cold. He felt he was swimming underwater, battling an Angel Face repeating over and over: "Another stripe! Another stripe!"

"What was your wife's name? I gotta tell you, I knew most of the girls there. . . ."

"It won't matter 'cause she just came and went. Our little baby died and that made her go crazy. See, when something doesn't work out . . . Now she works in the hospital laundry helping the nuns. She wasn't cut out to be a whore!"

"Well, I think I knew her. I knew her well enough to get permission for her to go to the baby's wake at Doña Chón's. I had no idea that little baby was yours!"

"I was in the clink, totally fucked up, without a cent to my name. . . . Really, whenever I look back at all that's happened, I just want to take to my heels and run for my life!"

"And I didn't know anything until a fucking bitch fed the President a bunch of lies about me . . ."

"And this Angel Face was in cahoots with General Canales; he was all lovey-dovey with his daughter, who then became his wife, so said some people. He refused to carry out the President's orders. I know all this because Vásquez—Velvet—met him in a tavern called the Two Step, just hours before General Canales's escape."

"The Two Step," repeated the major, suddenly remembering.

"It was a tavern right there, just on the corner. Oh yeah! They had two marionettes painted on the wall. On each side of the door. A woman and a man. The woman with a twisted arm—I still remember the sign—saying to the man, 'Come dance the Two Step.' And the man with a bottle in his hand saying: 'No, thanks. I prefer the Bottle Dance!' "

The train pulled away slowly. A patch of sunlight rose above the blue ocean. The town's straw shacks, the distant mountains, the miserable ships on the seacoast, and the commander's building, a little matchbox with crickets dressed like soldiers, appeared out of the shadows.

XL

BLIND MAN'S BLUFF

"He left so many hours ago!"

On the day of departure, one counts the hours until they run together. There are enough to say, "He left so many days ago!" But two weeks later, one loses track of time and says: "He left so many weeks ago!" And then it's a month. And one loses track of the months. And a year goes by. Then one loses track of the years. . . .

Camila waited for the mailman by a window, hidden behind living room curtains so as not to be seen from the street. She was pregnant and knit baby clothes for her child.

The mailman knocked like a lunatic on every door. Knock by knock, he came closer to the window. Camila put down her knitting; when she saw him, her heart stirred in anticipation. "Here's the letter I've been waiting for! 'My beloved Camila: . . .'"

But the mailman didn't knock on her door. . . . Maybe he . . . Maybe later . . . And she would go back to her knitting, humming songs to stanch her fears.

The mailman came by again in the afternoon. Impossible to put in a stitch in the time it took her to run from the window to the door. Cold, out of breath, all ears, Camila waited for the knock. When she was sure nothing had disturbed the silent house, she closed her eyes in terror. Tears and nausea overwhelmed her. "Why didn't he come to the door? Maybe the mailman forgot. How in heaven's name is he a mailman if he doesn't bring mail? Tomorrow he'll bring a letter, that's for sure. . . ."

She almost ripped the door from its hinges opening it the

following day. She went out to await the mail carrier, not only for him not to forget her, but also to increase her luck. But the mailman passed by as he did every day—dressed in his pea-green outfit, the color of hope, with his little toad eyes and his skeleton teeth ready for an anatomy class—and escaped her inquiry.

One, two, three, four months . . .

She no longer went to the window on the street, she was so overcome by a grief that yanked her to the back of the house. She was like a piece of coal, a clay jug, loose garbage.

"They aren't whims but cravings," explained a neighbor, a kind of midwife to Camila's servant's questions, more out of the need to talk than to offer remedies. They already knew what to do, not to get jammed up: light candles to the saints and relieve the house's poverty by selling whatever was of value.

One day, however, the sick woman went out into the streets. Corpses floated by. She was hunched in a carriage, turning her eyes away from people she knew, and almost everyone avoided her eyes. Many times, she tried to see the President. A tear-laden handkerchief was her breakfast, lunch, and dinner. She chewed on it, almost swallowing it as she entered the President's vestibule. So much misery, to judge by the waiting crowds! Country folk seated on the edges of gold cloth chairs; city folk reclining against seatbacks.

Women led Camila to an armchair, speaking in low whispers. Someone was talking by the doorway. The President! The thought of him stiffened muscles. The baby kicked in her belly, as if to say, *Let's get out of here.* People shifted in their seats. Yawns. Murmurs. Footsteps of office staff. A soldier cleaning the windows. Flies. The baby kicked again in her womb. *Not so hard! Why are you angry? We're here to ask the President for information about a man you don't know, but when he returns, you will love him a lot! Oh, you can hardly wait to come out and take part in this thing called life! No, it's not that I don't want you to come out, but you're better off inside, protected!*

The President refused to meet with her. Someone told her

she needed an appointment. Telegrams, letters, written and sealed . . . Nothing worked; he didn't answer her.

She went to bed and woke up with eyelids hollowed out from lack of sleep. She had dreamt of a huge courtyard. She was lying in a hammock, playing with a candy straight from *A Thousand and One Nights* and a little black rubber ball. The candy in her mouth, the little ball in her hands. While passing the candy from one side of her mouth to the other, the ball got away from her, fell to the floor, rolled under the hammock, and bounced into a second courtyard, while the candy grew in her mouth, growing larger by the second, until it was no longer small. She wasn't fully asleep. Her body shivered when it touched the sheets. It was a dream lit by a night lamp and an electric light. The soap slipped out of her hands two or three times, just like the little ball, and the breakfast roll—she forced herself to eat—swelled in her mouth like the candy.

People attended Mass. The streets were empty. She visited government ministries, not knowing how to win over the porters, nasty old men who wouldn't answer her questions and shoved her hard, those clusters of moles, if she persisted.

But her husband left to pick up the ball. Now she remembered the other half of the dream. An enormous courtyard. The little black ball. Each time the ball rolled away, her husband ran after it, slipping farther off, shrinking as if reduced by a telescope, until he disappeared from the courtyard, while she forgot about her baby and felt the candy swelling in her mouth.

She wrote to the consul in New York, to the ambassador in Washington, to the friend of a friend, to the in-law of a friend, asking for news about her husband. She might as well have thrown the letters in the garbage. She found out from a nearby Jewish grocer that the distinguished secretary of the American Legation, a detective and a diplomat, was certain that Angel Face had made it to New York. "Not only do we have proof he arrived—it's in the harbormaster's registry, in the hotel registry where he stayed, and in the police registry—but also because of certain newspaper articles and oral accounts of people returning recently from New York. And they are looking for him right now," said the grocer. "Dead or alive, they'll find him, although it seems he left New York on a ship bound for Singapore."

"And where is Singapore?" Camila asked.

"Where do you think? In Asia," answered the grocer, clacking his dentures.

"And how long would it take to send a letter from there?" she asked.

"I don't know for sure, but I guess some three months."

She counted her fingers. Angel Face had been gone four months.

In New York City or in Singapore . . . She felt a load lifting from her shoulders! What relief to have him alive, even if far away. That was proof he wasn't killed at the port, as many people said. Far away, in New York or in Singapore, but with her in his thoughts!

She leaned against the grocer's counter. She was so happy she was dizzy. She walked on air, without touching the hams wrapped in aluminum foil, the Italian wine bottles in straw, the tin cans, the chocolates, the apples, the herring, the olives, the dried cod, the grapes—she was visiting new countries on her husband's arm. "How dumb I was to torment myself. Now I know why he hasn't written; I'll continue playing my role in this farce, the role of the abandoned wife who goes looking for the man who left her behind, blind with jealousy . . . or the wife who wants her husband at her side during the hardships of childbirth."

Cabin reserved, suitcases packed, everything ready for the trip, but her request for a passport denied. Cigarette-stained teeth moved up and down, down and up, to tell her that her passport had been denied. Her lips moved up and down, down and up, rehearsing to repeat words she had not understood.

She spent a fortune sending telegrams to the President. He never answered. The ministers couldn't help her. The Under-Secretary of War, a kind man who had a way with the ladies, advised her not to push it, she wouldn't get a passport no matter how hard she tried: her husband had tried to pull the wool over the President's eyes and nothing could be done.

They advised her to see the little priest, a very powerful man, who raised toads. Or one of the President's lovers who went horseback riding in the Presidential stables. Rumor had it that Angel Face had died of yellow fever in Panama; friends offered to go with her to consult spiritualists.

They didn't have to ask her twice. The medium was a bit reluctant. "I don't like the idea of having in me someone who was the President's enemy," she said. Her dry legs shivered under her frigid dress. But entreaties, gold coins, nutcrackers, and begging made her relent. The light flicked off. Hearing the medium summon Angel Face's spirit, Camila was terrified to the point of fainting. They dragged her out by the feet, almost unconscious. Apparently, she had heard her dead husband's voice. He had died on the high seas and was now in a place where nothing becomes everything. He was in a great bed—water for a mattress, fishes for springs, and a comfortable pillow of nonbeing.

She gave birth to a boy. Thin as a rail, with old cat wrinkles on her face, though she was barely twenty. Her green eyes bulged with rings around them as large as her transparent ears. Her doctor advised that she go to the country as soon as she could get out of bed. She was hanging on by a thread—wrecked by progressive anemia, tuberculosis, lunacy, a baby in her arms, and the anguish of knowing nothing about her husband. She looked for him in mirrors where only the shipwrecked appear; in the eyes of their son or in her own eyes, when night brought dreams of being with him in New York or Singapore.

Nevertheless, on Pentecostal Sunday, while walking among the shadows of pine trees, fruit trees in the orchards, and trees in the fields taller than clouds, she had a vision that shed light on the night of her grief. On this day, her son received salt, oil, water, the priest's saliva, and his name, Miguel. The turkey vultures pecked one another. Two ounces of feathers and countless trills. The sheep amused themselves licking their lambs. What an amazing sensation came from the licks of that motherly tongue over the body of the suckling lamb, who batted his long lashes in pleasure. Foals ran with damp-eyed fillies. Calves nuzzled the spigots of happiness of their mother's udders. Without knowing why, as if life had been reborn inside her, she pressed her son against her heart during his christening.

Little Miguel grew up in the country; he was a country boy. Camila never again set foot in the city.

XLI

NOTHING UNUSUAL

Once every twenty-two hours, light penetrated cobwebs and blocks of stone all the way to the vault. Once every twenty-two hours, a knotted rope lowered a container—more rust than can—with food to the prisoners in the deepest dungeons. The prisoner in cell 17 turned his face as soon as he saw the can with the greasy broth, slivers of fatty meat, and chunks of tortillas. He would rather die than eat that garbage. Day after day, the can would come down and go back up untouched. But hunger slowly tamed his glassy eyes. His eyes grew swollen. He screamed aloud while he paced back and forth in his narrow pit. He brushed his teeth with his fingers, threw himself onto the ground, and one day, when the can came down, he ran and stuck his mouth, nose, face, and hair into it, choking as he swallowed and chewed at the same time. He ate everything. When he heard them pulling up the empty can, he smiled like a contented beast. He kept on sucking on his fingers, licking his lips. However, this was a short-lived pleasure; he soon vomited up his meal, groaning and cursing. The meat and tortillas stuck to his guts like glue, but each time he felt pressure in his stomach, he couldn't do anything but open his mouth, pressed against the wall like someone leaning over a cliff. Finally, he could breathe again; everything was spinning; he brushed his damp hair with his hands, which he then slipped behind his ears to wipe the drool from his beard. There was a ringing in his ears. A freezing sweat—sticky, acidic, like water from an electrical outlet—bathed his face. Already the light was vanishing, that light that began to vanish as soon as it appeared. Clutching his weakened body as if fighting with himself, he could half-sit, stretch his legs, rest his head against the wall, and fall asleep under the weight of his eyelids as if under the control of some powerful narcotic. He never had a restful sleep: he struggled to breathe despite the lack of oxygen, his hands running up and down his body. Compulsively, he stretched his legs. His fingers rushed over the tips of his nails to rip from his throat an ember burning him from the inside. Now half awake, he opened and closed his mouth like a fish out of water, tasting the cold air with his dry tongue and wanting to shout over and over again, awake now, although drugged and feverish. He struggled to lift himself, stretching as much as he could so that they might hear him. The vault reduced his howls to mere echoes. He banged on the walls, kicked the floor, howled over and over for water, broth, salt, grease, anything: water, broth. . . .

A trickle of blood from a crushed scorpion touched his hand . . . from many scorpions, because the blood kept coming . . . from all the dying scorpions in the skies turning to rain. He quenched his thirst with his tongue, not knowing whom to thank for a gift that later would become his greatest affliction. He spent hour after hour standing on the rock that served as his pillow, trying to keep his feet above the puddle of frozen water that formed on the dungeon floor. Hour after hour, soaked to the crown of his head, distilling water, damp to his very bones, between yawns and shivers, restless because he was hungry and the can of greasy broth was late coming down. He ate like a bony man wanting to fatten his dreams. With his last mouthful, he would sleep standing up. Later, the can that satisfied the bodily functions of prisoners in solitary would come down. The first time that the prisoner in cell 17 heard the can coming down, he thought he was getting another dinner. Since this was during the period when he ate nothing, the can would go back up without his guessing that it was full of excrement and stank as much as the broth. This can went from cell to cell and reached cell 17 half full. How awful to have the can come down and not need to go, and then

have to crap when he had possibly lost his hearing from banging on the clapper of a dead bell. A greater torture was when
his desire to shit left him thinking about the can that might
come down, that wouldn't come down, that was late in coming down, that perhaps they had forgotten about it—which
happened often—or the chain would break—something that
happened most every day—to shower some of the prisoners in
shit. Just thinking about the whiff that disappeared, the heat
of human idleness, the sharp edges of the square can; feeling
the urge and then, when the desire to shit fled, having to wait
for the next opportunity, twenty-two hours between cramp
and copper-tasting saliva, hunger, cramps, tears, more cramps,
coarse words, or worse, shitting on the floor, to bust your gut
there like a dog or a baby, alone with death.

Two hours of light, twenty-two hours of total darkness, a
can of broth, a can of excrement, thirst in summer, and floods
in winter: that was life in these underground cells.

"Each day I weigh less," mumbled the prisoner in cell 17,
not even recognizing his own voice. "And when the wind
blows, it will bring me to where Camila waits for me. She has
gone crazy waiting—she's become a little insignificant thing!
Who cares about her frail hands—she would fatten them up
against her chest. . . . Dirty hands? . . . She could wash them
with her tears. Her green eyes? Yes, like that Austrian countryside pictured in *La Ilustración* . . . or the golden bamboo or
flecks of sea blue . . . And the taste of her lips, her teeth, the
taste of her taste . . . And her body? Where will she leave it?
Like a figure eight with a narrow waist, or the guitar-shaped
cloud of smoke left by fireworks when they go out and the colors disappear . . . I stole her from death on a night of fireworks . . . The angels strolled, the clouds strolled, the roofs
strolled with the little steps of night watchmen. Houses, trees,
everything strolled in the air with her and with me. . . ."

And he felt Camila lying next to him, the silky powder of
her touch: in his breathing, in his ears, between his fingers,
against his ribs that shook like the eyelashes of the blind eyes
of his entrails. . . .

And he possessed her. . . .

The spasms came unexpectedly, softly, without contortions, a light shiver going down the length of the spine, a quick contraction of his epiglottis, and his arms dropped as if amputated from his torso. . . .

The repugnance he felt when he crapped in the can, multiplied by the guilt of satisfying his physical needs when he thought of his wife, left him without the energy to move.

With a piece of brass that he ripped off from one of his shoelaces, the only metal utensil he had, he carved and intertwined his and Camila's names on the wall. Taking advantage of the light, which appeared every twenty-two hours, he added a heart, a dagger, a crown of thorns, an anchor, a cross, a little sailboat, a star, three swallows shaped like the tilde on an ñ, and a train with smoke spiraling upward. . . .

Luckily, his weakness saved him from the tortures of the flesh. Destroyed physically, he remembered Camila as one remembers a flower or a poem. He yearned for the rose that bloomed year after year in April and May on the windowsill in the dining room where he ate breakfast with his mother. Her ears were rose petals. The rush of childhood mornings left him bewildered. The light slowly disappeared. Vanished . . . the light that began to disappear the second it appeared. The darkness swallowed the thick walls like wafers. Soon the can of excrement would be coming. Oh, such a beautiful rose! The rope that banged and the can crazy with happiness going down the intestinal walls of the prison vault. Trembling to think of the stench that accompanied such a noble visitor. They would pull the container back up, but not the stench. Oh, to remember that rose as white as the morning milk!

As the years went by, the prisoner in cell 17 grew old, more from grief than from age. Countless deep wrinkles formed on his face, and white hair appeared the way ants shed wings in winter. Neither he nor his body . . . Neither he nor his corpse . . . Without fresh air, without sunlight, not able to move, with bouts of diarrhea and rheumatism, suffering from wandering neuralgias, almost blind. The only thing that gave

him any hope was the possibility of seeing his wife again: the
love that sustains a heart with emery dust.

The Chief of the Secret Police pushed back on his chair, put his
feet under it, got on his tiptoes, and propped his elbows on his
black cinnamon desk. He brought his pen to the lamplight and
then, brandishing his big teeth, he pinched and removed the
hair from the pen tip that had been giving his lettering prawn
whiskers. Then he continued writing. . . .

. . . *According to instructions,* the pen scratched over the
paper,

> the aforementioned Vich became friends with the prisoner in
> cell 17 after two months of imprisonment. He created a ruckus
> by crying at all hours, shouting each and every day and wanting
> to kill himself. Going from friendship to words, the prisoner
> in cell 17 asked what crime he had committed against the
> President to be locked away in such a hopeless place. The
> aforementioned Vich did not answer him, content to bang his
> head on the floor and curse aloud. He asked Vich so many
> times that finally he spoke up: polyglot born in a country of
> polyglots. News of the existence of a country where there were
> no polyglots. A journey. An arrival. An ideal country for
> foreigners. Job here, friendship there, money everywhere.
> Soon, a woman on the street, the first few steps pursuing her,
> not sure, almost by will . . . Married? Single? Widowed? The
> only thing he knew was that he had to follow her. What
> beautiful green eyes! What pink lips! What a sashay! What a
> princess. . . . He wants to get to know her better, he walks by
> her house, makes advances, but when he tries to speak to her,
> she disappears forever, and a man that he doesn't know and
> has never seen begins to track him like a shadow. . . . Friends:
> What's this all about? Friends turn away. Cobblestones.
> What's this all about? The cobblestones tremble as he walks
> by. House walls? What's this all about? The house walls
> tremble from hearing him speak. Only his imprudence clears
> everything up: he had wanted to make love to the President's

mistr—a lady, he later discovered. She was the daughter of a general and he did this to avenge her husband, who abandoned her just before he was jailed as an anarchist. . . .

In reply to this, the aforementioned Vich said there was a weird noise of a reptile in the dark: the prisoner approached him and in a fish-tin voice begged to repeat the lady's name, which the aforementioned Vich repeated for a second time. . . .

From that moment on, the prisoner started scratching himself as if his inert body was consumed by itching. He scratched his face to wipe off tears but there were only bones, no more skin, and he tried to put his hand on his chest: a cobweb of damp dust had fallen to the floor. . . .

According to instructions, I gave the aforementioned Vich (whose testimony I have transcribed down to the letter) eighty-seven dollars, a secondhand cashmere coat, and a ticket to Vladivostok to compensate him for his imprisonment. The departure of the prisoner in cell 17 was duly noted as such: Nomen Nescio: amoebic dysentery.

It is my great honor to inform the President of all this. . . .

EPILOGUE

The student stopped at the sidewalk's edge as if he had never seen a man dressed in a cassock before. Yet it wasn't the robe that amazed him so much as what the sexton had whispered in his ears as they hugged, happy to find themselves freed:

"I'm dressed like this on orders of my superiors. . . ."

The student would have stayed there, if not for a line of prisoners that walked along between two rows of soldiers extending for half a block.

"Poor people," muttered the sexton, when the student got back on the sidewalk. "Such an effort to bring down the walls of the Portal! Some things must be seen to be believed!"

"There are things you see," exclaimed the student, "and touch, but you still can't believe. I'm talking about City Hall—"

"And I thought you meant my robe."

"It wasn't enough to get the Turks to paint the Portal. The protest against the murder of the Man with the Tiny Mule led to tearing down the building."

"Shut your mouth. Someone might hear you, for God's sake. We don't really know that."

The sexton was going to say something, but a very short man not wearing a hat came running across the square, stood between them, and shouted:

Figurine, figure maker,
who figured you
made you a figure
so figured and flaunting!

"Benjamin! . . . Benjamin! . . ." called a woman running after him, looking ready to break into tears.

> Benjamin, puppeteer,
> didn't figure you . . .
> swear who made you
> so figured and flaunting?

"Benjamin! Benjamin!" the woman shouted. "Don't pay him any mind, gentlemen, ignore him, he's lost his marbles. He can't swallow the idea that the Portal del Señor doesn't exist anymore."

And while the puppeteer's wife apologized to the sexton and the student for his behavior, Don Benjamin raced off to sing the praises to a grousing policeman:

> Figurine, figure maker,
> who figured you
> made you a figure
> so figured and flaunting!

> Benjamin, puppeteer,
> didn't figure you . . .
> swear who made you
> so figured and flaunting?

"Officer, don't arrest him. He doesn't know what he's doing. I think he's lost his marbles," intervened Don Benjamin's wife, standing between the police officer and the puppeteer. "You can see he's crazy, don't arrest him. . . . No, no, don't hit him. . . . You can't imagine how nuts he is. He says the whole city has been destroyed like the Portal."

The prisoners continued walking by. To be them, and not to be the onlookers so happy not to be prisoners. Behind the train of people pushing wheelbarrows passed a group carrying tools as heavy as crosses on their shoulders, and behind them, in formation, more men dragged chains like hissing rattlesnakes.

Don Benjamin escaped from the hands of the police officer

arguing with his wife and ran to greet the prisoners with whatever words came into his head.

"He who sees you and he who saw you, Pancho Tanancho,
the guy with a knife that bores into leather and points with desire into a bedroom of heather. . . . He who sees you and he
who saw you made you into a Juan Diego, Lolo Cusholo, you
with the hummingturkey machete! He who sees you walking
and he who sees you on horseback, Mixto Melindres, sweet
water for a dagger, you fag and betrayer! . . . He who saw you
with the pistol when your name was Domingo, and sees you
now sad as a worker during a weekday! She gave them nits,
now she can delouse them! . . . Tripe under a cloth that isn't
pepián for the troops! . . . He who has no lock to seal up his
mouth, put handcuffs on his wrists."

Workers began leaving their shops for the day. The trams
ran with no room to spare. A carriage, a car, a bicycle passed
by. It took the sexton and the student a split second to cross
the Cathedral atrium, the refuge of beggars and the trash can
for nonbelievers, and say goodbye at the Archbishop's Palace
door.

The student avoided the Portal rubble by going over a bridge
of connecting planks. A cold gust of wind had just raised a
thick cloud of dust, smoke without flames. The vestiges of
some distant eruption. Another gust forced a rain of shredded
office papers over what used to be City Hall. Remnants of tapestries glued to the fallen walls stirred like flags whenever the
wind blew. The shadow of the puppeteer appeared riding on a
broom against a blue curtain covered with stars—at his feet,
five tiny volcanoes of fragments and rocks.

Chiplongon . . . The eight o'clock night church bells plunged
into silence . . . Chiplongon! . . . Chiplongon!

The student reached his house, which was at the end of a
blind alley. As he opened the door, he heard—interspersed
with the coughs of servants preparing responses to the litany—
his mother's voice reciting the rosary:

"For the dying and the wanderers . . . So that peace will
reign among Christian rulers . . . For those that suffer judicial
persecution . . . For the enemies of the Catholic faith . . . For

the hopeless needs of the Holy Church and for our earthly
needs . . . For the Blessed Souls in Holy Purgatory. . . .
   "*Kyrie eleison.* Lord Have Mercy."

Guatemala, December 1922
Paris, November 1925, December 8, 1932